The Whims of War

A historical novel

by

DON R. SAMPEN

BOOKS

Adelaide Books
New York / Lisbon
2021

THE WHIMS OF WAR

A historical novel

By Don R. Sampen

Published by Adelaide Books, New York / Lisbon
adelaidebooks.org

Editor-in-Chief
Stevan V. Nikolic

For any information, please address Adelaide Books
at info@adelaidebooks.org

or write to:

Adelaide Books
244 Fifth Ave. Suite D27
New York, NY, 10001

ISBN: 978-1-955196-81-9

Printed in the United States of America

To my wife and best friend, Hee-jeong Im

The WHIMS OF WAR is an historical novel taking place in Philadelphia between 1775 and 1780. Unlike other accounts of this period, it tells the story of a family business man drawn reluctantly into taking sides in the Revolutionary War. In the process it explores both conflicts among family members and friendships between ideological foes.

Chapter One

Trial Proceedings

Finally, his turn to speak arrived.

He had been living in a prison cell for three months. As prison stays went, he could not complain. He played cards with the guards, usually whist, while his wife and sister brought him food. His children visited occasionally, as did a friend or two. His anger rose, not from the conditions of his confinement, but from the idea of being confined at all. He had served Pennsylvania and the Patriot cause well, so he thought. But then they arrested him, in front of his family, and brought him here in chains. The charges ranged from treason to fraternizing with the enemy, to conspiracy, to stealing captured enemy property. He would be hanged if found guilty.

The court martial began a week ago. Half a dozen witnesses testified for the prosecution. They told about anti-American statements he had made, his trading with the British, his camaraderie with British officers, the supposed assistance he provided to the British Army, his stealing of war booty belonging to the Continental Army. Some things were true, some false, but all could be easily explained. Today he would begin giving his side of the story.

Three guards came to his cell. After placing his hands in irons, they marched him to Carpenter's Hall to resume the trial. While the Hall could accommodate sixty onlookers, only twenty showed up today. Among them were family members. Five guards with muskets kept watch over the proceedings.

The court consisted of thirteen officers from different regiments. All were a rank of captain or higher. An army colonel served as the court's president. He sat at a table in the middle of the row of officers, six on each side. A fourteenth officer served as the Judge Advocate who prosecuted the charges. When not questioning a witness, he occupied a table on the right facing the court. Daniel sat at a table on the left. When testifying, witnesses stood in the middle. A clerk wrote furiously to chronicle their accounts.

"Daniel Thompson," the president called out. "Please rise. We have come now to the stage of the proceeding where you may offer a defense to the charges against you. I take it you intend to speak in your defense . . . is that correct?"

"Yes, sir."

"Do you expect to have any other witnesses?"

"At least one, Mr. President. Captain Samuel Johnson, 7th Pennsylvania Regiment, my commanding officer."

"You will now proceed with your own testimony, and we'll see where things stand. Is that agreeable?"

"It is."

"The Judge Advocate will ask questions as you proceed. Do you understand that?"

"I do, Mr. President." Daniel hesitated before stating, "A lot of evidence has been offered against me, spanning the last five and a half years. Where would you like me to begin?"

The president of the court thought for a moment. "Why not start from five and a half years ago."

Daniel nodded.

Chapter Two

My family is Anglican. My father's father was an Episcopalian who came from Wiltshire in south England. He helped organize Christ's Church in the City during the 1690s and passed on the religion to my father. My father passed it to his four children, although my older sister, Missy, later joined a Scotch Presbyterian church. That year, 1775, we all attended the picnic. It marked the start of everything changing.

I'm talking about the annual Quaker picnic held in Governor's Woods. Back then, the Penns still owned the woods. The picnickers gathered in a clearing on Schuylkill River's east bank.

I call it the Quaker picnic because they started it back before I can remember. They are a tolerant lot, the Quakers. Not so good at revolution. But religious tolerance was a strong point. The picnic expanded over the years to include all the City's other religious groups. It was the one time of the year when the Quakers actually reached out. Among those attending were families from the Anglican, Lutheran and Reformed churches, along with Catholics and Baptists. The Scotch Presbyterians came, too. They typically never spoke to Quakers with civil tongue. But they came to the picnic. Members of the African Methodist Church showed up, and a Delaware Indian tribe even attended now and then.

Sarah and I rode together in our two-wheeled chaise with our twin girls. Jonathan followed on a borrowed stallion named Swift. He would be riding in the horse race later in the afternoon. We reached the main picnic area in late morning, shortly before dinner. As I unhitched Dobbin and tied her to a tree, I saw Papa engaged in an animated discussion near the Anglican fire pit. He had brought his housekeeper, Mrs. Pickering, and my younger sister, Molly, both nearby. I also saw my brother, David, with his wife, Helen.

"There you are, Daniel," David called out while walking our direction. "Can't even make it to a picnic on time."

Sarah interceded before I had a chance to respond.

"Don't get into it today," she said, handing over a basket from the chaise. "Help me out with these things."

Sarah aptly came between me and David. From the time we were kids, he and I never got along. We always tried to out-do the other for Papa's approval. One time Papa asked us to chop firewood. Being three years older, David was stronger. To demonstrate I could keep up, I picked out the easier-to-cut soft pine logs from the pile and left him to gather the solid ash and maple. He quickly caught on, and when I dragged over my next pine log, David said, "Just leave it, that one's mine."

I persisted. When I turned my back to him, David said, "I told you to leave it!" He threw a hatchet in my direction and it stuck in a log a few feet away. It startled me and David started laughing. I lit out after him in a blind rage. We tussled for several minutes. Knowing I could never take him, I tried nevertheless to inflict at least some damage with my fists. Papa, who was working nearby in the back yard, walked over and broke us up.

"He's only cutting the easy pieces," hollered David before I could catch my breath.

"He threw a hatchet at me and almost killed me," I snapped back.

"It didn't come close. If I wanted to . . ."

"Boys!" Papa stopped us. "Try to get along, all right? You're brothers. Quit fighting. David, do not throw things at Danny, you hear me?"

"It was three feet away," David insisted.

"It doesn't matter. You scared him. As for you, Danny, don't just take the easy pieces. You take whatever comes next. You understand?"

I nodded.

"Go on, then, get out of here." Papa shook his head. "You've done enough damage for today."

I thought about that incident every time David and I got into a bickering match, which was frequent. But no bickering today. I had to deal with David on a daily basis in our family business. This day I set my mind to having a good time with my family.

Sarah and the girls began helping out at our church's picnic area, and I went over to talk with my son, Jonathon.

At eleven-years-old, he was a slight kid. We sent him and the girls to a private academy on the south side of the city. In his third year of schooling, he did well at most subjects. But he had been a mama's boy for years. Even now he had little interest in what I regarded as the normal boys' pursuits, like hunting and swimming. Around the house, he spent an inordinate amount of time playing a beat-up old fiddle Sarah gave him. It was an antique passed down through her family. So, while other kids were playing cricket outdoors, Jonathon stayed in his attic bedroom scratching out tunes. It about drove me nuts. That was one of the reasons I pushed him into the picnic horse race.

"Today's the big day, Jon," I smiled, "you ready?"

"I guess so."

"You 'guess so'? You've been training nearly every day for the last two months. Are you going to win this thing?"

"I don't know."

I could have kicked his backside for his lack of enthusiasm.

"Jon, you're never going to win unless you think you're going to win. Swift is a good runner. You're a good rider. You have the training. And no reason exists why you can't come out on top. Are you with me on this?"

"I guess so." He flinched, knowing I would not like his response.

"Now go find the starting line and practice a few starts before it gets too crowded. I'm going to try my luck in the musket shoot."

★

I grabbed my musket and cartridge box and headed a hundred yards upstream the picnic area. About thirty men with muskets gathered for the competition. Another forty or fifty onlookers and judging officials stood nearby. The shooting range consisted of five big rocks topped with clay bricks easily shattered when struck. The competitors would shoot in groups of five standing fifty yards away. The object was to load, fire and see how many bricks a shooter could hit within a minute.

"I'm surprised you had the courage to show up after your pathetic showing last year," said a voice in my direction. It was Peter Barclay, my brother-in-law and sister Missy's husband. Peter was a partner in a print shop. They printed mostly hand bills, pamphlets, some poetry, and a weekly newspaper. While eight years my senior, I liked Peter and gave him a hug.

"Courage I've never lacked. It's luck I'm short on. But that's never been your problem. As I recall you somehow got into the second round last year, and without your spectacles you're as blind as a bat."

"You're absolutely right." Peter nodded. "It was pure dumb luck. At least I remembered my spectacles this year, although they probably aren't going to help much. How are Sarah and the kids?"

I seldom got to see Peter and Missy. They lived with their son, Nathan, south of us in Chester County. Peter rode into the City daily. A long standing rift between them and Papa contributed to our lack of frequent contact.

"Doing well. Jonathon is riding in the horse race today. He's been training for the last two months. The easy money says he'll win."

"That so," said Peter. "He'd have to beat Nathan, and I don't think that will happen." Although his comment would be a boast from anyone else, Peter spoke matter-of-factly.

While Peter's son was only six months older than Jonathon, Nathan had all the physical skills and interests Jonathon lacked. He stood tall and was a good looking lad with lots of friends. I was envious of Peter. But I worked hard at suppressing any blatant comparisons between the two boys. Jonathon will grow into his own stride, I kept telling myself.

"We'll see about that," I said. "So what brings you to the musket range today? You expect to take home a silver cup?"

Peter shook his head. "No, just brushing up for when the redcoats start marching toward Philly."

"Come, now, surely we're not going to war. What a disaster that would be."

"It's coming. Maybe not today, maybe not next week, but it's coming."

"Peter, please." We'd had these conversations before. And one more time I would try to dampen his enthusiasm for war. "We've been prosperous here. We have our ups and downs, but the European demand for flour, meat and lumber is strong. Pennsylvania buys tons of dry goods from England on easy credit. A war will ruin it all."

"Daniel, my young friend, your head is in the clouds . . . yours and the other merchants'. Where do you think we've been heading these last few years? There was the Stamp Act in '65."

"Repealed within a year, old buddy."

"Then the Townshend Acts of '67 putting a tax on virtually every import."

"All repealed by 1770," I said, "except for tea."

"Yes. But not before the redcoats massacred five men and wounded a half dozen more in Boston trying to enforce it. And the tea tax was not resolved until the East Indian tea got dumped into Boston Harbor in '73."

"The tea was dumped, but not because of the tax. It was undercutting smuggled tea from the Dutch West India Company."

"Your facts are off, young fella." Peter shook his head. "But no matter. Just this past September, the Continental Congress voted that no obedience is owed acts of Parliament if Congress thinks they're unfair. And you think we're not headed to war? *That* was an act of rebellion."

"No, old man, that was an act of idiocy. And, by the way, the Continental Congress has no power to do anything anyway. Except pass idiotic resolutions, like that one."

"I could go on but the point is we . . . ."

"Yes, we have a Tory sympathizer among us." A new voice spoke up.

I looked to my right and became aware of the man standing there listening to our conversation. I turned back to Peter and shook my head.

"Who's this?"

Peter gave a sheepish grin. "It's Henry Waddy." He looked as surprised as I that someone had been listening, and embarrassed it was someone he knew. "He's a member of my church. How are you, Henry?"

"Good, until I saw the kind of company you keep." Waddy rolled his eyes.

"Don't be a boor, Henry. This is Daniel Thompson, my brother in law and a good friend. He is as loyal a Pennsylvanian as you or I."

"It didn't sound like it to me," Waddy said, "but I'll let it go."

He was a squat man, my age, mid-thirties, but a head shorter. Dressed a bit on the shabby side, he spoke with regal arrogance, and his tone irritated me – he would "let it go."

Peter looked at me and slowly shook his head, warning me not to exacerbate the situation.

Of course, I paid no attention. "What do you mean by 'Tory sympathizer'? You think it's wrong to oppose going to war with the country that gave this colony its birth, protects us in war, keeps the sea lanes open?"

"Yes, I do . . . if that's the same country that closed the port of Boston, and replaced the elected officials with royal appointments, and has been quartering thousands of British troops for the last year under the command of General Gage."

"I'm not responsible for those hotheads in Massachusetts," I responded. "This is Pennsylvania. We're more civilized here, and we have no British troops. So what's your point?"

Waddy looked exasperated. "My point is we're all in this together."

"Since when has Pennsylvania ever been in anything 'together' with Massachusetts?"'

He looked surprised, as if "in this together" was supposed to end the conversation. He stammered, "I said I would let it go, but only this time."

I squinted at him quizzically. "And just what do you do . . . when you don't *let it go*?" My tone was mocking, intended to spark a reaction.

It did.

With venom in his eyes, he muttered, "I'll show you, asshole!" and suddenly came at me with one hand grasping for my waistcoat and his other arm rearing back to strike with a fist.

I have never been much of a fighter, and how I avoided a blow to the head I shall never know. But somehow when I saw his fist coming I grabbed it with both hands, pulled it down, and yanked his arm up behind his back in a hammerlock. Holding it with one hand, I wrapped my free arm around his neck and pulled his head against my chin.

I held him there just long enough to whisper in his ear, "Go fuck yourself." Then pulling further up on his hammer-locked arm to make sure he felt it, I gave him a shove to the ground.

All this took place in a matter of seconds, before Peter could intervene. With Waddy now on the ground, Peter stepped between us and turned to Waddy.

"Henry," he said, "you started it, and that's enough. I agree with you on politics. But attacking my friend is not useful to our cause. Let me help you up and you should leave."

Declining Peter's assistance, Waddy got to his feet and brushed himself off. "I'll leave," he said, "but you tell your friend he's not seen the last of me."

As we walked away, I asked Peter, "What's wrong with that man?"

"He is a mechanic, at least that's what they call themselves. You know Ben Church, Paul Revere and their group. They grew out of the Sons of Liberty and keep track of British troop movements."

"I thought those folks operated in Boston."

"Here, too. Henry is one of them."

"Damn, he's irritating. At least with you, I can disagree and not get called a traitor. Talking with him, there are all his implied threats. He will 'let it go' . . . I've not 'seen the last' of him . . . what's that supposed to mean?"

"Danny, just be careful who you talk to these days."

★

At the time, I mightily impressed myself with the way I handled Waddy. Goodness, I thought, I showed him, and barely broke a sweat! But reviewing the incident in my mind, I concluded it was a move I could never replicate in a hundred years. I startled myself even more than I did Waddy. I learned some time later, to my chagrin, I should have taken Peter's advice, and just ignored him.

Chapter Three

The shooters began lining up in front of the targets. Starting out in groups of five, we progressed through a series of eliminations. The first round required only that each man hit two clay bricks within the stipulated minute. Those who did moved onto the second round, which required each man hit three clay bricks in a minute. That involved considerably more skill. Those hitting three moved on to the third round, and subsequent rounds. In each the contestants would continue to shoot until, either, a contestant faltered and hit only two bricks, in which case he would be eliminated. Or, someone hit four bricks in a minute. Someone loading and firing a musket four times in one minute with precision is an expert.

Anyone familiar with musketry knows the greatest skill is not the shooting. That's the easy part. It takes some skill, of course. Holding the piece steady in your arms, anticipating the target, allowing for air movement, knowing how quickly the ball drops at different ranges. All those things are important. The real skill, however, comes in loading. Doing it the right way, by using consistent amounts of powder, properly wadding and tamping, and having musket balls nicely sized to the inside of the barrel, an average marksman can hit his target eight times out of ten. But mess up during any part of the loading process? Even the best marksman will miss.

As I stepped to the front of the line, I opened my cartridge box and arranged several paper rolls containing powder and a ball. I also loosened the rammer from the underneath side of the barrel and rested the butt on the ground at the ready position. My father had bought the piece for me, and one for my brother, too, when he took us bear hunting in the Allegheny foothills in the fall of '56. Each was an English Brown Bess, and he paid five pounds apiece. I kept mine well-oiled and cleaned over the years and replaced all the moving parts once or twice. My initials, DT, carved deep into the stock marked my ownership.

The starting official shouted, "Load and fire!"

The first round I regarded as a practice round as I moved methodically and deliberately. I had plenty of time to get off two shots and wanted to be sure things went smoothly. After loading, firing, and shattering the clay target, I removed the musket from my shoulder, pulled the hammer back to half cock, and loaded a second time. As I lifted the piece to my shoulder, however, I sensed something was off. I pulled the hammer back to full cock and fired anyway. Poof! I felt a hot flash on the underneath side of the musket. The pan holding the primer charge had not properly closed. The flint on the hammer nevertheless struck against the frizzen, which emitted sparks igniting the primer. But the primer charge failed to ignite the powder in the barrel.

Now I was in trouble. I had only about thirty seconds to re-prime the pan, and to fix whatever malfunction had occurred. I bit open a new cartridge, sprinkled in the priming powder, and worked the hammer and pan mechanism back and forth to try to detect the malady. Some debris apparently caused the pan to remain open. I cleaned it off as best I could, and the pan this time seemed to close properly.

I lifted and fired just as the starting official yelled "Halt!"

I hit the clay target, but was not sure if I was in time. The official came over and looked at me. A Quaker, I knew him from Market Street. He ran a successful haberdashery selling beaver hats and fur.

He said good-naturedly, "If you were a Presbyterian, I would call you late. But as an Anglican, you go to the second round." He gave a friendly smile, and I nodded my appreciation.

Peter, I noticed, had not been so fortunate. His musket also misfired, but he had not recovered. He dropped out of the running.

The next round went smoothly. I fired three shots in rapid succession and hit three targets with time to spare.

By the time we got to the third round, twelve shooters remained. The real competition now began. It was only a matter of time before someone hit four. A round later just eight of us still stood, so we divided into groups of four. I joined the first group, and with heightened concentration, I focused on short-cutting the loading and firing process wherever I could. No double tamps with the rod. Faster lifting and firing once loaded.

The haberdasher gave the call. "Load and fire!"

Half cock, bite cartridge, prime, fill barrel, tamp, lift, full cock, fire one! Things were going well and my concentration felt good. Fire two! This would be the year, I told myself. Fire three! All I had to do was to avoid misfiring on this last shot, and . . . fire four!

"Halt!"

I did it. My heart leapt. I felt like dancing about and letting out a holler. Wow! I restrained myself, though, and tried to appear dignified as I looked around, receiving congratulations. The only problem was one other guy in my group also hit four targets. And when the second group of four fired, one of them hit four targets as well.

God damn! The one year I have a perfect round, and I have to go through a tie-breaker with two other guys. And one of them was . . . a Negro. I had seen him walking around, and thought he was there as someone's servant. Only now did I realize he was a competitor, and I wondered how he got so good with a musket. As the boys were setting up clay targets for the three-man shoot off, I decided to find out something about the man.

"That was fine shooting," I said to him. "What is your name?"

Medium built with short kinked hair and black skin, he looked to be in his upper twenties. He glanced up, wary of a stranger, but curiosity more than distrust showed in his eyes. Other black men walked around the shooting area, but he was the only one competing. I thought he looked familiar but could not place him.

"Thanks," he said. "I'm Willie Howell. And you, sir?"

"Daniel Thompson. Nice to meet you." I gave a nod. His expression told me his encounter with most white men was not as cordial. "You slave or free?"

"Slave."

I should have known. Thousands of blacks lived in southeast Pennsylvania, both free and slave. While the laws of Pennsylvania required better treatment for slaves than in other colonies, those same laws treated free blacks worse. Depending on the time and locale, they were banned from carrying firearms and barred from taverns. Their children could be bonded out like indentured servants for years at a time by local judges. Severe penalties were imposed for marriage or fornication with whites. And they were subject to arrest for the pettiest of crimes or just mere laziness. Although the laws were sporadically enforced, no free black man in his right mind would show up at an event like this with a musket in hand.

"But I believe you know me, sir," he added.

"Maybe so. Who is your master?"

"Mr. Marvin, over yonder."

Of course, now I recalled I had seen Willie out at the mill. On the edge of the shooting area a white-haired middle-aged man sat next to a woman in the driver's seat of a two-horse-drawn utility wagon. I walked over to say hello to Marvin Swenson, the manager of the grist mill owned by Thompson & Sons Trading Company.

"Marvin," I said, "I had no idea you owned such talented property. Your man just hit four targets."

"Willie knows how to shoot," Marvin said. "He brings home game for us at the mill. I thought it would fun to see him compete. But you did well yourself, Daniel."

"I got lucky. I doubt I can do it twice in a row. How are things going at the mill? I'm overdue for a visit." Our mill was located on French Creek in Chester County, about fifteen miles from the City.

"Winter wheat has started to come in, but we busted a pulley that shut us down for a day last week. We're back up at capacity."

Marvin had been our manager ever since we bought the mill eight years ago. He ran a tight operation. Most millers had a reputation for dishonesty, keeping more than their due of their customers' ground wheat. Marvin was the exception and dealt with both us and our customers with perfect honesty. His health was poor, though.

"Well, I wish your man good luck, but not better than mine," I said.

The haberdasher called the three of us to the ready, as a crowd gathered to watch. No one could remember a shoot-off of competitors who had each hit four targets.

"Load and fire!"

Half cock, bite cartridge, prime, fill barrel, tamp, lift, full cock, fire!

I did it four times, and within seconds of my shot each time I heard two others. I figured we all three had tied again and was anticipating yet another round. But I noticed out of the corner of my eye Willie starting the loading sequence a fifth time. In the instant I had to think about it I was confident he would never get the shot off. But instead of tamping with his ramrod, he banged the butt of his musket on the ground, and in one effortless motion lifted, pulled the hammer and fired simultaneously with the command to "Halt!" An instant later a clay target shattered to pieces fifty yards downrange.

I was stunned, the crowd quieted. The haberdasher stood in an apparent quandary over what to do. Five precise shots in the space of a minute, and that last shot alone was nothing short of miraculous. The only question was whether it would be judged in time.

The haberdasher shook his head and walked over to Willie. "The ball struck after the signal," he said.

I could tell where this was going, and could not let it happen.

"But the shot was fired before the signal," I blurted out. "So we have a winner!" I started applauding. I glanced over in Marvin Swenson's direction and nodded vigorously. He stood up in his wagon.

"Yes, yes!" he yelled, joining my applause. The rest of the onlookers, not sure whether this ruling was the official's or mine, joined in. By acclamation we donned Willie the winner.

The haberdasher gave me an evil look. Quakers officially opposed slavery, but that did not mean they took kindly to black folk, slave or free. He obviously disdained the thought of a Negro winning the Quaker-sponsored contest. But he lacked the ambition to buck the crowd favorite.

"No more favors for you," he told me under his breath.

An assistant brought over the silver cup trophy. The haberdasher held it aloft for a moment. Once the crowd calmed, he said to Willie, "I award you this trophy as winner of the 1775 musket competition. Congratulations." As reluctant as he was to hand over the trophy to a black slave, his words sounded genuine.

Chapter Four

When I got back to the picnic area, the feasting was about to begin. The Anglicans were roasting mutton this year, and I was hungry.

Before we began, the clerk of the Friends' Philadelphia Yearly Meeting, James Pemberton, took to a ridge just above the picnic area to welcome the collection of churches and members. Middle-aged with a broad-brimmed hat, he spoke as a Quaker with an air of authority.

"I would like to take just a moment to reflect upon our blessings," he said. "These are troubled times. High taxes, trade restrictions, uncertainty on our frontiers, rampant distrust, sabotage of the mother country, troops assembling in one of our sister colonies, suspicions running high, talk of militias being formed . . . who is to say what lies ahead? Yet here we are on a sunny day in April, shielded from fear, shielded from want, and eating our fill of the earth's abundance. So let us give thanks, among our many faiths, by joining in and singing Praise Ye the Lord, the Almighty."

Pemberton began the familiar old tune, a little high-pitched for most of us. By the time everyone joined in, the pitch took a noticeable dip. Still, it was a memorable moment. Some four-hundred-fifty picnickers, many with unintended harmony, filled the banks between river and forest with song.

"All ye who hear, now to His temple draw near, join me in glad adoration!"

I was never a particularly religious man. But as we finished the first verse and began the second, looking at Sarah the twins, and Jonathon a few yards away, I felt an uncharacteristic surge of contentment. For all that bore down on me personally – challenges facing our family business, the growing political divide among my own family members, a myriad of other daily difficulties – somehow we would struggle through whatever disasters might befall.

I hoped.

The singing ended, and Pemberton announced, "If I could hold your attention for just a few minutes longer, Joseph Galloway is here today." A murmur went through the crowd. "Joseph has been speaker of the Pennsylvania House of Assembly for the last five years. He also was our delegate to the Continental Congress last year, and he would like to share a few words with us today."

This will not go over well, I thought to myself. Wrong speaker, wrong time. So much for my moment of contentment.

Scattered applause emerged, mostly from the Quaker and Anglican congregations. Galloway took to the ridge and raised an arm to acknowledge the crowd.

"Many of you disagree with my politics," he began.

"Amen to that!" someone shouted out, provoking laughter. Galloway smiled and pointed his finger at the person now nodding.

Not a bad start, I thought. A little humility goes a long way.

"At least we can agree on that," he said. "And I suspect we can agree on a few more things, such as the utter insanity of the British Parliament, which alone has done more than anything else to unite the colonies of North America. What we disagree on, I suspect, is how we deal with that insanity and where we go from here. I don't pretend to have all the answers. No one does, not even our revered Dr. Franklin with whom I correspond regularly. What I do know, however, is most colonists want a legitimate government. Most colonists want freedom from overbearing taxes, and freedom to expand their frontiers and elect their own representatives. Most colonists want the same rights the citizens of Great Britain enjoy. For all of its faults, the British Empire provides its citizens more rights and liberties than any other country on earth."

The rumbling started.

"I know further that most colonists want to avoid the ravages of war. And I know the peace and welfare of this great land is undermined by the insurrections and conspiracies and illegal assemblies facing us daily. I know we as a people owe fidelity to a king who earnestly desires the restoration of harmony . . . ."

He had crossed the line.

"Go home, Tory!" someone yelled out from the crowd. Others joined in with, "Kill all the redcoats!" and "Down with King George!" Most of the outright shouting came from the Presbyterian congregations.

The Quaker groups looked appalled at their rudeness.

We Anglicans sided with the Quakers, while the Lutherans, Mennonites, and Amish leaned toward the Presbyterians.

It was not long before a chant began, "We want freedom! We want freedom!" It quickly spread throughout the crowd. Catchy as it was, even some of the Quaker children joined in, much to the chagrin of their parents.

Up on the ridge, Galloway made a couple of false starts to get back on track. Then he looked at Pemberton, shrugged, and they both descended to join their congregations. Under other circumstances, his pro-British rhetoric might have caused a riot. But these were church people, and they had not yet had dinner. So the chants tapered off. And the eating began.

★

The horse race in midafternoon highlighted the day's events and evoked a good deal of friendly wagering. Eight competitors, all young boys, participated. The course wound around the forest for half a mile and ended along the same straightaway where it began.

Jonathon and I led Swift over to the starting line where the crowd gathered. I wanted him to do well, so badly. His image of himself needed a boost, and I yearned to tell him how proud I was of him. He looked around at all the spectators and other competitors as we approached, displaying no emotion. I fancied he was experiencing an inner confidence that might just put him out in front. It mattered not to me whether he came in first. As long as he made a decent showing. Then, I would flatter the hell out of him.

As the boys were lining up, I saw Peter, my brother-in-law, assisting his son, Nathan. Within earshot of Jonathon, I said to Peter, "If you really think Nathan has this won, you ought to be willing to go even money, Nathan versus Jonathon. What do you say?"

Peter smiled. "Now, Daniel, you know I'm not a betting man. I'd go a shilling with you, though, just to keep things interesting."

"A shilling?" I replied in mock disgust. "That doesn't show much conviction. A pound sounds better. I have a lot more confidence in Jonathon, but at least a pound bet will make it worth my while."

"You have a deal," said Peter with a skeptical look.

I looked up at Jonathon sitting atop Swift. "I've got money on you, son. "Make me proud."

He gave a nod.

I found Sarah and the girls standing with Papa along with David and his wife, Helen. I joined them. "I've got a wager with Peter. Jonathon will beat Nathan in the race," I announced joyfully.

"I hope it's not for more than a pence," said David, "because you know you're going to lose."

I almost strangled him with my bare hands. His comment cut through my heart like the hatchet he threw when we were kids. Only this time it hit closer. No matter he might be right. It just griped me. David lacked the ability to demonstrate even a hint of encouragement. My head still fuming, I put my arm around Sarah and moved her up closer to the starting line.

"How much?" she asked.

"A pound."

She looked dubious. "At least your heart is in the right place."

The starting official walked to the front of the line and stood closest to Jonathon, who had managed a favored end position. Raising his pistol, he announced in a bold voice, "On your marks, get set . . . ."

Eight boys on horses, lined side-by-side, crouching forward, stick whip at the ready, their faces determined, breaths held, waiting eagerly for the start.

Bang!

In a cloud of dust, they took off down the dirt roadway, each prodding his equine charge with kicks, whips and yells while jockeying the others for better position.

All except one. The starting official had stood too close to Jonathon, and the pistol shot spooked Swift. The horse reared up and threw the boy to the ground. My heart sank. At first, he looked as if he might shake it off, remount, and charge after the others. But then he paused, sat back in the dirt as if to say, "What's the use?" He rose slowly with reddened face, took hold of the horse's bridle, and coaxed her across the roadway past Sarah and me.

He paused long enough to say, "I'll make up that lost wager, Papa." We did not see him again until evening.

Only a few short minutes passed before seven boys on horses crossed the finish line. Nathan led, the crowd cheering wildly during the last forty yards. Once they crossed the finish line, every rider was treated like a hero by family and friends, being lifted off his horse and congratulated with back slaps, handshakes, whoops and hollers. It was the celebration I had looked forward to bestowing upon Jonathon. But not this year.

An hour later Sarah and I stood near our church's cooking fire with Peter and my sister Missy. Peter refused to accept my wagered pound, saying Jonathon's fall had not been his fault. He and Missy had come over for a chat and to help finish off our church leftovers from dinner. About half the picnickers had left for home.

In the late afternoon chill of early spring, the fire coals were feeling good.

"All I wanted," I said to Missy, "was for Jonathon to finish, and maybe beat someone. I knew he would never place in front of Nathan, but that wasn't the point. You know how he is, so shy and keeping to himself. To finish the race in front of a crowd of spectators, and to have something to talk about and look back upon. It would have done him good."

Missy was five years my senior, and many more years than that in wisdom and maturity. Ever since Mama died giving birth to Molly, I always looked to Missy for maternal guidance. At twenty, she married Peter, but still came home several times a week to help keep peace between David and me and oversee the housekeeping. Always wanting a big family of her own, it was her fate to have only one child, Nathan. Still, she never complained and compensated by getting involved with Peter's printing business. She envied me and my family of three children and encouraged Sarah and me to have more.

"I wouldn't get too worked up over the fact it didn't turn out for Jonathon," she said. "He's just a kid, eleven-years-old. These things happen. So what? And, true, he may not be the most athletic boy in the City, but that's all right. Jonathon is a thinker. He's smart. He needs to find the right outlet for his talents. It just may not be horse racing."

I nodded. They were the kind of words I needed to hear. Leave it to Missy.

When we heard a commotion on the road leading from the picnic clearing, we turned and saw a man on horseback shouting as he made his way in our direction. He stopped from time to time to speak briefly with picnickers making their way back to the City by carriage and foot. It took a good ten minutes before he was close enough where we could hear what he was saying.

"British regulars fired on the militia at Lexington and then did battle at Concord!"

He repeated this message a couple of times before his horse got close enough to ask for more details.

Peter grabbed hold of the horse's bridle before he passed, and asked, "How many killed?"

"At Lexington, maybe a dozen militia. At Concord a lot more, but the British took heavier losses than the militia. Maybe a hundred dead, hundred-fifty wounded. It's hard to say."

"How many men were engaged?" Peter wanted to know.

"Best estimate is seven hundred British regulars to start, but they were reinforced by another twelve hundred from Boston. On the Massachusetts side, three thousand militia or more at Concord. The engagement began Wednesday morning. It ended with the militia chasing the regulars back to Charlestown."

Peter turned to face Missy, Sarah and me. "It's a genuine battle, not just a standoff."

"What were the British trying to accomplish?" I asked.

"They apparently were after John Hancock and Sam Adams at Lexington and a militia weapons stockpile in Concord. Hancock and Adams escaped and are on their way to Philadelphia." With that, he galloped off.

"It's a battle," repeated Peter, "the first of a war. We've actually engaged the British in battle." A determined eagerness inflected his voice. It depressed me.

I made a mental note of the date. Today was Friday, so Wednesday was April 19, 1775.

Chapter Five

Trial Proceedings

"You admit to being a Loyalist, then?" asked the Judge Advocate.

"I admit to making pro-Loyalist statements in 1775," Daniel answered. "The war had not even started. The Declaration was not signed until more than a year later. My views were no different from half of the City."

"Who by now have fled the City, correct?"

"No. A lot of people left over the last five years. But a lot of Loyalists are still here, and people who never chose a side. Many of them are being harassed, even though they aren't a threat to anyone. They could be won over with a little encouragement."

"Focus on the question, Lieutenant. No need to editorialize."

"I want the truth brought out."

"Mr. President?" The president of the court gave an irritated look.

"Lieutenant, focus on the question," he ordered.

"Yes, sir."

"You did choose sides though, correct?" asked the Judge Advocate. "I mean, you didn't just make pro-Loyalist statements.

You were committed to continued British rule of the colonies, at least in 1775, is that not true?"

"It's true my family were merchants and had business ties with the British. We had an interest in continuing that relationship."

"And you were fully committed to that position?"

"My father was fully committed to that position. I was less so."

"Tell us about your business."

"I'll do as best I can."

Chapter Six

"The governor has been pushed aside," Papa said. "Not even the Assembly pays attention to him anymore."

Papa, David, Molly and I, along with Papa's house guest, George Logan, were sitting in the counting house in early June. The counting house occupied what would otherwise have been the first floor parlor of Papa's house. It was the house where I grew up, where David and I fought as kids, and where we still fought as adults.

Papa lived with Mrs. Pickering, his housekeeper. She was more than just a housekeeper, but no one pried into details. Molly, my younger sister, had moved back into the house two years earlier, following her husband's death from smallpox.

"So, who's in charge?" asked Logan. "Someone has to run the government."

"Morton's the new Assembly speaker," Papa was quick to answer. "He does all right, but he gets swayed sometimes by the Whigs and their rebel friends. He's also a delegate to the Continental Congress."

Papa had been elected to the Pennsylvania Assembly for the last four years. He was not much of a politician. When asked to run for election by a Quaker business acquaintance, he saw it as a business opportunity.

"When you ask who is in charge," Papa continued, "it's a mare's nest. We have half a dozen self-appointed committees. Each one thinks it's in charge while the Assembly is in adjournment. The Committee on Safety is the only one with any authority, headed by Ben Franklin. It might be he is in charge."

He shook his head in disgust. The great colony of Pennsylvania, first in trade, prosperity and religious freedom, ruled for the last ninety years by a tidy, pro-business government of Quakers, now teetered on the brink of chaos. It was brought on, not by the British, but by pedestrian masses of farmers, artisans and trades people who wanted to overthrow the British. And that was only part of the irony. The other part was the Quakers, having been persecuted in England for generations, bore no natural affinity toward the Anglicans. Now, however, they found themselves reaching out to the Anglicans, like my father, to assist in maintaining their pro-British government and lifestyle. That's how bad things had become.

"So what do you hear from other Assembly members?" Logan asked. "Are we going to have a full-fledged war on our hands?"

Papa sighed. "Not if the Assembly can help it. We have a few Whigs from the western counties. But the rest are pretty level-headed. That said, we've begun issuing loan certificates to finance the militia." He shook his head. "Had no choice in the matter."

He referred to the mob of eight thousand descending on the State House yard after the details of Lexington and Concord arrived.

"It was either agree to provide funding or be tarred and feathered." Papa shook his head again.

"The real question," David said, "is how we go about riding this thing out. Your best guess is what, Papa, another six months before things get back to normal?"

"That's my expectation. Connecticut troops took Fort Ticonderoga in northeastern New York a few weeks back, but it was a fluke. A loss for the British, but not significant. The bulk of the British army is in Boston. Ten thousand colonial troops surround the city. But at some point the British are going to break out and the siege will end. I expect that to take a few months. You hear anything on your end, George?"

Logan was a factor with the dry goods house in England where we bought most of our wool, canvas, glass, hardware, china, and other dry goods we sold locally. His company sold to us on credit with the expectation of repayment within a year.

"I'm probably behind the times," said Logan, "because I spent the last six weeks getting here. But the scuttlebutt in London before I left was about three major generals on their way to Boston to assist General Gage. They should have arrived by now. I don't know what strategy they have up their sleeves, but your estimate of six months sounds about right."

"Are you able to continue supplying us?" asked David.

"We want to." Logan looked solemn. "Politicians squabble and armies shoot at each other. Which is what they are paid to do. We are businesspeople, we trade with each other. That's what we do. The only problem I see is getting past the naval blockade."

"How did you manage this trip?" I asked.

"It was touch and go for a while. We were flying the Union Jack, but a man-o-war still detained us for two days away from the City. They wanted to make sure we were not carrying munitions. They eventually let us through."

"That's not good," warned Papa. "Most of the British fleet are tied up in Boston, and yet they are still able to bottle up the mouth of the Delaware."

"We may not be so lucky next time." Logan looked worried.

"What does that mean?" asked Papa. "You're not shutting us down?"

Papa's question hung in the air as Mrs. Pickering entered the room with a tray laden with teapot, cups and pastries. "You can stop your business talk long enough to take a little tea," she said in a cheerful, high-pitched voice.

She had to step carefully to find her way to a table in the center of the room. The counting house was neatly cluttered with tools of the merchant trade. Two desks with oil lamps faced each other on either side of a fireplace built into an inside wall. A cabinet of shelves filled with papers, rolled parchments and books nearly reached the ceiling along another wall. Lead-framed glass windows supplied the daylight and were open to the fresh late-morning breezes. Sprawled out over several tabletops were books of accounts, maps, rulers, writing implements, wax seals and candles of varied vintage and size. And in a darkened corner squatted a heavy safe whose combination was known only to Papa and David.

Mrs. Pickering sensed the serious mood generated by Papa's question. "Oh, come now," she said, "nothing is so bad a cherry tart can't make it better. Isn't that right, Mr. Logan?"

She handed him a cup of tea and a pastry.

"Yes, ma'am."

Papa grinned. "Thanks, Elsie. You're right. Nothing is ever that bad."

"Exactly what I thought," said Mrs. Pickering. "If you need more tea just let me know. We'll serve dinner in about an hour and a half." She left as quickly as she arrived.

I sipped my tea in the silence that followed trying to figure out how we were going to survive if Logan really did intend to stop shipping inventory.

Molly spoke up. "You can't do that," she said.

In her early thirties, Molly had a dark complexion, a well-maintained figure, and quiet demeanor, but spoke her mind when pushed. Having lost interest in socializing when her husband died, she now spent most of her time supporting Papa and our family business. Much of the accounting work fell into her hands.

"I beg your pardon?" Logan responded. If not used to dealing with a woman in business, he was too much a gentleman to show it.

"You can't shut us down," Molly showed her emotion. "We're your best account. We always pay on time. Setting up with another supplier could take us a year, maybe longer."

"I didn't say we were shutting you down," Logan corrected her, "but we have to do something. The house can't afford to have one of its ships and cargo tied up in detention, whether by the British Navy or the rebels."

"What do you have in mind?" Papa asked.

"I've been trying to figure out something," Logan said thoughtfully, "ever since we were stopped by the man-o-war. The shipping lanes to the West Indies are always going to remain open. The best I can come up with is a plan where we could deliver the freight to, say, Jamaica? Or even closer? Perhaps, we could deliver to New Providence, north of Cuba. Then it's just a matter of getting it a few hundred miles from there to here."

An idea began forming.

"If your ships won't carry it the distance, what makes you think someone else's ships will?" David was quick to ask.

"The problem," said Logan, "is our trans-Atlantic ships are big and slow. What we need is to transfer the freight to a smaller, sleeker vessel capable of outrunning the naval blockade."

"About the size of a schooner," I suggested.

"Yes," Logan nodded, "a schooner or sloop. It would need a skilled captain willing to take a bit of risk. But the vessel ought to be able to outrun any British gun boat."

"We don't have a schooner," David interjected.

"No, but we could have one built," I offered.

The concept was one I had before. Thompson & Sons Trading Co. engaged in two types of trading activities. One was the dry goods business, whereby we imported household goods from England, and resold much of it to small shops from our warehouse on Front Street. The rest we sold directly to customers out of our own retail shop on Second Street.

After I joined the company, I developed the second part of our business, the provisions trade. We would buy or produce *provisions*, mostly flour and lumber, for resale abroad. Since we owned no ships, I acted as a middleman purchasing wheat and timber from farmers or millers. We processed some of it in our own mill, and transported it to the docks. We then sold the goods to one of the big firms, like James & Drinker, or Joshua Fisher & Sons, who handled its shipping and sale abroad.

I always thought our profits would grow a lot faster if we owned our own ship. The idea of purchasing a small ship like a schooner to handle trade between Philadelphia and the West Indies seemed like an ideal start. We could ship out with flour and lumber and fill up with dry goods for the return trip, making both going and coming profitable.

Papa brought me back to the discussion. "She would cost a good five-hundred pounds, son," he shook his head, "and that would be before outfitting her and paying the wages of captain and crew."

"And it would be five-hundred pounds sterling up front," added David with a scoff. "Shipyards don't take payment on the back end."

I knew all these facts, but in the rush of the moment I had spoken too soon without thinking things through. Then a lightning bolt struck. The man with the credit terms was sitting in our midst.

Trying to appear as if I had fully anticipated the financing obstacle, I turned to Logan. "George, what do you think? Is this an investment your firm could help us out with?"

As Papa turned his head in surprise, David rolled his eyes.

"Well," Logan sighed, "maybe we could work something out. Let me think about it."

"This is brilliant," Papa said excitedly. "It could be the start of a whole new era for us."

"Papa," David broke in with an exasperated tone, "what's gotten into you? Our business strength is importing and sales, not shipping. You said so many times yourself."

"That I did, David," Papa agreed, "but times change."

Turning to Logan he said, "Tell you what, George, we'll both give it a couple of days and talk again."

Chapter Seven

I left the counting house that afternoon to prepare for my overnight trip to our mill the next morning. With school suspended for the hot summer, Jonathon was coming with me. It would give me an opportunity to reconnect with him and try to improve his mopish outlook.

I took the long way home by Market Square. Our colony's militia had begun training on the square's open cobblestone. Their frequent exercises, and troops in brown uniforms that accompanied meetings of Congress in the State House, had begun giving the City a military feel. Nonetheless, Philadelphia remained many miles away from armed confrontations. I hoped things would stay that way.

From Market Square I took a turn east to the waterfront. Although shipping activity had fallen off from a year ago, the wharves remained the lifeblood of the City. Walking past the building where we rented our warehouse space, I saw it was locked up for the day. Most of our wholesale trading took place from early morning to noon. Our retail shop on Second Street, though, would still be open, and I decided to stop in for a brief visit.

The shop was the lower level in a row of two-story commercial establishments, with our shopkeeper's cramped quarters just above. As I entered, a bell jingling atop the door brought Mathew scurrying to the front.

"How are things?" I asked.

Mathew O'Leary squinted in the glare of the opened front door. Papa's Irish second cousin, Mathew had served as the company's shop-keeper for the last fifteen years. I do not recall ever seeing him without the leather apron he wore as he approached me with a friendly smile.

"Master Daniel, how good things are. And what is it that brings you to see me this fine afternoon?"

I looked around at the well-stocked shop. Bolts of cloth, died yarns and sewing supplies lined one wall. Next to them were coils of rope and chain of different sizes, with cooking utensils nearby stacked on tables and hanging down from racks suspended from the ceiling. Garden, farm and smith tools occupied another wall, mixed in with all kinds of building supplies, buckets and baskets. The shop maintained a good stock of glassware for drinking, windows, lamps, vases and bottles, along with a myriad of other things.

"Just taking a walk before supper," I replied. "While I'm here, I should pick up a few balls of yarn to take with me to our miller's wife. I'm sure she would be appreciative."

"Of course," said Mathew, "just help yourself. Have you heard the latest from our esteemed Congress meeting in the State House?"

"The latest? Probably not," I said while stuffing a dozen yarn balls into a burlap bag. "What are they up to now?'

"Appointing George Washington from Virginia to command the army."

"What army?" I asked. "Congress has no army. Who will he command?"

"The Boston Army, or militia, or whatever it is they are calling themselves these days. You know, the guys with the muskets holding the British at bay in Boston."

"If that's who he's going to command, why didn't they just appoint John Hancock from Boston? Wouldn't that have made more sense? He wouldn't have to travel as far."

Mathew shook his head. "Master Daniel, I just report the news, I don't try to figure it out."

The news disappointed me. If a man like Washington, one of the richest in the colonies, favored war with England, many others from the upper echelons of society would join him.

"You have to wonder why a man like that would accept," I said with disgust. "He's got more to lose than anyone if this thing escalates and the hostilities go sour."

"A lot to lose, true, but maybe a lot to gain if the effort succeeds."

I wondered vaguely whose side Mathew was on.

"How is Jonathon working out?" I asked, changing subjects. I had arranged for Jonathon to work in the shop a few hours a day to help clean up and restock merchandise from the warehouse.

Mathew gave me a sidelong glance before answering. "He does just fine when he comes in. He's getting to know when we're low on an item and goes to the warehouse on his own to restock. Very bright boy."

I almost ignored his answer, but asked off handedly, "When he comes in? What do you mean? Hasn't he been coming in every day?"

"Not every day, Master Daniel. I'm sure your wife has him busy with other things."

He was probably right. "When was Jonathon last here?"

"It has been several days." Mathew avoided eye contact.

I thanked him, burlap bag in hand, and finished walking home. The principals of Thompson Trading were far from being among the merchant princes of the City like Robert Morris, or Thomas Willing. Neither, though, were we among the paupers. We were middling merchants, and I felt comfortable where we were on the social ladder.

Our house reflected our position. It was neither sumptuous like some of the mansions along Front and Penn Streets, nor cramped and dingy like the townhouses in Elfriths Alley. It stood two stories tall, with an attic, where Jonathon slept, and cellar for storage. Alphonse, our bonded man, stayed in a closet-sized sleeping room in the stable, heated by a Franklin stove.

I found Sarah in the kitchen setting the table for supper with the help of Janie. Sarah had been the love of my life ever since I met her in the early 1760s. I was attending the College of Philadelphia at the time, where I completed two years before joining Papa's company full time. Sarah was the daughter of an Anglican priest who served, not at Christ Church where we now went, but at a smaller congregation on the north side. One Sunday morning our churches met together for a combined mass, and I ended up sitting next to her. I promptly fell asleep, whereupon my sister Missy, sitting to my other side, jabbed in the ribs. I woke up with such a start everyone in the pew in front of us turned around. Sarah could not stop laughing, and that was when I noticed her. I always thought myself a handsome guy, but I was not nearly as handsome as she was beautiful.

I kissed Sarah and Janie, saw Annie in the corner reading a penny book, and stooped down to kiss her as well.

"So, what are we having for supper tonight?"

"Pork pie from the baker's," Janie answered. "And boiled turnips. Mama made them."

"And sliced apples," Annie called out from the corner. "I helped cut them."

"I'm sure they will be sweet, then," I said to Annie, rolling her eyes. At thirteen, both girls considered themselves too grown up for sweet talk from their father.

Sarah did not cook much indoors during the summer months. Tonight she boiled vegetables on the wood-burning cook stove. Any serious cooking she did outside in an earthen oven.

"Alphonse coming in for supper?" I asked.

"As soon as he finishes up in the garden."

Alphonse was from Prussia by way of Scotland. That was where the authorities convicted him of theft when he was eighteen. They forced him onto a ship headed to the colonies. We had purchased his contract soon after he landed in the City. He now was in the third year of a seven-year indenture. Gruff looking though he was, he worked hard at maintaining the house and the garden.

"Mathew says Congress is appointing George Washington to command the Boston Army," I said to Sarah.

"I heard the same from Mrs. Lisle. Her boys have been members of the Association for a couple of months. They're hoping to be assigned to Washington's command."

"That will never happen."

"Why not?

"Because the militia protects the colony. It doesn't fight in another colony."

"They are happy with the choice in any event."

"I think it's a disaster."

Alphonse came in, washed up in a sink that drained through a tile to the outside, and sat down quietly at the table.

"Any blooms on the tomatoes yet?" I asked him.

"A few, sir, but we're behind last year due to the dry spell."

"How early tomorrow, Papa?" Jonathon cut in after coming down to join us for supper.

Goodness, I thought, he was actually showing an interest in our trip to the mill. I had been half afraid he would find an excuse not to go. Still, I did not want to appear over anxious about his coming along. Funny thing about kids. You push too hard in one direction, and they will resist every time.

"I have some stops to make before we get to the mill," I said pensively, "so I would like to get an early start. As soon as Mama packs our dinner, we ought to be on the road. Maybe seven-thirty."

I wanted to leave earlier but did not want to press my luck.

"Can I bring my fishing pole and knife?"

I could not believe it. He actually was looking forward to the trip.

"Sure," I answered nonchalantly.

We all sat down to eat, and I said the blessing. Our main meal, dinner, we ate at noon. Supper was lighter, sometimes not more than a snack.

"Why do you think he's a disaster?" asked Sarah.

"You mean Washington? He's not the disaster. His appointment is. It means the rabble-rousing commoners from the northeast no longer spearhead the movement. Support has spread to the south, and worse yet, to the wealthy. Not a good day for those of us who prefer peace."

"Oh, now, Daniel, things can't be that bad. The ships are still getting through, are they not? Logan arrived a few days ago."

"Who knows how long it's going to last. Speaking of ships and Logan, we talked today about his helping Thompson Trading finance one of our own."

Sarah grimaced involuntarily. The girls looked up. Jonathon turned in wild surprise.

"Our own ship? Really, Papa?" he asked in amazement. "You think I could become a sailor?"

"You must be joking!" Sarah was fast to answer her son.

"Don't get too excited, or upset," I said. "It's only in the talk stage.

"Could we go around the world?" Jonathon's eyes lit up. This was the most excitement he had ever shown about anything.

"No, Jon, this would be a small ship, a schooner. It would only go as far as the West Indies."

"We are merchants, not sailors." Sarah shook her head.

"You sound like David."

"What did your father say?"

"He sort of liked the idea."

"I could become the captain." Jonathon raised an arm and struck down as if giving orders to the crew from the point of a cutlass.

"You don't know anything about sailing," Janie snapped. "Besides you get sea-sick and barf." She giggled.

Annie joined in laughing. "You'd barf on the poop deck, which is why they call it the poop deck."

The girls laughed hysterically, and even Alphonse let out a guffaw. I had to suppress my own smile. But none of this seemed to bother Jonathon, who continued giving his imaginary captain-of-the-ship orders.

"All right, enough," I said. "Time to move to something else. Jonathon, what did you do today?"

Jonathon suddenly became motionless and stared down at his food.

"What's gotten into you, boy?" Sarah asked him. Turning to me she added, "He spent most of the day helping Mathew at the shop."

"No, he didn't," I said without thinking. "He hasn't helped out for several days."

Sarah looked startled. "What do you mean?" She turned her head to face Jonathon. "Young man, you told me you were at the shop. Were you or not?"

The atmosphere at the table thickened. I half hoped Jonathon would lie again. That would buy him some time, and maybe it would just blow over.

"No, Mama," he said sheepishly.

"Where were you?" Sarah wanted to know.

"With my friends at Elfrith's Alley."

It was not just that Jonathon's friends at Elfrith's Alley were sons of trades people and day laborers. We had tried to discourage these connections and to coax more of an interest toward the children of professionals and merchants. The more immediate problem was that we had caught him in a lie. And that meant I had to punish him.

Sarah looked expectantly at me. This was my job, and one I hated. Hitting our kids never set well with me. We did from time to time. But I avoided that option whenever I could, which is why I sat there, trying to think of some other form of punishment. Only one thing occurred to me.

"Jonathon," I said gravely, "you lied to your mother. On top of that, you failed to perform the job we assigned you. You proved yourself dishonest and unreliable. So you will stay home tomorrow and not go to the mill."

He gave me a look of desperation, his lips quivering. "Papa, you said I could come."

"I know what I said. But I didn't anticipate your lying to your mother and not showing up for work with Mathew. You stay home tomorrow and help Alphonse in the garden. And no playing the fiddle. The next day you report to Mathew at the shop and we'll see how things go."

He stood up. "You promised I could go. You cannot . . . ."

Looking mad and sad, he turned and ran up the stairs to his attic bedroom, crying like the immature kid he was. I wanted to cry too, for him.

All I could do was sigh and shake my head.

We sat at the table in silence for several minutes.

Then Janie spoke up. "What about me, Papa. Annie and me."

"What do you mean, honey?"

"If Jonathon's not going to the mill with you, can we go?"

"All the way to the mill?" I gave Sarah a quick glance.

Sarah shook her head. "Girls, remember we were going to get together with Mrs. Lisle and work on our sewing. She's offered to show you how to stitch letters onto a quilt."

"But Mama," Annie almost whined, "Janie and I haven't been to the mill in years. Jonathon went last summer. Why can't we go?"

I tried to think of a reason why not and concluded it would actually be nice to have some company. "It's fine with me, if your mother approves."

"Daniel." Sarah used her tone of disappointment. She did not like to be the one saying no.

"Three can squeeze onto the chaise," I said. "We'll arrive in a couple of hours, and they can play around the mill and creek. We'll return Thursday and be back by midafternoon."

"Where will they sleep?" Sarah wanted to know.

"Swenson and his wife are nice people. They have an extra room where the girls can sleep, or in the parlor."

She gave me a woeful expression and I guessed her real concern.

"It is only fifteen miles," I responded. "It's safe . . . not like we're going to Pittsburgh."

When Sarah nodded her begrudging consent, the girls whooped with excitement.

Chapter Eight

We started on time the next morning. Although destined to be a warm day, it started cool so the girls wore their shawls. One would sit next to me in the chaise's two-person chair, and the other on the platform in the back looking to the rear. Then they would change places, or both sit in the back, or both try to squeeze in the chair, or trot alongside the chaise for a piece. We traveled light, with just a bag containing a few overnight clothes. I brought my musket, with the idea of doing some shooting with Swenson's slave, Willie, if we had time the next morning.

Chester County had upwards of a hundred grist mills along one or another waterway. Most grist mills served local farmers by grinding grain for their personal use in return for a portion of the final product, one eighth being the going rate. The Thompson mill, however, was a merchant mill that actually bought the grain from the farmers, ground it, barreled it, and shipped it for sale afar. In the last few years we handled upwards of six-hundred barrels per year, both our own production and some purchased from other mills.

I spotted the stone cottage, frame barn and barrel shop about a quarter mile away and pointed the buildings out to the girls. The mill itself was down an embankment alongside the creek and out of view from the road.

Marvin Swenson, our manager, oversaw six to ten workers depending on the time of year. They included bonded men who stayed on the mill premises and day laborers who lived nearby. They hauled bags of grain to the top floor of the three-story mill by pulley. Or, they worked in the sifting process or bagged ground grain. Sometimes, they worked in the barrel shop fashioning barrels out of staves and hoops. When grinding operations were converted to a sawmill for the winter months, everyone helped cut timber, both for our use and for sale. Mill operation involved plenty of work.

As we approached, Marvin and his wife emerged from the cottage. He did not look at all well, walking with a cane and one arm on his wife's shoulder for support. Both smiled broadly when they saw the girls were with me.

"Daniel," Marvin said, "I knew you would be showing up one of these days, but I had no idea you would be bringing such pretty helpers with you."

Annie and Janie were on their best behavior. Stepping down from the chaise, they curtsied politely. "It's nice to meet you, sir. It's nice to meet you, ma'am," they said simultaneously.

"You two are so nice to come way out here to visit us." Mrs. Swenson looked pleased to have some female company, even at their age. "You must have gotten up so early today. Come in and I'll fix you some nice tea and toast."

"You're sure we're not imposing?" I asked.

"Not in the least. And of course you're staying overnight so I'll fix the two girls up right nice in our extra bedroom."

We stepped into the central room of the cottage, which served as both parlor and kitchen.

While chatting amiably I gave Mrs. Swenson the balls of yarn I had brought along. While Marvin managed the operation, she took charge of the cooking, including dinner at noon for the whole crew and three meals per day for the bonded men.

I asked Marvin about his health.

"Damnedest thing," he said. "I sometimes get tired and run out of breath no matter what I do. I walk from here to the mill and I'm panting. And then my legs get bloated. Doc says I need to keep my legs up to help with the swelling. But if my legs are up no work gets done."

His description sounded worse than I remembered. He had become a friend over the years, and his condition caused me concern.

"We have no interest in replacing you, Marvin," I said. "But maybe you ought to think about taking some time off, or even retiring. Your health comes first. How old are you, anyway?

"I'm 52, and what you say is nothing different from what Ruth's been preaching for the last two years. I'll give it some thought, but I can tell you this. I would not have made it this far without Willie."

"Willie knows how to handle a musket. I can attest to that. But what does he know about milling operations?"

The Swensons owned both Willie and his wife. They lived in a shanty about a hundred yards from the Swenson's stone cottage. Being property of the Swensons, Marvin had no obligation to use either one in the service of my family's milling operations. So Marvin's revelation about Willie being involved in the business surprised me.

"What does he know? What doesn't he know? He's been my eyes and ears for the last eight months. He can operate that mill as well as I can, and when something goes wrong, he knows how to fix it."

I had to ask, "The men take orders from a black man, a slave no less?"

"Has not been a problem."

Most Pennsylvanians, including the Quakers until recently, never had moral reservations about owning slaves. Unlike in the south, our small Pennsylvanian farms never supported a widespread slave-holding community. We also lured more northern Europeans to our part of the country who were willing to indenture themselves for several years in return for ship passage. Nevertheless, many households owned slaves, and those that did almost always used them for menial and hard labor. Willie, however, appeared to have become Marvin's right-hand man. I was not sure what to think.

When Marvin sensed my unease he said, "Daniel, they're just like us. You just have to give them a chance is all. And a little training."

It was time to get down to business. "I promised the girls they could play outside along the creek while you and I talked shop. Any place they ought to stay away from?"

"They should stay downstream from the mill works," Marvin said. "But other than that, it's pretty safe. The creek is shallow, and you can cross maybe fifty yards to the south. If you girls get lucky, you might see some deer in the forest on the other side."

"That's right," Mrs. Swenson said. "And this time of year a lot of fawns are around. I'll show you where the apples are and you can feed them."

"What about bears this time of year?" I asked.

"We see them once in a while." Marvin assured me, "They are just curious and don't stick around. They won't bother the girls any."

With the girls off on their own, Marvin and I spent the next several hours inspecting the mill, going over accounts, and discussing operations.

Thompson Trading owned about sixty acres of forested land around the mill, which assured us plenty of lumber to maintain the mill structure, waterwheel, and adjoining gates and canals with plenty to spare for other uses. We examined the mill works and talked about needed repairs. We also went inside the mill to view the huge two-ton grinding stones. There we found Willie just having taken the stones out of gear and in the process of adjusting their cut.

"A problem?" I asked.

"No real problem," he answered without looking up. "We just had them sharpened last week, and they're grinding a bit uneven."

"How can you tell?"

"Texture of the meal."

"He feels the ground meal with his thumb and fingers," Marvin explained. "Here, I'll show you."

Marvin lumbered slowly down a stairway with me behind to an area directly beneath the millstones where the wheat grind escaped the stones through a chute onto a bolter. Two men were filling and sealing barrels of ground flour nearby. Marvin picked up a handful of meal before it descended onto the bolter.

"Here, feel this," he said. "It's not consistent throughout. Compare it to this." He picked up a sample from a bag on the floor. "This handful is properly ground."

While I gave a knowing nod, I could barely tell the difference. We returned back upstairs, where Willie was putting the runner stone back in gear.

"That should do it," he said. The room instantly came alive with moving shafts, wheels, gears and grain sliding down from an upper floor through a spout.

"Willie, tell Daniel your idea about loading the hopper by wagon instead of by hand."

That I had to hear. Milling raw grain began with hauling it in bags up three stories, either on backs of laborers or by rope and pulley. It was then fed into a hopper that would guide it back down through a hole in the runner stone for grinding.

Willie looked at me sheepishly. "It's not that much of an idea, sir. Basically, we could build up the earthworks around the mill, to allow a horse to pull a wagon up to the third floor, and then unload right next to the hopper."

The simplicity of the idea stunned me. Implementing it potentially meant a farmer could deliver the grain to the hopper himself. We could eliminate two or three mill workers. Of course, logistical issues existed, but the end result was a wagon-in and wagon-out facility. A great idea.

"Nice thinking," I said. "Let me run that by some friends of mine in the City. You may be onto something."

Marvin and I spent the rest of the afternoon going over the accounts back at the cottage and talking about what effects the hostilities with the British might have on business.

★

It was late afternoon when I glanced out the window and saw Annie walking up the path from the creek. Her clothes were soiled from playing on the banks near the water.

I leaned out the window and yelled, "Where's your sister?"

She walked closer and shook her head. "I lost her. She went into the trees to feed a deer, and I never saw her after that. I thought maybe she came back."

"You left your sister in the woods?" My tone reflected my irritation.

"No, Papa, she left me. I waited almost an hour."

"Janie has been gone for an hour?"

I turned to Marvin, "Where is Ruth. My daughter is missing."

The three of us found Ruth in the garden behind the cottage, but she had seen nothing of Janie. I felt a sick, panic-like sensation begin to form in my stomach.

"All right, Annie, we'll go back and find her. I'm sure she'll be fine."

"I'm too slow to come with you." Marvin looked sad. "Let me call Willie and a couple of the boys to help look. She can't have gone far."

Annie led four of us to a shallow area of the creek a few hundred feet downstream the mill. She explained how she and Janie had been building a mud castle on the far side of the creek when Janie decided to try to feed a doe and her fawn that had ventured close. When she looked up a few minutes later, Janie had disappeared into the foliage. Annie climbed the embankment, looked around, called Janie's name, and returned to the side of the creek to await her sister's return.

Annie pointed to the spot she last saw her sister. The five of us then spread out fifty feet apart and began walking northwestwardly away from the creek, shouting Janie's name. We had not progressed more than twenty-five yards when it became evident to me how thick the woods were and how easy it would be for anyone to lose her way. The sick feeling returned. Looking toward Annie, I could not see her clearly through the trees, but I could tell from her voice she was worried, and her worry worried me.

The time was getting on past seven o'clock, and the light in the forest was fading.

Willie came over. "Mr. Thompson, I'm going to send one of the boys back to pick up a few lamps. That way we can continue a little while longer."

"A little while?" I responded. "We're staying out here until we find her."

Willie nodded.

I spoke with determination, but I knew staying out there much longer, even with an oil lamp in hand, would do no good.

By the time the lamps arrived, I was feeling my way blindly through the underbrush. I convened a meeting of the search party, and we gathered around the lamps.

"Willie," I kept my voice emotionless, "you've hunted these woods before?"

"Yes, sir. Many times, at Master Marvin's request."

"Tell me what's in here. Any houses or shelters or paths or even clearings she might have found and could lead us to her?"

"You keep heading this direction another mile or so," Willie pointed in the direction we had been walking, "you'll come to the Rock Run which branches off the French Creek. If she made it that far, which I doubt, she would have to turn to the north and east. No houses, though, it's all forest. A trail runs southeast to northwest the Lenape still use, but it's pretty far to the east of here. She would never have made it that far by now. She probably would not recognize any of the foot paths."

"Do the Lenape ever get close to the mill?"

"We see Indians from time to time, but they mostly steer clear of the Thompson property."

"What else is back there? Bear, wolves, coyote?"

Willie's eyes shifted. "No, sir." He was lying.

"You're familiar with this forest," I said. "What do you suggest?"

"I can probably track her," he said, "but not this dark."

I thought about what my daughter probably was going through right at that moment: tired and hungry, sitting uncomfortably under some tree, maybe in pain, she would be shivering and feeling terrified of the dark. And who knew what dangers lurked? Bears maybe, we occasionally saw coyotes, sometimes wolves, even cougars were known to stray into these parts, not to mention creeks and rivers, precipices she could fall down, and thick underbrush that might entangle her. Yet nothing I could do this moment would make things any better.

"All right, here's what we'll do," I said. "Willie, you and I will stay out here and keep the fire going over night. If Janie is able to move somewhere close, maybe she will see the fire and shout out. At daybreak we'll track her. Just the two of us. We'll be able to move faster. And we will take our muskets. The rest of you go on back, including you, Annie."

"But, Papa," Annie said, looking scared. "She's my twin. She needs me."

"Annie, you go back and stay with Mrs. Swenson. It's not your fault, you did nothing wrong. Janie will be just fine, I promise. She's probably fallen and hurt herself somewhere, and we'll find her in the morning. One of these men should bring us back some jerky and ale to get us through the night, and a couple of blankets. Now, go!"

★

In my youth I spent many a night outdoors next to a campfire on hunting trips with my father and brother. So the concept was nothing extraordinary for me. This was different because I was worried as hell. My stomach was in knots. With every piece of wood I put on the fire, I looked to the east to catch the first hint of daylight. In the darkness I thought gravely about how I would face Sarah if we came home without Janie. I knew I could not do it.

When finally I did see the first sun rays, I jostled Willie.

He glanced up and said, "Better give it another half hour. In the meantime, eat and drink a little. We have some walking to do."

A Negro telling me what to do. Under other circumstances I may have gotten upset. But he gave good guidance.

We soon extinguished the fire and went back to the spot where Annie said she had last seen Janie. Instead of moving blindly to the northwest as we did the night before, Willie searched around for evidence of Janie's movements. Annie said she was following a doe and her fawn, so he looked for fresh deer tracks and a child's shoe print together. Eventually he found them and observed that, instead of moving to the northwest, they tracked more to the northeast. Willie had a good instinct about the path a deer would follow. And for the first hundred yards or so he was able to confirm his guesses with tracks in the dirt.

At that point, Willie pointed out bits of apple and core on the foliage.

"She finally got them to eat out of her hand," I said. "It took her long enough." I wanted to smile but could not.

"My guess is she loses her four-legged friends here, and now is on her own."

I nodded, and we looked for evidence of her movement. I had never been much of a tracker. But with Willie's instruction I soon caught on to subtle impressions in the grass and dirt, broken twigs, fallen or bent foliage and other signs. We eventually found her shoes' wooden heel markings along a narrow gulley. Possibly on the supposition it would lead her back to the French Creek, she appeared to have walked along the gulley for a good five-hundred yards or so. The water in the gulley, however, was too low to flow. So, instead of walking in the direction the water would have flowed had it been higher, she walked in the exact opposite direction, away from French Creek.

What Willie pointed out next startled me: hoof prints.

"Deer? Cattle?" I asked.

"No, horse, but not shoed."

"Being ridden?"

"Probably."

"What do you think, Indian?"

"That's my guess."

"Are we close to the Indian trail?"

"Not far away," Willie shrugged. "Maybe another half a mile east."

Most of the Lenape tribe remnants this far east were friendly, but one always placed caution before trust in dealing with Indians. The colonial government had been pushing the Indians westward for decades, not always by the most ethical means. Many Indians harbored resentment. The atrocities from Pontiac's rebellion in the '60s still loomed large. One could debate whose atrocities – the British or Indian – were more heinous. Such a debate would only corroborate how the civility of the Lenape could not be taken for granted. Add that to the danger any young and pretty girl in back country might face, and my concern for Janie's safety heightened.

"How late you think it was when she reached this point?"

"Dusk," said Willie. "Too late for her to have been brought back to the mill from here."

"So . . . they could not have gone far."

We traced the hoof prints northeast about mile when we began noticing a second set of hoof prints, then footprints, bits of clothing and a bird carcass. We slowed our pace and moved more cautiously.

Upon hearing a horse's whiney, we dropped to hands and knees knowing we were getting close to whatever it was we had stumbled upon. A hunting camp. Peering through the trees and brush from about sixty feet away, we saw two dome-shaped wigwams made of birch bark stretched over bent poles. A squaw bent over a cooking fire, and a horse pulled on its tie rope nearby. But no sign of Janie.

I whispered to Willie, "I'm going to walk into the camp. You stay here and cover me."

He nodded. I handed him my musket, stood up, held my arms out to my sides to show I was unarmed, and began walking toward the squaw.

"Hello," I shouted, "I come as friend."

An Indian wearing a breechcloth, leggings and moccasins appeared from nowhere to my right. I stopped. He was bare from the waist up and carried a spear in hand and a tomahawk in his belt. He eyed me warily and then nodded deliberately in the direction of Willie. I sensed he was telling me Willie should disarm. I wanted no trouble.

"Willie," I called out, without taking my eyes off the Indian, "put down the musket and come forward."

Willie joined me unarmed near the center of the camp, and almost immediately two more men, dressed similar to the first, emerged from behind trees. At the same time a boy about fifteen-years-old stepped out from one of the wigwams. He looked similar to the others but wore a leather tunic. They all appeared to have been waiting for us to make our move. And now we were their prisoners, if prisoners they wanted.

I knew nothing of the Lenape language, and had to struggle along in English and made-up sign language.

"Daughter," I held my hand out about waist high to indicate a short person. "Looking for." I held my hand to my eyebrows and looked around as if searching.

They watched me curiously.

"Papa, is that you?"

The voice came from the wigwam from which the boy had just emerged.

"Janie! Are you hurt, baby?"

An instant later she came bounding out of the wigwam's opening and leapt into my arms. My tears of joy competed with pangs of anger over the last twelve hours of anxiety and exhaustion.

"Where have you been, young lady? You have no idea . . . ."

"Papa, I'm so sorry. Please . . . ."

The tears of joy won out as she pressed her face against my mine.

I looked around and suddenly realized I had not yet determined if we were among friend or foe.

"Did that boy touch you?"

"No, Papa," she laughed, "he was very nice to me. I've been teaching him English. They let me sleep in the hut last night with the lady."

My fears were allayed. These were nice people. I took a deep breath and put Janie down.

"Thank you," I said to the Indian who first appeared and who acted as the leader of the group. He gave no evidence of having understood me. Another Indian walked over and handed the leader our muskets. The leader took the muskets and handed one to me and one to Willie. He then pointed to the three of us and made a sweeping gesture with his finger to the forest beyond the camp. He was telling us to leave.

"Janie," I said, "which one picked you up last night and brought you here?"

"It was the boy."

I pointed to the leader and then the boy; and then I pointed to Janie and me. It was a clumsy gesture but I think he understood I was asking if the boy was his son. The leader, expressionless, nodded his head.

I took a few paces over to the son and with both hands I handed him my musket. I then took off my cartridge pouch and handed that to him as well. They were the best and only gifts I had available for the safe return of my daughter.

Holding Janie's hand, I nodded to Willie for the three of us to leave. We walked out of the camp in the direction from where we came.

Not more than twenty feet away, a voice called out from the camp, "Jane, good bye."

"Oh, Papa," squealed Janie, jumping around in delight. "He remembered!"

Chapter Nine

Trial Proceedings

"That began your friendship with the Indians?" asked the Judge Advocate.

"My friendship with the Indians?" repeated Daniel. "What kind of question is that?"

"You find it offensive?"

"I find it asinine. The Indians are no more my friends than the white people are. Some are and some are not."

"Let me clarify. Did you continue to have dealings with the Lenape tribe?" asked the Judge Advocate.

"No," Daniel said, "not the tribe, but the Indian boy later became a problem."

"Just out of curiosity, did you ever see your musket again?"

"I did as a matter of fact, a couple years later. In the meantime, I bought a new one. Brown Besses were still easy to come by in those days.

"You said earlier you were a less committed Loyalist than your father. What did you mean by that?

"I meant I was open to considering independence. My father was not."

"Be specific. Did you actually do anything at that time that evidenced the fact you were less committed than your father?"

"At that time? I'd have to think." Daniel paused. "As a matter of fact, yes, I did. I tolerated my sister Missy. She was a handful to begin with, but an ardent Patriot on top of that. My father had virtually no contact with her, in part because of her political views."

"Your sister? That's her, sitting in the front row?"

"Yes, of course. That's my sister."

Missy nodded.

"She seems nice enough," said the Judge Advocate. Missy scowled. "Anything else?"

"Yes, I overheard some confidential information that could have caused a problem for the Continental Army. If I had been a staunch Loyalist I would have disclosed it publicly, but decided not to."

"Really," said the Judge Advocate with skepticism. "I'd like to hear about that. But I take it, despite your lesser commitment to the Loyalists, you continued to trade with the enemy?"

"The enemy? No. We continued to do business with our British supply house. They were not shooting at anybody."

"So even though your supply house paid duties to the King of England, you felt it was all right to do business with them because they were not shooting at you, is that right?"

"Of course we did. It was not a matter of being Loyalist or Patriot. No one told us to stop. And if all the merchants had stopped importing goods from England, we would have had a lot of angry citizens on our hands. Of all political persuasions."

"Didn't the trading become more difficult?"

"It did after a while, yes. That was why we built the ship."

"Tell us what you recall."

"The next year went quickly," Daniel began. "It ended in tragedy, so I have to think carefully what occurred."

Chapter Ten

We arrived back from the mill safely and gave Sarah the minute-by-minute version of Janie's rescue. Angry at first, Sarah eventually made me commit to never taking the girls out of the City again without their mother coming along. She need not have given such an edict. While this adventure ended with few ill effects, I was not about to take another chance. I loved all my children dearly, but the girls were the special prizes of their mother.

I say few ill effects because I began noticing a growing distance between Annie and Janie. Prior to that time, I rarely saw one without the other. Like two peas in a pod, they agreed on everything. Janie, however, never tired of telling how she was *captured* by an *Indian prince*, who took her to a *forest palace* where she educated him by *teaching him English*. While the details varied with the telling, she made Annie jealous. The fact Jonathon's respect for Janie grew with each rendition did not help matters.

Before the end of June 1775 we received word the British attempt to break the Boston siege turned out to be . . . unsuccessful! Papa's prediction had been wrong. In the battle, the British took control of key positions: Breed's Hill and Bunker Hill, near Boston. From that perspective they had won. But in the process they lost more soldiers than the colonists. And they remained under the siege begun in April. The colonists' success did not bode well for an early end to hostilities.

"I can't believe it," said Papa to George Logan toward summer's end. "General Howe controls the coast and his troops are well equipped. He doesn't have to remain besieged. He can outflank that army of rabble by land and sea."

Logan shook his head, embarrassed for his homeland.

By the end of August our own church pastor at the time, Dr. William Smith, could be heard preaching Pro-Whig sermons from the pulpit, at least to my family's ears. He would talk about the colonists as having chosen lands different from their fathers, similar to the tribes of Israel occupying opposite sides of the River Jordan. And although the English and Americans had many common goals, the Americans . . . like the Jews against the Egyptians . . . were entitled to use force to resist oppression and protect their common safety.

"From the mouth of an Englishman, no less!" said Papa to Dr. Smith one Sunday following the service at Christ Church. "You're giving license to take up arms against the very powers who put you where you are today."

His raised voice, and the delicacy of the subject matter, drew a crowd. The pastor took a moment to reflect, perhaps knowing Papa was hardly alone in his sentiments. But he knew as well the growing support for military action against the British.

"Steven," said Dr. Smith, "I don't presume to grant license to do anything. I encourage people to do good and discourage them from evil. That's the limit of my authority. My message today did nothing more than urge our members to resist oppression and take heed for their common safety. It's what I've been preaching for the last twenty years."

"Let's cut through all this," said Papa. "Who do you support, the treasonous Whigs or his Majesty's Royal troops who have protected our common safety for most of our lifetimes?"

"You're asking me a political question." Dr. Smith shook his head. "I never take sides in politics. But I will say this. I support neither treason nor oppression. I also don't favor war, but if war comes, let it be short and decisive, and fought in the name of peace and prosperity."

Just like a preacher, I thought, never a straight answer. We did not stop going to church after that, but Papa's grumblings continued.

Hope for peace had not been completely lost, however. Peace feelers occasionally made their way from London to the Continental Congress meeting in Philadelphia. Sometimes they made the return trip. Even though unsuccessful they made me think the world had not lost all its senses.

Our own John Dickenson sent back a peace proposal to England, aptly named the Olive Branch Petition. Dickenson was one of Pennsylvania's delegates to Congress, and also held a seat on the Pennsylvania Assembly. He drafted what might best be described as an apology to King George, asking for understanding and reconciliation. The petition was carried across the sea by a descendant of William Penn himself. In November we learned of the King's rejection.

★

In December I took Sarah and the kids to the City Tavern to celebrate Sarah's birthday. It was only once in a great while our family ate at a public establishment. The City Tavern was one of the nicer ones. Members of Congress, Pennsylvania Assembly members, wealthy merchants and bankers often dined there. Rich tapestries adorned the walls, and a huge chandelier able to be lowered by rope to add new candles every night, lit the main dining area. Sitting at tables, not just trestle benches, diners chose among huge joints of meat roasted on an indoor fire pit. The place was one of the few allowing families with children, at least if they arrived before the heavy drinkers and men in search of prostitutes.

Going out for dinner once a year on Sarah's birthday had become something of a family tradition. That year, a few days before her birthday, Sarah had announced she was pregnant. Missy and her husband, Peter, brought their son, Nathan, to join the celebration. We had a table off to the side of the main dining area big enough to accommodate the eight of us.

"Just remember," said Peter as we finished eating, "if you ever want to give the kid up for adoption, Missy will take him or her off your hands."

"In a heartbeat," said Missy.

"That's very generous," Sarah laughed, "but we'll manage. The girls are old enough to help out. It'll be good training. We do, though, want you two to serve as god-parents."

Missy lit up. "We'd be honored."

"Where's the baby going to sleep?" asked Annie.

"For a while he'll sleep with us," Sarah said. "And we'll use the upstairs parlor as a maternity room for a couple of years. After that, we'll have to see."

"I'm not giving up the attic," Jonathon announced.

Missy turned to me. "I'm very happy for both of you. Actually all five of you. We've not had an addition to the Thompson family for years now, so it's about time. What does Papa say?"

"When did you last talk to him?" I asked.

"At the picnic in April. But you know how things are. He has to force himself to say 'hello.'"

I felt bad for Missy, being deprived of a big family of her own making, she would have been content with a big extended family. Yet Peter's side of the family offered little opportunity for participation, his only relative within a hundred miles being his ailing mother. Our father, on the other hand, found her and Peter's politics intolerable. Ever since Papa became interested in the Assembly and took his politics more seriously, the acrimony between them grew to the point where Papa now barely recognized their existence.

True, I stood in Papa's camp when it came to England, but I was much more pragmatic than either Papa or David. Compared to them, on the one hand, and Missy and Peter on the other, I was practically a-political. I simply favored what seemed to work best, and what to me worked best was the status quo.

"Papa's happy for us," I said. "Not as happy as Mrs. Pickering is." Missy laughed. "But at least he seems pleased."

"So tell us what happened in school the other day," Sarah said turning to Nathan. "Jonathon came home laughing so hard we could barely understand what he was talking about."

Nathan held up his hands, as if to show his innocence. "I know very little about it."

"Yes he does," Jonathon laughed and pointed. "He was at the center of it."

"He almost got the whipping of his life," offered Peter, frowning. "That's what happened."

"I swear," said Nathan, maintaining a half-convincing show of innocence, "all I did was furnish the twine. It was out of my hands after that."

"The twine for what?" asked Annie. "I heard nothing about this."

"Go ahead," said Peter, "tell them."

"It was twine that got threaded through a loop in Mr. Mc Gillicutty's wig during study period."

"Threaded through?" asked Annie. "What do you mean?"

"One end was tied around the loop, and the other end was tied to the handle on the door to the hallway behind him."

"Didn't he see it?"

"No," Nathan answered. "He'd fallen asleep in class."

Jonathon could not restrain himself and burst out laughing. "And then the headmaster comes through the door, and swoosh, the wig flies onto the floor!" Jonathon was almost convulsing. "And the headmaster says, 'What's going on here,' and even he starts laughing."

Annie and Janie shrieked with laughter. The boys told a good story, and Missy, Sarah and I could not help but join in. Even Peter, who tried to maintain the role of stern parent, had to smile although he shook his head at the same time.

"Poor Mr. McGillicutty must have been pretty upset," Sarah said. "Did he catch the culprit?"

"Upset?" Nathan echoed. "That doesn't come close. He was furious. The poor kid got a whipping. But he said it was worth it."

"You boys," Missy said. "One of these days, you're going to be the one getting caught."

"I swear, Ma," Nathan put up his hand, "I didn't even know why he wanted the twine."

The large center table in the dining area erupted in shouting. Although it soon subsided, we all looked to see what was happening. A dozen distinguished looking men occupied the chairs around it. All were in waist coats and breeches, along with several well-dressed ladies.

"Who are those people?" Jonathon asked.

"Mostly government officials," I said.

"Tory or Whig?"

I looked at the table's occupants. "I'd say more Tory than Whig. Peter, what do you think?"

"Maybe," said Peter, "but pretty evenly split."

"Well, now, I see Joe Galloway, former speaker of the Assembly, who spoke at the picnic in April; and John Morton, the current speaker. Definitely pro Tory."

"No question," said Peter.

"Next is John Bayard who has Sons-of-Liberty connections. George Clymer and Thomas Fitzsimmons, both merchants, but both dislike the British. You agree?

"Staunchly Whig," said Peter. "Unusual for merchants."

"All right. Robert Morris and Thomas Willing, the wealthiest merchants in the City. What say you?"

"Definitely pro Tory," Peter nodded, "but they're also pragmatists. I could see them changing sides depending on how things go."

I continued around the table. "Then we come to James Wilson and Ben Franklin. They're both moderates, too close to call."

"Wilson, I agree," said Peter, "but Franklin, he is a Whig. He was pro-British for many years, but then he appeared before the king's Privy Council last year in London, and they ended up calling him a thief. Our own Dr. Franklin. That was when he realized the direction of things."

"I hope you're wrong about his being a Whig," I said. "He gets a lot of credit from us Tory merchants. We stand to lose a lot if he turns Whig."

"So, it's now official," said a distinct voice from the government table. It was John Morton, speaker of the Pennsylvania Assembly. He was speaking to the others seated at his table, but his voice carried.

"Let's listen," I said to our table.

"The Howe brothers are in the charge of our military," continued Morton. "William has taken over from General Gage, and Richard replaced Admiral Graves. They are very talented, and they come from an old-line British military family. The rebels have put up a good fight, and at the moment they have our boys bottled up in Boston. In deference to my good Whig friends sitting here, I give credit where credit is due. But I also want to be realistic. I have to think British ingenuity, not to mention military superiority, will soon prevail. If I were to give advice to the rebel leaders . . . and I mean this in all sincerity . . . I would urge them to use this period of temporary advantage in Boston to negotiate a settlement of the conflict on favorable terms. Because if they do not, it's all going to be over in six months on British terms."

Here, here! I thought to myself, what an imminently reasonable point of view. Morton was as clear-headed as anyone I had heard speak on the subject. He expressed my own thoughts exactly: bring the fighting to an end, not with malice nor a view toward punishing either side, but for solid, practical grounds, and on terms that recognized a modest level of validity in the causes that prompted the colonists to arms in the first place.

I almost expressed my like-mindedness to Peter but thought better of it. He sat red-faced, visibly trembling. I held my peace and waited for someone at the government table to respond. It was Franklin.

"It's hard to argue with your logic," he said, "but I'm not sure logic is the driving force behind either side of the conflict. For their part the colonists favoring separation are looking to the benefits of ending the domination by a sovereign power thousands of miles away, which I think we all admit has a mixed record in the fairness with which it governs. One can debate, of course, whether the colonies could do any better on their own. But it's a fair debate, and arguments exist on both sides. I for one believe the quest for separation has sprouted roots sufficiently deep and wide, that it will take a lot more than a few

British military victories, and a lot longer than six months for the movement to be defeated."

Franklin, who was sixty-nine and the oldest member of the Second Congress spoke matter of factly and with such a simple eloquence that even I, a Loyalist, was captivated and momentarily energized. When he finished, the entire room sat in silence.

And then, to my great surprise and consternation, Missy stood up. She began clapping her hands and calling out in a voice for the whole room to hear, "Bravo! Bravo!"

At first she stood alone, but Peter soon joined her, followed by about a third of the restaurant patrons around the room. The remaining patrons donned expressions similar to those sitting at the government table. Some looked delighted, others scowled, while others pretended to ignore the whole event.

The room returned to normal with conversations humming all about, dishes clashing and waiters taking orders and serving food. I leaned over and said to Missy, only half in jest, "I'll never take you out to dinner again."

She responded dismissively with, "Your loss!"

★

As the guests at the government table started leaving, Franklin walked toward the door with James Wilson and Wilson's wife, but then had second thoughts and returned to the dining room on his own and worked his way toward our table. Philadelphia's most famous citizen, Franklin was known almost as well in Europe as in the colonies as an inventor, printer, writer, statesman and skilled politician. Even I felt honored by his attention.

He stood near Missy, gave a polite bow and asked, "To whom do I have the pleasure of speaking?"

Peter stood and said, "Dr. Franklin, this is my wife Missy Barclay, and I'm Peter. We have long been your admirers."

"That is so nice of you," Franklin said. "And is this a family gathering I am intruding upon?"

"Not intruding at all," said Peter. "This is Daniel Thompson, Missy's brother and my brother-in-law, his wife Sarah, their three children and our boy, Nathan."

"It is so nice to meet you all," said Franklin. Then turning to Missy, he continued, "I want to thank you for your kind support of the humble words of encouragement I offered for the separation movement."

"Your words were restrained," Missy said, "but the perfect rejoinder to Morton. Peter and I have always supported independence and we want to do everything we can to help."

"I wish we had more families with foresight as clear as yours," said Franklin.

"Unfortunately," Missy said, "not even our whole family agrees with Peter and me." She shot a disapproving glance at me.

I expected some words of reprimand from Franklin. Instead he replied with a wink at Missy, "These are tough decisions. Maybe he will come around some day. By the way, what do you and Peter do for a living?"

"Peter's a partner in a printing shop, and we both work in the shop."

"A printer," Franklin said with approval. "I may soon have need of your services. How may I contact you?"

"We're on the southwest side of the City," Peter offered. "The name of the shop is Barclay and Black. We have special rates for supporters of independence."

Chapter Eleven

We departed the restaurant basking in the glow of our encounter with the City's leading citizen, and walked to our house where the Barclays had parked their horse-drawn chaise. After they left, I began questioning my own sense of values and ability to make a decision. On the one hand, I heard Morton speak about the advantage to the separatists in negotiating a good deal and letting bygones be bygone. And then I hear Franklin speak, and I'm nearly convinced to join the rebel cause.

Dammit! Had I no principles at all?

Suffering this frame of mind, I took a walk through the lamp-lit streets of our central Philadelphia residential area to sort things out. The air was cold but above freezing. I walked slowly, thinking about how easily I could be swayed from one camp to the other, and wondering how many other Philadelphians had equivocal minds like mine.

As I approached Carpenter's Hall, I noticed candles burning on the ground level floor. At this time of night, it seemed unusual. I then saw two men walk toward a side door, knock, and the door open. Simultaneously I heard Franklin's voice issue a greeting in French from the inside. My initial inclination was to continue walking, but my curiosity got the better of me. What was Franklin doing greeting French visitors so late? I knew it was none of my damn business. But then I saw the light go dim on the first floor, and candles begin to glow in Franklin's lending library on the second floor.

What could they be meeting about? Of course, they could have gathered to talk about anything from business, to art, to inventions to politics. But it also occurred to me the side door probably was not locked. With the light out on the first floor, someone, such as me, could walk in unnoticed and listen in on the conversation. Now why would I want to do that? Curiosity for one thing. But I also had a feeling the meeting was not just a social visit. I fancied it had something to do with the ongoing conflict with the British. I determined to give it a try.

I slipped inside the door and made myself comfortable on a chair close to the door, for a quick exit if the occasion required. The voices from the second floor easily found a path down the stairway or through the ceiling planks without my ears having to strain. I learned Franklin was meeting with John Jay, a moderate member of Congress from New York, a French emissary by the name of Julien Achard de Bonvouloir, and someone else.

Since much of the conversation was in French, and my French limited, I could understand only half the discussion. Basically, de Bonvouloir said he had been sent by France's foreign minister to assess the commitment of the colonists to separating from England, with a view toward French assistance if the commitment were genuine. The Americans assured him it was, and much of the conversation thereafter centered on the kind of assistance the French could provide, payment terms, and the need for secrecy. De Bonvouloir explained how public disclosure of the French government's interest in assisting the colonists could not only make delivery of supplies more difficult, but also cause embarrassment for the king of France, who was uncomfortable with the basic concept of overthrowing a monarchy. While the French hated the British, French assistance needed to be discretely channeled. That was the gist.

When the meeting seemed to be coming to an end, I exited quickly.

So, the French wanted to assist the American separatists. And not just in a passive way. France's interest was sufficiently heightened that the French foreign minister initiated contact with the colonists to assess their receptiveness. That seemed like a prime piece of intelligence for which any high-ranking British official would pay dearly!

★

I held it to myself for a few weeks. But one morning in January when Papa, David, Molly and I were reviewing accounts in the counting house, we got to talking about Boston.

"So what's your best guess at this point, Papa," I asked, "about how much longer the siege will last?"

"I've stopped guessing," Papa said. "Six months ago I thought it would be over by now. But the longer it goes on, the more time the Whigs and rebels have to gain support."

"Once the siege ends, what do you think?"

"Depends how it ends. The two sides could negotiate a peace deal. But if they don't, the worst outcome would be for the militias under Washington to remain intact. That would force the conflict to spread. So far we've been fortunate. We've maintained our imports through the islands. And once our ship is built, I expect our business will increase. Thanks to your idea, Daniel."

"And a little help from Logan," I added. Logan's company had come through with the financing, and we were expecting delivery of the ship in the summer.

David frowned at the prospect. He frowned at any idea of mine.

"But if the fighting spreads outside of Massachusetts," Papa continued, "who knows what's going to happen."

"Pennsylvania ought to be safe, don't you think, Papa?" asked David. "The Assembly is never going to vote for independence. At least so long as the eastern counties have control."

Papa nodded. "Yes. But retaining control is getting difficult."

"Why do you say so, Papa," asked Molly.

"Because the Assembly retains its pro-Loyalist majority through voting restrictions . . . like requiring land ownership. And some of the committees are calling for a convention to change the colony's constitution and open up voting. If that happens? The Scots, Irish and Germans will be in the majority, the western and northern counties will take charge, and we're down the road to revolution."

"Maybe we can do something to stop it," I offered.

"Like what?"

"The British cannot lose a war with the colonists if the colonists are acting on their own. British troops are too well equipped and organized. The only thing that would make a difference would be if the colonists get some outside assistance."

David looked up skeptically. "What kind of assistance do you have in mind?"

"From another country," I suggested, "like France. Military assistance, muskets and supplies."

"That would make a difference," said Papa. "But how would you stop it?"

"What if we could find out exactly who was negotiating on behalf of the French and the Americans . . . the kinds of equipment coming in, financial arrangements, the supply routes. You think that would help put a stop to the fighting?"

My father and siblings looked at me with suspicion. I had never been so forthcoming with pro-British proposals.

"Have you heard something, son?"

I was about to disclose the meeting in Carpenter's Hall but thought better of it. My hesitation had to do with the fact that David was there, and I was not sure what he might do with the information. I wanted to keep control of this secret, and David would never let that happen. Also, though, I had not yet decided I should take an active role in harming the separatists' cause. True, I considered myself loyal to England, but that did not mean I wanted to hurt those who were not. So, here I was equivocating again.

"No. I guess not," I turned back to my work. I would keep the secret a while longer.

"Why did you bring it up, then?" David gave me a disgusted look.

★

By the time of the annual church picnic in April of 1776, we received word the British had broken out of the Boston siege. But it was hardly a celebratory occasion for us Loyalists. A few weeks earlier Washington's artillery offer, Colonel Henry Knox – a former bookseller! – showed up on the outskirts of Boston with sixty pieces of artillery he had hauled three-hundred miles from Fort Ticonderoga in northern New York. That sealed the fate of the British. With the artillery staring down at them from the hills over the city, they had no way to fight through the siege by land without a needless waste of blood. The entire British Army vacated the city by ship and headed to Nova Scotia.

The picnic itself turned out to be my worst nightmare, but not because of Boston. It started out pleasant enough. The Barclays dropped by our house on the way to Governor's Woods, and we drove our two chaises together. Peter brought with him a copy of a booklet Franklin had recruited his shop to help print, called *Common Sense.* It sold for two shillings.

"This is going to change everything," said Peter.

"Why do you say so?"

"Because it refutes every conceivable reason offered to support the British."

"Like what?"

"Like what you're always telling me why you're so pro British. What's your main reason?"

"Many reasons. It's good for business, that's one."

"All right, so let me look." He fingered through a few pages of the booklet. "Here, right on point. For the argument that we need the British for our prosperity, here is what it says: 'We may as well assert that because a child has thrived upon milk, that it is never to have meat. . . . But even this is admitting more than is true, for I answer roundly that America would have flourished as much, and probably much more, had no European power had anything to do with her. The commerce, by which she hath enriched herself are the necessaries of life and will always have a market while eating is the custom of Europe.'"

He paused and looked up, perhaps expecting my favorable reaction. When I refused to give it to him, he summarized what he had just read.

"He is saying we don't need the British because we'll have markets for our goods, maybe even more markets, without them."

"I understand what it's saying," I said with aggravation, not wanting to be preached to. I had to admit – to myself only – it had a certain logic. "Who wrote it anyway?"

"It's published anonymously," said Peter, "but Franklin told me it was a guy by the name of Thomas Paine. He lives here in Philadelphia. Moved from England two years ago."

The name, Thomas Paine, was hard to forget.

By the time we arrived at the picnic most of the congregations were already cooking dinner. Attendance was down this year. Recent developments in Boston dominated conversation. And moods changed depending on whether those doing the talking leaned pro-British or pro-Colonist.

I participated in the musket shooting contest but got eliminated in the third round. Then on my way back to our church group, I spotted something from a distance that made me pause. It was a tribe of Lenape around a fire pit on the outskirts of the main picnic area. About twenty-five or thirty men and women were not only preparing food but also selling animal skins and crafts they had brought with them or were still in the process of making. They attracted a small but steady group of curiosity seekers willing to negotiate for a good deal.

The presence of the Lenape was not unusual at the picnic. Their dress and look, however, reminded me of the hunting party we had encountered out near the mill last summer. I began looking closer for faces I might remember. Then I saw her. Janie was talking and laughing excitedly with the Indian boy who had found her in the forest. He looked much the same as he did last summer, with a deerskin mantle hanging down over his breechcloth and leggings.

She waved me her direction, barely containing herself.

"Papa, he's here! Lightfoot. You remember him, don't you? He rescued me from the wilderness. I'm so happy to see him again!"

I did not like the look in her eyes as she fawned over her Indian rescuer who now was all of sixteen-years-old. The boy smiled expectantly and nodded, apparently not quite sure how to greet me. I knew I should have been happy to see him again, but I was not. I wondered vaguely what had happened to the musket I gave him.

"Hello, sir," said Lightfoot.

"See, Papa," squealed Janie, "he has learned more English. I'm going to make him good at speaking English, and he is going to teach me Unami." She danced around, pleased with her idea. "Can he come over for dinner with us, Papa, please?"

Lightfoot nodded at me eagerly. I did not know if he understood what she said, but he obviously was not reading my glaring eyes. I frowned and shook my head. Still, he gleamed at me.

"Janie," I said, "we eat with only our congregation. You and I must return to our group and you can invite him over to visit later in the afternoon to help clean up the leftovers."

I thought it an imminently reasonable suggestion.

"Papa, he rescued me from the wilderness. I can't leave him now."

"Yes, you can!" I said. "He has his whole tribe here. He will be fine."

"He's my friend, Papa, let me talk to him a while longer. You go on."

"Janie, please, he is not your friend. You don't even know him."

My words of reason went unheard. They already had turned to walk toward the center of the tribe, talking partly in English, partly in Unami, and partly with hand signs. I thought about going after her but did not want to create a scene, of which Janie was fully capable of creating. I prayed she would return alone.

"A problem in paradise," I said to Sarah once I isolated her for a moment alone. "The Indian boy who found Janie over at the mill, he's here. And she's eagerly talking with him in many languages."

Sarah gave me a dismissive glance. "I'm sure she will be fine."

"You don't understand," I said. "He's an Indian boy. He's wearing a – what do you call it . . . a breechcloth. And it's not difficult to see what's underneath. He has his whole tribe here. I don't want to have difficulty."

"It's just their culture, dear. Janie is fourteen. She can take care of herself. Besides, he rescued her. He would not try to hurt her now."

I was not reassured. My eyes kept wondering to the direction from where Janie should have been coming by now. It felt like an eternity, but she eventually did appear pulling the Indian boy by the arm. His outward reluctance to being thrust among such a large group of strangers was betrayed by his broad smile and obvious pleasure he took in being near her. I had to admit he was a good-looking kid with a muscular upper body and square jaw. Still, my shock in contemplating the possibility my daughter might develop a serious interest in the young man was overcome only by the outright mortification I felt in the way they walked around together. Who had the greater prize, the Indian boy showing off his white girl, or my daughter showing off her muscular Indian lad?

Comments from my brother David did not help.

"Looks like your daughter landed herself a live one," he said sarcastically. "Don't know if I'd want that to go on too long, though."

"Stick it up your ass, David."

Here I was warding off my daughter's critics at the same time I was nearly paralyzed with embarrassment. I went back to Sarah.

"Talk to her, please! Tell her she cannot walk around with him like that. It's not normal. It's not healthy. He's an Indian for God's sake! We're Anglicans."

"Oh now, Daniel." Sarah tried to soothe me. "They are a couple of kids having fun. Leave them alone and relax."

"You want your daughter going off with an Indian boy like that?"

"Who said anyone is going off? They are only walking around. Don't you trust your own daughter?"

"I trust my daughter. It's the Indian boy I don't trust."

I spent the rest of the afternoon fuming. The reaction from my friends and family was split. Some clucked their tongues and shook their heads, while others took it all in stride. By the end of the day I had had my limit of being fed up. I loaded Sarah, Jonathon and Annie into the chaise, and when Janie did not show up, I sent Jonathon on a mission.

"You find that sister of yours, and you tell her if she wants to be a part of this family, she better get herself over here right now. You understand? You tell her to get over here right now. And she better come alone."

I rarely got so angry, but when I did, Sarah knew better than to intervene. She would stay silent for a few hours until I cooled off, and then excoriate me.

Jonathon soon returned with Janie.

"Sorry, Papa," she tried to explain, "I was just talking with . . . ."

Sarah waived her hand to cut off the chatter, and the five of us rode back home crowded onto the chaise in silence.

Chapter Twelve

By July of 1776 we were readying our ship for her maiden voyage to the Indies. Thompson Trading was four-hundred-fifty pounds in debt, but looking at the ship made me wonder how anyone could have doubted our decision. Even David seemed aglow standing alongside her with a few of our business friends, while the ship's crew made preparations.

With two masts, she was not a huge ship. She measured a sleek ninety feet along the main deck and twenty-five feet across the beam. Both the fore and main masts were gaff rigged to support four-cornered main sails. Triangular top sails flew atop the mains, and a jib jutted forward to the bowsprit, which looked like a spear shooting out from the tip of the bow. With fourteen feet of hold depth, she could carry ten tons of cargo.

We named her the Thompson Trader and had given her a test launch a month earlier. Papa, Molly, I and my three kids had gone along to observe the captain and three-man crew at work. With no cargo in her hold she skimmed along the water's surface at speeds Captain Bart estimated at fourteen knots. While she would move slower with cargo, the captain predicted being able to make the round trip between Philadelphia and the islands once every twenty-five to thirty days, including loading and unloading time.

My entire family gathered for the first real launch, although Sarah, almost nine months into her pregnancy, stayed in the chaise. As the kids scampered around the gangplank barely staying out of the way of the longshoremen loading barrels of wheat, Mrs. Pickering chatted amiably with Molly and Helen, and David and I talked with several small traders about their future shipping needs. At the same time, Papa was doing his best to quell any concerns of Logan about the soundness of his company's investment.

"I heard the ringing from the State House bell last night," said Logan to Papa, as the final barrels were being loaded. Logan was once again staying at Papa's house, having just returned from a trip to Virginia.

"What was that all about?"

"Don't you know?" asked Papa. "We have a Declaration of Independence now."

"What do you mean, 'we have'? Who has?"

"It was passed by the Second Continental Congress five days ago."

"Congress? Independence? I thought you said something like this could never happen."

"No," said Papa, "I said it could never happen without Pennsylvania going along."

"Did Pennsylvania go along?"

"Not at first. The idea came up in June and our delegates voted 5-2 against. They carried most of the other colonies along, and it was defeated."

"So what happened this time around?" asked Logan.

"3-2 in favor. One delegate switched, and two who voted against abstained. Dickenson and Morris. With Pennsylvania's support, the resolution passed."

"Why in bloody hell would they abstain on something like this?"

"To let it pass," said Papa. He shook his head in disgust. "They felt pressured and didn't want to be seen supporting it. But look, it doesn't change anything. It's just a piece of paper. The war has been good for business. We've got a brand new ship, and we're going to make you a lot of money. And also for ourselves."

"Yes, but it gives people something to fight for."

David joined the conversation. "Not here in Philadelphia. We see a few redcoats and a few brown and bluecoats from time to time, but that's about it. Not much fighting is going on anywhere right now."

"That's just my point," said Logan. "Things are quiet, and maybe the fighting will just peter out, but with this noble-sounding Declaration, people might just get the wrong idea the war has some noble principle behind it. What happened in the Assembly to turn things around?"

"It's been gradual over time," said Papa. "The fact is the Assembly is dissolved at the moment, and frankly, the Quakers may never regain control. We are supposed to have a convention start up in a few days to write a new constitution for the colony. If the voting rules change, the Quakers and Anglicans are sure to be in the minority. Franklin may take charge in the short term. He's reasonable, but pro-independence. None of this means anything, though. Really. It's all on the political side." He emphasized the word *political.* "The business side is the only thing you should be concerned about, and we can't keep up with demand. The ship couldn't have come at a better time."

Papa had a way of explaining bad news in a way it no longer sounded bad. Logan nodded.

Captain Bart approached looking hearty in his mid-forties. He wore a blue, double-breasted blouse, a captain's hat to match, and a dark beard cut short. We had advertised for an experienced sea captain who knew the West Indies, and he was one of three who applied. He had been hoping for a larger ship, but the Thompson Trader was the only one with an opening. He impressed us with his enthusiasm and professionalism.

"We're set to shove off," he said matter-of-factly.

"You have our shipping instructions?" I asked, knowing full well he did, but wanting to make sure for about the tenth time.

He nodded, apparently having dealt with nervous new owners in the past. "Yes. It's all in the ship's log, sir. We're first to New Providence to make contact with the dry goods establishment. With any luck the goods will be waiting for us, and it will be a matter of finding the right market for seventy-five barrels of flour. We're authorized to sell for British bills of exchange at a price of no less than four pounds per barrel. If we can get that price on New Providence, we'll offload. If not, we're off to Antigua and as far east as St. Vincent. We will return with dry goods, but if for some reason they don't show up, we'll return with sugar, rum and molasses."

"Excellent," I said. "And your home port?"

He grinned. "Toronto, of course, depending on the circumstances."

The cover of home port was Logan's idea. The Thompson Trader would be carrying two sets of logs: the true set, and a second set showing Toronto. If inspected by British authorities, Logan thought it less likely for the ship to be detained if the log listed a British home port.

"Best of luck," I said, "and Godspeed!"

"Thank you, sir, and best of luck to you and your wife on your addition. She actually looks as if she might be a little overheated. You might want to check on her."

★

I had lost track of the time talking and watching the ship being loaded. When I turned to look at Sarah in the chaise I realized she had been in the hot July sun for nearly an hour. Although she had a parasol for protection, Captain Bart was right. Sitting at an angle, she looked flushed with heat.

I dashed over to the carriage, calling her name. Sarah did not respond. I jumped up to see she was all but unconscious and breathing heavily.

"Sarah, what's wrong?"

She shook her head and mouthed, "I don't know."

"Girls! Come now," I ordered. "Jonathon, go find Dr. Wagner, and have him come to the house."

Molly hurried over to the chaise along with the girls.

"Anything I can do?" she asked.

"Sarah's not well. I'm taking her home."

Molly and the girls helped Sarah recline in the back of the chaise, but whatever the problem, I knew it was serious. She vomited several times along the way, and by the time we reached the house, the front lower part of her dress was soaked red with blood. It was her pregnancy. I told the two girls to get pillows and blankets and bring them to the parlor. Somehow I suppressed my frantic impulses in front of the kids. Molly assisted in removing her dress.

"I'm so hot," Sarah kept saying. She began to convulse from cramping in her abdomen, and groaned from the pain.

"Get some wet towels and a pail of water," I commanded.

Janie scampered out of the parlor.

"Please, I'm so hot, do something."

Jonathon arrived to report. "Dr. Wagner's on the way."

"Help Janie get wet towels"

Sarah convulsed again from the cramping. Squeezing her eyes shut, she grimaced and began panting heavily. The bleeding had not stopped from her pelvic area and Molly was using a towel to mop it up. I was kneeling on the floor holding

Sarah's head. Annie kept hold of her mother's hand, trying to give her comfort.

"Everything's going to be fine," I said without much conviction. "The doctor will be here soon. Try to relax your body."

"I'm so warm! Why am I so warm?"

Janie and Jonathon returned with the towels and water.

"Ahh, here we are," I tried to assure her. "This will help."

We placed wet towels all around her, but they seemed to have little effect. By now, Sarah was beside herself suffering with both pain and heat. Her whole body writhed in pain.

"Cool me off, Daniel. Do something. Please. I can't take much more."

"I know!" exclaimed Jonathon tearing out of the parlor before I had a chance to stop him.

"Where in God's name is he going?" I asked no one in particular.

"I'm going to lose my baby," Sarah screamed out in anger, between her labored breaths.

"When did you start feeling it?" I asked. "Just today?"

"Week ago. Back pain, bloating, sore shoulders."

"Why didn't you tell me?"

Sarah shook her head. "Water. Sip of water"

Molly filled a cup and held it to Sarah's lips as I propped her up.

Moments later Jonathon burst back into the room with a bucket in hand. It was filled with . . . chipped ice?

"Look what I have, Mama," he said with tears in his eyes. "The ice will help cool you off."

"Where did . . . ?" I stopped mid sentence. Where my son found ice in July did not matter at the moment. My wife was dying from the heat.

"Wrap the ice in towels," I said, "and hold next to her. That should help."

Sarah's body finally cooled and she relaxed a bit as Dr. Wagner arrived with Mrs. Lisle our neighbor in tow.

"Hello everyone!" He immediately took charge.

"Sarah, we're going to do everything for you and your baby. Mrs. Lisle is here to help. Molly, you stay here. Everyone else out."

He turned to me, "Boil a pot of water and let me know when it's ready."

Two hours passed before Dr. Wagner emerged from the parlor. He and Mrs. Lisle came into the kitchen. Molly had left an hour earlier, reporting only that progress was inconclusive.

"The baby's gone," he said. Sarah's resting. She's lost a lot of blood."

Hearing our baby was gone made me realize how much I had been looking forward to having a new little one. I turned my attention to Sarah and asked, "She's going to be all right?"

"She's hanging on by a thread." His tone sounded ominous.

"You cannot mean . . . ." My thoughts were jumbling up inside my head. I could not believe what he was saying. This was Sarah, the center of my life.

"I've done everything humanly possible."

"What caused her condition?" I asked.

"It's hard to say." Dr. Wagner kept his eyes down. "Lots of things can go wrong in childbirth. It may have been the position of the baby, or a knot in the umbilical cord. Medical conditions, sickness, maybe the heat, her age. It could be all sorts of things. I'm sorry."

"Can we go in and see her?" I asked. I was sitting at the table with the girls. Made somber by the loss of their newest sibling, they now agonized about their mother.

Jonathon stayed up in his attic room. He hated for people see him cry.

The doctor thought for a moment. "Daniel, you can see her in a little while. Annie and Janie, you should wait. Your mother doesn't need a crowd around her."

When I entered the parlor, it was still warm and now dark. The only light came from two candles. Sarah was lying on the floor in her nightgown. She looked comfortable with several blankets under her and her head propped up with pillows. I sat down beside her.

"How are you feeling?" I took her hand and kissed it.

"Numb," she said weakly.

"Do you want to go up to our room?"

"No. Just leave me here. It's cooler."

"I guess you were right about the baby. I'm sorry we lost it."

"He was a son, by the way."

"That would have been nice." I tried to smile. "Kids are wonderful. I don't know what I would do without the three we already have."

"Maybe, we could try again later?" Sarah wanted to give me hope.

I thought about what the doctor said. "You just rest and retrieve your health. That would make me happy. Three children are enough. We could be facing hard times with the war and all."

"Did you hear something new?"

"Just what Logan was saying. With this Declaration of Independence, there's no end in sight."

Sarah nodded. I could see she was losing strength. She wondered aloud, "Where did that ice come from?"

I was surprised she remembered.

"It was Jonathon's idea. Alphonse helped him with it last winter when they dug a pit inside the barn and lined it with straw. They filled the pit with chunks of ice hanging off the roof. They covered up pit and let it be. Jonathon wanted to see how long the ice would last. He kept it a secret all this time. Do you believe that?"

"Through the middle of July?"

"If he had dug it a little deeper, it may have stayed frozen the whole summer."

"Maybe he'll amount to something after all." Sarah smiled.

"Let's not get carried away. He's still the kind of kid who stays in the shadows."

"Jonathon will change. Are you still jealous?"

"Of Peter and Nathan? I am, I admit it." I could never fool Sarah.

"What do you think of our girls?"

"We could not have two nicer daughters. They are smart, pretty, and a lot more popular at school than Jonathon will ever be. They take after their mother."

Tears formed in Sarah's eyes, and she lay quiet for several minutes. "You were very upset with Janie."

"I was. The way she walked around with that Indian boy. And then for weeks after that was all we heard about . . . her Indian friend. I'm hoping it's over by now." When I heard no confirmation I had to ask, "It is over, isn't it?"

Sarah sighed. "I'm not sure, honey. She has toned it down, but I don't really think it's over. You need to be prepared."

"It didn't seem to bother you, her linking up with an Indian kid."

"Not like it did you. I just want her to be happy." Sarah turned quiet again, but after a few minutes she said, "Hold me, Danny. Hold me."

"Sure, baby. You want more water?"

"No. Just hold me until I . . . until I fall asleep."

I lay down next to her on the floor, and put one arm under her head and pillow, the other around her waist. I kept thinking if she just made it to morning, she would be all right.

Chapter Thirteen

Trial Proceedings

The Judge Advocate gave Daniel a moment to collect himself. "I am sorry to hear about the loss of your wife and child."

Daniel wiped his eyes and nodded. "We were devastated. It was all any of us could do to get through the next few weeks. Over two-hundred people passed through our parlor to say goodbye. Her father had been a priest. Sarah had lots of friends."

"How soon did you get back to work?"

"A few days after the funeral, I started going to the counting house on-and-off. My children remained my first priority. I wanted to make sure they were cared for. I could not leave them alone."

"What did you work out?"

"We had a lady come to help, one of my sister's friends. Missy introduced us. Margaret Fletcher. The kids called her Maggy. We paid her at first, but after a couple of months she refused to accept payment. She considered herself part of the family."

"Fortunate for you."

"There were pros and cons."

"Was this about the time you began trading with the enemy? And this time I mean the real enemy, the British Army. You would agree they were the enemy, would you not?"

"The British Army was the enemy. Yes, we sold flour to them. If that's what you mean. We also sold to the Continental Army. We were in business to sell. Why shouldn't we sell to a willing buyer, whoever it might be?"

"Why should you not sell to them? Because you're a Pennsylvanian, and an American. At least you claim to be. Did you have no sense of loyalty?"

"I do now, yes. But in the last half of '76, business was business. And not just for me. All of the traders in the City, particularly the wealthier ones, made money wherever they could, however they could, and probably still are."

"So even by the end of 1776, nothing moved you to join the independence cause?"

"I didn't join at that time, that part is true. But a lot of things moved me. My brother-in-law, Peter, joined the Continental Army. That really impressed me."

"When was this?"

"Some time around September of 1776. We heard the British were amassing troops in Raritan Bay in New Jersey, just opposite Staten Island, in preparation for an assault on New York. That was when Peter announced he would be joining the army.

Chapter Fourteen

On a Sunday, I took Jonathan with me to visit Peter and Missy. It was the day before Peter left for the army. The Barclays lived in eastern Chester County, less than half an hour drive in the chaise from our house.

The short trip gave me an opportunity to catch up with Jonathon's first few days in the new school year. He had come home after the second day without a toy flute he had carved. The organ player at our church helped him tune it and gave him some music. I was not enthusiastic about his interest in music. Still, I thought it a clever piece of work for a twelve-year-old kid.

"So what happened at school?" I asked as we plodded along behind Dobbin. We would arrive at the Barclays before dinner and return by late afternoon.

"Nothing, Papa."

"Come on now, Jonathon, this is just between the two of us. The girls aren't here to tease you. Tell me what happened."

"It's fine. Nothing happened."

"Did you get into a fight?"

He answered reluctantly. "Sort of."

"Did it have to do with the flute?"

"Yes."

"Did someone try to take it from you?"

"Not take it away. I gave it to them to look at."

"Who was it?"

"Tommy Anderson and his friends."

"Why did you give it to them?"

"They said they wanted to see it and then they would not give it back. They said it was stupid and smashed it against a tree. When I went to pick up the pieces, they began hitting me."

"Did you hit back?" I asked hopefully.

Silence.

His lack of response told me what I did not want to hear.

"What happened to the flute?"

"I left it."

"Why did you do that?"

"It was broken."

This son of mine! He showed streaks of promise and then retreated into his child-like ways. I wanted to tell him when someone hits you, you hit back. And you might come home with a black eye. But if you don't hit back, the bullying will never end. And when you create something as elegant as a flute able to be tuned to an organ, you don't just leave it. You bring it home, salvage what you can, and come up with something better next time. I wanted to say those things to my son, but knew my words would go unheeded.

We had Sunday dinner at the Barclays' house. The printing business had been good to Missy and Peter, but not so good they felt comfortable abandoning Peter's agricultural roots altogether. He had inherited twenty acres of farmland in Chester County, which he farmed with hired hands. Bad investments in western land speculation had cut into their savings, but things were turning around.

After dinner the two boys, Nathan and Jonathon, disappeared, and I was left with my sister and her husband to talk about Peter's upcoming soldiering. I wanted to make sure he knew I wished him well no matter what political differences we had.

"So where do you think the county Associators will be headed?" I asked.

"I'm not joining the militia," Peter said. "I've signed up for a Line outfit, Second Pennsylvania Battalion."

"Why the Pennsylvania Line? Any advantage over the Association?"

"It gets me away from some of the local politics. Also a Line Battalion is more likely to get involved in the conflict than a county Militia Battalion."

"You're taking this seriously," I said with both concern and admiration.

"It's a serious matter. And we always have room for one more, if you're interested. No advance training required."

I smiled. He and I both knew if I did join the army, it would not be on the side of the colonists. "How long are you in for, the standard six months?"

"Three years. Or until the war ends, whichever comes first."

"What happened to six-month enlistments?"

"They are creating havoc for Washington. He will be lucky to keep the army together at year's end. Everyone's enlistment is up."

I wondered vaguely if the British high command was aware of that piece of intelligence.

I turned to Missy. "What do you think about a three-year enlistment?"

"It was my idea," she told me.

"And the print shop?"

"Peter's partner is also a Patriot. He has agreed I can be responsible for Peter's end of the work with Nathan to help out, if necessary."

"Why the Second Battalion?"

"It's forming a new company to join up with the rest of the battalion in New York," said Peter. "The British already have taken the Flatlands on Long Island. You probably know that. Manhattan may be next. Who knows what after that. We could be looking at the end of the American cause within the next few weeks."

Peter's speculation was music to my ears, but I had my doubts. "It may be the end of the American cause in New York, but the British have yet to make inroads in a lot of other colonies. I don't see this war ending anytime soon."

"I hope you're right," Peter said.

I shook my head. "I was hoping you were right. But more important, I also hope you stay safe, no matter what happens."

"Thank you."

"What happened to the secret peace deal Franklin was supposed to negotiate last week with the Howes – the general and the admiral?" I asked.

"I guess it was not so secret if you heard about it," said Missy. "And how did you hear about it?"

"I hear lots from other merchants, Sis. Most of them are Loyalist. I don't know where they get their information. Half of it turns out to be wrong, and I don't know who exactly told me about the peace negotiations. Did a peace meeting take place last week?"

"Yes," Missy answered, "that's what we've heard too, but nothing came of it. General Howe touted his great authority to negotiate a deal. But when push came to shove, he admitted everything had to go through London. At that point Franklin and Adams walked out."

"That's too bad. What about the French. Are they in yet?"

"The French?" Missy asked. "Is this from another one of your merchant friends?"

"Actually no, I overheard it directly from the horse's mouth a few months ago."

"You come across some interesting information. Did you take it to the British?"

"No." I answered, feeling her anger building.

"Why not, Daniel?" asked Missy.

I had to think myself why not. "A lot of good people are on both sides. I guess I didn't want anyone to get hurt because of me."

"You're a Patriot at heart," Peter said. "I knew it all along."

"No, not really, I'm just not hardline British."

"As for the French, that would be the best news I've heard all year, if they actually reach a deal."

"You are off to fight the British in New York, then, that's your best guess?" I asked.

"I'm off to New York. I hope they will let me fight."

"You're not too good with a musket."

"I'm terrible. And if I break my spectacles, I am blind as a bat."

"Maybe they will recognize you have other talents, like writing and publishing."

"Probably won't find a printing press on the battle field."

"Missy, are you and Nathan going to be all right out here in the country by yourselves?"

"Sure, we'll be fine. The road by here is well traveled, and we have neighbors close by. Our hired men can help out with any problems."

"If you ever need to move temporarily, we'll make room in our place."

"Thanks, Danny."

I gave a shout for Jonathon and Nathan to join us, and all five of us put our arms around each other and said the Lord's prayer in one voice.

Chapter Fifteen

Our business continued at a brisk pace that fall of 1776. On the import side, our ship, the Thompson Trader, kept us stocked with dry goods more reliably than the suppliers of other mid-sized merchants. Between the British blockade and the American privateers, it was a wonder any ships at all made it through to the Philadelphia waterfront. But nothing phased Captain Bart. He continued to make regular four-week round trips to the islands until ice floes developed on the Delaware River in early January.

In our flour trade, we could not keep up with demand. The growing hostilities brought on increased opportunities for sale in the colonies. The excess inventory we loaded into the ship's hold and filled up any extra cargo space with lumber for sale in the islands.

One day in early November, a large and a distinguished looking man by the name of Emil Higgins showed up at the door of our counting house. Papa, David and I were all present as Mr. Higgins explained Thompson Trading had been recommended to him as a reliable trading firm able to deliver good quality flour by the barrel.

"Is that true?" Higgins asked.

"Of course it's true," I answered. "That's our business, or a good share of our business, selling flour. Why do you ask?"

"Because I have need of a sizable quantity. Higgins answered.

"How sizable?"

He hesitated, glancing up at the ceiling. "Forty barrels. More later if things work out."

We occasionally sold quantities of forty barrels in single transactions, but always to a shipper interested in reselling to a different market. Higgins gave me the distinct impression he was not interested in reselling.

Papa also was intrigued and asked, "What are you going to do with it?"

"What do you think I'm going to do with it?" Higgins retorted. "I'm going to bake it into bread."

"Who are you anyway?" Papa demanded. "And why forty barrels?"

"I'm an agent for the British Army Royal Commissariat." His tone suggested we should be impressed. And we were. "I'm here to purchase on behalf of the British Crown to supply the army. We're willing to pay four and a half pounds per barrel in British bills. You interested?"

"Of course we're interested," Papa rose out of his chair and walked over to give Higgins an embrace. "Everyone is a Tory in this household. It would be a delight to do business with the army of the people who settled this land and the institution seeking to return it to peace and prosperity. I'm surprised you didn't show up months ago. Where have you been?"

"We're very selective with whom we do business. Most of our provisions come over from Cork, arrive in Montreal or New York, and are distributed from there. But if we have to purchase from the colonies, we want to make sure we're not feeding a rebel sympathizer."

"Don't worry about us," David spoke up. "No one is more loyal to King George than we are." He turned to me. "Right, Daniel?"

He was testing my loyalty, and I did not like it one damn bit.

"That's right," I responded. "How soon do you need them and where do you want them to be delivered?"

"I need them today if you have them," said Higgins. "But they have to be delivered to New Brunswick in New Jersey. The price is free on board. I can give you up to twenty-one days. We're stockpiling supplies for use in the New York campaign and upcoming winter. You'll receive payment in New Brunswick from the Royal Paymaster, who controls the largest war chest on the continent."

"That's fifty miles," I said, "and pockets of Pennsylvania militia are up and down the border. How much of the countryside do the British control in New Jersey?"

Higgins looked offended. "Sir, you are asking for military intelligence."

Papa spoke up. "Daniel is a little too direct sometimes. He's trying to figure out how much difficulty we're going to have getting wagons through to New Brunswick."

"Of course." Higgins seemed mollified. "The situation is fluid. Washington is still ensconced around New York City. But after his loss at White Plains in October, he has only one stronghold left, and that's Fort Washington on Manhattan. Once the fort falls, we expect him to pull back into northern Jersey. All of which is to say wagons coming up from the south to New Brunswick probably will not encounter any difficulty from militia troops in the next few weeks. I'll let you know where we think they are, and I can give you a letter of safe passage to deal with British forces."

"What's your assessment at this point?" David asked. "Are we close to concluding this thing?"

Higgins gave a shrug. "The upper echelon feels optimistic. With these latest victories, we'll control all of Manhattan, southern New York and the Jersey bank of the Hudson, so things are looking good. Unfortunately, Washington has been on the brink of disaster before, and managed to slip through. So, who knows?"

"What else can we help you with?" Papa asked. "We've been able to keep our warehouse stocked, despite the efforts on both sides to shut down shipping. We can get you whatever you need in dry goods, from building material to cooking equipment."

"Let's start with the flour. If that goes well, I'll be back for more."

I started to make the arrangements. We maintained an inventory of fifteen to twenty barrels in our City warehouse, and our mill could supply the balance. We also had other merchant mills we could purchase from, and a network of farmers who regularly did business with us. Four and a half pounds was a good selling price and gave me room to negotiate on the buying end.

Then something surprising happened. When I arrived at the counting house a few mornings later, David was talking with a man who wore neat but well-worn clothes. His grey cloak and three-cornered hat lay over a chair.

As I entered David announced, "And here he is, late as usual, the man who handles our flour sales." He spoke in a slightly animated, condescending tone. "Daniel, I would like you to meet Mark Ableson. Mr. Ableson is interested in buying some flour."

"Hello Mr. Ableson. How much are you looking for?" I was glad for the opportunity of more business.

"Twenty five barrels," said Ableson.

"That's a nice size quantity. Almost enough to feed an army."

David burst out laughing. "Yes. Ask him what army he is planning to feed."

My brother's laugh had a devious quality about it. "Are you really purchasing for the army?"

"Yes," said Ableson, "the Continental Army."

Now, I understood why David was so animated.

"You do sell to the Continental Army, don't you?" asked Ableson.

David laughed again. "Yes. What about that, Daniel, do we sell to the Continental Army?"

He was testing me again. He suspected me of rebel leanings because of my closeness to Missy and Peter. If I now appeared eager to do business with Ableson, David would inform Papa. On the other hand, if I refused to do business he would make sure Missy and Peter found out.

I needed time to think. "Willing & Morris supplies most of the army's needs." I referred to the City's most successful merchant firm. "Why would you be coming to us?"

"Maybe that's why," Ableson said with a shrug. "To give some smaller firms an opportunity. Are you able to sell?"

I had an idea how to handle this. "Business is business. We deal with anyone willing to pay a fair price. What price are you offering?" I looked at David. His expression was noncommittal. I had scored a victory.

"Four and a half pounds per barrel."

That seemed to be the going government purchase price. "Payable in what form?"

"Continental currency."

I had to think for a moment. "We can't accept Continental currency at that price. It's too shaky. We can supply you twenty-five barrels at four pounds sterling, four and a half pounds British bills of exchange, or five and a half pounds Continental. That's our delivered price by land within fifty miles. It's the best we can do."

I hoped he would decline, and David would then be forced to tell Papa I drove too hard a bargain with the Continental Army.

"It is a little steep," said Ableson, "but within my authority. Five and a half pounds Continental it shall be. We'll need it delivered to Belvidere in northwest New Jersey within fourteen days. Is that agreeable?"

"I think we can do that."

"Is the Continental army going to last that long?" David asked with a guffaw.

Ableson gave a frown.

"Don't pay him any attention," I said.

"What else do you need from me?"

"We'll prepare a contract. Twenty percent payment now with the balance due on delivery. That's everything."

David asked, "What about a letter of safe passage through any Continental troops?"

"Sure, I can give you that."

"Any troop movements in the area?" asked David.

Ableson looked at me, as if asking whether the information was necessary.

I thought a moment and decided against it. "That's all right. I'm familiar with the area."

I was not familiar with the area but I did not feel comfortable with Ableson sharing the information with David. What my brother might do with it was anyone's guess. I would find out later about the troops.

The transactions with the British and Continental Armies made me wonder again about my own sense of ethics. Sure, we were businessmen, we did not ask for the war, and we had an obligation to ourselves and to our families to make a living. On the other hand, what of life's basic principles? If I were a Loyalist, as I held myself out to be, what justification existed for giving assistance to the rebels, even for profit? And if I sympathized with the rebel cause, then how could I justify trading with those whose purpose was to crush that cause?

The real problem: I had divided loyalties and had been sitting on the fence too long. I knew it, and I kicked myself for it, but I could not do much about it. I was not yet ready to commit.

Chapter Sixteen

Peter came home on leave from the Army for a few days in mid-December. It was close enough to Sarah's birthday that, upon hearing he was home, I arranged to have our annual supper with the Barclays at the City Tavern. Sarah was gone, of course, but I promised the kids we would celebrate her birthday and keep up the tradition. Margaret, our housekeeper and Missy's friend, offered to go in Sarah's stead. She was hardly a worthy substitute, but I did not turn her down.

I was half afraid Peter would show up in a Continental Army uniform. But he exercised common sense and wore a civilian waist coat. Philadelphia, at least so far, had been spared the ravages of war. Living within its borders were as many British sympathizers as rebels, and as many Quakers who were officially neutral. Uniformed American soldiers made their presence known whenever Congress was in session at the State House. And British uniforms were occasionally observed in isolated parts of the city. In most public areas, however, it was considered ill form to wear partisan colors. Publicly the Loyalists and Patriots detested one another. Privately, friendships formed before the war continued, albeit with awkwardness at times.

The dining area was busy as usual with well-dressed patrons. No telling who was Loyalist or Patriot simply by appearance.

As our two families sat down at our usual table, Missy and Margaret chatted amiably as if oblivious to the battles recently fought in New York.

"Are you planning to go to Papa's for Twelfth Night again this year?" Missy asked me.

"I'm sure we will. He asks us every year and we cannot turn him down. He always invites his Assembly friends and they can be entertaining. They love Mrs. Pickering's old family recipe for wassail."

"You should take Margaret with you then."

Margaret smiled expectantly.

She was not an ugly woman, and she actually looked attractive on good days. Still, I did not appreciate being prompted to include her. "We'll think about it," I offered cheerfully. "What are your plans this year, Missy?"

"Probably nothing special. Nathan and I will go to church on Christmas, but with Peter away, we'll not have much of a celebration. We used to have a group who would get together and the men would shoot off their muskets and fireworks. Now, most of them are away in the army.

I looked over at Peter. He appeared older, more reserved, less exuberant and perhaps more pessimistic. Missy sat extra close to him while we ate, and Nathan seemed enthralled with the prospect of his father having already become an army veteran.

"Tell them about Kip's Bay," Nathan said, beaming at his father.

"It's not good conversation over a meal."

"Sure it is," Nathan pressed. "What you told us about General Washington. He's a hero."

"We lost the battle," Peter dropped his eyes. "So he was not much of a hero. I cannot imagine they would be interested." He looked at Margaret and me, seeking confirmation.

"Not so, we would like to hear about it," I said. "Were you there during the battle?"

"I saw part of it," Peter answered reluctantly.

"Come on now, tell us about it. This was the battle before New York fell?"

"Yes, a few weeks ago just after I joined in mid-September."

"What were you doing?"

He sighed and kept his eyes down. I suspected he was concerned about offending my Loyalist proclivities.

"I was assigned as an aide to General Greene," Peter began. "A debate arose over how to proceed with Manhattan. General Greene wanted to burn it down to keep it from the British, but Congress forbade it. So Washington tried to defend it by assigning troops to various areas because the island is so vast. It became an impossible job. He sent Generals Putnam and Knox to the southern tip. Washington himself commanded from Harlem up north. And he assigned General Greene to defend any invasion at Kip's Bay along the East River."

"Were these troops of the Second Battalion you joined?" I asked.

"No. They were militia troops. I started out in the Second Battalion, but they found out I was a printer and took me for an educated man. Since General Greene was looking for an aide with some education, I got transferred."

"So what happened at Kip's Bay?"

"General Greene took charge of this unit of militia men, I don't even know where they were from . . . probably Connecticut . . . and they were supposed to act as a front line defense in the bay. So the British start coming up the East River. First, there was a flotilla of war ships bombarding us in the late morning. Then the redcoats and Hessians began coming ashore in flatboats by the hundreds. And our breastworks fell apart. They were not well formed in the first place. And when they disintegrated, the militia men started running backwards away from the river. They were backed up by Line troops, and then the Line troops started running. I was watching from the rear with General Greene. It turned into complete chaos. These were our men, and they could not retreat fast enough. Running, tripping over each other. And then . . .."

As he paused, I looked over at Jonathon and the girls. They had stopped eating and were staring at Peter in amazement, completely absorbed.

So this was war? Tactics and maneuvers, guessing where the enemy will land, defending the territory. How different from the world in which I lived only a hundred miles away, where public enemies still managed to maintain an awkward peace as we carried on business pretty much as usual. Peter volunteered to put himself in the middle of the fray, while I volunteered to stay home. He wore thick glasses and could not shoot straight to save his soul, while I needed no eyewear and was an expert shot. He was a brave man, and I?

I was a businessman sitting here listening to him tell of battle, almost as entranced as the kids.

Peter continued, "And then, I heard a commotion in back and to my right and what do we see but General George Washington on a white stallion charging toward the river against the retreat of our militia men. He was whipping at them with his riding crop, men and officers alike, ordering them to turn around and engage the enemy.

"I could not believe what I saw. He was charging at the enemy, musket fire all around, men falling down dead, still he moved forward, yelling at the soldiers to get ahold of themselves and be soldiers, to fight like men, just yards away from a line of Hessian invaders."

Peter hesitated. "It only lasted a few short minutes, but it's an image I'll take to my grave." He paused again as the image sank in.

"Did he reach the Hessian lines?" I had to ask.

"No. Someone grabbed his horse's bridle and led him back to safety."

"How badly did we lose?"

"Wait a minute," Jonathon interjected. "I thought you were on the other side."

"What do you mean, 'other side'?" I asked.

"I thought you were on the British side, which makes you and Uncle Peter enemies, right?"

"Peter and I would never be enemies."

"You know what I mean."

I was not in the mood to justify my fence sitting, so I rephrased the question. "How many men were lost on your side?"

"I don't know. A lot. But Washington kept the army together. Just as the British and Hessians were flooding ashore on the east side of Manhattan, Putnam's and Knox's troops were marching back north in columns on the west side to meet up with Washington's main body. But it was not long after that we evacuated Manhattan except for one fort."

"Who was commanding the British?" I asked.

"General Howe."

"Any more encounters with him?"

"Yes. We met up with his troops again at White Plains near the end of October. They beat us off a couple of hills after a day's engagement and we ended up withdrawing further north. Then two weeks later our sole remaining fort on Manhattan fell and Washington retreated to New Jersey."

Peter sounded dejected. I had lots of questions I would have liked to ask, such as where Peter was when Howe's troops prevailed at White Plaines. Was he in the front lines? Was he shooting at the British? Did he actually kill anyone? Were they shooting at him? How close did he come to being injured? I nonetheless restrained myself. The details of the mayhem would serve only to heighten the anxiety of Missy and Nathan.

"Are you still in New Jersey?" asked Margaret.

"No." Peter answered, "we crossed into northeast Pennsylvania a few days ago. Howe dispatched Cornwallis to come after us when we left New York. He was making things fairly unbearable in New Jersey."

"Do you think you will stay for the winter?" asked Margaret.

"It looks like it for the moment."

"At least you'll be closer to home," I said. "How much time do you have off?"

"Not more than another day or two. I could be called back at any time."

"I don't understand, Uncle Peter," said Annie. "If Cornwallis's men were chasing after Washington in New Jersey, why wouldn't he just come after you in Pennsylvania?"

It was a good question, and one I did not expect out of Annie. She was growing up.

"We don't know what they're going to do," said Peter. "They haven't tried to cross the Delaware River so far and they may not before spring, but things could change if the river freezes. It wouldn't be easy for them because we're pretty well spread out along the river."

"How many men does Washington have under him?" I asked.

"Perhaps six-thousand troops under his direct command. Remnants of the army are elsewhere."

"You think he is going to hold it together until spring?"

Peter stopped to look around the eating area and then back at Missy. He was not anxious to continue.

"Go ahead and tell him, Peter," said Missy. "Daniel's not going to talk to anyone. And the kids realize whatever you say here goes no further." Her eyes darted over to my son. "Right, Jonathon?"

"I swear, I'm not saying anything to anyone." Jonathon looked sincere. "No one would believe me anyway. They never do." He gave a grin.

No matter, Peter looked around the room again and spoke in a low voice. "What I can tell you is not a military secret. The British already know as much about our situation as we do. Intelligence leaks out of headquarters like water through a sieve. On the other hand, we never want the British to get too confident in what they know. We leak as many false rumors as true."

Peter's voice softened even more. "Here's the truth of the situation. It's dire. The men are ill-clothed, many without shoes, and winter is upon us. We're short on food, short on powder, short on every conceivable supply. And that's not even the worst of it. Enlistments for about five-thousand soldiers are up on New Year's eve. Even if half re-enlist, I don't see how we can continue. The cause is doomed or nearly so. Can Washington hold out until spring? If that's your question, my answer is I don't see how."

The frankness and intensity in the man's voice stunned me. Peter had always been gung-ho for independence, and he always gave a positive interpretation to any setback. My Loyalist friends, of course, had predicted the rapid end of the American cause from the onset. I took everything they said with a grain of salt. But Peter predicting defeat actually meant something. I could feel the courage and disappointment from the words he spoke.

"I would like to give you some encouragement," I said, "but you know my views on this war. My main interest is in having it over and you, my friend, coming home safely and for good. I hope it ends honorably on both sides. Apart from that," I paused a moment to gather my thoughts, "I can think of one piece of information I picked up that might be considered intelligence. I'll pass it on for whatever it's worth. We sold a load of flour to the British Army in November."

Peter's eyes squinted and he looked at me sharply. "You what?"

"Now don't get all excited. We sold a load of flour to the Continental Army just a few days later. Business is business. But the British agent told us they were stockpiling supplies in New Brunswick for the winter. I don't know whether that's any indication one way or the other of how anxious they are to be leaving New Jersey to cross into Pennsylvania this season. I'll leave the interpretation to your folks. He also told us the royal paymaster has his headquarters in New Brunswick. If Washington is looking for a good target to raid, he might consider New Brunswick."

Peter looked at me with uncertainty over how he should deal with my sin of trading with his enemy. "Thank you," he finally said, "I will pass it up the ranks. You think you can develop any more information like that?"

Apparently, I was not only forgiven but now being looked to as a source for further intelligence. Before I could formulate a response, a man wearing a gray cloak and black three-cornered hat still wet from the outdoors entered the dining area and began making an announcement at each table. The noisy conversations covered his words so we could not make out what he was saying until he got closer. Soon we became aware of his mission.

"Officers and enlisted men of the Continental Army, report immediately to the duty officer in the State House square."

His statement elicited varying reactions from those sitting around us, ranging from complete disinterest, to ridicule from Loyalists, to a few men rising and leaving immediately. Peter was among the latter. He looked at Missy, kissed her, gave Nathan a pat on the shoulder and stood up.

"Duty calls." He gave a nod in the direction of Margaret and me before he turned and left.

"May God speed your return," said Missy. She spoke with a determined voice, but I could see the anxiety in her eyes. Nathan had his arm outstretched to touch his father one more time, but Peter was gone.

It was only then I spotted Papa sitting in a corner with Mrs. Pickering. He looked in my direction as Peter exited the dining room. Seeing him at that moment made me feel embarrassed and awkward. He knew I socialized with Missy and Peter. Yet his seeing Peter answer the Continental Army duty call placed me closer to the enemy camp than comfort allowed.

When I nodded in Papa's direction, he turned and resumed his discussion with Mrs. Pickering.

★

Papa was away on business the following day. When he returned to the counting house two days later, I thought he had forgotten the incident altogether. Instead, he said in a gruff voice loud enough for David and Molly to hear, "I hope you're not taking up sides with that rebel husband your sister married."

"No, Papa, all here are on the same side."

Chapter Seventeen

The end of the year came, followed by our Twelfth Night celebration at Papa's, which I had expected to turn into something of a victory celebration for the end of the war. But even before Twelfth Night we heard reports of a battle gone bad for the British on Christmas night, and then another American win about a week later. I remained optimistic the news of these British losses would blow over and the war would grind to a halt. My hopes were dashed at a meeting of merchants at the London Coffee House in mid-January.

Papa went there often to meet with other merchants, get updates from the far side of the Atlantic, talk trade and money, and dabble in politics. He usually went alone. This time, he invited me and mentioned that some of the larger traders – the "Tall Oaks of the waterfront" is how he put it – were in the City and likely to be on hand before dinner. He thought it might be a good time to get some insights on the recent American victories and longer term business outlook.

The London Coffee House sold not just coffee but also cider, wine and spirits. Plus, it boasted a dozen private rooms for guests. People knew it best for its great room with huge stone hearth at one end. It was fully fired in the winter time, providing not only heat for the entire ground floor but also cooking and baking space for the many varieties of warm treats served with libations. Chairs, tables and sofas clustered around the room so groups of businessmen could confer in private if they chose. But often as not a conversation would become loud and interesting enough that patrons would join in from all quarters.

We arrived in late morning and joined some former colleagues of Papa on the Assembly who, like us, were small to midsize merchants. Off to the side of the great hearth a distinguished looking group drew our attention.

"Washington's not a brilliant general. Still, Trenton was his best move so far," said William Bingham. He was an Anglican and member of our church. I knew him as a successful merchant and member of one of the wealthiest families in the City. He certainly met Papa's description of a Tall Oak.

"It's beyond comprehension how he could have routed the Hessians," said Thomas Clifford, another merchant of about the same stature as Bingham, only Clifford was Quaker. The thought flashed through my mind how virtually all the major merchants in Philadelphia were Anglican or Quaker.

"My sources tell me," continued Bingham, "twenty-five hundred of Washington's men crossed the Delaware Christmas night in whale boats, then marched the nine miles to Trenton and took the Hessians by surprise at daybreak on the 26th."

"I understand the element of surprise," Clifford said, "but what's so confounding is that he even gave it a try. A maneuver like that gives rise to all sorts of risks. He could have been detected at any time. He could have lost half his men in the river or bad weather. So what I want to know is whether he is an incredibly lucky moron, or has he just been hiding his brilliance?"

"Maybe neither," chimed in Thomas Willing, another Tall Oak. "Maybe he's the same average general we've known all along and was desperate for a victory to raise morale and keep the army intact."

"You think it worked?" asked Bingham.

"I think it had an impact," Willing answered. "The capture of the Hessians at Trenton, and taking Princeton a few days later, raised Patriot morale. At the very least, it will make it difficult for the British Army to replenish supplies from the New Jersey countryside."

"Speaking of average generals, Cornwallis is right up there," noted Bingham. "Washington left a garrison of forty men at Trenton as a diversion, and Cornwallis took the bait. He thought it was the whole Continental Army. So he is about to attack with eight thousand redcoats from Princeton, and Washington's main body advances into Princeton with hardly a shot being fired."

"Rumor has it he had his eye on the weapons stockpile at New Brunswick, but thought better of it," said Clifford.

"And not just weapons," Bingham reported. "The Treasury Department was sitting on a stockpile of sterling in New Brunswick to pay British troop wages. But lacking the manpower to pull it off, Washington retreated, to his credit."

I never found out whether Washington's interest in New Brunswick was the result of the information I passed on to Peter. But I was beginning to learn the value of well-placed intelligence.

"These victories," said Willing, "bought Washington another season of fighting."

"How so?"

"Instead of the army collapsing, he's been able to extend enlistments six weeks, and that will give him time to raise enough troops for the spring."

"The whole season?" asked Bingham. "The Continental Congress can't buy a pot to piss in. How is it all getting paid?"

"Ah, now we're getting down to the good stuff," said Willing. "Robert, how is this war getting financed?"

A large man sitting a few feet away, his head down and eyes focused on a lap full of papers suddenly looked up. It was Robert Morris, a business partner of Willing, former member of the Pennsylvania Assembly, and member of the Second Continental Congress. He had voted against the Declaration of Independence early on but abstained in the final vote to let it pass. He signed his name to the document a month later. Although he attended St. Peter's on Pine Street, an Anglican church, he sometimes visited Christ Church.

"Now that's a loaded question," said Morris.

Willing winked at the others. "I have reason to think you have personal knowledge of the subject."

"Why's that?" Clifford looked eager to know. "You've not been making loans to Congress, have you?"

"No, not to Congress," said Morris.

"To Washington," Willing said. "Twenty-five thousand in Spanish milled dollars."

Clifford shook his head. "Good Lord! Are you out of your mind?"

"I expect to be fairly remunerated," said Morris.

"Yes, but only if the Americans win."

Morris thought for a moment. "Yes. I'll be better off if the Americans win, but I'm sufficiently hedged so I should do well regardless."

It occurred to me these men may not have been indifferent to the war's outcome, but their principal preoccupation by far was business. And chances were good, whatever the outcome, each, like Morris, would come out ahead.

"I think you're daft," said Bingham. "Twenty-five thousand doesn't keep the army afloat."

"Not by a long shot," added Morris. "But it can help out in a pinch."

"In a pinch, yes," agreed Bingham, "but the war is being financed mainly through emissions. Congress has emitted upwards of twenty-five million in paper currency. Unfortunately for Washington, it can't go on like that for much longer."

"Is it being redeemed?" asked Clifford.

"No," Morris answered, "and that's why it cannot go on much longer. Congress prints and spends the currency, and the colonies are supposed to *withdraw it from circulation* by accepting it as tax payments. If they did, the value could be sustained. But that's not happening."

"How long before it becomes worthless?"

"I don't know." Morris shook his head. "Soon. Its value is already declining."

Their discussion of war and finance utterly fascinated me. I decided to get a better understanding of what to expect going forward. With some trepidation, I took a half step forward and blurted out, "Mr. Morris, what is your best business advice for smaller size firms over the next year or so?"

I half expected to be laughed at or have my question brushed aside as unimportant. Instead, the room went quiet in anticipation of his response. Although a known opportunist, Morris was well regarded as an adept financier and congressional insider. Businessmen sought out his financial advice.

"You're Steven Thompson's son. Am I right?"

"He certainly is," Papa spoke up. "Nice to see you, Robert."

"And you, Steven." They gave each other a formal bow. "You think we'll ever get our Assembly back?"

Morris referred to the fact that, following Pennsylvania's constitutional convention in September, the colony's Assembly had succumbed to the control of pro-independence radicals.

Morris favored independence but stayed a moderate and pragmatist. So much so that Papa and he retained a cordial relationship.

"Not with the riff-raff we have right now," said Papa.

Morris chuckled. "I suppose not. Your son, though, raises a good question, for all size firms, Tory and Whig."

Eyes danced around the room to the uneven rhythm of nervous laughter. Allegiances were in such flux among those present it was hard to tell whether Loyalists and Tories outnumbered Patriots and Whigs, or even who fell into which camp. About the only thing we all had in common was retaining the fortunes we already possessed, large and small, and improving our lots when possible.

"So what is the prudent course for businessmen like us?" Morris continued. "One thing I would caution against is taking payment in Continentals. And if you have to accept Continentals, turn them around quickly, because they aren't going to hold their value."

"The preferred payment?" asked Clifford.

"Specie is always number one," said Morris. "Gold and silver coin. Spanish dollars next; they are stable. British bills of exchange if you can get them, bearing in mind they are good only for British foreign trade. If you have a choice between Continental loan certificates and currency, take the loan certificates; they pay interest. Continental currency comes last, which means you spend it first."

"Anything else?" I asked him.

"Just the obvious," said Morris. "Try to negotiate payment in weaker money if you are buying, and stronger money if you are selling. Another thing, if the war continues, stored goods will not be safe."

"Why is that?" I asked. "Looters?"

"Yes. If you consider the Continental Congress a looter. As the Continental currency goes down in value, Congress and the army will confiscate goods out of necessity. It's already happening. They issue impressment certificates as payment, but who knows if you'll ever be able to use them for anything. It's best not to store much inventory. If you do, keep it well hidden."

★

I went home that day thinking about our company's business prospects. Much of our profits were tied to being able to purchase large quantities at low prices and storing for sale at a time when market conditions seemed right. We would have to re-evaluate our strategy. Our shop and warehouse inventory needed to be reduced, moved or hidden. Who knew when some American quartermaster, backed up by a company of soldiers, might ride into the City and decide to re-stock using our wares. Mark Ableson, the Continental quartermaster buyer, negotiated this time around but next time there may not be any negotiations, leaving us no control over the terms of sale.

And no more sales based on future payment in Continentals. Barter exchanges were still safe. But with Congress's spending out of control, and Continentals soon to take a dive, we had to eliminate credit sales or risk being paid in worthless currency.

The safe in our counting house stored stacks of Continentals. We needed to spend them, invest in land, or convert it all to specie, but not all at once, and hopefully not in any way that would work to the detriment of our friends or family. Still, we had to get rid of it. Morris was a Whig and supported independence. If he was advising not to hold Continentals, the action we needed to take could be no clearer.

Another thought occurred to me on my way home. A fellow could learn an awful lot hanging around places like the London Coffee House. Today it was finance. Tomorrow it might be foreign trade or maritime insurance. The next day maybe troop movements. Yes, a fellow could learn an awful lot.

Chapter Eighteen

Trial Proceedings

"So you're telling us Robert Morris advised you not to hold Continentals?" asked the Judge Advocate.

"Absolutely! The same man who signed the Declaration. Business is business. People were losing fortunes with Continentals. And that was happening in early '77. Things got worse after that."

"Continentals were financing the war effort. It was an act of patriotism to accept them."

"Tell it to Mr. Morris. You think I did something awful by selling a few barrels of flour to the British. He dumped his worthless currency on unsuspecting farmers and tradesmen, making them paupers."

"Mr. Morris has been essential to the war effort. He and his firm have supplied the Continental Army with its basic needs. You said it yourself. He personally lent General Washington twenty-five thousand. How can you question his loyalty?"

"He is doing it all for profit. He uses Continental government shipping rights to haul his own freight. He overcharges for everything he sells. It's no wonder he had twenty-five thousand he could lend Washington."

"Yes, well he never consorted with the enemy, like you did."

"He traded in enemy ports. They all did, all the big merchants. They partnered up on both sides of the war effort. It looked like consorting to me."

"Let's get back on track, Lieutenant. We're here talking about you, not them. Did you end up selling off your Continentals?"

"As best I could."

"You talk about Mr. Morris profiting. What about your family's business. Did it continue to profit and prosper?"

Daniel thought back. "Things continued all right through the first half of 1777. I had to replace our mill manager, but apart from that we had no major problems. The war had not really reached us yet, at least in any negative way.

Chapter Nineteen

In the spring of that year I decided it was time for Jonathon to have his own musket. At thirteen, he was about the same age I was when Papa gave David and me our muskets.

I had taken Jonathon with me on a few half day hunting trips outside the City and taught him how to load and fire. But he never expressed much interest. Part of his reluctance stemmed from the fact he remained small for his age. At only five feet tall, the musket was almost his height. Still, he needed to learn how to shoot. The younger the better.

Brown Besses were generally available from local gunsmiths. Acting with uncharacteristic foresight, the Continental Congress issued specifications for the firearm to help assure it would become standard equipment for the troops. Unfortunately when I made an inquiry, my usual smith had none on hand. He explained he could craft only about twenty per month. And all currently in production were under contract to the Continental Army or private customers. He also told me I was not likely to find a new Brown Bess anytime soon, unless I was willing to fork over fifteen or twenty pounds. That was not going to happen! I ended up going to an importer and purchasing a piece from Holland. It fired eleven-gauge lead balls similar to my Brown Bess and cost just eight pounds.

I put it in the cellar to await an opportune time to give it to Jonathon.

About that time Margaret announced we were going to start attending weekly evening Bible study services at Christ Church. Though not overly religious, I did not mind going. The weekday services were more informal than on Sundays and the pastor sometimes invited an open discussion. It was a chance to discuss things other than family and business.

Church attendance had been dwindling and many Anglican churches ended up closing altogether. The problem had to do with the Anglican clergy. They had sworn oaths of allegiance to the King of England, who sat as the head of the church. In addition, the Book of Common Prayers contained prayers for the monarch. Many in our membership leaned toward independence. In July of last year the vestry went so far as removing the references to the King in the prayer book and adding prayers for the Continental Congress. While the rector, Reverend Duche, was not happy, he went along.

Tonight, one of our then assistant pastors, Reverend White, officiated at the adult prayer service. About twenty of us adults listened as he read the story of David and Goliath. My children were in a prayer service with kids their age at the other end of the church.

The story had always fascinated me. The Philistines standing on the side of a mountain, the Israelis facing them on another mountain. "Out of the Philistine camp came Goliath whose height was six cubits and a span!" Goodness that sounded tall! "Wearing a coat of mail, and carrying a spear having a head weighing six-hundred shekels of iron he shouted out, baiting the Israelis. Then David, the son of a servant of Saul, ran toward the Philistine line. Having earlier selected five smooth stones from a brook, he loaded one into his sling, hurled it toward

Goliath, the stone sinking into his forehead, killing him." My mind wondered. Could a stone hurled by a sling actually pierce someone's forehead?

"So why are we told this story?" Reverend White asked rhetorically. "What validity might it have for us today?"

I started to have a bad feeling about this Bible lesson.

"It's obvious," said a parishioner to my right, Hugh Sanders. Reverend White looked startled, not expecting a response. "Good always triumphs over evil, no matter what the odds."

"Yes, quite, Mr. Sanders," said Reverend White. "And we can surely . . . ."

"It's like the Americans and British," continued Sanders.

"You better be careful where you're going with that," a parishioner to my left interjected.

"You can have your interpretation and I'll have mine," said Sanders.

"It's not really a matter for debate," answered Reverend White.

"No. It's not," said parishioner John Lawrence. "And just to make things clear, the British represent the good who, though stronger than the rebel traitors . . . ."

"That's absolute rubbish," said Sanders, waiving his hand dismissively. "It's not the Patriots who kept Boston under siege for more than a year and massacred militia farmers at Lexington in April of '75." He now yelled over a growing chorus of supporters and detractors.

Reverend White tried to take control. "All right, then, let us try to . . . ."

"Look," said Lawrence, "I didn't come here to listen to a bunch of insults. Not within the walls of the Church of England where I've been a member now for thirty years. And . . . ."

"Please!" shouted Reverend White. "Hugh, sit down."

"This is just as much my church as . . . ."

"Sit down, Hugh," commanded Reverend White. "And you, too, John." Lawrence started to speak. "And button it up. I don't want to hear anything more from either of you."

"Here is what I think . . . ." began another parishioner.

"Or from anyone else," shouted Reverend White. "Let us just have a moment of silence and think about what just occurred in this House of God."

We obeyed.

"These are difficult times," he resumed. "We are fortunate in that, so far at least, Philadelphia has been spared. But I've prayed long and hard and still I cannot tell you who is right or who is wrong. Good, honest, hard-working men and women exist on both sides of this conflict. But in this church, we are all on the same side . . . the side of God. I am not going to dictate what friends you should have or which side you should take. But I am going to dictate that so long as you are in this church, you are going to tolerate everyone here. You two shake hands."

No one moved.

"Sanders, Lawrence, please shake hands."

"I'm not shaking hands with no traitor," said Lawrence.

"You will not be welcome in this church until you shake hands," said Reverend White. "That goes for you too, Sanders."

"If you want to kick me out of this church, then you go right ahead and do it. But I'm not shaking hands with a traitor."

"Hugh?" asked Reverend White.

"He has gall, calling me a traitor. My son was wounded by redcoats at White Plaines," said Sanders. "He'll be walking with a limp for the rest of his life, because he was fighting for my country. I'll not be called a traitor, and I have no interest making up with any damned Tory."

Reverend White looked at both of them, trying to decide what to do. His threat of banishment was not working. He tried a different tact.

"You're both good men," he said. "Please go home and cool off. And then come see me and we'll talk. We're done with our prayers for the night."

As we got up to leave, Lawrence approached me. "Daniel, can I talk to you outside?"

"I almost thought we had seen the last of you for a while," I said with a grin as we walked to the steps outside the church doors.

He nodded. "It's an ugly situation. I don't mind Sanders. He and his family have always been friendly. Still, I'm not going to stand for us British subjects being compared to Goliath."

"I agree, John."

"Here is what I wanted to tell you. Marvin Swenson died."

"What?"

"We were out by your mill earlier today visiting my sister, and she told us. So we stopped by the mill to pay our respects to Ruth, Marvin's wife. It happened yesterday. She wanted me to tell you, so you could decide what you wanted to do with the mill."

"I'm shocked," I said. "I knew he had health problems, but he was in his early fifties."

"His heart gave out kind of sudden. Ruth is still deciding what to do, but will probably move in with one of her kids closer to the City."

"Thanks for letting me know. I'll go visit right away. Be well."

As I waited for Margaret and the kids, I noticed a woman wearing a bonnet and light cloak, standing on the other side of the church doors. I did not recognize her but thought she had likely attended the service with Reverend White. Under the bonnet I caught a glimpse of strikingly pretty features with a dark complexion and straight black hair. Her face appeared reserved.

If I had seen her before, I had taken no particular notice. I decided it was time to introduce myself and find out more. The fact she was pretty, however, triggered feelings of guilt. Sarah had died less than a year ago. How could I abandon her spirit on the spur of the moment? What would she think of her husband, drawn to another female so quickly? What would the kids think of their father? Did I have no sense of fidelity?

For goodness' sake, Danny, just go over, say hello, and move on.

"So what did you think of the Bible class tonight?" I asked as I approached the stranger.

She looked up, slightly surprised. Her dark eyes caught the moonlight and sparkled.

"Hard times strain friendships," she answered.

Her statement eloquently summed up my thinking. She impressed me.

"And sometimes create new ones," I added.

I had not intended my statement as being anything other than friendly conversation, but she now viewed me suspiciously as if I had been forward.

"Have you experienced new friendships lately?" she asked.

She was challenging me. I could feel it. And it left me almost speechless. I could only think of something vague to say.

"I'm always hopeful."

The shadow of a male emerged from the church. "Ready, Elizabeth?" It was a young man close to her age. My heart sank.

"Yes, Albert," she turned in his direction. Then almost as an afterthought, she hesitated.

"Albert, this is Mr. . . . ?"

"Hello." I gave him a little bow. "I'm Daniel Thompson.

"Nice to meet you."

"Albert is my brother," said Elizabeth. "Good night."

I was not sure what to make of this encounter. But one thought buried itself in the back of my brain. He was her brother, not her husband.

★

I told Margaret about Marvin Swenson as we walked toward the house that evening. She suggested I leave early the next morning.

"With Marvin gone, who knows what might happen."

"I guess that's best," I said. "My hope would be to put one of the hired hands in charge for the short term. But I don't know what to do with the bookwork. Marvin always kept good accounts. We need someone literate. I may have to ride over to the Town of Chester to see who is available. It could take a couple days. I'm thinking of taking him with me." I pointed to Jonathon now walking with Annie ahead of us.

"He would have to miss school," Margaret reminded me.

"That's true but it's been a while since he's been there. And I could give him his musket. Maybe even do a little hunting with him."

She gave me a look of disapproval, which sparked my ire. While I knew she meant well, Margaret sometimes overextended her role in our family. This was not the first time. Jonathon was, after all, my son, not hers. I began evaluating anew whether we needed to continue her services.

Chapter Twenty

Early the next morning Alphonse hitched Dobbin to the chaise so Jonathon and I could get a good start. We ended up waiting an extra half hour to allow Margaret's fresh beef and liver pie finish cooking to take along for Mrs. Swenson.

Jonathon had been acting true to his usual form of late. He never took much of a role at church or school, and showed an interest in little other than his friends in Elfriths' Alley. I continued to assign job responsibilities under Mathew's tutelage at the shop. But since his mother's death, he fell back into the habit of showing up late, or not at all. When he did present himself, Jonathon moved with such lethargy that Mathew inquired whether he might be ill.

The one exception to his overall malaise was his violin. He had begun playing almost every day. Our church organist, Mr. Lochmond, approached me the previous fall to say Jonathon had musical promise. A month later he suggested Jonathon take music lessons. I expressed my disinterest, saying I regarded the fiddle as a passing boyhood fancy. Mr. Lochmond countered that Jonathon ought to be encouraged. He said he could help Jonathon with the fundamentals for a modest fee. And if things went well for a few months, he would find him a better teacher.

Just like a clergyman, I thought, always trying to find new ways to extract money from the congregation.

I put the subject aside. But we had not gone more than a couple of miles on our way to the mill when Jonathon brought it up again.

"Have you had a chance to think about the lessons?" he asked.

"A little, but I didn't think it was something you would appreciate."

"Why would you think that, Papa? I'm never going to improve much on my own."

"That's true, but I was thinking more in terms of how you really want to spend your time. When I was your age, my father took David and me hunting. I got pretty good with the musket."

"We hardly ever go hunting, and I don't even have a musket."

Eureka! My timing could not be better. I had wrapped the new musket in burlap and placed it under my musket and a few other supplies on the floor of the chaise to keep it a surprise.

"Besides," continued Jonathon, "I like playing Mama's old fiddle. I think I could get good at it."

"Mr. Lochmond is an organist. Has he ever played the violin?"

"He has played some, but even so, he knows a lot about music. He can help me understand it. It's something Mama would have wanted me to do."

He had me there. That was exactly what Sarah would have wanted. I kicked myself. For her sake, I would have to give in. "I guess it wouldn't hurt to try a few lessons, just to test it out."

Once we got within a few miles of the mill, the time was right for the musket. I reached down, pulled it up, held it aloft, then handed it to him. I wanted him to like it. I really did not mind if he pursued the violin as a pastime. But certain things I regarded as mandatory for a young boy, and interest in a musket was one. Being able to handle a musket was a milestone for coming of age. In my view, Jonathon never would become a man until he could use a firearm efficiently. I realized, though, if I were to push him too hard, I would lose him.

"Here, I picked this up the other day," I said as casually as I could, "and thought you might be able to use it."

I watched my son's young face. It went from genuine surprise, to amusement, to disappointment, to being mildly resigned, which I took as an indication he would try to please me. At least for a while he would not reject it. As he removed the burlap from the long barrel, I thought: Come on, Jonathon, can't you show a little pleasure in this expensive gift?

Holding it up to his shoulder as if to take aim, the piece looked awkward and unsteady in his arms. He then placed it back down on the floor of the chaise.

"Thanks, Papa, it's nice."

That was a start.

"Maybe we can work in a little hunting while we're out here as soon as I get things at the mill under control."

"Sure, if you want."

I sensed the battle between the musket and the violin had just begun.

★

Closed window shutters still protected the Swensons' stone cottage from the cool temperatures. The black bunting nailed over the threshold reminded me of the purpose of our visit. Next to a tree not far from the house were a horse and wagon, announcing the presence of house guests inside. A young black woman, met us at the open door.

"Good day, I know you're Willie's wife," I said as she ushered us inside, "but I can't remember your name."

"I am Mary Jane, sir," she answered politely. "Mrs. Swenson is inside with her son and daughter-in-law, Mr. Robert and Ms. Beth." She gave a curtsey.

"Thank you, Mary Jane."

They were sitting in chairs around the stone hearth and stood as we approached. "Robert, ladies, nice to meet you all."

I turned to Mrs. Swenson, "I'm so sorry for your loss." I gave her a hug and handed her the covered pot with the meat pie. "Margaret, our housekeeper, insisted you have it."

"Bless her heart." Mrs. Swenson said, "This will make a nice dinner for us this noon."

"I wish it were under more pleasant circumstances. Marvin was a good man, and we'll all miss him dearly."

Mrs. Swenson told us about Marvin's difficulties over the last few weeks. He had been on a slow decline for the last several years, and the local doctor had not been able to do anything for him. The worse he got, the more he relied on Willie, his slave, to keep the operation running. Then a couple of weeks ago he woke up and could not get out of bed. That was the beginning of the end. Ruth spent full time tending his needs until he died three days ago.

"Why didn't you send word so we could get you some help?" I asked.

"Marvin thought it was just temporary. And besides Willie was running the mill and we didn't want to bother you."

"So what's in your future?"

Her son, Robert, answered. "That's why we're here. Mom is going to come live with us for a while. We live in Germantown north of Philadelphia. We'll spend a couple of days loading things into the wagon. Then it won't take us long to get there."

"No rush for you to leave, Ruth," I said. "Take as much time as you need."

"That's very decent of you," she said.

"What about Willie and Mary Jane? You planning to take them with you to Germantown?"

"Mom wanted to talk to you about that," said Robert. "My wife, Beth, doesn't believe in slavery. She's a Quaker and an abolitionist."

Beth nodded. "I just think it's wrong."

"So, Mom, tell Mr. Thomson what you had in mind."

Mary Jane was beginning to prepare dinner, but I saw out of the corner of my eye she looked our direction and moved a little closer.

Mrs. Swenson began slowly. "Marvin was always fond of Willie. Mary Jane, too, but particularly Willie because he is so talented. You know how well he can handle a musket. It's not just that. He can track in the woods, he is good with people, and he knows the mill. Marvin taught him everything about the mill and Willie caught on fast. So we were thinking, and this is partly Beth and William's idea, maybe you might like to hire Willie to manage the mill."

I heard a muffled "What!" behind us, glanced around, and saw Mary Jane wide eyed, turning her head and covering a huge smile. This obviously came as a surprise to her. I almost spoke, but could not think of what to say. It was just as unexpected to me.

"Now before you say anything," Mrs. Swenson continued, "don't get me wrong. We're not trying to tell you what to do. Your family owns the mill and maybe you have other plans, and that would be all right. But if you don't, and if you were interested, we would release Willie and Mary Jane from their bondage. It would be a comfort to us to know Willie had employment and was provided for, at least so long as you and he agreed he could stay on here."

I stared at her, still trying to think of what to say. "That's an interesting idea," I managed. "What about the accounts? How would we handle those?"

Mrs. Swenson paused. "Why, I hadn't thought about that, but now that you bring it up, I've been teaching Mary Jane reading and arithmetic. Isn't that right, Mary Jane?"

"Yes, Ma'am. I know reading and how to figure."

"You have been teaching a black woman how to read?" I asked incredulously. It was contrary to everything I had learned about slave owners. They usually kept their slaves uneducated, isolated and well away from firearms. They discouraged independent thinking which led to ideas of freedom. Marvin and Ruth had turned those concepts on their head. "Why did you do that?"

"I taught school," said Mrs. Swenson, "years ago of course, before Marvin and I married. But I missed it, and was thinking about doing some teaching around here, and Marvin suggested I start with Mary Jane. He said if I could teach her, then I could probably teach anyone." She laughed. "But Mary Jane's been a good student. She was not difficult at all. And it gave me something to do besides cooking and cleaning."

It was an odd thing to do, teaching a Negro to read, and enjoying it no less. But I could not think of anything wrong with it. A lot of white women, and men, especially in rural areas, did not know how to read. I had to think Mary Jane was probably one of the very few of her race who could. I admired Mrs. Swenson for the effort.

"Can you cook, Mary Jane?" I asked.

"Oh, yes, sir, Mr. Daniel, I'm a right good cook."

"And she is, too," echoed Mrs. Swenson. "She helps cook every day."

"I have to think about what to do with the mill," I said, "but if we were to try something like this, where would you be living, Mary Jane, where you are now?"

"Oh, yes, sir, the shanty is just fine for Willie and me. We like it real good."

"Then you could either sell this cottage or rent it out to someone else," said Mrs. Swenson.

"Well, like I said, I'm going to need to think on this a spell, and have a talk with Willie, and some of the hired help to see what they might think about it. That is certainly very generous of you, Ruth. I just don't know, though."

After eating dinner, Jonathon and I walked the short distance to the mill. The mill foundation was located on the French Creek bed well below the grade of the stone cottage. So it was not until we got almost there when I noticed the dirt path leading to the mill had been raised about thirty feet. At its upper-most height, the path came up even with double doors built into the third story. The project was still in progress. But already atop the path were timbers taking the form of a wooden bridge to span the eight-foot distance between the top of the path and the mill doors. The bridge was wide enough to allow a wagon to back into the mill and offload.

"Willie!" I called out. He came running.

"Yes, sir, yes, sir, oh, it's you Mr. Daniel. I didn't know you were here today."

"Willie, what's going on here? This path to the top of the mill is raised?"

"That's so we can haul the grain to the top by wagon."

"I didn't authorize this."

Willie gave me a quizzical look. "Master Marvin and I thought you did."

"When did I do that?"

"Last time you were here, or, maybe not the last time but two times ago, last fall."

"What did I say that led you to believe that?"

"Mr. Daniel, we were talking about building this wagon road up to the top of the mill. You said you had not yet had a chance to talk to your engineering friends, and were concerned about damaging the mill wall, but other than that you wanted to go ahead with it."

"And you took that as authorization to begin elevating this path?"

Willie looked at me carefully, not certain whether he may be in trouble. "Yes, sir, I did, so long as we found a way not to damage the side of the mill."

I examined the work that had been done. A retaining wall abutted the earth works beneath the path and looked well-braced. A lot of time had gone into hauling dirt to raise the path level. The bridge at the top appeared strong enough to hold three or four wagons. I would prefer to have gotten a design from an expert, but I could not fault what Willie and Marvin had figured out on their own.

"Well, then, complete it. It looks good to me."

"Yes, sir! Me and the boys work on it mostly in our spare time, when the other work is slow. But we'll get it done."

I spent the rest of the day watching farmers pull up in wagons, observing how they interacted with Willie, and talking with the workers about how they all got along together.

The following morning I set up Jonathon for some target practice with his new musket near the creek. He seemed none too enthusiastic. Throughout the morning I kept listening for his musket to discharge. It occurred only sporadically. Obviously his heart was not in it, and I began wondering if this were another failed attempt at parenting.

I also went over the books with Mary Jane. Mrs. Swenson was right. Mary Jane was literate and had a good handle on what needed to be done.

Most of our transactions were recorded through bookkeeping entries. Farmers under contract delivered their crop at our agreed-upon price, currently three and a half pounds Continental per barrel. Instead of cash, the mill would issue a receipt, which the farmer could negotiate to make purchases of his own or take for payment to our business agent in the City. If the farmer wanted us to grind the wheat for the farmer's own use, the charge was one eighth of the wheat milled. Most supplies we purchased on account and reconciled with the supplier at year's end. It was all pretty straightforward for someone with a little patience.

By mid-afternoon we finished the bookwork, but I still had not made up my mind yet about hiring Willie and Mary Jane. For everyone's sake, I wondered if it was the right thing to do. My concern was how a black man and woman would work out in a white world. Willie had the respect of our workers, but up to now his authority had been backed up by Marvin. Could he handle the employees on his own? And what about our customers and surrounding community? How would they react when they saw two former slaves in charge? Hiring the couple would be a nice gesture to Mrs. Swenson, but this was business. The mill had to run pretty much on its own. I could not be trekking out here every two days.

Chapter Twenty One

While I pondered what to do about a manager, Willie approached me. "Mr. Daniel, you trying to get that son of yours to learn how to handle a musket?"'

"I am and it has not been easy."

"What he needs is a little hunting trip to perk up his interest."

"I think you're right." I had almost concluded our hunting excursion would have to wait for another trip. Willie's suggestion made me reconsider. "What kind of game do we have this time of year?"

"Almost anything you want. Rabbits, squirrel, beaver downstream the creek."

"Anything larger?"

"Sure, there's plenty of deer north side of the creek. They'll eat apples out of your hand." He spoke with a knowing glance. "And bears sometimes come up from the south or west."

"Bears? They huntable?"

"This is a good time for bears. They been out of their dens for a month or so, nice full coats. The boars are just starting to look for sows."

"Where would we go?"

"I know a place not far," said Willie, "maybe five miles. I could set up a bait pile yet today. Good chance we'd attract one or two. Best time to shoot 'em is daybreak or dusk. They get shy during the day."

"I say we do it then. You set up the bait, and we'll leave here before daybreak. Mrs. Swenson's son might want to come along."

"I'll bring Larson, too. He's a bonded man, and can help cut up the meat and haul it back."

Early the next morning, Jonathon was none too happy to get up, and I had to drag him by the scruff of his neck. I figured he would liven up once the hunt got under way. Robert, Mrs. Swenson's son, lent us the use of his wagon to get us part way to where Willie had set up the bait. We walked the remaining distance.

Willie had chosen the site carefully. To a sturdy young tree he and Larson had tied several beaver carcasses. They then smeared honey and jelly high up the trunk to make it more difficult for a bear to reach. They also burned some bacon grease, and we still could smell the smoke on the nearby trees. For the blind where we would wait, they piled up dead branches and bushes partway up a ravine and downwind of the bait. It gave us a good vantage point from which to take aim.

At daybreak we arrived and set up our positions a few feet away from each other.

"I want to give Jonathon the first shot," I said to Willie and Robert. "Is that agreeable to everyone?"

They both nodded.

Jonathon wore a look of satisfaction, his interest increasing. "Why isn't he carrying a musket?" he asked, pointing to Larson who stood behind our firing line with burlap bags, knives and a tomahawk at the ready.

"Four of us can handle a bear," I said. "He'll help skin it once we have it down."

"Yes. But what if the bear comes from behind us?"

It was a good question. We had no idea from which direction a bear would arrive.

Willie answered. "Don't worry, boy. Larson's done this before. He'll keep a good look out and let us know in plenty of time."

"How'd you get to know so much about hunting?" asked Jonathon.

Willie looked at me as if inquiring whether it was permissible for him to answer. Slaves were not always allowed to talk to white kids. I nodded.

"Master Marvin said I had to earn my keep, or he would sell me off down in Virginia, and I would end up picking cotton or cutting tobacco. He was only half jostling."

"Why did he buy you then in the first place?" asked Jonathon.

Willie looked at me again, and I nodded again. I wanted to hear his answer.

"Actually he didn't buy me. He inherited Mary Jane and me when his papa died. His brother got the farm. I don't think Marvin intended to keep us, but things worked out. Now, young man, if you want to shoot a bear, you got to be quiet."

We waited behind the underbrush as the morning light turned from a faint ray to a soft glow and westerly breezes pushing gray clouds began signaling the start of an overcast day. It was then that Willie held up a hand to get our attention. I moved only my head to peer through the branches and beyond to the baited tree. At first I saw nothing, then fifty yards upwind, I sensed movement. It was only a feeling, but soon the shadow in a wooded patch moved. The shape of a big black bear appeared.

I moved my arm only slightly and pointed in the bear's direction to guide Jonathon's searching eyes. His mouth opened in awe as he picked up the view of the huge dark creature sniffing around like a dog. It advanced cautiously toward the tree, retreating, standing on hind legs, sniffing, listening, back on all fours, looking around, and advancing again.

I pointed at the bait tree and then to Jonathon, motioning him to take his shot once the bear reached the tree. He had only to get the shot off. Anywhere near the bear would be fine, it did not matter. His shot would be immediately followed by three more.

Slowly but surely the bear worked its way up to the bait tree. Then looking around, as if curious why a beaver carcass was lying so far from the creek, it began nibbling. I nodded at Jonathon. Now was the time. The bear was on all fours, its broad side making a nice sized target from forty yards away. Jonathon took aim, hesitating. I listened in anticipation, heard nothing, looked in his direction. He was sweating and shaking his head, the barrel of his musket wavering. I wondered if something was wrong. His right hand squeezed the trigger.

"Oh, no!" he said aloud, "I didn't cock it."

Hearing that cry of despair, the bear made a sudden jerk. With the agility of a squirrel on a limb, it took several quick leaps toward the safety of the woods. Robert got off a shot, and may have nicked it at the far end of his range, but the bear was gone. Willie could still have hit it but held his fire.

"I'm sorry, Papa!" Jonathon was near tears. "I thought I was ready to shoot. It was my fault."

I sighed. "It's all right, son." I looked at Robert, beginning to re-load, shaking his head. I turned to Willie. His face was non-committal. "Worth tracking?" I asked him.

"A mighty fine bear, Mr. Daniel."

"How big do you think?"

"Four hundred pounds, maybe more. We could track it."

"Robert, what do you think? You up for a chase?"

He was doing his best to restrain his irritation. "Sure, why not."

"Willie, you lead the way."

"Maybe that boy of yours could walk with me, give a hand?" asked Willie.

"Good idea." I was liking Willie more and more. The man did not need help. If anything, Jonathon would be in the way. He was just trying to calm down my son and repair his confidence.

We headed out in the general direction of the bear, Willie and Jonathon in the lead, Robert and I a few yards behind, and Larson bringing up the rear.

"Here's what the track looks like," Willie showed Jonathon as they paused. "The one looking like a man's fat hand is the rear foot, except his big toe is on the outside not the inside. The smaller half hand is the front foot. You can see the claw marks."

"The tracks are here but not up ahead," Jonathon noted. "What happened to him?"

"The tracks are hard to spot. Bears run with flat feet, so the tracks only show up in mud or dry loose dirt."

"So how do we find him, once we get into the brush?"

"We keep looking for his tracks, or his scat, or scratch marks on trees, or places where sprouts or twigs or leaves are damaged. But mostly we got to think like a bear."

Jonathon looked at him curiously. "How does a bear think?"

"If I were a bear, I'd run as fast as I could away from people and take an easy path, but soon I'm going to get tired and slow down, and start looking for food. Maybe acorns or the soft part under tree bark, or buds on trees, or a nice nest of insects. I'd be interested in dead meat if I could find some. I'd never stray far from the creek or a water hole. And I'd probably stay down low until I was sure no one was following me."

We trudged through shallow marshes, low brush thick with thorns, and stands of tall pine. We climbed hills and ran down their sides to deer paths or rippling streams below, pausing now and then to let Willie check out a track or claw mark on a tree. All the while he kept Jonathon engaged in the hunt by asking questions, testing his answers, soliciting his input. He had a good instinct with people.

Around midmorning Willie called our little troop to a halt and went ahead by himself. On his return he motioned to be quiet.

"He's over there," he pointed, "eighty or ninety yards out. To get closer we first move away and go northwest, then back south, and approach from downwind. There's plenty of cover to the west, so we ought to be able to get close in. We'll go single file, Jonathon you stay behind me."

Willie led us in a huge arch for half an hour before we started heading back in the direction of where Willie saw the bear. As we moved eastward I began hearing the faint rush of water through a small rapids. That was encouraging. The flow of water against the rocks would mask the noise from our movement through the forest.

Willie motioned us to stay put while he went forward a few yards and came back to report. "He's just ahead about thirty yards," he spoke in a whisper. "Beyond those two trees in a clearing near the stream. He can't smell us downwind or hear us with that stream so close. And his eyesight is not that good. How you want to take him, Mr. Daniel?"

"Here's what we'll do. The four of us with muskets will spread out a few feet apart and approach in one line across. And let's not mess it up this time. Can you handle it, Jonathon?"

"Yes, sir."

"You got your musket fully cocked and ready?"

"Yes, sir."

"As soon as you see that bear, you advance one more step and take your shot. No matter what happens, the rest of us will fire after you. I want you to shoot first, all right?"

"Yes, sir."

"And, Larson, you come in afterwards with the hatchet to finish him off."

We spread out with Jonathon between me and Willie to my left and Robert on my right. In unison we moved forward and around the trees, took a couple more steps and there it was . . . bigger than life, a huge furry black bear, none too happy to see visitors. We were much closer than Willie had estimated. Not more than ten yards away, I could hear it breathe.

"Now, son," I glanced over to see he was fiddling again with his musket.

The bear rose up on its hind legs, let out a terrible-sounding roar and leapt forward toward us. Simultaneously, Jonathon threw down his musket, screamed, began running backwards, and tripped to the ground. An instant later three musket shots rang out, hitting the bear mid stride and causing it to drop half the distance from where it started. Larson charged forward with his tomahawk in one hand and skinning knife in the other. Without hesitation he cut its throat to assure its demise, and turned it on its back to give us a better look.

The danger was over, but Jonathon's hurt feelings were just beginning. "You almost killed me," he wailed. "Papa, you almost killed me."

Looking at the dead bear, a dozen feet away, I sighed. Yes, we had a tense moment, but Jonathon had not been in any real danger. All he had to do was pull the trigger. Then I would be able to tell Margaret and the girls how he had shot the bear and make him feel proud. But it was not to be. Dammit! I thought back to my experience with my older brother, David, and the wood chopping years ago. David threw a hatchet, and I accused him of almost killing me. I had been in no real danger, just embarrassed. So it was with Jonathon. Maybe I was pushing him too hard. Or maybe, I was not cut out to be a good parent in the first place.

We hauled the bear back to the wagon in pieces and arrived back at the mill in early afternoon. Willie and Robert maintained a lively conversation along the way, grateful for an abundance of bear meat to divide up. Jonathon, on the other hand, sat silent and sulked. As for me, I took the opportunity to come to a decision about what to do with the mill.

★

On our arrival I assembled the hired hands and bonded men in front of the mill. With Willie at my side, I announced, "Willie is taking over as manager." It was the only logical decision. Not only could he operate the mill, but he had leadership skills and an ability to deal with people.

I continued on in stern words how they were to give Willie all the respect, support and loyalty they had shown Marvin. If anyone thought he would have trouble taking direction from Willie, I said to let me know now; and advised I would be visiting frequently to make sure things were running smoothly. Everyone nodded, a few even looking relieved they would not have to break in a new manager.

I then took Willie aside to make sure we were thinking alike. "You're in charge now. Is this something you can handle?"

"Yes, sir, Mr. Daniel."

"Great, and I never want you to call me Mr. Daniel again. That sounds like you're still a slave. You are a free man, or soon will be once the paperwork is completed. So act like one. Call me Daniel or Mr. Thompson. Understood?"

"Yes, sir . . . Mr. Thompson."

"You are the Thompson family representative at this mill. You are to treat our customers fairly and with respect. If they don't like you, or if they think you are cheating them? They aren't going to want to do business here and we're all going to lose. On the other hand, you can't let the customers take advantage of you. If that happens, again, we'll all lose because the mill will not be profitable and we'll have to shut down. So, you can see it's just as important you're honest with our customers as it is you keep them honest. Are we in agreement?"

"Yes, sir, . . . Mr. Thompson."

"My family has owned the mill eight years now, and we know what to expect. We're looking to you to maintain the same results we've had in the past. If you do better, you'll get a bonus. If you do less, I'll want to know why."

"Yes, sir."

"I'll try to get out here once a week for the next few weeks to make sure everything is running smoothly. You have questions?"

"No, sir."

"All right, Willie, you're in charge once I leave. Don't let me down."

"No, sir"

"One other thing. After Mrs. Swenson moves out, you and Mary Jane move into the stone cottage."

Willie eyed me curiously. "We should what?"

"You are to move into the cottage. You are the manager, so you live in the house. It's your right. The house comes with the job."

His lips quivered as he repressed a smile. "Yes, sir. That's very nice of you, . . . Mr. Thompson."

"You'll get used to the place."

Before we left I made a gift of the bear skin to Mrs. Swenson. I wanted nothing to remind me of today's hunting trip. We also divided up the meat among Robert, Willie and me. I gave my share to Willie for the work crew.

Jonathon remained quiet for most of the ride back to the City. He managed only to ask, “You don’t have to tell Janie or Annie, do you?”

“No, of course not, at least not about the last part. I might tell them how you helped Willie track down the bear. You want to try it again some time?”

“No, Papa.”

Chapter Twenty Two

Trial Proceedings

"You actually put a Negro in charge of the mill?" asked the Judge Advocate skeptically.

"I put the most qualified man available in charge." Daniel nodded. "And yes he is a Negro. And he did a pretty good job running the place. I had no regrets."

"Until he disobeyed your orders."

"I don't know he ever disobeyed my orders."

"We'll get to that," said the Judge Advocate as he picked up his notes and studied them. "Let me see here, you told us earlier in the fall of 1776 you were willing to sell barrels of flour to anyone willing to pay, and you ended up selling to both the British and Continental Armies. Is that correct?"

"That is true."

"Business is business, I think is how you put it. Is that correct?"

"Those were my words, yes."

"But by the summer of 1777, you refused to sell to the Continental Army, isn't that correct?"

"Refuse to sell? Not that I recall. That was the summer General Washington paraded through the City, correct? Oh, I know what you're talking about. It was right before the battle down on the Brandywine. No, we never refused to sell. We could not reach an agreement on price."

"You were over-charging and trying to gouge, weren't you? The very kind of thing of which you accused Mr. Morris."

"No. We were not gouging. We were asking what the flour was worth."

"That is what you call it. Maybe that's what Mr. Morris was doing, too."

"No, not when he is charging the army two or three times more than he charges everyone else."

"So you claim. You also disobeyed Continental Army orders concerning your ship that arrived in port after the battle?"

"I didn't violate orders of the Continental Army. I did have a run-in with the local militia. That part is true. I still believe they caused us an unnecessary loss."

"I'm not surprised by your attitude. You also mentioned earlier you had further contact with the Lenape tribe, or at least the boy who rescued your lost daughter. When did that occur?"

"That was earlier in the summer . . . about the time we heard rumors the British were going to attack Philadelphia."

Chapter Twenty Three

A few weeks after the bear hunt, Papa returned to the counting house with some unsettling news.

"General Howe's troops are making preparations for Philadelphia."

David, Molly and I were all busy with paperwork, but we looked up incredulously.

"What?" I asked.

"You heard me. He wants to take the City."

"What happened to meeting with General Burgoyne up in Albany, dividing up the colonies along the Hudson, and isolating New England?" Molly asked. "Wasn't that the master British plan for winning this war?"

"That's what I thought," said Papa, "and it was a good one. But Bill Bingham doesn't lie. He has contacts all over. His people in New York are telling him the British regulars are starting to pack up for a move south."

"It's about time." David spoke triumphantly. "This City is full of Loyalists. It will be a piece of cake. They should have taken this town a year ago. It will decapitate the rebels and end this war within six months. That's great news, Papa."

Papa sighed. "Maybe. I was sort of hoping this thing would end without dirtying up Philadelphia. Being occupied by an army is never good. And who knows what we're going to have to go through before our troops actually set foot here. Look at Boston. It was under siege for months. We could find ourselves in the middle of a battle."

"You're right to be worried," said David. "But in the long run coming here has more advantages than disadvantages. It will shorten up the war and a lot of the rebel riffraff will flee. We will also have a chance to make friends with some of the top brass in the army, which could be good for business. Maybe we can even get in on the ground floor of helping to plan the structure of the colonies after the war ends."

"How soon does Bingham say this is going to happen, Papa?" I asked.

"No one knows for sure. Howe moves with the speed of a crippled tortoise. If they are only starting to pack up, it will be a few months. And Washington will be tracking their moves. You have to figure him into the mix."

"Should we move the warehouse?"

"Let's think about it. Better keep this to ourselves for the time being. It's not yet public."

I returned home late that afternoon with a lot on my mind. If the British were coming, I had my family to think about. Should we stay or go somewhere, and if the latter, where? And if we had to go, how much money could I put my hands on? I had twenty-five pounds in silver hidden in the cellar, and I could probably withdraw some reserves from the company, although the company's finances were getting tight. How much was enough? Who would look after our property while we were gone?

These thoughts percolated through my mind as I opened our front door, saw Annie reading in the parlor, and heard her shout, "Maggy, Papa's home."

Margaret's immediate presence in the parlor raised warning flags.

"What is wrong?" I asked.

"Daniel, we have to talk." Margaret turned to Annie. "Go to the kitchen."

I looked skeptically at Margaret. "Did Jonathon do something?"

She gave me a solicitous, now-aren't-you-glad-I-am-here kind of look. She had a habit of giving me those looks. I loathed it. "No, not Jonathon."

"Who, then, Janie? What happened to Janie?"

"Nothing happened to Janie . . . other than the fact she is growing up." This time she spoke with a touch of arrogance, as if growing up was something only women knew about.

"Of course she is growing up. What's this all about?"

"Sit down here and I'll tell you. Janie will be home soon and she has something to ask you."

"Yes, so what is it?"

"She is going to ask your permission to be courted by a young man."

That hit me like a brick. "Well." It took me a moment to regain my bearings. "She is a little young to be courted. She is only fifteen."

"Half the girls her age are thinking about getting married, if they aren't married already," Margaret informed me. She gave me a worried, but understanding smile.

"Do you know the guy?"

Her too-long pause made me uncomfortable. "I'll let her tell you about him."

"Do you know him or not?"

"Actually, no. But please, don't be hard on her. She is a young girl and needs our support."

Our support? I hated when Margaret was so assuming.

Margaret, though, was right to be concerned about one of my daughters being courted. I wished Sarah could be here to take charge. She always knew what to do. With Margaret I was not so sure.

Within the half hour Janie bounded through the front door and into the kitchen where we were ready to sit down for supper. She had a wild, happy expression on her face.

"Oh, Papa, I have the most wonderful news." Her eyes sparkled as she looked at me expectantly.

"Really," I said nonchalantly, trying not to let on my advance warning. "Let's sit down while you tell me."

"I'm getting married!" She blurted out. "I cannot believe it. And he is going to stop by here tonight. Isn't it wonderful?"

I looked at Margaret whose eyes had now popped wide open. Even Annie looked surprised, although she tried not to show it.

"Just a minute, young lady." Margaret grit her teeth. "What do you mean, you're getting married?" Margaret could be stern on occasion and I applauded her for that, even though these were my children.

"Papa, you and Mama always said you wanted me to choose my own husband." Janie looked at me.

"What's your point?"

"Now I've chosen, and he is going to be here tonight."

"Slow down! I don't know who is coming here tonight, but you're not getting married to anyone anytime soon."

"Papa," Janie began to wail, "you always said I could choose."

"Of course you can choose. At the right time and the right place and after we have all talked it through and decided it's the right thing for you." I tried not to be too obvious about adding a few conditions to her freedom of choice.

"We can talk now, Papa, and it is the right thing for me."

"Sit down," I commanded, "and be quiet."

Janie looked to Margaret and her sister for support, but they were nodding in agreement with me.

"Papa . . . ."

I held up my hand. "Quiet." I had to think about what to say. The situation caught me unprepared. Finally I took a stab. "Getting married is one of life's most important decisions. People go through a courtship period for good reasons. The time together allows you to get to know the other person, so he can meet your family, so your family can give you advice, and so you can be certain he is the right person for you."

"Papa, I'm aware of all those things and I know you're concerned because you love me. I already know he's the right person for me. I've been seeing him for more than a year now."

"You what?"

Janie's eyes shifted and she looked embarrassed, having let the cat out of the bag. Margaret shook her head, obviously taken by another surprise.

"Who gave you permission to be courted by a boy?" she asked.

"Mama said I could choose my own husband. I thought you would want me to also. Besides, he didn't really court me, we only spent time together."

We heard a knock at the door.

"Who could that be?" I asked angrily.

"It's probably . . . ." Janie's voice trailed off as I went to the front door.

Opening it, I saw a young man maybe eighteen years old with long, black braided hair, a wrinkled white shirt adorned with multiple strands of a beaded necklace, ankle-length wool trousers and wearing moccasins.

"There is an Indian boy here," I shouted. "Anyone know what he wants?"

"It's him, it's Lightfoot," cried Janie running to greet him. "You remember, Papa, he rescued me in the forest?" She took his hand and pulled him into the kitchen.

I stood speechless at the front door, in utter shock.

They all shared a few awkward *hellos* and *how do you do's,* in the kitchen but the place returned to silence once I entered.

Then Jonathon came down from his attic hideaway.

"What's the Indian doing here?" he asked.

"Quiet, Jonathon," I said. "Get an extra chair from the parlor."

Alphonse joined us from the barn and without any apparent surprise said something to Lightfoot that sounded like gibberish to me.

Lightfoot responded, "Wanishi," which I later learned meant "thank you."

I looked askance at Alphonse.

"What did I do?" he asked defensively. He added, "I know a little Unami," in a tone suggesting I had underestimated him.

As we sat down to eat supper, Janie spoke with characteristic obliviousness. "This is just wonderful, our first meal together as a family."

I was not sure if she saw my scowl, but if she did, it did not prevent her from exchanging glances with Lightfoot and whispering messages in his ear. After several minutes' worth of exchanges, she announced, "Papa, Lightfoot has something he wants to ask you."

She then nodded at him, and in halting English he said, "Sir, I would like to ask for the honor of your daughter's hand in marriage."

"What," asked Jonathon, "Janie's getting married to an Indian?"

"Jonathon, please. No, Janie is not getting married to an Indian. Either this one or any other." I spoke emphatically.

"Papa!" The wailing returned in Janie's voice. "You said I could choose, and I've chosen."

"Have you heard nothing I have said?" My voice showed anger.

"Papa, you cannot . . . ."

"This has gone far enough," Margaret said sternly. She was finally coming through, and more or less taking charge, and none too soon. "Annie told me you were bringing home your Indian friend you wanted us to meet. And now we find out you have been seeing him for a year behind our backs and you want to get married. You have been deceitful, and we'll have no more of it in this family."

I flinched at the word "family" coming from Margaret, but let it slide.

"Maggie, I'm in love. I can't help it. You're in love with Papa. You know how it is, don't you?"

"Enough of that, young lady." Margaret turned beet red and gave me a furtive glance.

"She's in what?" I asked. I could not believe what I just heard, and concluded I had not heard it. "Janie, please, this is really starting to irritate me. You finish your supper and Mr. Lightfoot can finish his supper. Then he's going to leave and you are going to stay here. And once he has left we're going to set up some rules so nothing like this happens again. And no, you are not getting married."

I heard Jonathon snicker as I gave my little speech. "Mr. Lightfoot!" he said under his breath.

"Papa, don't say never." Janie was close to tears, no longer wailing, but begging and clutching Lightfoot. "Please don't say never. I know I've been deceitful, and it was wrong, and I'm sorry.

But don't say I can never marry him. Tell me what I need to do. Tell me how long I have to wait. Just tell me, please, so I know what needs to be done."

My daughter never ceased to amaze me. I had been about ready to wring her neck, but now I almost felt sorry for her. This was the first nearly-reasonable thing she said all night. The truth of the matter was the last thing in the world I wanted was an Indian son-in-law. An Indian for God's sake! How would I ever live that down? But she was right. Sarah and I had always said we would never choose their husbands. Now Janie was asking what she had to do to make this particular prospect acceptable. She was putting our liberal parenting to the test. I had to come up with a nice-sounding justification for why she had to wait. Not a long time. Just long enough for her to forget this Indian boy.

"For one thing," I began hesitantly, "before you get married, you need to grow up. No more of this running around behind our backs and then making surprise announcements. It only demonstrates you have not fully matured."

"I know that, Papa, is that all?"

"No. It is not all and I will let Margaret speak to this as well." I paused, but Margaret was nonresponsive, still reeling from the revelation I was her secret love.

I continued. "Another thing, you need to plan out what you will be doing after getting married. Where you would live, where he would work, all those sorts of things. That kind of planning takes time, and my guess is you have not given it much thought."

"But we have, Papa. His tribe holds rights to some land not far from the City. We've talked about building a home and farming."

That was more planning than I expected. I had to come up with something else. "That's good, but another problem with Mr. Lightfoot . . . ."

"Just call him Lightfoot, Papa, it sounds better." Janie smiled.

She was actually becoming likeable again. I had to do this gently. "Another problem I have with Lightfoot he is from a different world from ours. I'm not saying that makes him bad or that you should never consider making friends with an Indian. Lightfoot himself seems like a nice person." I was on a roll. "He found you in the forest and protected you. So he cannot be all bad. But we, all of us, need to learn more about his customs and his way of life, so we'll know what to expect. And I am not confident he knows enough about us or our way of life to make him comfortable living among white people."

"What do you want us to do?"

"He could be doing a lot of things while we're getting to know him, such as" – come on, Danny, think – "maybe getting a job in the City for a while, working on the waterfront. Or you mentioned farming. How much experience has he had? Maybe he ought to spend a year or two working on a farm so he knows what it's all about. Or joining the army. That would give him a lot of experience with white people. It might even help him learn the language. My guess is both sides are looking for young Indian guides and scouts who know the territory and who know some English."

"For how long, Papa?"

"For a while, not forever. Until we all feel more comfortable with this whole idea. Margaret, what do you think?"

"Your father is right." Margaret was still a little pink. "Getting married is always a big step but this step is bigger than usual. You're asking a boy from a different race, from a different culture, to join your family. Have you thought about church? Does he have any religion?"

"He is willing to learn," Janie said quickly.

"Yes, but you need to make sure. He needs to meet Reverend Duche, and we need to ask for his blessing."

Finally, Margaret had come up with something worthwhile. As we continued to talk through supper, the mood lightened. Alphonse even joined in the conversation, exchanging a few words with Lightfoot in Unami.

Jonathan asked what he said.

"I asked if he had any sisters who might like to meet me," said Alphonse, "and he said no."

"No sisters, or no to wanting to meet you?" asked Jonathon.

"I didn't clarify."

Everyone laughed, even Lightfoot. As we finished eating, I took a good look at him, and understood, anew, why Janie would find him attractive. He was tall and muscular, dark bright eyes, high cheek bones. Except for the long braided hair, he could pass for a white man with a nice tan.

As he was about to leave, Janie turned to me and asked, "Papa, Lightfoot wants to know, if he did join the army, which one should he join?"

Goodness! The question was music to my ears. If he ended up joining the army, he would be occupied away from the City for months, if not years. I wanted to do nothing to discourage him.

"Let your consciences guide you," I said. "Your Aunt Missy is pro American, your grandfather is pro British. Arguments can be made on both sides. You decide."

Chapter Twenty Four

The next few weeks of summer went slowly. Our dry goods inventory was getting low, and the Thompson Trader was overdue. We were beginning to wonder if she had been detained by the British fleet, or waylaid by an American privateer. The thought of losing her was sickening. She had kept our business alive, and we still owed more than two-hundred pounds on her. What a disaster if she sank.

In mid-July we received word the British had retaken Fort Ticonderoga in New York. We Loyalists had downplayed the American capture of the fort in 1775, but with it now back in British control, many celebrated with predictions the war was all but won.

Papa was not convinced. "It was a fluke when the Americans captured it back then," Papa declared, "and it's a fluke we have taken it back. The British mission was to disable the rebels holding the fort and that we failed to do."

By August everyone knew of General Howe's plan to take Philadelphia. He loaded fifteen-thousand troops onto the British fleet at the end of July. Instead of floating down the Delaware River from New York, he decided to take the much longer ocean route around the coasts of New Jersey, Delaware and Maryland and turn back north through Chesapeake Bay.

"It adds weeks to the voyage," Papa shook his head, "and once they land he's going to have a bunch of sick soldiers and dead horses on his hands. This guy is a frigging idiot."

By this time, a sense of uneasiness had come over the City. Philadelphia had always been a bustling place with a dozen merchant vessels tied up along the docks at any given time, along with many schooners and scores of fishing boats. Hundreds of free laborers worked alongside the enslaved and indentured servants with the sounds of industry and commerce drifting well inland.

As the summer wore on, the diminishing number of ships arriving and leaving caused commercial activity to slow down. People still congregated outdoors during daytime, but they no longer talked of business ventures, holiday visits, or the latest cooking recipes. Rather, they focused on the British Army creeping our direction, whether to stick it out or leave for the countryside, and stocking up supplies in anticipation of shortages.

In a matter of a few short weeks that summer of 1777, the City shifted from peace to war.

True, for some, the war had never been far away. It was always in the forefront of the minds of the pro-independence radicals who had taken over the Pennsylvania government. Unfortunately, they lacked the leadership skills to manage and organize. Franklin was now in France on behalf of the Continental Congress. And many other would-be leaders were too conservative for those who had managed to wrest control. As a result, the new Pennsylvania colonial regime lacked popular support. Had it not been propped up by the Continental Congress, it would have collapsed entirely.

Another sign of the war's close proximity was the growing presence of Continental Army recruiters who sought to entice our boys to join up with promises of bonuses and glory. Service in the army, though, was voluntary, and no stigma was attached to those whose families declined the invitation. Pennsylvania militia duty, by contrast, was theoretically mandatory, but easily avoided by paying a fine or hiring a substitute.

Thus, along with the summer's coastal winds blowing the flotilla of British ships closer, came the growing realization that the City stood in the crosshairs of the best equipped and organized army in the world. Whether one regarded the British as the enemy or the overlord of order and virtue, change was coming and everyone knew it.

Instead of driving a wedge between the Patriots and Loyalists, as one might expect, the impending sense of danger and uncertainty in some ways drew the two sides closer together. Certainly, radicals existed on both sides who were prepared to inflict harm on anyone espousing the wrong point of view. And in public forums Patriots championed God-given independence, Loyalists railed against the ungrateful rebels, and Quakers denounced the ravages of war in general. But in the local communities, neighbors for the most part continued to act like neighbors who sought and gave friendly advice regardless of political views.

The Continental Congress reacted to the approaching British by enacting regulations designed to make the City less of a prize once they arrived. It forbade citizens and merchants from stockpiling various goods, such as flour, iron, weapons, and blankets. It also required excess supplies to be moved to rural areas. To enforce the regulations, Continental soldiers confiscated stores of material found to be in violation. Frequently, they issued receipts for what they took, but on occasion the confiscations looked more like outright thefts than attempts to keep goods of military value away from the British.

Washington's troops congregated in southeastern Pennsylvania to begin preparing for the British. Toward the end of

August, postings appeared around the City announcing the army would march through the streets in a grand parade. How could anyone not be interested?

Patriots wanted to see just what it was that protected them from the loathsome British. Loyalists were curious to find out how formidable were these rebels. The streets that Saturday swelled with City folk and rural visitors alike. They stood along the parade route, which extended north on Front Street and then westward up Chestnut to the State House.

In anticipation of a huge crowd, the five of us took Dobbin and the chaise to a side street where we could sit on the chaise and get a better view. Once we heard the drums beating in the distance, we began looking for the lead column turning the corner and march our direction.

"Look," I called to our family group, "General Washington in the lead!"

The man was unmistakable, wearing a blue waist coat and buff colored breeches, cross-belts, and black boots to his knees, a general's hat atop his long powdered hair tied in back in a queue. Riding a white stallion, he strutted in front of a double row of horses.

With saber in hand the general waved and smiled as his horse crossed from one side of the street to the other. On occasion, he sheathed his saber and stopped to greet someone in the crowd. His frequent reaching down to shake hands brought cheers from the spectators. He knew how to work a crowd.

Behind him officers on dark brown horses rode in formation, walking or trotting in tandem. Once in a while one waved to an acquaintance on the street side. But mostly they stayed focused on looking dignified.

Then came the columns of infantry. Column after column. Each appeared to consist of a regiment four or five-hundred strong.

Most of the men carried muskets upright at the shoulder, cartridge belts secured around the waist, haversack strapped on the back, and three-cornered hats decorated with fresh green leaves.

"They're wearing different colors," Jonathon noted. "Are they all in the same army?"

"Yes," I said. "They just disagreed over what color to wear. Either that or they're color blind."

"They are not," said Annie, brushing aside my attempt at humor. "They're from different colonies."

Annie was right, of course. The regiments were organized by colony and the men in each regiment wore similar colors, but the colors varied among regiments. Leading each regiment were field officers on horseback with horse pistols on their saddles, flag bearers with colonial flags, and sergeants holding aloft halberds with regimental banners. Drummers up front helped maintain the pace, although keeping step to the drumbeat was the exception.

The condition of the troops varied. Some dressed sharply with clean, handsome uniforms. Others wore tattered clothes looking as if they had not been washed for months. A few wore only stockings on their feet or were entirely barefoot. Still others marched with wounds from combat, arms in slings, or limping with crutches.

Following each regiment, wagons carrying tents, tools, food provisions and ammunition kept space between the columns. The artillery pieces assigned to a regiment were drawn by horses next to the wagons. On occasion, a company of sixty or seventy mounted cavalry rode in formation behind the regiment of which they were a part. The heavy cavalry horsemen all carried sabers and pistols and wore leather or steel cuirasses. They led the charges into enemy lines. Riding on horseback but wearing no armor were the light cavalry and dragoons.

Heavy artillery and a wagon train marked the end of the parade. The big cannons were pulled by teams of horses. Weighted with ammunition, the wagons rolled up the street two or three across and stretched on for two blocks. They were the charge of the quartermaster staff and carried extra supplies and munitions for the army as a whole. A few of the wagons transported women who performed laundry services and assisted with cooking.

"That's not fair," said Jonathon. "The women get to ride?"

"Because we're special," Margaret smiled.

The entire parade took two hours, and none of us thought about leaving before the end. Never before had I seen so many people all marching in relatively good order. Nor had I ever seen so many muskets, cannons, horses, wagons and supplies. It was a long, flowing river of fierce manpower and weaponry.

★

As the parade wound down, soldiers on leave began mixing with family or friends. It was then I spotted Elizabeth with a female companion, followed by her brother in a blue uniform. They worked their way through the crowd, both women carrying parasols on the hot, sunny day.

I had seen her several times since first meeting her in the spring. I found out she regularly attended St. Peter's Church, which was affiliated with Christ Church and shared its pastors. With that intelligence I made up some excuses for attending St. Peter's. I found her always assisting an elderly woman, who turned out to be her mother. They lived together on the north side of the City, and she worked out of their home as a seamstress. Her brother, who served in the Continental Army, lived in nearby Germantown.

Today was the first time I saw her away from church. I had thought about calling at her home, but every time I worked up the nerve, I considered the kids and Margaret. What a commotion my calling on another woman would cause. But now here she was, alive and looking fresh in a crowd wilted from standing hours in the hot sun. Her dark hair was tied in a swirl atop her head with a few locks extending down her forehead. She wore a white blouse with ruffles down the middle, frills on the cuffs with a knotted ribbon around her neck matching her long gray skirt. Looking prim and proper, yet young and exuberant, not a drop of perspiration showed on her forehead. If I was going to talk to her, I had to act fast, or risk losing her in the crowd.

"Margaret," I said, "you and the kids go back home. I see someone I need to speak with."

"But, Daniel, I thought we were . . . ." Margaret looked quizzical.

Already out of ear shot, I glanced back seeing her scowl. I just kept going, hoping she would lose sight of me.

Catching up with Elizabeth, I tried to make our meeting look like a chance encounter. As she and her companions were turning north to walk up Third Street, I darted to the outside, turned, and donned what I fancied was a startled expression.

"Why, Elizabeth, did you enjoy the parade?"

"Mr. Thompson. A surprise seeing you here. You remember my brother Albert, and this is his wife, Helena."

"A pleasure. Call me Daniel." I gave a little bow while Helena curtsied.

"Daniel attends St. Peter's," Elizabeth explained, "at least he does sometimes."

"Yes, as the spirit moves me." I turned to Albert. "Elizabeth says you're from Germantown."

"We are indeed," said Albert, "and I hope you will not think me rude. But we must find our carriage and be getting back. I have only a day's leave before rejoining my regiment. Would you mind so much walking Elizabeth home?"

Would I mind? The fates were smiling on me today! I restrained myself from showing too much enthusiasm.

"Of course not. Maybe you and I could further our acquaintance when you have more time."

Once away from Chestnut Street the crowd thinned, and Elizabeth and I walked together.

"What regiment is Albert in?" I asked conversationally.

"The Fourth Pennsylvanian. They have had engagements in New York City and northern New Jersey."

"You must be proud of him. I take it your entire family is pro Patriot."

"Of course we are. And what about your family, Daniel?"

It was not the most auspicious of topics for winning Elizabeth's affections. I treaded carefully. "We are of conflicting persuasions."

"I see. And you? Are you conflicted?"

"I feel conflicted now." I smiled.

She eyed me with a playful but serious look. "Which is it, Daniel? Are you a Patriot or are you a Loyalist?"

Here was a direct, no-nonsense person, which could be good in some circumstances. Just not now. How can I turn this around, I wondered. "If I said I were a Loyalist would that mean I could not call on you next week?"

Her pause made me think she was about to turn me down. Then she seemed to have a change of mind. "I would like you to call on me, but not in a red uniform."

Not an enthusiastic invitation, but good enough. "That's fair. But you have to tell me one thing."

"And what would that be?"

"Why is a beautiful woman like you not married by now?"

She blushed and averted her eyes in a feminine way. "It must be I have high standards."

A good answer, I thought.

"And now you must answer me."

I turned with curiosity. "And what might that be?"

"Who was the woman in the chaise I saw as we passed?"

I laughed, with a touch of embarrassment. Elizabeth did not miss much. "That's Margaret. She's been helping out at home."

It took ten minutes to reach Elizabeth's cottage located in a row of small houses on the north side of the City. On the way, I opened up to Elizabeth about how my life had changed since Sarah died and explained the role Margaret played in my family.

"She and I get along," I said, "but she goes home after helping with supper." Elizabeth eyed me in a way that made me laugh again. "Most of the time, at least. And when she does stay over, my children are always home. So everything is perfectly innocent. That's the honest truth. I swear." I felt like a teenager denying having eaten the whole mince pie.

I did not know if Elizabeth believed me. But one thing became clear after I left her at her door: I would think about her constantly until I saw her again.

★

"I was impressed," I said to Papa, David and Molly two days later.

"You were supposed to be," Papa responded. "That was the whole purpose of the parade. To give confidence to Whigs and rebels, and break the spirit of us Loyalists and Tories."

"How many troops you think we saw?"

"I heard over ten thousand," Molly spoke up. "That would seem right. I counted twenty regiments and that didn't include the horsemen or wagons."

"Anyone know where they are headed?"

"Southwest," said David. "Howe is landing at Head of Elk in Maryland, if he hasn't already. The battle will take place somewhere between here and there."

"Are we still planning to wait it out?" I asked.

"It's a close call," Papa said. "After thinking it through and talking to Bingham and the others, I think we're all right. It's in no one's interest to bombard or burn the City. On the American side, Philadelphia is the capital of the colonies. And for the British, too many loyal supporters live here. Howe's plan is to lure Washington into a battle somewhere nearby. Staying put may be the safest strategy."

We heard a knock at the door, and a familiar face entered.

"Good day, my friends," said Mr. Ableson. "I hope life has treated you well since my visit."

I spoke up. "Yes, quite well, thank you. I believe you already met my brother, David, and this is our father, Steven Thompson, and sister Molly. Papa is the founder of our company." Papa nodded without rising. "Mr. Ableson is a buying agent for the Continental Army."

"Nice to meet you all. I trust you saw the glorious parade on Saturday?"

"Yes, we were just discussing it."

"All those soldiers need to be fed. And I'm here to see if we can work out another purchase of flour."

"That's Daniel's end of the business," Papa grunted.

"What did you have in mind?"

"If you can tell me where you keep your stock, and how much you have, I can have it picked it up and save you the cost of delivery."

Ableson may have taken us for fools, but he was the last person with whom I would share such details. In fact, I had already given instructions to Willie that flour no longer was to be stored at the mill. It was a sitting target for marauding army supply officers. Rather, it was to be taken to out-of-the-way warehouses near Turks Head in the center of Chester County. One warehouse there was built into the side of a hill, and the other was an old barn. Both attracted little attention. With the Thompson Trader six weeks overdue, we had accumulated well over a hundred barrels. We needed to sell it soon because our company was running short of capital.

"We might be able to put our hands on a few barrels," I said, "for the right price."

"How many?"

"I don't know for sure. We would have to check our sources. I think your last order was for twenty five. We could probably handle that."

"We need a hundred barrels or more," said Abelson. "Can you do it?"

"Like I said, we have to check our sources. What's your asking price?"

"Five and a half pounds Continental. Just like before."

"Can't do it," I said. "The Continental is not worth what it was last September. We could do five and a half pounds in British bills or Spanish dollars, but not Continentals."

"What is your price in Continentals?"

I had to think quickly. With Papa listening to every word, I had to show myself an effective negotiator. True, we needed the cash, but Morris's predictions about Continentals were coming true.

"Fourteen pounds per barrel Continental."

Abelson looked mortified. "Fourteen pounds? That's highway robbery. It's gouging, nothing more nor less."

"I'm sorry, it's the best we can do."

"Maybe we could ask your father for something more reasonable," said Abelson. "He looks like a good Patriot."

Papa turned his head away. "My son has the final say."

Abelson looked back to me. "Let me put all my cards on the table. The army needs flour, you have it to sell, and I'm willing to pay a fair price. We've been paying other mills seven pounds per barrel. I will pay you eight, but that's my best price."

"We can't help you at that price," I said. "Not in Continentals."

His face turned a dark red and his voice was sullen. "So you're not a Patriot after all, just like the rumors I heard. Let me tell you this. I know your mill on French Creek in north Chester County. I will find the flour. Once I do, we will impress it for use by the army, and you will receive certificates worth five pounds per barrel Continental, if that."

Abelson stormed out and slammed the door behind him.

I sighed and looked around at Papa, David and Molly.

Molly shrugged.

David smiled.

"Good riddance," Papa snorted.

"What if he finds it?" I asked.

"Let's just hope our ship comes in soon," said David. "If it doesn't, that eight pounds per barrel could start looking pretty good."

Chapter Twenty Five

The battle took place two weeks later, on September 11, at Chadd's Ford along Brandywine Creek in northern Delaware, thirty miles from the City. It was far enough away no one in the City could see what was happening. Still, we heard distant cannon roars throughout the day, providing a constant reminder men were dying and our fates may be decided in the balance. Of the battle itself, we received scattered reports from stragglers separated from their units, mostly American, who found their way into the City beginning late that day and for the next several. They told us Washington had anticipated the British advance from the southwest and positioned his troops at key ford crossings on the eastern side of the creek with the center focused on Chadd's Ford.

In typical fashion, however, Washington had not thoroughly investigated the terrain and left a crossing upstream unguarded. Twelve British regiments surged across and outflanked him on the right.

In the meantime General Howe sent Hessian forces under the command of General Knyphausen against the American center at Chadd's Ford, resulting in the capture of a cache of Continental artillery. The Hessians used it to blast the retreating Americans. Washington pulled back for the night to camp in the Town of Chester, in south Chester County. The next day he retreated further north.

While the Continental Army went down in defeat, Washington managed once again to hold the army together.

The decisive victory Howe had sought continued to elude him.

For the next two weeks Washington successfully kept his army between the British and Philadelphia. It was an anxious period inside the City for Patriots and Loyalists alike. Both American and British wounded were brought in by ambulance wagons for treatment at the hospital on Pine Street or the makeshift field hospital set up nearby.

Continental Army supply officers, accompanied by armed soldiers and wagons, also arrived daily to purchase needed equipment and food. For the most part they paid reasonable prices for the goods, but no haggling took place. The goods were in plain sight, and the presence of armed soldiers made clear the goods were leaving the premises at the offering price. If no agreement was reached, the merchant was left with an impressment certificate which, if he were lucky, could be redeemed from the colonial government in payment of taxes. They were not good for much else. Our own dry goods shop on Second Street was the victim of several such forced sales, but our inventory was so low our losses were minimal.

The uncertainty in the days after the battle was sufficient to cause many families, especially those with children and Patriot leanings, to pack up for the countryside. And who could blame them?

While the Continental Army's losses were not so great it would never fight again, Washington could not keep Howe out of the City indefinitely. Congress itself fled the City a week after the battle to take up quarters at York. The Pennsylvania

Executive Council made a stab at erecting fortifications. But the effort was soon abandoned and the Council withdrew to Lancaster.

★

Movement in and out of the City's harbor came to a standstill. The vessels remaining were ordered upstream on the Delaware by the Executive Council to keep them from British capture. I lost hope of seeing the Thompson Trader any time soon. But as David and I were leaving the counting house one morning to review our inventory, we heard a familiar voice approach from behind.

"David and Daniel, hold up."

We turned to find a smiling Captain Bart. Our ship had finally returned.

"Where in God's name have you been?" asked David. "We figured you must have been captured or detained, or even sunk."

"Sorry to have caused you worry," said the captain. "We started out from New Providence three times. Had to turn back. Twice due to storms, the third time because of the rigging. We eventually got it repaired and here we are."

"You and the crew all right?" I asked. "What about the British blockade?"

"We were chased, but never caught. We got us a great ship, swift and maneuverable."

"Come on, we must tell Papa."

We returned to the counting house and brought Papa up to date. He was delighted. "Goodness gracious," he said, "both you and the ship are safe. A load off my mind. You have cargo?"

"Filled to the brim, and then some," said the captain. "We're at the pier just east of the warehouse. The crew secured the ship.

No longshoremen anywhere in sight. The place is dead. What's going on here. An epidemic?"

"Worse," said Papa. "Let's take a look and we'll fill you in on the way."

As we walked toward the pier, David explained the absence of activity along the waterfront. "No ships have come in for the last two or three weeks. The British are about to take the City. It's going to happen any day now. No one wants their vessel confiscated."

"Last I heard when we left the islands was they were on their way," said the captain. "I cannot believe it has taken this long."

"It has," I answered, "and now is an incredibly bad time for you to arrive. Glad you are here, but a week or two earlier or later would have been better."

Papa explained, "The colonial government ordered the harbor cleared. I don't know what they are going to do when they see our ship. David, what do you think?"

"We need you to sail her upstream," he said to Captain Bart, "cargo and all. Find a safe harbor, and sit there awhile. Once the British have taken over, we can negotiate her return."

When we got to the pier, the Thompson Trader stood out like a sore thumb in the absence of the usual sea traffic along the river. She sat low in the water and had big crates strapped to her deck, evidencing the much needed merchandise she carried above and below deck.

"Is that what you want me to do then?" asked the captain.

"Daniel, your view?" asked Papa.

The idea we could curry favor with the British Army by having what would probably be the only fully-stocked dry-goods shop in the City at the time they arrived had planted itself firmly in the back of my head.

"I think we ought to unload her first," I said. "That will make her easier to handle on the river. We need the cargo. Once the Brits arrive, we'll make a good profit."

"No!" David cut in. "Imports are my end of the business. We should play it safe. Once the rebels figure out the only ship on the waterfront is owned by Tory sympathizers, no telling what they might try to do. We need to get her out of here. How soon can you do that, Captain?"

"Give me an hour and a half to take on fresh water and provisions and we'll shove off."

I was not convinced. "Bart, can we unload her first?"

This was not the first disagreement Captain Bart had witnessed between me and my brother. He knew better than to take sides.

"I don't know. I've been at sea for the last few weeks and before that in the islands. You have to tell me. I don't want to do anything to endanger the ship."

"How long would it take?" I asked.

"To unload? With plenty of hands, we could get it done before noon."

"Papa," David looked to our father, "don't take chances. Let the captain get this ship out of here now."

Papa looked at each one of us, trying to decide. He eventually spoke. "I respect you both. But here is how I come out. If the captain is confident he can still get out of the harbor by noon, then I say get her unloaded."

"You never listen to me anymore, Papa." David looked angry. "We have too much invested in this ship to take a chance."

"Daniel thinks we can do it," Papa told him. "Let's hope he is right."

I felt exhilarated. Papa usually sided with David, but recently he seemed to be listening to my side of our debates, especially when it came to things involving the ship. I was gaining an edge with Papa.

David left in frustration, but Papa stayed to help oversee the unloading. I located six longshoremen in a local pub and offered them a day's wages to offload the cargo before noon. They came with their own dollies, wagons and pushcarts along with ropes and pulleys. As the operation got underway, a small crowd gathered around the ship. They were curious to see what was happening with the sole vessel of any size arriving in the last two weeks. Among the onlookers was Henry Waddy, the Sons of Liberty spokesperson I encountered at the Quaker shooting match a couple years back.

"Who's ship is this andwhat's it doing here?" he shouted out.

At first, I ignored him. When he repeated his question, I walked over to him and looked down into that squat little face. He was just the type of fanatic who made me question the legitimacy of the whole pro-independence movement.

"It's my family's ship," I answered. "We're in the process of unloading her. Once we're completed, we'll remove her from the area. I'd be pleased if you caused us no trouble."

He gave me a look of recognition and nodded. "I told you you'd not seen the last of me. You forgot all about me, didn't you, asshole? Well now *you're* going to get fucked. We're torching the ship."

At first I thought he was joking, but then those beady eyes of his told me otherwise. "You will do nothing of the sort." Turning, I walked toward the pier. After a few words with Papa, I shouted out, "Captain Bart, have your crew stand at the ready with arms if anyone but longshoremen try to board." The ship had no cannon, but it did carry a supply of small arms.

"Yes, sir," answered Captain Bart.

He and the crew readied their weapons and took up positions on the deck of the ship. Waddy looked on for a few minutes, shaking his head.

As he turned away he said, "We'll see about this," and quickly left.

The offloading continued for another hour. I was convinced we were rid of Waddy until I heard the drum beat and marching of a dozen armed but non-uniformed Pennsylvania Associators coming down Front Street two abreast. Several carried lighted torches, followed by a mule pulling a cart. My heart sank. The group was led by George Bryan, Vice President of the Supreme Executive Council, and Waddy. The marching stopped in front of the pier, and Bryan stepped forward.

"Steven Thompson," Bryan said to Papa, "I understand this is your family's ship."

Bryan and my family were never friends largely because of his ardent views on independence. He nonetheless had a reputation for fairness.

"Mr. Vice Governor," Papa nodded to him, "it's always a pleasure. Yes, this is my family's ship. As you can see we're unloading her and will have her out of the harbor yet this morning."

"I wish that were going to be possible," said Bryan. "We differ on politics, but that has nothing to do with what needs to be done now."

Papa stared at him in disbelief. I stepped up next to my father. "What needs to be done, Mr. Vice Governor," I said, "is for the wharves to be cleared. That's the only order I've heard coming from the Executive Council. And our ship will be out of here before noon."

"Not soon enough. A British foot brigade crossed the Schuylkill four miles south at five o'clock this morning. Washington has retreated to Stowe. The British have a free pass at the City. If they have not reached the fringes by now, they will be here any minute. They will take control of the waterfront first, and a British man-of-war and frigate sit five-hundred yards downstream to assist. If we don't destroy this ship now, it will be taken by the British, outfitted with cannon, and used against us. So, I am asking your sailors to stand down."

"Absolutely not." I walked the gangplank to the ship and stood on the deck with the four sailors now holding muskets. "What are you going to do, shoot us?"

Bryan turned to the commander of the militia.

The commander responded, "Right face!"

The dozen men turned and formed two rows facing us.

"Front row, kneel! Make ready!"

With the front row kneeling, all twelve men held their muskets vertically in front of them, the trigger guards facing forward.

"Why are these men not out fighting the British?" I blurted out from the deck of the ship. "Instead, they are harassing the citizens of Philadelphia." I was desperate and could think nothing else to say.

"Steven," Bryan called to Papa, "we don't have time to negotiate. Please, tell your son and sailors to stand down. I don't want to hurt anyone."

"Pre-sent!" ordered the commander. Twelve muskets were brought up to firing position, aimed at the deck of the ship.

If we had not tried to unload the cargo, the ship might have been on its way out of the harbor by now and we could have avoided this whole mess. I had face to lose, and I felt sick and angry and tired.

"Daniel and Captain Bart," Papa said in an irate voice, "come down from the deck and bring your men."

Captain Bart looked at me, paused, and said to the four sailors, "Come on, we must go."

I could not blame him. I stood on the deck alone, unarmed.

The standoff did not last long. "Have your men escort him off the ship, and then burn it," said Bryan.

"Ground your arms," ordered the commander. "Smith and Lincoln, remove the younger Mr. Thompson from the ship. And then, let's get to it."

They boarded quickly and walked me down to stand next to Papa. I could not look at him. I knew he was blind with rage, some of it directed toward me. We watched as the militia men took buckets of liquid tar and pitch from the wagon, poured the thick liquids in various areas of the ship, and lit them. They also placed kegs of powder in the hold to blow a hole in the hull once the deck was ablaze. After untying the ship, they pushed it away from the pier toward the middle of the river.

Papa had enough. "I hope you go to hell," he said bitterly to Bryan as he stalked away. I almost left with him, but knew he had no interest in seeing me.

★

Bryan had been right about one thing. The British were already at the fringes of the City. Within minutes after ship's release, an advance platoon of redcoats with bayonets fixed came marching from the south on Water Street and turned our direction. Upon seeing them, Bryan and the militia men quickly dispersed.

Then one of the redcoats yelled, "Look, they're burning a ship!" They broke rank and ran in our direction and out onto the pier, but the ship by this point was burning twenty-five yards from the dock. The commander of the platoon looked around and saw me sitting on a box of cargo with Captain Bart, a couple of our sailors nearby.

"What goes on here?" he asked.

"Ship caught fire," I said.

"You have anything to do with it?"

"I tried to prevent it."

"A couple of ships are coming upstream. We could push it back to shore and salvage what we can."

I looked down the river and could see the frigate and behind it the much larger man-o-war. They would dock within the hour. "I would not do that," I said. "Powder kegs in the hold. It could blow any time."

An entire company of redcoats arrived. Soon the waterfront was swarming with them. Wagons rolled up with cannons, equipment and supplies. Drums beat, officers shouted orders, checkpoints and guard stations were set up. Before noon at least half a dozen more ships had followed the frigate and man-o-war into the wharves and began unloading cannon, gear and more soldiers. The dormant waterfront had finally come alive again, except everyone was wearing red.

In the meantime, I sat with Captain Bart waiting for the Thompson Trader to blow. It took longer than I expected, but I had never seen a ship sink before, and felt a morbid sense of curiosity.

"So what do you think you will do?" I asked the captain.

"Oh, I don't know," he said. "I will probably sign on with another ship. With the war going on, it should not be too difficult."

"Which side, British or American?"

"I could be loyal to whichever side pays me a fair wage."

I looked at him skeptically.

"What is wrong with that?" he asked. "I'm not the only opportunist in this war." I nodded. "The more important question is what about you and the company? Is your family business going to survive?"

"I don't know," I said. "We only owned that ship for a little over a year, but it became a real mainstay of our business. Now that the British have arrived, maybe the shipping lanes will open up. We'll have to contact Logan and see what he's willing to do. I am hoping he will forgive part of the loan."

"For your sake I hope so."

"I'm also worried how this is going to affect my relationship with Papa."

"I could feel the tension."

"Papa tries to be fair, but he goes with whoever is more likely to make the company a success. I thought I was making progress in winning him over. But now, whatever advantage I had is gone."

We heard three rapid explosions. For a few minutes, the ship burned brighter than the sun and cast an orange glow along the riverside. But it quickly split apart and sank. And with its sinking, the wharves returned to their more typical day-time drab, which today with all the activity was a little gayer than usual.

By early afternoon two-hundred mounted light cavalry troops and a military band playing *God Save George Our King* led several British and Hessian regiments through the streets of the City. They took much the same route the American Army did five weeks earlier. The columns of troops also vaguely resembled those in the American parade with officers on horses leading columns of marching soldiers. But there were important differences.

The British had a lot more equipment, horses and heavy artillery. The troops had a uniform appearance, looked smart and well-trained, and marched in step.

Now *here* was a professional army. It made the Americans look like a ragtag bunch of dirt farmers.

The British parade had much the same purpose as General Washington's to bolster the spirit and confidence of those supporting the English cause and to intimidate those who would undermine it. The river of redcoats flowing sharply up Chestnut Street, however, failed to achieve its intended effect on me. Maybe it was just my compassion for the underdog. But whatever the reason, I began feeling an appreciation and apprehension, for those tattered, multi-colored uniforms that passed through here a few weeks ago.

If one side deserved victory over the other, it was not these regiments of paid professionals who came from three thousand miles away. Most of them would leave once resolution was reached. They came, moreover, to preserve a way of life for an ancient monarchy that looked upon the colonies as just another stream of income. The side most deserving of victory was the one whose soldiers and families would remain living in the land most directly affected by the difficulties leading to the war in the first place.

Realizing the moral righteousness of the American cause translated to a deep-seated anxiety in the back of my mind. I now knew all the predictions of a British victory just around the corner were for naught. Many months of fighting lay ahead, and uncertainty clouded the future for both sides.

Chapter Twenty Seven

Trial Proceedings

"You actually felt sympathy for the American cause?" asked the Judge Advocate.

"I did," Daniel nodded.

"Or, was it sympathy for yourself having lost the ship?"

"I was feeling sorry for myself as well."

"At least you're honest. Did you stay in the City during the occupation?"

"For most of it, yes."

"This was the fall of 1777. Did things get a little crowded with the British Army here?"

"It was not the entire army. Only a third of the British and Hessian troops were actually stationed in the City. The rest were in Germantown to the north, or along the road between."

"Where did the soldiers stay?"

"Initially, temporary camps on the Commons around the State House. But a lot of houses were left vacant by the Whigs and Patriots who fled. As the weather turned colder, most of the men moved into houses. Some of the houses were still occupied by their owners."

"Any soldiers move into yours?"

"No. We didn't have the space. For the most part they took possession of vacant rooms, and the owner continued to live there. A lot of people welcomed them, and not just Loyalists. They paid rent. A lot of folks were in need of money. Still are."

"British officers are not known for traveling light, are they?" asked the Judge Advocate with a smirk.

"I should say not," said Daniel. "Those in the upper echelon had baggage measured by the wagon load. They also came with servants, valets and cooks, along with animal livestock."

"Did the British place any restrictions on what people could say or do?"

"Absolutely. You would never want to complain too loudly about anything. And they censored everything printed by the local shops."

"How did the Patriots hold up?"

"After Brandywine, many Patriots questioned General Washington's competence, at least at first. Then in early October, to everyone's amazement, he counterattacked at Germantown where the British were the strongest. What effect did that have? Well, as you know, Howe still held Philadelphia at day's end. But criticism of Washington eased up. Just like at Trenton. I suspect his purpose was to send a signal to the colonies and the French. The Americans were not giving up."

"What about the American victory at Saratoga?"

"That came, when, just after Germantown? General Burgoyne was a top commander. To have him surrender five-thousand troops sobered a lot of Loyalists and energized the Patriots."

"And the loss of the American forts along the Delaware River, Mercer and Mifflin in October and early November? Did that put a damper on things?"

"Not as much as you might think. Fort Mercer had been reinforced by French engineers, and it caused the Hessians a lot more trouble than anyone expected. Even though it fell, people felt good about the American effort."

"What about your dry goods business? How did that fare during the occupation?"

"Good initially, and then poorly."

Chapter Twenty Seven

With the initial arrival of the British, Thompson Trading enjoyed a spike in business. We were, after all, one of the few establishments with significant inventory since we had managed to unload most of the cargo off the Thompson Trader. Without the restrictions imposed by the Continental Congress, we actually did quite well for a few weeks selling to the British Army.

The problem was it did not last. The British brought with them scores of English and Scotch merchants and artisans who set up business in many of the shops and stalls vacated by Whigs and Patriots. Once their inventory started to arrive, the City became awash in dry goods. For most Philadelphians, the influx of goods provided little benefit. The army paid in gold, silver or British bills, and those forms of payment set the standard. Most shop keepers, including ours, flatly declined Continental currency.

Most civilians also experienced shortages of food and fuel. The Continental Army, assisted by the Pennsylvania Executive Council and militia, did its best to patrol main roads into the City and to block food and other provisions from being brought in. The idea was to make it difficult for the British Army to maintain itself. The blockade probably had that effect, but it had an even a greater impact on the residents who remained.

Apart from the Continental Army restricting the entrance of supplies, the British limited the areas around the City where wood could be cut, reserving the prime areas for the army. And they purchased, rented, or simply confiscated whatever they needed, including most of the horses and wagons in the City. The end result: Tories and Loyalists with good connections fared well; everyone else suffered.

It was at this time Papa walked into the counting house with George Logan. They had just eaten breakfast with Mrs. Pickering in the living quarters.

"Look who showed up on my doorstep last night," Papa said to David, Molly and me. "We've been talking about the loss of the Thompson Trader."

My heart sank. I knew Logan would find out sooner or later, and we would have to face the consequences. I did not anticipate it would be this morning. I straightened up in my chair and tried to look nonchalant and businesslike. I did not want him to realize, if he did not already, he held the fate of our company in his hands.

"It was my idea to unload her before she left port," I said, shaking my head. "Perhaps if we had not taken the time . . . ."

Papa interrupted me. "We've been through all that, Daniel. Captain Bart himself says he could not have turned her around to leave port in time. Don't go blaming yourself."

"Your father's right," Logan added. "This is wartime and things happen. Even if she had gotten out of port, the Continental Army might have requisitioned her for its use anyway. You were lucky you got the cargo off and available for sale once the army arrived."

Things were looking up for me. David scowled.

"As I mentioned to your father," Logan continued, "we had a policy on her written by an underwriter at Lloyd's. It covered our interest in the ship. The only problem is once the underwriter pays us off, he will be assigned our interest, and he may end up coming after Thompson Trading for what is owed. We'll try to talk him out of it, but I cannot guarantee it. I suspect we'll at least be able to talk him down, so your company will not bear the entire loss."

Hearing Logan tell how he still had faith in our company and would work on our behalf was music to my ears. "That's right decent of you."

"We want to keep you as a customer." Logan smiled. "How's your inventory?"

"We need supply," David said. "I've heard tell you're no longer accepting Continentals."

"That's right," Logan sighed. "The home office fully expects us to win this war. And once we do, Continentals will be worthless. I am sure you can appreciate that. They're already worth a lot less than they were a year ago. We would be fools to accept them."

"I'm not sure we can sell for specie," David nodded. "And if we can't sell for specie, we can't buy from you in specie. As long as the British Army is here we'll be able to take in some hard coin and continue on for a while, but the competition is killing us. What's the long-term outlook for Philadelphia from your perspective?"

"Hard to say. We don't foresee the army moving out anytime soon. On the other hand, the defeat in Saratoga was not helpful. And if the French get into the war in a big way, then things could change. What about barter? You have anything to trade?"

David shook his head and Papa looked at me. "Daniel?"

"We may have some flour," I said. "I just don't know. We tried to hide it from the Continental Army, but a Continental buying agent threatened to confiscate it if he could find it. I have tried half a dozen times to get out and visit the mill, but never made it."

"Roads blocked?" asked Logan.

"Most of the time," I answered. "The British patrol the immediate perimeter west of the City, and American patrols are a few miles out. Every once in a while they get too close and start shooting at each other. That's when all the roads and ferries get closed. The closings last for two or three days. They eventually open back up but they can close again because of bad weather. I'll try again in a few days."

"I will be in town for a couple weeks," Logan said. "A market always exists for flour. You could sell it to the British Army; they will pay you in coin. But your profit is higher if you trade it to me for dry goods and then sell the dry goods to the army. If you can find a way to get it here, I can put it on a ship for you, and we'll be in business."

I had several reasons for visiting the mill. The main one, as I told Logan, was to see for myself if we had any flour left. Abelson's threat to confiscate it caused me sleepless nights. Then, too, I wanted to see the condition of the mill and how Willie and Mary Jane were holding up. I had not been there since before the Battle of Brandywine. My last instructions to Willie were to buy at seven and a half pounds per barrel Continental. I could not imagine he was doing much buying at that price due to the rate Continentals were losing value. We would have to make an adjustment.

I also was curious to see what the countryside looked like after the big battle. If I could get out of the City, it would be an interesting trip.

★

Alphonse and I departed a week later. I asked him to come along because I was concerned about vagrants and marauders along the way. As for soldiers. I figured we could negotiate our way through the check points, one way or another. Our horse, Dobbin, was not much of a prize or the British would have taken her by now. The chaise itself was not big enough for military use.

We left just as long rays from the sun broke through the morning mist. We made good time to Middle Ferry west of the City to cross the Schuylkill River. Mostly military traffic crossed at this location. Still, no one seemed particularly interested in why we were crossing, although the British captain in charge kept us waiting nearly an hour and then charged us ten shillings for the privilege.

So far so good.

The route took us ten miles west on Lancaster Road before turning north to French Creek. We had to pull over several times to allow British foot patrols and a wagon train pass by. About seven or eight miles into the journey we came to a check point where the Brits had a guard station and gate across the road. We pulled up to the gate and redcoats approached.

"Where would you be headed?" asked a soldier, apparently the commander in charge.

"I own a mill a few miles west and north of here," I answered. "I'm going to see what damage it took, and what supplies are needed."

The commander looked at me skeptically. "Who's this you got with you?"

"His name is Alphonse. He is our bonded man. I brought him along to help out with any problems along the way. I have not been out this way since before the battle down on the Brandywine."

"Where you from, son?" he directed to Alphonse.

"Originally Prussia, then Scotland."

"What brought you over here?"

"I got into trouble a few years ago, and they put me on a ship."

The commander took this all in and apparently was convinced of the genuineness of our mission. "About all I can say is this is as far as we control. You pass here at your own risk. A lot of rebels out here."

"You think they'll let us through?" I asked.

"You look harmless enough," said the commander, "so they might. I hope you don't have much in coin with you. If they find you do, they'll take it. They're desperate."

"A pound is all I have. Just enough to pay the tolls."

He nodded to a man under his command. "Open the gate, let them pass."

I felt relieved as we passed and glad I had not told any lies. If I had, I would need to remember and tell the same ones on the way back home.

The commander told the truth about the rebel activity. We had not traveled half a mile before I began seeing unusual movements in the woods. About the time to turn on the trail north, four men with muskets stepped out in front of us. One wore a blue coat and the others wore tattered civilian clothing. Alphonse reached for a musket on the side of the chaise, but I motioned him to leave it be.

The man in the blue coat held up a hand to stop us while the other three held their muskets at the ready. Rustling sounds in the nearby underbrush told me more soldiers accompanied them.

"Who goes there? And what's your purpose?"

"Hello fellows," I said amiably. "I'm Daniel Thompson on the way to visit my mill with the hope it hasn't been destroyed." I looked ahead and saw more activity and a tent in a shallow clearing on the side of the road. It appeared to be a temporary outpost to keep tabs on movement in and out of the City.

The blue coat was humorless. “Where’s your mill located?”

“A little further west and about five miles to the north on French Creek.”

“Are you American or British?”

I paused before answering. I sensed even if I were to respond pro-British, they probably would not detain us. The Continental Army had enough problems on its hands that civilians, even British civilians, were not priorities. On the other hand, I figured our passage might go smoother if I gave the impression of being pro-American.

“I’ve lived in Pennsylvania all my life,” I said. “I guess that would make me an American.”

“So you’re a Loyalist?” asked the blue-coat.

“I didn’t say anything about being a Loyalist.”

“How did you make it past all the British patrols?”

“In all honesty they didn’t ask us what side we’re on. If you are now asking, I will tell you my father is Loyalist. My sister, however, is a Patriot, and her husband is with the Continental Army in Saratoga.”

My explanation appeared to come across as truthful. The blue coat asked in a less accusatory tone, “And you?”

“I’ve not declared my views in any official way. I’m just trying to make a living and it’s becoming more and more difficult.”

“You a Quaker?”

Answering in the affirmative would have been an easy out, but I had not lied so far and I tried to maintain my record. “No. If you must know I’m Anglican, same as Ben Franklin.”

“All right then, you can be on your way to your mill,” said the blue coat wearily. “But so you know, you can’t bring anything back with you. No food provisions nor wood for fuel.”

“How about one barrel of flour for personal use, not for sale to the British?” I held out no hope but gave it a try.

"No. No flour," said the blue coat. "We can't make exceptions."

"How about two barrels of flour?" I asked. "One for me and my family, and the other for you and your men."

His interest perked up. "You have that much?"

"No guarantee we have anything. Still, if we have two barrels, I will bring them both. Is that a deal?"

"Maybe we can work something out," he nodded

I saw three or four soldiers in the clearing standing around a fire, and nearby a cluster of the same number of Indians seated in a semi-circle with their backs to the soldiers.

"Looks like you're making good use of our native population."

"We do what we can," answered the blue coat. "A lot of them fought for the British back in the fifties and now don't want to fight against them. But some of the Delawares left around here, especially the younger ones, have taken an interest in our side. They know the terrain and can get through just about any blockade."

"Speaking of getting through, will you be here all day if I have trouble?"

"Yes. Ask for Captain Samuel Johnson, Seventh Pennsylvania Regiment."

"You know anything about the Second Pennsylvania Battalion? I'm only interested because that's the unit my brother-in-law, Peter Barclay, originally joined before he was transferred."

"Actually, the Second Battalion dissolved into the Third Regiment. Don't ask me how that happened, it's too complicated. Battalions are now regiments, and he's in the Third. I once did meet a Peter Barclay. Nice guy, thick glasses, smart as hell."

"That's him! Couldn't hit the broad side of a barn with a musket."

Captain Johnson laughed. "You're right, he's not much of a shot. But any friend of his is a friend of mine. Just ask for me on your return trip. Even if you are a Loyalist."

Chapter Twenty Eight

A short while later, we approached the stone cottage near the mill. Along the way we saw an occasional burnt-out building, or the remains of a broken-down wagon, but not much else to evidence the area had been invaded by opposing armies. We pulled up in front of the cottage and I banged on the front door.

"Yes, sir, yes, sir, I'm coming, I'm coming." Mary Jane opened the door. "We can only help . . . oh, my, Mr. Thompson! You're a sight for these sore eyes. I thought you were more soldiers come begging for food."

"Have you had many soldiers by here?" I asked.

"Every few days. They are usually lost and sometimes wounded. We do what we can and send them on their way. Come in, come in."

"We don't mean to intrude unannounced. This is the first I could get out here in the last two months."

"It's no intrusion. Willie will be glad to see you. He ought to be coming in for dinner any time now. Here, let me get you some cool cider."

The place looked much the same as when the Swensons lived there, but less cluttered.

Willie arrived momentarily, and we began talking as he washed up for dinner. "One of our hired hands quit the other day to join the army," he said matter of factly. "I'm hoping we can replace him without too much trouble."

Mary Jane set four places on the trestle table for dinner.

"You and Mary Jane both look well," I said, "and the mill, still intact?"

"Yes, sir, Mr. Thompson, it's up and running."

"That's good news. What about the wagon ramp up to the top?" I asked. "Finally finished?"

"In use for several weeks. Business has been off a little with this war going, so we had time to work on it. But things will pick back up."

"What makes you think so?

"So many mills down. They all have mechanical problems and can't get parts. We've made do with what we got."

"Are you drawing more farmers for their own accounts?"

"Yes, sir, they take back what we grind . . . less our fee, of course."

"What about our farmers under contract?"

Willie shook his head. "Some of them still deliver, but you're going to have to pay more. Seven-and-a-half pounds Continental is not enough to keep them coming, not with what the Continental is worth these days."

"We'll raise it to nine per barrel." Now came my big question. "The flour inventory; do we have any left in Turks Head?"

Willie hesitated. "We do in one of the warehouses. The Continental Army took everything in the other one."

"Tell me what happened."

"It was after the battle down on the Brandywine and the Continental Army was camped in Chester. A big sweaty guy, name of Abelson, came riding by here with a dozen solders. He asked if this was the Thompson mill, and I answered yes. He told how he knew we had flour for sale and he wanted to buy it for the army. I told him we don't have any here, and he demanded to know where it was. I thought he might wreck the place and figured I had to give him something. So I told him it was in a warehouse in Turks Head. He demanded to see the warehouse receipt, so I pulled out the receipt for the Atkinson barn. We had forty barrels there. And I told him that was everything we had in the warehouse."

"Willie didn't lie, Mr. Thompson," Mary Jane chimed in. "Willie told him 'the warehouse.' And that was everything in that warehouse. He didn't say anything about the other warehouse in Turks Head, the Blackson warehouse, a half mile away."

They looked at me as if I might reprimand them for being deceitful. Instead, I breathed a sigh of relief. "So we have what, eighty barrels left at Blackson's?"

"Yes, sir, plus another fifteen here at the mill that we filled over the last few weeks."

"Did he pay for the forty?"

"He gave us these." Willie pulled out a stack of preprinted paper slips. "He called them impressment certificates. Said they covered the forty barrels at five pounds per barrel. I have here what's left after paying for some supplies."

"If you can find a way to spend them, then do it. Just keep track of where. You have done well, both of you. Once we finish up here, we'll ride down to Turks Head and take a look."

Our ride to the Blackson warehouse proved uneventful. When we asked the owner about visits from army supply officers, he explained the main road through Turks Head by-passed his facility.

"You're lucky," he said. "Everything is safe and sound. I have to warn you, though, the storage rates are double if you're paying in Continentals."

I said we would pay double. At least I would have some place to spend our Continentals. I counted the barrels inside the earth-and-timber hillside warehouse – eighty-four in all – and discussed with the owner his views on how we might get them to market.

"It's a tough spot to be in," he said. "The Continental Army controls this far out from the City and if you don't want to sell to them – and I can't say I blame you – you're going to take a real risk moving these barrels into British territory by wagon."

"You don't think we could haul it in on back roads?"

"No. Even if you could find the wagons and horses, it would take forever, and once a Continental patrol sees you, it would be all over."

"I guess we'll leave it here for a while."

We returned to the mill, where Willie assisted Alphonse and me in strapping two barrels of flour onto the back of the chaise. With our mission accomplished, we started back to the City.

★

Before we reached the turnoff for Lancaster Road, however, two soldiers in green coats on horseback overtook us and ordered us to a halt.

"What's that you're carrying in the barrels?" asked one of them. The other held a musket upright ready to swing into action.

"Flour," I said. "We have the permission of Captain Sam Johnson, Seventh Pennsylvania Regiment, to return it to the City."

The soldier eyed our horse and carriage carefully. "You'll have to come with us," he said. "Private Fitch will relieve you of the muskets."

"I told you we have permission to carry these two barrels."

"Not from Colonel Dean. And not from me either. I am Corporal Lance."

"Who is Colonel Dean?"

"Colonel William Dean. Fourth Battalion, Philadelphia County Associators."

"Well Captain Johnson is with the Continental Army. And this is Chester County, not Philadelphia County. You're outside your jurisdiction."

"We're assigned here by the Executive Council. You are coming with us. I will ask you one more time to hand over your muskets to Private Fitch."

The two green coats took us to an encampment of Pennsylvania militia men south of Lancaster Road. It consisted of a dozen or so tents. Corporal Lance retrieved Colonel Dean, escorted by two more musket-bearing soldiers in civilian clothes. A hefty middle aged man with a beard, the colonel chewed tobacco and spit as he spoke. Alphonse and I still sat in the chaise as he approached.

"The corporal tells me you're taking food provisions back into the City," he said. "You know it's contraband."

"We have the permission of Captain Samuel Johnson, Seventh Pennsylvania Regiment, Continental Army," I repeated. "Just ask him."

"Private Fitch, Corporal Lance," asked the colonel, spitting, "you know anything about this Captain Johnson?"

"The Seventh may be patrolling Lancaster Road," Corporal Lance answered, "but I never heard of a Captain Johnson."

Colonel Dean shrugged and looked at me. "There you have it. We don't know anything about Captain Johnson. Anyway, no renegade officer in the Continental Army is going to violate the contraband order of the Pennsylvania Executive Council. So here is what I'm going to do. I will let you two boys go, and I'll even leave you with your horse and carriage. But for violating the contraband order, I will relieve you of those barrels of flour. It will lighten your load and make your journey go that much faster." He laughed and spit. "Private Fitch, take down those barrels of flour."

"Yes, sir." The private began untying the barrels and lifted one down from the chaise.

Before he removed the second, however, we heard galloping horses coming from the dirt road leading to the encampment. Within moments three soldiers in blue coats and an Indian wearing a leather blouse and leggings rode up beside us. The lead soldier had a saber drawn, and the others brandished muskets. Their quick arrival and weapons drawn took us all by surprise. Colonel Dean looked genuinely offended.

"To what do we owe this intrusion?" he demanded. Militia men from other parts of the encampment turned to watch.

"I'm Captain Samuel Johnson, Seventh Regiment, Continental Army," said the blue coat with the saber. I had not recognized him in the three-cornered hat he now wore.

Colonel Dean gave a look of satisfaction. "That's quite a coincidence," he said. "I just caught these two civilians trying to take contraband back into the City. One of them told me this cockamamie story how you gave him permission. I knew it was all a bunch of horse shit!"

"It's not horse shit," said Captain Johnson. "He offered to bring my outpost a barrel of flour if he could take one back into the City for his family's use. It was a steep price for him to pay, and my men need the flour. I agreed."

"That's all right nice and dandy," said Colonel Dean, "but my men need bread too, so here is what we'll do. We will split them. You take one barrel and I will take the other."

"That's not the deal, sir. The deal is he takes one barrel and the other comes to my outpost."

"Now, I'm trying to be fair with you, Captain," said Colonel Dean in a menacing tone, "but you are starting to irritate me."

"Yes, well I gave my word to this man, and I intend to keep it."

"You're acting outside of your authority, Captain, and the Executive Council is going to hear about this."

"That may be, but General Washington is going to hear about how a piss-ass green-coated Pennsylvania militia officer by the name of *Dean* tried to steal two barrels of flour from a civilian trying to feed his family."

Colonel Dean looked flabbergasted. "I was doing no such thing. I have every intention of giving him receipts for those barrels."

"You eat the receipts and he'll keep the flour," said Captain Johnson. "I am going to ask your private to tie that barrel back onto the man's carriage, and then step back and we'll be on our way."

Private Fitch did as he was told as the colonel looked on in anger. I thought he might summon soldiers in camp to come to his assistance, but he apparently felt sufficiently uncertain about his relationship with a Continental Army officer and held back giving more orders. As between a local militia colonel and an army captain, I had no idea who had seniority.

With the two barrels back on the chaise, I turned Dobbin down the dirt road and headed out of the encampment toward Lancaster Road. Once on our way, Captain Johnson trotted his horse up alongside the chaise.

"How in God's name did you know we would have trouble getting back?" I asked in amazement.

"We've been keeping an eye on you since this morning," he said.

"You've been following us?"

"I had one of my Indian boys do it." He nodded in the direction of the Indian scout. "Just trying to keep you honest. Besides, some of these militia units get pushy with civilians. I wanted to protect my investment."

"So now you know all my secrets," I said, testing how closely his scout was following us.

"Any you want to share with me, just to get them off your chest?"

"None other than the fact my mill is operational, and one of the few around here that is. But I have no reason to keep that a secret."

"Not unless you're selling to the British."

"Not much chance of that," I said, "with all the patrols and roadblocks you have set up. The fact is we'll deal with anyone who will give us a fair price, so long as we have something to sell."

"I'll keep that in mind."

We found our way back to the captain's outpost in short order, untied one of the barrels, and thanked him for his protection and courtesy.

"I have a feeling we've not seen the last you," he said as Alphonse and I took leave.

★

Within half an hour, heading back east on Lancaster Road, we began spotting British patrols once more. I thought they might give us trouble about the flour barrel, but no one did.

It was then a thought struck me: the Indian scout. To my white man's eyes, all Indians looked much the same. But as I focused my memory on the one glance I had of the scout, I realized I had seen him before.

God damn! It was Janie's suitor, Lightfoot. He actually joined up with the Continental Army. A sense of guilt, and feeling of satisfaction, struck me simultaneously.

Chapter Twenty Nine

A few days later we celebrated Sarah's birthday at the City Tavern. This was our second annual supper without her, and no one wanted to end the tradition. Having asked Elizabeth to meet us, I looked forward to introducing her to my family for the first time. Walking with the kids I asked Janie about Lightfoot. He was a topic I usually avoided on the theory: the less said, the better. It was my hope Janie would forget about him. I nevertheless wanted to hear what she might say about his whereabouts to test whether my memory was correct.

"Have you heard anything from Lightfoot of late?"

"Not really," she said. "I get information about him from time to time, but nothing directly. He joined the army like you suggested and liked the idea. I was surprised."

That was not the reaction I had anticipated. I expected her to be either reluctant to say anything, or giddy about the opportunity to talk about him. Instead, she spoke matter-of-factly, making me wonder if her relationship with the boy was going sour. Maybe she was coming to her senses.

I pretended to be hurt. "I guess we old folks are able to come up with some reasonable notions part of the time."

She smiled.

"What side did he join?"

"We talked about it and I told him you didn't care. He joined the Continental side."

"You talked to him? Have you been seeing him again?"

"Papa, it was after he came to our house. I thought you wanted me to."

"I did, but any further conversations are to be in my presence, or Margaret's."

"Yes, Papa, I'm sorry."

"Do you know where he has been assigned?"

"No, but I don't think it's far from the City."

For once I felt my parental guidance might be succeeding. Janie's infatuation was ending.

We met Missy and Nathan outside the main entrance of the City Tavern, and the six of us entered. I spotted Elizabeth in cloak and bonnet waiting in the foyer and drew our group together.

"I have someone I would like you all to meet," I said. "This is Elizabeth. I met her at St. Peter's a few months ago."

She looked as radiant as ever. I took pride showing her off. I had been seeing her once a week, and she occasionally invited me in to chat with her mother, who was remarkably open and pleasant. Elizabeth herself was more reserved. Making arrangements for her to join us tonight had been no exception. I ended up having to ask her twice before she agreed.

After bows and curtsies all around, I noticed the kids seemed to take meeting a female friend of their father in stride. It was Missy who gave me a wry look as we entered the dining area.

"Have you been holding out on us, Danny?" she asked under her breath.

I could not help but laugh. "She's just a friend," I said meekly.

"Just a friend, my ass. She's stunning."

"You really think so?" Missy's views always mattered to me. "Unfortunately, she is pro American."

"You've chosen well, then."

The inn had not lost its luster. Two smaller chandeliers now hung on either side of the huge center one, and newly installed oak paneling clad the walls. Choice cuts of meat roasted on the open fire pit, filling the entire room with a warm, rich aroma promising a delectable meal.

We had not seen Missy and Nathan for several weeks now and I hoped they would bring us up to date on Peter. The only problem was the place swarmed with redcoats along with Tory civilians trying to curry their favor. We nearly had to shout across the table to be heard.

A fiddler's lively music for a table of British officers and their mistresses added to the overall festive atmosphere. Our particular corner of the room contained mostly civilians and I recognized a few of them as having Patriot leanings. They seemed to have a calming effect on Missy, who showed her anxiety whenever British soldiers were around.

Servers brought a big plate of beef, veal and mutton for the table with a bowl of boiled potatoes and onions alongside and freshly brewed ale. It was a meal fit for royalty, the likes of which we rarely ate these days. The whole Thompson family was feeling the pinch of harsh times with our store inventory dwindling, sales squeezed by competition, and the prospects of any immediate turnaround bleak. Logan had promised to put us back in the thick of things if we had goods to barter. I now knew we had a warehouse full of flour and yet getting it to market would be nearly impossible.

How much longer we could hold out was anyone's guess. All the uncertainties translated into skimping on food, clothes, and all but the basic necessities. So much so I considered skipping this year's outing at the City Tavern. I ended up justifying our coming here since it was our only splurge all year, even if I had to dip into my cellar reserve to pay for it.

"With the great American victory at Saratoga a few weeks ago," I asked Missy as we began eating, "do you expect Peter home any time soon?"

"I wish," Missy shook her head and looked tired, and for good reason. Peter's partner in the print shop had fled the City before the British take-over. Missy and Nathan had been running the printing business by themselves for the last two months. They had to close down after the British first arrived. Later they re-opened but only upon agreement to submit samples of all print work to the British Information Office for censorship prior to publication. That meant setting the press, printing off a sample, seeking approval, and waiting. And if the censor did not like it? Then re-setting the press and seeking approval a second time. Missy struggled to keep the shop in operation.

"He was scheduled to come back, but now he has smallpox."

Her statement brought a halt to our eating. This was the first I had heard, and we all stared at Missy.

Elizabeth broke the silence. "Oh Missy, I am so sorry."

"We all are," I added. "I thought he had been inoculated."

"We talked about it," said Missy, "but had no time. Recovering from inoculation can take weeks. He decided to take his chances to stay clean."

"When did you find out about it?" asked Elizabeth.

"Two days ago. We received a letter."

"How bad is it?" asked Elizabeth.

"He was well enough to write the letter. And of course, he told us not to worry and he would get well soon. But he also said he was not in good enough shape to travel. Nathan wants to go up there to get him. I will not have it."

"I should say not," said Elizabeth.

"You were not really going to travel all the way to Saratoga, were you, Nathan?" Jonathon asked.

"Yes, I am."

Another moment of silence settled around the table. Obviously the matter had not been resolved.

"I could go with him, Papa," Jonathon suggested.

"Absolutely not. And Nathan's not going anywhere either."

"You can't tell him that, Papa." Jonathon tried to enforce Nathan's right to be told what to do only by his mother.

"I don't have to tell him," I said. "His mother already did. And I can tell both you boys, no one should plan on traveling outside the City. Not these days. I had trouble getting to the mill, and that's only fifteen miles away. You could get stopped by one army or the other, or by vagrants or by deserters looking to take the clothes off your back. Who knows what else might happen. Besides, Nathan, your mother needs you in the shop."

"Papa needs me, too," said Nathan.

"I'm sure he does," I said. "But if you were to ask him if he wanted you to come up, he would say no. You know that. You're barely fifteen-years-old."

"I could pass for sixteen," he argued. "And there are plenty of drummer boys fourteen or fifteen. They're taking more risks than I would be."

"The army may have a few drummers who are that young," I agreed, not knowing a lot about it, "but that's rare. And when they are that young they usually have their fathers or close relative serving in the same unit." At least that was my best guess. "Your father's letter said he expects to get well soon. Give it a week or two, and then we can revisit the issue together . . . as a family."

The fiddler was playing the same song the British Army marched to as it entered Philadelphia in September, *God Save*

George Our King. I had not been familiar with the tune, but now regarded it as the song of conquerors, the song of dominance, the song that told the world or at least the Americans, that the British were still in charge. It was not a catchy tune, more like a hymn. The fiddler played it with long strokes and a sense of pride.

A few British officers began humming and then singing along, and before long the diners at the far side of the dining room were singing in unison, not loudly, but reverently. As more soldiers and civilian Loyalists joined in, a British officer stepped out into the center of the room waving his arms as if directing and trying to get the whole room to sing. The fiddler kept playing louder and more deliberately. A few officers hoisted their cups and began toasting each other and the volume increased as did the camaraderie.

I heard Missy say something from across the table, but it was lost in the din of the music and singing.

"What?" I called out.

She raised her voice, almost to a shout. "That's the best they can do?"

I was not sure what she meant, but it sounded like a challenge. "Take it easy, Missy, we don't need any problems here."

She looked around as if assessing the possibilities. "That's the very best they can do?"

I hissed sternly, "Missy, don't do anything silly. These are British officers. They are tough guys. Just let them sing their little song. There is no shame in being silent."

Missy would have none of it. She stood up and began singing, softly at first and I thought she had actually joined in with the British. I soon realized it was a different song. No harm in that, I thought, and then discovered how wrong I could be. Missy was now getting others near us to join in with her. Just a few at first, timidly, and then more. Our kids did not start in fortunately, but they looked around in astonishment. Elizabeth wore a bemused expression, obviously enjoying Missy's singing war.

Before long, our side of the dining room was singing *Free America*. It was an old British Grenadier tune Papa had taught me, but a militia man from Boston had popularized it with a new title and new words:

> Lift up your hearts, my heroes,
> And swear with proud disdain,
> The wretch that would ensnare you
> Shall spread his net in vain;
> Should Europe empty all her force,
> We would meet them in array,
> And shout huzza, huzza, huzza
> For brave America.

Upon ending the stanza they repeated *For Brave America* with emphasis and started over again. In the meantime, Missy moved out near the center of the room not far from the British officer trying to rouse enthusiasm for the British hymn. He continued on with fervor to overcome the *Free America* forces but he lost ground to the livelier tune on the American side. Even some Tories joined in, thinking perhaps it was time now for a new tune. The officer in charge did not accept defeat gracefully and began to stare at Missy with evil in his eyes.

I wanted to fade into the woodwork. The British to their credit had not made merely associating with Patriot civilians a crime. But crime or not, associating with a defiant Patriot who humiliated a British officer in public could not be advantageous to one's career.

After singing *Free America* through a third or fourth time Missy topped it off with a verse or two of *Yankee Doodle*, another British tune with Americanized words. The American side of the room burst into applause, laughter and back slapping. By that time many of the British officers had lost interest in the singing. Some took the event in stride, shrugging it off or even offering a good-natured nod to their American acquaintances. The officer directing, however, would have none of it and started conferring with his associates and pointing in our direction.

It was time to go. I looked at Elizabeth and motioned to the door with my nod. She understood and started helping the kids on with their cloaks. Missy kept talking and laughing with some of the singers. When she saw me prepare to leave, she initially gave me an angry look as if I were betraying her in her moment of triumph. Her demeanor changed when she realized the British were not taking humiliation lightly.

I ushered Elizabeth, Missy and the kids toward the exit. Out of sight, out of mind . . . that was my intention. Before I could make it out of the room, a British orderly took hold of my arm. "Sir, may I have a word?"

I turned and pulled away. "What is it?"

"Who was the woman accompanying your party tonight, the one doing the singing?"

I gave him a disgruntled look. "What difference does it make? We're a good Loyalist family and she was only having a little fun. And a little too much to drink. I'm sure you understand."

"But her name, what is it?"

"Who wants to know?"

"Captain William Cunningham. He stands there." He pointed to the officer leading the singing. The captain looked in our direction, frowning.

"Tell the captain I am a firm Loyalist. I regret any hard feelings from this evening. I enjoyed his singing, and I will personally deal with the woman in question to make sure she never sings again in public. She was really quite awful by comparison."

I nodded and left, hoping to have defused the situation.

★

To curry favor with the local population, General Howe encouraged schools and other institutions to remain open. Thus, the following day when I returned home for dinner at noon, the kids were in school, but Missy's carriage on the side of the house took me by surprise. As I entered, I found Margaret and Missy sitting in the parlor with somber faces. Margaret had been out of town visiting relatives, and I had not expected her to return so soon. Seeing them together at first raised concern about Peter, and my heart sank. Margaret quickly cleared up my misapprehension. But what she told me did not make me feel better.

"Nathan's gone."

"Saratoga?"

Missy nodded.

"You couldn't stop him?"

"He took off before I woke."

"No goodbye? Nothing?"

"He scrawled a note saying I should not worry, he would be back soon."

"Did he take anything with him, food or clothes?"

"He may have stuffed clothes into a bag and perhaps a little dried meat."

I sighed. "I'm so sorry, Missy. It's a long walk to northern New York, unless he can hitch a ride somewhere. My guess is he'll be fine. He's mature for his age and he has a good sense about him."

"I don't know," Missy sobbed. "I miss him already. I am afraid I will never see Peter again and now I've lost Nathan. I just don't know."

Margaret and I tried our best to comfort her, but I knew she had cause for concern. The chances of Peter surviving in an army camp with smallpox were not good especially during the cold of winter. And even if Nathan got that far, what could he do for Peter? The best chance for Peter was to stay there, meaning Nathan would stay with him and expose himself to the disease.

"He'll be all right," I kept repeating. "He's young and strong and resourceful. And Peter's a smart guy. He'll tell his son what to do. It might be good for both of them."

"Perhaps you should stay in Daniel's home for a while?" Margaret suggested. I did not appreciate Margaret extending invitations on my behalf, but in this case she was right to do so. "No need for you to stay out in the country all by yourself."

"No. I couldn't impose," said Missy.

"It's no imposition at all," I reassured her.

"No, thank you for the offer. And I am sorry about last night. I wanted to put down those British officers. So much arrogance, I couldn't help myself."

"That may not have been the smartest thing to do." I said. "They asked me for your name on the way out. I didn't give it to them, but I did promise that, with your voice, you would not sing in public again."

Missy looked at me, half alarmed, half amused. "Was I that bad?"

"Watch yourself."

When Missy left, Margaret looked at me suspiciously. "So you went out for supper when I was out of town?"

"I didn't know when you would be back."

Later that day I received word Missy had been arrested. She was being held at the British Provost, a prison on Walnut Street that held about nine-hundred Americans. Captain Cunningham oversaw the prison.

Chapter Thirty

Trial Proceedings

"That was your first encounter with Captain Cunningham?" asked the Judge Advocate.

"Yes," Daniel answered and added, "unfortunately not the last."

"You were not aware he used to be the Provost Marshal in Boston, and then again in New York, where he needlessly sent hundreds of American prisoners to the gallows after nearly starving them to death?"

"I heard about some of his past exploits before he came to Philadelphia."

"And you're going to tell us Captain Johnson was willing to cut a deal with you, to help you with Captain Cunningham, even though he knew you were a Loyalist?"

"I would not put it like that. Captain Johnson would do anything to advance the interests of the troops serving under him. Including cutting a deal with someone he thought may have Loyalist leanings."

"Your sister, the singer, the same sitting here in the front row?"

"Yes, sir."

The Judge Advocate turned again to Missy. "I congratulate you, Madame. Whatever your singing ability, I am certain it sounded beautiful that night at the City Tavern. I regret I was not there to hear it." He gave a little bow.

"Ending this farce of a trial against my brother," Missy said without hesitation, "would do even more to resolve your feelings of remorse."

The president of the court looked up with a scowl. "The audience will refrain from any further outbursts. Is that understood, Mrs. Barclay?"

Missy stared intently at the Judge Advocate. The president nodded to the Judge Advocate and said in an irritated voice, "You may continue."

The Judge Advocate turned back to Daniel. "Did you free your sister?"

"I did . . . eventually. It was a drawn-out process."

The Judge Advocate studied his notes for a moment and without looking up, and asked, "This was about the time you started trading with the British again?"

"I what?"

"You said earlier you should not be criticized for selling a small quantity of flour to the British. But now you decided it was acceptable to engage in a major financial transaction with the enemy. Isn't that true?"

Daniel chose his words carefully. "I did make a large sale to the British. Ultimately, it was for the benefit of the American side."

"You didn't benefit from the sale?"

"I didn't say that. I did benefit. But the primary purpose was to assist the Americans."

"You have a lot of explaining to do on this one."

Chapter Thirty Two

I went to see Captain Cunningham the following day.

The British Provost already had a bad reputation. In barracks-style enclosures, the facility held American prisoners captured at Brandywine and Germantown. Rumors circulated about the filthy living conditions for prisoners, the beatings, the routine executions, and food rations consisting of a couple of pounds of raw pork per week.

Up to that time, I did not know what to believe and had not been particularly interested. The incarcerated men were volunteers and had the bad judgment of choosing the wrong side. Besides, what could I do about their living conditions? I was having a hard enough time putting food on my own family's table. Now, however, my sister was locked up and I had a personal interest. I had to get her out.

Cunningham maintained quarters in a two-room hut inside the prison compound. The main room contained a desk, table, writing materials and chairs, while the back room slept several men in bunk beds.

Although he kept me waiting for an hour outside in the cold, Cunningham started our meeting on an air of cordiality. He directed me to a chair beside his desk and offered a cup of tea. He then chatted at length in an Irish brogue about his military career and coming to America. A sergeant sat at the table nearby while another soldier stood at attention at the door.

Finally, he asked, "And what brings you here today?"

"I'm here about my sister."

He tried to look surprised, but we both knew it was only an act.

"Oh, yes, the woman we arrested yesterday. So she's your sister."

I nodded.

"I should have recognized you from the City Tavern, singing with the so-called Patriots."

"I was not singing."

"Well you were sitting with them."

"I was sitting with my family to celebrate my wife's birthday."

"The pretty young lady you were with is your wife?"

"Actually, my wife died in the summer of '76. The lady I was with is a friend. My father, my brother and I are staunch Loyalists."

"Your sister is not."

"She was drunk and trying to have fun. It was our only family outing all year. Times have been rough here in the City."

"And her husband . . . where was he?"

I hesitated. "He's in Saratoga."

"Oh, really," Cunningham's eyes began to squint. "He is a staunch Loyalist too, I take it."

"No. I never said he was a Loyalist. He is actually not much of anything right now. He has smallpox and is too sick to return."

"Hmph! Smallpox in a rebel camp. The man is as good as dead. At least it tells me I was not wrong to arrest your sister."

"Arrest her, why? Because she was singing in a public inn?"

"That's not why she was arrested."

"Why, then?"

He looked at me before pushing a piece of paper on the desk in my direction. "Because of this."

It was a page from Thomas Paine's Common Sense, the part about why America need not rely on the British and would do just fine on its own.

"Yes. So what does this have to do with Missy?"

"She printed it."

I had underestimated Cunningham. Missy never printed this page. The style was not hers and she dutifully cleared every pamphlet she printed with the British Information Office. Cunningham knew arresting her for embarrassing him at the City Tavern would never pass muster.

"How do you know she did this?" I asked.

"My men found copies of it in her printing shop. We were tipped off by the Information Office."

"This looks pretty serious," I remarked.

"Oh, it is. Sedition is very serious. Serious enough for me to keep her locked up until this war is over."

"I don't suppose I could do something, as a staunch Loyalist of course, to win her early release. To help out in some way, I mean, to show my family's loyalty to the British cause. On the understanding, of course, she would never do something like this again, and I would be personally responsible if she did."

"The army can always use another soldier. Is that what you had in mind?"

He knew exactly what I had in mind and played dumb. "I guess I was thinking something more tangible."

"Well, the army has many needs. Blankets, fuel, liquor, flour, meat. I don't know what you could possibly offer. Would you have any ideas?"

He wanted a bribe but did not dare ask me outright. I would have to oblige him. "The army is so vast I'm sure I could not do anything to help the whole army. I was thinking on a smaller scale to demonstrate my loyalty to General Howe or perhaps other high-ranking people under his command such as yourself. Would you have any thoughts?"

"Every journey starts with the first step as they say, and that would be a step in the right direction. What would you be in a position to do?"

I was not sure myself. Moreover, I had to play this carefully. Whatever I offered, Cunningham would want more. Once I delivered, he could start demanding something else.

"I will need a day or two to think it over," I said. "But in the meantime, I want to make sure my sister is safe. I don't want any harm coming to her."

"Of course not. There is no safer place than right here in my custody."

"Can I see her? Now? I need to make sure she was not accidentally injured during her arrest, so I can report back to my family."

He thought about it and said to the sergeant, "Collins, go fetch Mrs. Barclay. Be sure to use the shackles. She's a feisty one."

The sergeant arrived back with his prisoner within a few minutes. Missy had a blackened eye and an unhealed scar on her face. She looked disheveled in the same dress I saw her wearing two days ago. But even with iron shackles around her wrists, she had not lost her spirit.

Upon seeing me she let out a surprised, "What are you doing here?" And wasted no time letting me know what was on her mind. "Daniel, don't dare give this scum anything. You should see how he keeps his prisoners. They are starving and freezing to death. They wear rags and eat mice and . . . ."

The sergeant cut her off by pushing her forcefully to the floor in the corner of the room and he was about to land a kick into her ribs.

"Please don't kick her," I said quickly.

The sergeant stopped mid-stride and looked at his captain. Cunningham waved off the sergeant.

Missy was not to be intimidated. "I don't care what they do to me, I will rot here in prison. Don't give any bribe to this bloody . . . ."

"Missy, you're not helping things," I said before she could go further.

"I mean it, Daniel."

"Missy, quiet!" This time I commanded her and for once she obeyed.

Cunningham sighed. "You see what we're dealing with here? No one wants to harm your sister, but we need to have discipline. This is a prison. For her own good, your sister needs to learn to hold her tongue."

"I understand, Captain," I said. "Let me see what I can do. Why don't you give us some time alone? You don't want to get the reputation of causing harm to women, and I think I can help smooth things over. Just post Sergeant Collins outside the door, and I'll knock when I'm finished. Would that be possible?"

"You seem like a level-headed person," said Cunningham. "I'm going to grant that request, but only on the condition you get some results. If she continues in this way of behaving, things will get worse. I have to go anyway. It's nice to have met you. I'll be looking forward to hearing back."

When Cunningham and the soldiers left, I went over to the corner and sat on the floor next to my sister. I knew we had only a minute or two before the sergeant would return.

"Who would have thought thirty years after Mom died," I began, "that you and I would be sitting together on the floor of a British prison."

She nodded. "It's entirely my fault. I'm making things worse for you. This is not what I wanted, and I'm sorry."

"No. Don't apologize. I'm blaming no one."

"What are you going to do?"

"I don't know, Missy. I really want to get you out of here. I'm not sure how. I don't think I can come up with enough silver to pay off Cunningham."

"Daniel, please, don't even think about it. I meant what I said earlier. The man is a bloody piece of lying filth. Whatever deal you make with him, he'll break it. He'll make you pay dearly to get me out of here and it will never end. He'll hang it over your head. I will be fine. Let me stay."

"You are too good a person to leave you here."

"I'm a rebel, Daniel."

I kissed her on the cheek. "I know, Sis. I care about you anyway. I will do what I can. Behave yourself."

★

I went back to the counting house where I found Papa, David and Molly going over books and records and talking about Quebec. I had not yet told them about Missy's arrest and was debating how to bring it up. Papa and David would not have much interest in helping her, but I thought Molly might. Maybe she could help me prevail upon Papa for money from the company to pay off Cunningham. Without it, I had no confidence in being able to do anything for my sister.

Before I had a chance to formulate my thoughts, Papa gave me the news. "Daniel, we are going to Quebec."

"You are what?"

"You heard me. We're moving to Quebec."

I had the impression he expected me to accept the idea enthusiastically. And I might even have done so, except that my mind just then was focused on Missy. I had no intention of leaving her to fend for herself.

"When are you thinking about leaving?"

"It's not just me . . . it's all of us," Papa said matter of factly. "The ship is scheduled to arrive in a week or ten days. If the river's not frozen, we ought to be able to leave a day or two after."

"Is now the right time to make a big move, Papa? I mean, we're Loyalists. The City is now occupied by the British Army. Isn't that what we wanted?"

"Don't be so naïve," said David. "We're not going because the army is here. We're going because business is so bad. We have to buy in specie, but the only customer who can pay in specie is the army, and they aren't buying from us."

"You think Quebec is going to be any better?"

"Logan thinks so," said Papa. "It was his idea. It makes sense. He is willing to extend us credit to set up shop there. He is not willing to extend us credit any longer here."

I was beginning to catch on. "What about our houses, Papa. David rents, but you and I own."

"I've talked with some folks. The army needs more quarters for the winter. We can rent out the space for the immediate future. At some point we may sell. I don't think we'll take a loss."

"We're not returning?"

"I would never say never, but if the business goes well up there we may have no need to return. We can decide that later."

I sighed. "Now is not the best time to bring this up, but in case you haven't heard, Missy has been arrested."

"What?" Molly's eyes popped open.

"What did she do now?" David asked.

"I'm not sure," I said. "I went to see the Provost Marshall this morning, a Captain Cunningham. I don't believe what he told me. Which is not to say he didn't have grounds to arrest her. I don't think she printed any treasonous literature, which is what he's accusing her of doing."

"Is she all right?" asked Molly.

"She's alive with bruises and a black eye. They beat her up."

"Beat her up? Was she hurt?"

"A little, but Missy is as fearless as ever. We can't leave her there. It will only get worse."

"We?" asked David.

"She's your sister, David, and she's your daughter, Papa. I know she's on the wrong side of this war, but she is our blood. We need to get her out."

"And how do you propose getting her out of there?" asked David. "We storm the place with bayonets?"

"No. We bribe Captain Cunningham. I have every reason to believe he will take it."

"How much?"

"I don't know."

Silence fell over the room. I hoped for an offer of assistance.

Papa and David were no doubt waiting for a more definitive proposal. But I had no understanding how much it would take to pay off Cunningham, a high ranking military man. Would he be the only one? Or, would there be many more hands ready to take our money in the process?

Papa broke the silence. "I, for one, am not interested."

"But Papa, she's your daughter."

"You already said that."

"Why can't you help, then?"

"One reason, son, we don't have the money. Are you totally oblivious to the condition of our business? What little inventory we have left is not selling, and we have no money to buy new inventory. Whatever is in the safe will barely set us up in Quebec, even with Logan's help. I'm not willing to spend the forty or fifty or however many pounds it would take to bribe a British officer who most likely had good cause to arrest Missy in the first place."

"Yes, but . . . ."

"And I'll tell you something else, if you'll not interrupt me. Even if we had the money the company would not use it on your sister."

"Why, Papa, because she is a Patriot?"

"That doesn't help."

"Then why? She raised David, Molly and me as if we were her own children. Don't you owe her something for that?"

"Not a bloody thing. Not after she . . . well, you know what she did.

"Because she didn't ask your permission to get married?"

"Not only did she not ask my permission, but she ran off with a Scotch Presbyterian. And then, she lied about it."

"Missy had to lie. You would never approve and she didn't want to hurt you. It happened more than fifteen years ago. Isn't it time to get over it? She's raised your grandson, Nathan, who you hardly ever see."

"No. It is not time to get over it. And let me make it clear. We're not spending Thompson Trading Company assets on your sister Missy. If that decision makes you not want to move to Quebec, that's your choice."

"Just like that, Papa? You've written Missy out of your life and now you're going to write me out, too?"

"Your sister chose her path and you can choose yours."

"After everything I've done for this company? I've built up the flour trade, which kept us alive these last five years. It was my idea to purchase the ship, which would have made us a fortune if . . . ."

David cut in, "If your Patriot friends had not sunk it and almost driven us into bankruptcy."

"My Patriot friends? You ungrateful son of a bitch, if it hadn't been for that ship we . . . ."

"You watch what you call me or I'll put you in your place."

David came at me and with both hands pushed me hard. I recoiled and struck back.

"Boys!" Papa shouted, "now stop it."

"He's been on my back ever since I joined the company. I've had all I can take."

David shot back, "I've been on your back because of your poor judgment. It's just about ruined this company more than once."

I turned to Papa. "Is that what you think . . . that I ruined this company?"

"No. That's not what I think."

"It's what I think," David repeated.

"Now, David, let me handle this," said Papa.

"Handle what?" I said. "Handle me? You both think you're handling me?"

"Not at all," Papa said deliberately. "You asked if that was what I think. It's not what I think. You have both contributed significantly to this company."

"Then why are you asking me to stay here instead of going to Quebec?"

"I didn't ask you to stay here. I said it was your choice."

"Yes, but you were quick to make the invitation. You didn't invite David to stay here."

"I didn't invite you, either. And David is a grown man, just like you, and he will make his own choice."

"I am going to Quebec with Papa," said David.

Looking around the room, I was not sure what to say or believe. David showed how he was clearly against me and always had been. That was no surprise. Papa? I was not sure about. I thought he generally approved of my contributions to the company. Still, his comments today made me wonder. I saw Molly with her head down at a table to the side.

"What about you, Molly, what are you going to do?"

When she looked up, I could see tears in her eyes. She had sunk comfortably into her bookkeeping responsibilities over the years and never took sides in our family disagreements. I could sense her discomfort.

"I thought we all would be going, Daniel." She spoke almost in a whisper. "I would like you to join us. These are hard times and we need to stay together."

"Thanks, Molly, I knew I could count on you. I must think about it."

Chapter Thirty Two

Over the next few days, I stopped by our shop on Second Street to talk with Mathew. In part I wanted to make sure he knew Papa, Daniel and Molly were leaving. I also wanted to check and see how he had been holding up and get his thoughts on what I should do.

While most of the shelves were empty, Mathew still had some glassware, sewing supplies and cooking utensils. All the tools and building supplies were gone, having been picked clean off the shelves by one of the two armies. Mathew sat in the rear of the shop with Jonathon playing a game of draughts. My son's reliability over the last year had improved. Now he seemed not to mind helping at the shop, and Mathew enjoyed his company.

"How are things going?" I asked, pulling up a chair.

"Not that great," Mathew said. "I'm about to get my backside whipped by Master Jonathon here."

"What about the business?"

He focused on his next move and did not look up. "You needn't ask. I go days between customers who can pay in silver."

"You are aware Papa is moving to Quebec?"

"Along with David and Molly and you, too, if you had your wits about you."

"Are we going, too, Papa?" asked Jonathon. I had raised the possibility with the kids. The girls were most resistant. Jonathon bordered on indifference. With all of us feeling the pinch of insufficient food, cold nights, and inadequate wood to keep us warm, I could get their cooperation if worse came to worse.

"I don't know yet." Turning to Mathew I asked, "What is the likelihood of a turnaround in business?"

Looking up from the game he shook his head. "You're asking the wrong fellow. I'm just the simple shopkeeper. Your family cuts the deals that make the business go. If you ask me, things won't improve until the British leave town and we're trading in Continentals again."

We heard some muffled musket fire and a cannon discharge. Jonathon went to open the front door so we could get a better read on the location.

"It's coming from over west, across the Schuylkill," said Mathew. "British patrols probably got too close to the Americans again. It'll stop soon."

"I guess you're right about the British leaving," I sighed. "My original thought was the British taking over would be good for business. It has come to have an opposite effect. You really think the kids and I ought to go?"

"What are you going to do if you stay?" Mathew looked back to the game board.

"I don't know. Maybe try to keep the wheat business alive."

"You could join the Americans."

I looked at him closely to see if I could discern any hidden meaning in his comment. "Why, Mathew, are you a secret Patriot?"

"What if I were? Would it make a difference?"

"Probably not. I will say you have kept it well hidden all this time. That raises another question. What are you going to do once Papa leaves? We'll have to shut down the shop."

"I know you will," Mathew nodded. "Your father already told me. Don't worry, I'll find something."

★

Apart from Mathew and the shop, I had Elizabeth to think about. I had made up my mind some time ago that, other than Sarah, no one else existed with whom I would rather spend the rest of my life. The kids, moreover, were still young enough to benefit from some female parental guidance. Elizabeth would be a perfect fit. Still, every time I asked what she expected out of life, or whether she was interested in having a family, she brushed aside the question saying she was "much too busy to think about those things."

To some extent I found her attitude refreshing. Many single women her age thought about nothing other than marriage. Margaret was one. I would not dare ask her that question. She would talk my ear off for the next twenty minutes about the importance of married life. Elizabeth was the opposite. She made me think something troubled her about getting too close, something she was not willing to tell me.

In my quandary over Quebec, I called on Elizabeth and her mother. Elizabeth welcomed me into the main room of their cottage, serving as a fitting room for their clients, a work room, parlor and kitchen all in one. Stacks of material and bolts of cloth were neatly stashed on one side and near-finished garments hung nearby. Elizabeth's mother, Grace Clyburn, rocked in a chair near the wood-burning cook stove.

She rose from her knitting as I entered and greeted me. "I was hoping it would be you," she said, reaching up to giving me a friendly embrace and peck on the cheek. "It has been awhile, Daniel."

"I was here just last week," I reminded her. "You sit back down and please don't let me interrupt your knitting. I see your daughter is busy, too. I will only stay a moment."

"Elizabeth, pour Daniel a nice cup of tea. It's time you take a break anyway. Mrs. Simpson's dress can wait."

"Yes, Mama."

"What news do you bring, Daniel?" She seemed anxious to know.

"One piece of news is about Missy." I sat down at the table near Mrs. Clyburn.

Elizabeth spoke up with a smile. "Oh, Mama, you should have seen her. She was just wonderful. The way she stood up to those British officers. It was amazing to watch and something I would never have the nerve to do. I admire her so much."

"It may have seemed wonderful at the time," I said soberly, "but she ended up getting arrested."

"What?" both Elizabeth and Mrs. Clyburn asked simultaneously.

I sighed. "I found out the next day. She is locked up in the British Provost."

"What are you going to do?" asked Mrs. Clyburn. "You must get her out."

"Yes. But I have no idea how. I will have to think of something."

"I am so sorry, Daniel." Elizabeth looked sad. "I would never have wished anything like this for you or for her. She is so sweet."

"We should all have been more alert to what was going on. But that's not the only news I bring. Papa is moving to Quebec. He is taking my brother, David, and my younger sister, Molly, with him."

Mrs. Clyburn wrinkled her forehead. "Why would he do that? He's lived here his entire life, hasn't he?"

"Yes," I nodded. "But business is bad. You would think being pro-British, Papa would have an advantage. But it hasn't worked out that way. The British Army has its favored merchants. Evidently, he's not one of them. Our British supplier offered to set him up in Quebec."

"You're not going with him, are you?" asked Mrs. Clyburn.

I had hoped that question would come from Elizabeth, and felt disappointed. "What do you think I should do?" I looked at Elizabeth, but her eyes were looking down at the floor.

"You should stay here," Mrs. Clyburn opined without hesitation. "We both want you to stay. Tell him, Elizabeth."

"Of course, we do." She still did not look at me. I felt disappointed a second time.

"Elizabeth wants you to stay more than she lets on," said Mrs. Clyburn.

"Mama, please."

"No. You let me talk. My late husband Alex and I are both of good Welsh stock and never fond of the British.

"Mama, please do not go on . . . ."

"I'm speaking my piece here in my home. Alex and I were both outspoken, but Elizabeth is different. She is adopted. You didn't know that, did you, Daniel? Elizabeth is shy about telling people. Which is not to say I don't love her to death. I love her more than my own natural son. Elizabeth thinks people will look down on her if they know the truth. I don't know why. She should be a little more open. It would do her a lot of good."

A pause followed

"So, we both want you to stay," Mrs. Clyburn continued. I know you have to think about business and supporting your family. All those things are important. But these bastard British aren't going to be here forever. Sooner or later they'll leave, and business will get back to normal. That would be my prediction." She ended this time with finality.

I sat there feeling stunned. It was a lot to take in.

Elizabeth finally looked at me. "I am sorry."

"What are you sorry about? Your mother is an open person and I like her for that. Why didn't you tell me you were adopted?"

"Does it really matter, Daniel?"

"Of course not. I'm interested in you . . . not your family history. But the more I know about you the better I like you. And being adopted is a part of you. Why should we have secrets?"

Her eyes roamed the floor again.

"Any other secrets I should know?"

"No, Daniel."

"Tell me, do you really want me to stay or, is that just your mother talking?"

"I want you to stay. I just don't know . . . ."

"Know what?"

"I want you to stay. That's all."

★

A few days later I went to the counting house to tell the others I was staying. Finding it vacant, I entered Papa's living quarters and saw half-full wooden boxes strewn about the place. Mrs. Pickering, in her work clothes, directed me up the stairway to Papa's bedroom where I found him taking apart a dresser and mirror to facilitate transporting it by ship.

"So, you are staying," he stated before I said hello.

"Yes, Papa."

"I'm not going to argue with you, son. I can't tell you how disappointed I am."

"Disappointed I am staying, or disappointed in the reason I am staying."

"All of the above."

"Papa, I can't leave while Missy is still locked up."

"That's not the only reason you're staying." He spoke in an angry tone.

"No. I have other considerations. My family is here. We have friends and connections here. I have met someone here, believe it or not, a woman I'm interested in. What other reasons do I need, Papa?"

"Your heart is not in the business nor is it in the British cause."

I could not believe his accusation. "Not in the British cause? I've done nothing to help out the American rebels. Is that what David is telling you?"

"No. But you think like your sister."

"That's utterly absurd. And how would my staying here help out the American cause?"

"Because it will give you the opportunity to change sides."

"Why in bloody hell would I do that? Helping the rebels win will only make things worse for business. And so far as the business is concerned, I've worked my ass off for our company. You told me yourself a few short days ago I made a significant contribution. Have you changed your mind?"

"I did say that and I meant it, but your contribution could have been a lot more. Except you held back."

"Held back? I've done at least as much for the company as David."

"Yes. You have."

Now, I was mystified. "What are you telling me then?"

"You have more talent and vision than David. You had so much more to give but gave so little. You could have been one of the Tall Oaks of this City by now, but you never took advantage of your opportunities."

I went from being mystified to being dumbfounded. Papa praised me, something he had never done before, while at the same time he leveled debilitating criticism at me. I wanted to hug him and to scream at him at the same time. I did neither.

I only stared at the man I revered. "I'm sorry, Papa."

He looked away. "There is no turning back, son, life is too short for that."

"I know, Papa."

"So what do you want?"

"What do you mean?" His question had an offensive tone, as if I was trying to use the threat of staying as leverage for something else.

"You're a partner in the company. Part of the assets belong to you. Unfortunately, most everything is tied up in debt or pledged for sale to the army to help finance the trip to Quebec. Since you are not coming with us, you're entitled to your share."

"Papa," I stammered, "I don't want anything. What I wanted most in this business was to please you. And I've made a mess out of that."

"Yes. You have." He paused and added, "The only thing the company can leave you with is the mill and whatever inventory we have left in flour. We can't take any of it with us, and it's free of debt. Unfortunately, it's all located in rebel territory, and who knows of its condition by the war's end. So, it's yours. I wish there were more."

★

I walked home in the cold, late-morning December sun, my head awash in second thoughts, regrets, and confusion. I had made the decision to stay, but now I felt guiltier than hell about it. A few days ago I was not certain about Papa's attitude towards me. Now, I was certain and that made a big difference.

As I approached the house the sound of conversation inside drew my attention. I expected Margaret, but then I thought I heard Janie and Annie and other voices as well. They should have been in school. It occurred to me something must be wrong.

I knocked on the front door to give fair warning to whatever was going on. Margaret opened it. Sitting in the parlor were my two daughters and three or four other girls about their age. Janie's eyes were puffed up and her cheeks were tear-streaked.

"What happened?"

Margaret took me by the arm and pulled me to the side. "Janie received word at school this morning. Lightfoot was killed."

I almost let out a relieved "Is that all?" but looked at Janie's weeping face, and quickly caught myself.

"That's only part of it." Margaret looked eager to tell me more.

"What do you mean?"

She hesitated, and then whispered, "Janie's carrying Lightfoot's child."

My mind went black. So that's what that Indian kid was doing, joining the Continental Army and staying so close to the City! He was sneaking through the British perimeter, meeting up with my daughter and raping her. All along I kept thinking he was out of her life. I did not want to imagine where or how the evil deed was done, or how many secret rendezvous there were behind my back. My hands began to shake and I wanted to vomit. That boy deserved to be killed, and I hoped it was a wretched death.

But here was my grieving daughter, surrounded by her sympathetic young friends and Margaret. Through a herculean effort I forced myself over to where Janie was sitting. I knelt down beside her, and said in a strained, raspy voice, "I am so sorry."

About to explode, I quickly ducked outside to walk around the City for a couple of hours, trying to decide what to do.

★

Today had been a turning point in my life, one almost as devastating as the death of Sarah. Not only had I learned what a disappointment I had been to Papa, but I also found out I had a pregnant fifteen-year old unmarried daughter, and a dead Indian would-be son-in-law. Add to that, my sister sat in a military prison.

The combined effect shook the very roots of everything good I felt about myself and my family. I had been living a lie of optimism, believing things would always turn out fine. Yet nothing had turned out fine. And I had no Sarah to help me figure out what to do. I had to face each one of these heartbreaks alone and try not to mess up even more.

I ultimately concluded my daughter was the most immediate problem. What she had done, sneaking around with an Indian boy behind my back, could bring shame to my family. My initial impulse was to turn her out of the house and never speak to her again.

But Papa came to mind. Isn't that what he had done with Missy? Missy had run off with her Presbyterian lover, Peter, never to be forgiven by Papa. He had grown so alienated from his daughter that he even refused to help get her out of prison. Is that how I wanted to end up with Janie?

No. It was not. Papa and Missy were the future of Janie and me if I were to follow my natural instincts. I had to come up with a better way. I did not condone what she had done. But throwing her into the street was not the answer. Her lover was dead, she was pregnant. If anyone ever needed a helping hand it was Janie. I was her father and the one most able to help.

I returned home in midafternoon. One of Janie's friends remained and the two of them, along with Annie and Margaret, were sitting at the kitchen table drinking tea. Their conversation stopped as I hung up my cloak and entered the room. Margaret rose to get me a cup.

Still standing, I faced Janie and said solemnly, "I am sorry for your loss, but I also am disappointed in you."

Janie stood, put her arms around me and her head against my chest. "I know you are, Papa, please don't get mad at me. I couldn't bear it." She started crying and I could feel her emotion. "I loved him so much. I could not help myself. And now I miss him, Papa, more than anything."

She was crying uncontrollably. Try as I might to prevent it, I felt myself tearing up. I had to turn away to regain my composure. I wanted to be stern in my disapproval but found it incredibly difficult.

"I will try to find out what happened. He was a soldier in the Continental Army and deserves a decent burial."

That seemed to be the right thing to say. Maybe it was just that Janie had never heard her lover referred to as a *soldier*. It gave him the same respected status as the many young white boys who had died in this war. Whatever it was, she began sobbing anew and hugged me tighter than before.

"He was a good soldier, yes, thank you, Papa." Her sister and friend put their arms around her and also started crying. Soon Margaret joined.

Chapter Thirty Three

The wind blustered about on the mid December morning when Papa, Mrs. Pickering, David, his wife Helen, and Molly were scheduled to set sail for Quebec. It was the same day I picked to cross the Schuylkill once again, this time in search of Lightfoot's remains. Dobbin was none too anxious to leave the warmth of her stable as Alphonse and I jumped aboard the chaise. We took extra blankets and started down the as yet unfrozen dirt roadway toward Middle Ferry. To their credit, the British kept the crossing open despite bad weather.

I had no idea whether Captain Johnson's unit would still be in the vicinity. My best shot at finding him, I figured, would be to head straight west on Lancaster Road. When we came to the gate that signified the last British outpost on the road west, we drew the same questions as before about where we were headed.

After responding, I asked, "And what about you boys? We heard a fire fight in this area a couple days ago. Everything all right?"

A redcoat corporal gave us a dismissive waive. "Don't worry about us. The Yankees got a little too restless. We had to teach them a lesson about warfare in the woods. You fellows going to be back through here yet today?"

"Hopefully, unless that lesson of yours didn't sink in."

A few miles later, five American soldiers stopped us and demanded to know our business. All were wrapped in blankets.

"I've come to talk with Captain Samuel Johnson, Seventh Pennsylvania Regiment."

"He expecting you?"

"No. But I want to find out more about one of his men who was killed a few days ago, an Indian scout."

"The captain's not here."

"Can you take me to him?"

The corporal looked back at his superior, who gave him a nod and told us, "We'll have to take you blind-folded."

"A blind fold is all right."

The journey led us to a creek-side clearing, which contained thirty tents staked around a log cabin. Soldiers milled about warming fires that dotted the area. After ushering us past check points, our guide pointed us in the direction of a large tent and told us to wait outside until summoned. Within a few minutes a guard grunted and motioned me in while Alphonse remained outside. The simmering coals of a fire just inside the entryway kept the place warm enough I could loosen my cloak and talk without my teeth chattering. Captain Johnson rose from behind a small table and gave a bow.

"Mr. Thompson, I believe, is that correct? And your bonded man outside?"

"You have a good memory, Captain. I had no idea you had such a sizeable outfit back here."

"My company runs the operation for most of the area west of Philadelphia outside the British perimeter," said the captain amiably. "We block supplies from entering the City from the west. If the British begin any westward movements, it's our job to alert General Washington at Valley Forge. What brings you out here?"

"One of your Indian scouts was killed a few days ago. His name was Lightfoot. He was a friend of our family. I came out to make sure he received a decent burial, and to return with any personal effects."

The captain nodded. "Lightfoot was a good boy. Fearless. He could track anything, and he easily slipped into the City almost at will. I was sorry to have lost him."

"How did it happen?"

"He and two other scouts were at the head of a platoon to check on British positions along the Schuylkill south of here. They were ambushed from the side. Two of my other soldiers were also killed and four wounded."

"That's too bad. What happened to Lightfoot's body?"

"His fellow scouts buried him yesterday over in the camp cemetery. While they don't mark their graves, I can have one of my men show you where it is. They wanted to return him to his tribe, but I could not allow it because I can't spare the men."

"Any possessions I can take back?"

"Funny you should ask. The Lenape tribesmen usually bury weapons or tools with their dead. But in this case they didn't bury his musket. When I asked them why, I was told they wanted to give it to his family. That's unusual. Maybe they thought someone like you might come along."

"I'd be honored to take his musket. I will see it gets into the right hands."

"Fair enough." The captain summoned the soldier to retrieve the musket and sat back in his chair. "So, how did you make out with that barrel of flour?" he asked. "Were you able to get it past the British patrols?"

"As a matter of fact it was not a problem. I appreciate your assistance with Colonel Dean. Have you had any more run-ins with him?"

"His unit was transferred to north of here. So no, I have not. How is life inside the City? Most people holding up all right?"

"Just barely," I said.

An idea occurred to me. Sitting before me was a military man who might have insight to offer. I felt desperate about my situation with Captain Cunningham. I needed to rescue Missy and had nothing to lose by asking Captain Johnson.

"If you have a few minutes, I could use your advice on a problem."

"Sure, go ahead."

"My sister has been arrested and is being held in the British Provost by Captain William Cunningham."

"Hmm. That's not good." He shook his head. "That man has a reputation. What'd she do to get arrested?"

"You're not going to believe it. You have to understand she's an ardent Patriot. I told you last time I saw you that she is married to Peter Barclay."

"I remember."

"She sometimes lets her emotions stand in the way of good sense." When I finished telling him about the singing contest at the City Tavern, Captain Johnson burst out laughing.

"It was kind of funny," I said. "There was Captain Cunningham trying to direct the British choir in a round of *God Save George Our King*, and half of them are singing *Free America*."

"I wish I could have seen it." Captain Johnson could not stop laughing.

"The next day," I continued, "Cunningham charges her with printing seditious literature and has Missy arrested. She will never last in that prison. I went in and talked with Cunningham and know he would take a bribe. I just don't know how to make it stick. He could turn around and arrest her again."

The captain stopped laughing and turned serious. "It's a tricky business. I've not had much experience with bribes."

"I'm not suggesting otherwise. But you're a military man, and I thought you might be able to give me some ideas."

"This is a special case. Cunningham is a fucking scoundrel. Take my word for it. He hates Whigs and Patriots. When he was in charge of the prison in New York, he confiscated what few possessions the prisoners had and sold it all for his own profit. The British Army shipped food to the prison, but the prisoners never saw it nor ate it. He sold it and let them starve. He hung more than three-hundred American prisoners for no good reason. He likes seeing people suffer and die."

"That's all the more reason she has to get out."

"And you? Are you in any danger of being arrested?"

"Not likely, I have good Loyalist credentials. You already knew that, did you not?"

He paused to look at me before answering. "I suspected so."

"Does that mean you're not willing to help?"

"No. Not necessarily, but I don't know if I can help. It seems to me what you have to do is go public."

"What do you mean by that?"

"If this amounts to secret payments between you and Cunningham, it's never going to end. He will suck you dry. You need to involve his superiors and someone who has a base level of integrity."

"Like who?"

"It depends on what you have to offer. Can you come up with silver coin or anything else that would get some attention. You got a mill, right? Is it producing anything right now?"

"I have flour."

"How much?"

"A warehouse full."

"You've been holding out on me."

I looked at him suspiciously. "Don't tell me you're going to confiscate my flour. It's all I have to work with."

"No. I'm not going to confiscate it. You have not even told me where it is. And I don't have time to search every nook and cranny."

"That's a relief," I sighed. "When you and I cut the deal last time, I truly didn't know what was left. I thought the Continental Army might already have impressed it. They did take part of it, but missed the rest of it. And that's what I'm holding."

"Why don't you sell it, then?"

"It's in rebel territory. All I could get would be Continentals. They're worthless in the City. I have no way of getting the flour to a British market."

The captain nodded, sat back, and thought for a moment. "Here is how I come out, Daniel. You need someone who can move your flour to where the British can buy it. I have men and wagons to do just that. But I am going to level with you. It's one thing for me to sit here and give you some thoughts off the top of my head. No charge for that. But for me to get my men and equipment involved and authorize movement of contraband into the City so it can be sold to the British? That's going to cost you."

"How many barrels this time?"

"It is going to cost you some barrels of flour. No question about it. We can negotiate something that's fair. But it's going to cost you a lot more than just flour."

"What then?"

He looked at me straight. "I want you to work for us in the City. I want your undivided loyalty. I want you to spy. That's the only way, and believe me I mean the only way, my superiors would authorize this."

I was surprised. Not that Captain Johnson made such a proposal. I was surprised his proposal did not shock me. To the contrary, it sounded reasonable. I could gather information of military significance without even trying. As for my loyalty?

What Papa had said a few days ago came back to me. "Your heart is not in the British cause."

I did not know how long my father had realized the truth about my political convictions. He seemed to know even before I did that my loyalty to the British had waned.

Still, the whole concept was so novel I had to think it through.

"Interesting proposition," I said. "Let's suppose we make such a deal. What do you propose would happen then?"

"I would arrange to have the flour hauled from your warehouse to a location near the British perimeter so it could be sold to the British."

"In violation of the contraband order prohibiting food into the City?"

"Yes, but only because I get a spy in return."

"You must have spies inside the City now. Why do you need another?"

"We do have spies, but the quality of information has been dwindling. We need a spy with a history of being a Loyalist to acquire even better access. What we need is someone like you."

"So you move the flour close to the City . . . and then what?"

"You negotiate a price with a British officer that would include the release of your sister."

"Who would that be?"

"Just thinking out loud here, I would say someone near the top that would not have any problem dealing with Cunningham. He would also have access to quartermaster funds to buy the flour. General William Erskine comes to mind. He is close to both General Clinton and Lord Cornwallis. He is rumored to be the next Quartermaster General. He also has connections with the Royal Commissariat, which is the branch of the Treasury Board that provisions the British troops."

"If I negotiate this kind of a deal, I'm going to need assurances the flour will be where it is supposed to be and the British are able to buy it. What I mean is, I don't want to negotiate a deal, only to find out you folks have confiscated it."

"That's not going to happen. For one thing, I will take personal responsibility for the operation. For another, I want you to be successful. With a sizeable sale of flour, you will be noticed and you will gain the confidence of the British high command. They will trust you, doors will open, information will start flowing. That's the kind of access we need, but don't have."

"How would we communicate once the doors open?"

"We'll work that out. Typically we would have you drop a letter at an agreed-upon location. It would be picked up and brought over here. If we need to contact you, we let you know where to pick up our message."

"And if I'm caught?"

"Spies are hanged. They don't get the courtesy of a firing squad. You will be placing yourself in danger. I know you have a family. It would be something you need to think about."

"Yes, I do."

"Can you get back to me within two days?"

"Probably."

"Then let's accomplish what we can now. First, you have to tell me how many barrels of flour you have and where it is."

When I hesitated, he added, "I promise you, if you decide you cannot or don't want to go forward, the information will never be used."

"All right. Eighty barrels and they are over in Turks Head."

"Hmm. Eighty barrels total. I will need twelve for my company. That will pretty much get us through the winter. Is that fair?"

"I suppose."

"So, if you give me the go-ahead, we'll move the remaining sixty eight for sale to the British. That should give you plenty with which to negotiate. At the corner of Front and High Streets there is an abandoned shop. Beside the shop is a wood pile with a broken rain barrel. Take the top off the rain barrel, leave a sealed letter inside with your initials on it. Be sure to put the top back on. The message should say nothing more than 'go' or 'stop.' If you give me the 'go' I will get back to you with further instructions."

I stood up to leave. "Lightfoot's musket?"

"I almost forgot." He summoned a private waiting outside, who entered and handed the musket to the captain. After examining it for a moment, he handed it over to me saying, "That Indian boy must have been special to you and your family."

"Yes, he was special." I wondered what prompted such a remark.

The captain's men blindfolded me and Alphonse, guiding us back to Lancaster Road. It was not until we passed the first British checkpoint I realized what had caught the captain's attention. Picking up the musket to check out its condition, I felt an indentation in the stock where my initials DT were carved deep into the wood. Yes. This was Lightfoot's musket, for those were the very initials I had engraved when I was a kid. And those initials were what caught Captain Johnson's attention and prompted his comment.

Still feeling around, I found another crevice an inch away. Looking closely, I saw more initials carved not quite so deep and not quite so large. "LF." Janie would cherish this remembrance.

Chapter Thirty Four

Trial Proceedings

"Let me get this straight," said the Judge Advocate. "With nine-hundred prisoners in the British Provost, you focused on one, your sister Missy Barclay. Is that correct?"

"Yes, I was most concerned about my sister," said Daniel. "But it's not fair to say I had no concern about the others. I just didn't know any of them. I became more concerned as time went on."

"And you now say the Continental Army agreed to assist you in selling flour to the enemy, which would be in violation of its own contraband order prohibiting foodstuffs to enter the City?"

"That's exactly what happened."

"Absolutely incredible."

"Not at all. The plan made a lot of sense. The Continental Army got the benefit of another spy inside the City. Captain Johnson would never have acted on his plan if he didn't have approval."

"And you expect this court to believe you put aside all your Loyalist leanings and became a flag-waving Patriot?"

"You have not been listening, sir. The deal I reached with Captain Johnson put me firmly into the American camp. I had been wavering for some time. My family was split. I don't think you can blame me for being undecided. Up until then, I had not taken any significant actions against the Patriot cause, nor did I stand staunchly in favor of the British. Now, I was committing."

"Did you in fact begin working for the benefit of the Patriot cause?"

"Once Missy was released, I focused on that cause pretty much full time."

Chapter Thirty Five

Arriving back in the City by midafternoon, I went to the counting house to see if Papa might still be there. I found the place empty and abandoned except for a few stray pieces of furniture, leaving me with an intense feeling of loss. True, Papa's departure made it easier to embark upon my proposed arrangement for freeing Missy. But Papa, Molly, and even David, had been bedrocks in my life until now. As I walked through the empty rooms, I realized I rarely had done anything of consequence, business or personal, without consulting, being advised by, or arguing with at least one of them. I would miss all three, and I had not even said goodbye.

Then it dawned on me. Their ship may not yet have left. They could still be loading in the harbor. I took off in a run toward the waterfront. A block away I saw a ship forty yards from the dock, its crew still getting her under way. Sure enough, it was the ship taking my family members to Quebec. A dozen or so passengers remained on deck waving to friends and family on shore.

I yelled out, "Papa, David, Molly!" hoping one of them might hear me.

I saw two figures moving along the rail as a voice called out, "Goodbye, Daniel!" It was Molly, waving. Papa stood next to her.

I shouted out to the ship again, wildly flapping my arms. "Godspeed!"

My misty eyes watched until the ship was but speck down river.

Returning to the counting house, I resolved now was the time to put aside my reservations. I found a sheet of paper and wrote the word GO and my initials. Sealing it in an envelope, I walked over to the corner of Front and High where I placed it in the broken barrel and replaced the lid.

The next day I found a folded paper slipped under the front door of our house. Handwriting on the inside stated, "George Street, Haverford, ready in one day. Access will be clear. SJ."

Haverford was a little town a few miles southwest of the City. It was not clear to me whether the Americans or British controlled the area, but Captain Johnson was telling me the flour would be moved to a warehouse on George Street accessible to the British.

It was time to meet General Erskine.

★

I put on my best waist coat and breaches, although my best were a bit shabby. Still, I looked presentable for a middling Loyalist-leaning businessman. If I looked overly well-to-do, even the reputable General Erskine might start making excessive demands beyond my finances.

The British high command was headquartered in the State House, and there I made my initial inquiries. The clerical staff sent me to the waterfront where the general was supposed to be meeting with the captain of an East Indiaman recently arrived in port with supplies. I found the huge three-masted merchant vessel as well armed as a man-o-war. Asking permission to board,

I was directed below deck to a waiting area outside the captain's quarters. I waited with other civilians and soldiers who also had business with General Erskine. Eventually, he emerged with two aides.

I approached him quickly. "General Erskine, might I have a moment with you about a business proposition of interest to the army?"

The general eyed me, not sure of what to make of the impromptu request from a would-be merchant. "If it's goods or services you're selling, you'll have to go through the commissary general's office over in City Hall."

"I know the usual procedure," I said, "but this involves not only a sale of goods but also a sensitive matter I would like to discuss with you personally."

He looked irritated and I feared my efforts may be going nowhere. "Have you done business with the army before?"

"Yes, sir, a year and a half ago."

"Through whom?"

"An agent of the Commissariat, Emil Higgins."

"Higgins. Really. It so happens I am having dinner with him today. Meet us at the London Coffee House at noon. We'll see about this sensitive business of yours."

"Yes, sir, I will be there."

Upon arriving, I was ushered to a private table where the general and Higgins were seated with two others. One was an officer they introduced as Lieutenant Masters, and the other a civilian who worked under Higgins.

I feared Higgins might not recognize me, but he promptly put my concerns to rest. "Daniel's family company is Thompson Trading," he said, "one of the few in the colonies we found reliable. They sold us a nice supply of flour and delivered in full and on time in New Jersey when Lord Cornwallis was chasing after Washington. How is your father these days, Daniel?"

That was as good an introduction as I could hope. "Doing quite well, thank you. As a matter of fact he and David are right now on a ship headed for Quebec."

"Why so?"

"Business has been off lately, and our British supplier offered to relocate us there. Papa jumped at the opportunity."

"And left you to tidy up the loose ends."

"Something like that, Mr. Higgins."

After they invited me to join them, the conversation resumed between General Erskine and Higgins. They talked generally about another East Indiaman to arrive in a few days; the several hundred tons of hay the army was stockpiling for winter livestock fodder in Olney, just northeast of the City; and a half dozen other matters of interest only to someone like Higgins whose job it was to keep the army supplied.

Erskine, I noticed, was a big but well-built man, maybe fifty. He looked resplendent in his red double-breasted army jacket with gold epaulets. Although having an over-prominent nose, he maintained an authoritative but likeable manner. Eventually, he turned to me.

"Well, sir, you mentioned a business proposition this morning and a sensitive matter that needed discussing. Tell us what's on your mind."

"As Mr. Higgins mentioned," I began, "part of our business involves the purchase and sale of flour. It so happens we have a supply near the City we could make available for sale."

"How much have you?" asked the general.

"Roughly 68 barrels."

"How is it such a quantity suddenly available?"

"Good question. We've been hiding it for months from the Continental Army for fear they would impress it for their own use. It has only been recently I was able to have it moved close to the City for sale to His Majesty's Army."

"How much are you asking?"

"We aren't looking to make a killing, General. Mr. Higgins and I negotiated a price of four and a half pounds per barrel a year and a half ago. If the army has purchased recently at a higher price, maybe you would favor us by paying the going rate."

The general looked at Higgins. "What have we purchased flour for recently, Emil?"

"It has varied from five to five and a half pounds sterling for good quality flour."

"And his barrels?" asked the general. "What of their quality?"

"Sturdy and tightly sealed," Higgins answered "We never had a problem. Your mill actually makes them, right, Daniel?"

"Yes, sir. Oak or cherry staves. They last the longest."

"I cannot tell you how many tons of flour we've lost due to flimsy casks," said the general. "But it has been many. So five pounds is your price. Now, what was so sensitive about that?"

"Nothing so far, General," I said. "The sensitive part is my sister. She is being held in prison in the British Provost. She did something stupid and was arrested by Captain Cunningham's men."

Higgins gasped.

General Erskine scowled. "What did she do? Is she a Whig?"

I sighed. "Every family has a black sheep, General. My father has not spoken to her for years. That tells you something. As for what she did? she sang some American songs too loudly for the pleasure of Captain Cunningham one night at the City Tavern."

The general turned to Lieutenant Masters. "I think I heard about this."

"Yes, indeed, sir," said Masters, "a couple weeks ago. Ugly incident."

"Very ugly," said the general stern-faced. "Cunningham is the type of person one needs to be wary of. What do you propose we do about your sister?"

"I'm prepared to sell the flour at a significant discount if that would secure the release of my sister. I would also guarantee she will never do anything so stupid again."

An awkward silence followed. I would have to be more specific. I had prepared myself to make an even exchange of the flour in return for Missy. But my merchant's instincts got the better of me.

"What about three pounds specie per barrel," I said, "instead of five, with the balance to provide compensation for your efforts."

"My good man," the general said with an accusatory tone, "are you offering me a bribe?"

"Absolutely not," I said quickly. "Securing the release of my sister involves time and effort. I can only imagine the headaches involved, or fine that may be owing. I wish to compensate the army in whole. I'm willing to sell at a price that reflects a reduction of two pounds per barrel, and however you or the army decides to account for that reduction is none of my business."

General Esrkine turned to Higgins. "I like this man." His tone had lightened. "Let's see what we can do. Daniel, you contact Emil in the morning, and he will make arrangements to pick up the flour and payment at three pounds per barrel. In the meantime, I will secure the release of your sister, and I will also make sure Cunningham is no longer a problem for you."

I nodded.

"You have to understand," he continued, "mistakes sometimes happen, and Cunningham was only trying to do his job."

"Of course, general."

He added as a warning, "You must also understand your sister has to stay out of trouble. No exceptions, or you will be facing dire consequences."

"I'm aware of that."

"Very good then," he said. "We've all done our duty. Let's finish our dinner."

I never found out whether General Erskine took the discount for himself or gave the benefit to the army. I received over two-hundred pounds in silver two days later. I had to make reimbursements for receipts being held by our business agent in the City and pay off some other expenses, mostly in Continentals. Still, a good share of the payment was profit.

★

That same afternoon I received word the British Provost was releasing my sister. I drove the chaise to pick her up, and waited outside the headquarters hut for an hour in the cold. Walking with a limp, she finally emerged. Her clothes were not much more than rags, and the shawl she wore was full of holes, offering no protection from the weather. She looked as if she had lost a good fifteen pounds, and I could see dark rings around her eyes and bruises all over.

But she was the same old Missy. "Why did you do it, Danny?"

Her lack of gratitude disappointed me. "You can't be serious. Look at you, Missy, you wouldn't have lasted another month."

"Those are the real American heroes. My place is with them."

"You're not going to do anyone any good if you are dead."

She looked at me with anger. "You think it's that easy? You pay a bribe and that's the end of it? Now that you have done it once, Cunningham will take you for more. He will have me arrested again and you will be right back paying another ransom."

"I didn't deal with Cunningham, and we are safe so long as you stay out of trouble."

She gave me a side-long glance. "Who did you deal with then?"

"It's a long story. We need to go home, get you some clean clothes, a warm bath and food. Then we can talk. In the mean-time, tell me a small part of you is happy to be out."

She offered me a tiny grin, fleeting at best, but one I could notice. "Yes, brother, I am happy to be out."

Over the next few days we made the decision Missy would live with us for a while. Part of it was the fact her house had been ransacked by soldiers from one army or the other. Then, too, we found out someone had pilfered a press, frames and type setting machine from her print shop. Missy was left jobless making her feel even more depressed. Another factor was Missy finding out Janie was pregnant. One might have thought a properly-bred aunt would chastise her teen-age niece now pregnant out of wedlock. If anything, the news of a baby on the way seemed to cheer up Missy.

"Those things happen," she responded with contented resignation. Whatever her reasoning, Missy took on personal responsibility for Janie's well being.

With Missy staying with us, I figured it was time to nudge Margaret out. Margaret had been helpful, no question about it. But I had come to the point where being civil with her was a struggle. It did not help she seemed totally oblivious to my growing dislike of her. She prattled on about how happy she was, and how much she had blossomed since coming to know me better. It got to the point I rarely came home for dinner to avoid talking to her.

In making arrangements for Missy to stay, I told her she would have to let Margaret go.

"She means well," said Missy.

"I'm sure. Just tell her not to come back. Preferably when I'm not here."

Unfortunately, Margaret stopped by unexpectedly while I was still at home. Missy handled the situation tactfully, and Margaret seemed to take the news in stride.

Then before she left, Margaret turned to me and said, "Daniel, I know you have been seeing another woman. She is not the nice person you think she is, and I hate to see you ruin your life. Know when you are ready to come back, I will be here for you."

Responding with a comment about shoving a cob up her ass sorely tempted me. But I managed restraint. When she was out the door, I turned to Missy, now raising her arms in exasperation and shaking her head.

"I can't believe what I just heard," she said.

"At least we agree on something."

★

Although the prospect of taking care of Janie helped, Missy's experience in prison continued to darken her attitude. She felt genuinely guilty about her sudden release. Here she was warm and comfortable, while her comrades were literally freezing and starving to death in prison.

She approached me a few nights later. "What did you do to get me out?"

The kids had gone to bed, and the two of us moved into the parlor, hot toddy in hand. Christmas was only a few days off and I wanted to get her thoughts on a few gifts. A week ago my thoughts focused on surviving the winter and keeping food on the table. Now, with the sale of the flour, I had comfortable wealth.

After swearing her to secrecy, I told her the story of my dealing with Captain Johnson. I concluded, "If you start acting up and get into trouble again, you're going to raise all kinds of suspicions. And that will destroy the confidence I've built up with my newly made British friends. Not to mention getting me hanged."

She gave me a hug. "I knew you were one of us."

I was not in a hugging mood. "I am not one of you," I said, wresting free. In truth, I was not exactly sure what I was. "Let me put it this way. I have no interest getting sucked into this war. But a deal's a deal, and I came into this with eyes open. I just don't know much about spying."

"Maybe I can help." I gave her a skeptical look and she held up her hands defensively. "I will stay out of trouble, I promise. I may be a diehard Patriot, but I'm not stupid. You're my brother. I owe you. I have a few ideas for Captain Johnson."

I sensed her darkness was lifting. She had found a way to help the Patriot cause.

I sighed. "What do you have in mind?"

"Let's begin with the simple stuff. You had dinner with General Erskine. Did he say anything that might be useful?"

"I'm not sure. He did mention things like another merchant ship arriving soon, and where they are storing winter hay."

"Those are the types of things you need to report. What else? The London Coffee House . . . you used to go there with Papa, right? It's a favorite place for British officers. You need to start having dinner there on a regular basis. And never alone. Always find an officer to sit at your table, the higher his rank the better, and you must always pay."

"That is going to get expensive."

"Yes. It's going to get expensive. But you're a rich man! You are holding two-hundred pounds in silver for goodness' sake."

"Not exactly," I tried to calculate. "Nearly half of that went for costs."

She waved off my argument. "Dining is just the beginning."

"What do you mean?"

"The brothels on Front Street. Ever partake?"

"Even if I had, I would not tell my sister."

Eyeing me, as if sizing me up, she said, "Probably not. Margaret's more your speed."

"I puke at the thought."

"Here's the point." She ignored my comment. "Nearly all the British soldiers are here without their wives or girlfriends. Madame Averell is a Patriot. She runs a fine brothel. You offer to pay for visits to Madame Averell's and you will not only make a lot of British friends, but you will be giving her and her girls the opportunity to pick up good intelligence."

I could see the wisdom of her suggestion. "You think it's safe? I don't want to be seen sending customers to a known traitor."

"It is safe. Believe me, I know what I'm talking about."

She gave me a few other ideas before saying, "You just get the information. Important stuff, unimportant stuff, whatever they talk to you about. You give to me, and I will write out the reports and take care getting them sent. And I will get it done without leaving this house. We'll be a team."

A team with my half-crazed sister. Good Lord!

★

The arrangement seemed to work well. I left the house by mid-morning to go to the London Coffee House or City Tavern or some other place where officers liked to gather. If I had no pre-arranged engagement, I sipped tea or ale and joined a game of cards or draughts and became friendly enough with one or two of the other players to buy dinner. All the while, I listened to conversations and picked up information about British troop movements and plans. I also listened closely for what the British knew about the Continental Army, which was just as important as the information I passed along concerning British activities.

In the afternoons I might drop in on Elizabeth, or attend a cockfight, or a game of cricket played by the soldiers, or watch a parade in honor of the Queen's birthday. Alternatively, I went down to the waterfront to check on incoming ships. I frequently spent the evenings at prayer services at Christ Church, where many soldiers attended. Often, I went to plays organized by officers, or a weekly ball at Smith's Tavern. I became sufficiently familiar to dozens of officers they had no inhibitions about freely discussing military matters in my presence.

At the end of each day, I gave Missy an accounting. She took copious notes and prepared a report. It was not clear to me how she got the reports out of the house and across the Schuylkill to Captain Johnson, but I suspected she made use of our neighbor, Mrs. Lisle. Missy also received information from Captain Johnson on occasion, and raised pointed questions she wanted me to investigate, or she suggested I subtly pass on information – presumably false – about Continental Army activities to my British contacts.

I never knew for certain how useful my efforts were, but I did hear occasionally from British sources about things I reported. One example was the winter hay storage dump, which was burned by the rebels. Or, an East Indiaman merchant ship, which was ambushed and sunk by a Continental privateer. Missy conveyed how pleased Captain Johnson was with the quality of information I provided. He constantly requested more.

Chapter Thirty Six

On a cold winter morning in late February while having breakfast, we heard a rap at the front door. I unlatched the door and saw a young man bundled up in a military-style brown cloak and knee-high boots. The sides of his three-cornered hat were pulled down over his head and ears and tied with a string around his chin. He wore wool stockings on his hands and an old drum hung from a shoulder strap at his side. It was open at the top and carried what appeared to be a few belongings and scraps of food.

I looked at him skeptically wondering why he was there, until he spoke.

"Uncle Daniel."

Nathan stood in front of me and I felt a burst of relief, like a dark cloud being lifted from the back of my mind. The darkness quickly returned as it dawned on me he stood alone without his father. I knew what that meant.

I called out for Missy, and the kids followed her into the parlor. She was overjoyed her only child had returned. Still, I could see as she hugged him how she, too, realized the significance of his returning alone.

We helped him take off with his outer clothes and took him into the kitchen to warm up in front of the kitchen hearth. Soon we got into the details of his journey.

"You made it to Saratoga and saw your father?" Missy asked without much enthusiasm.

"Yes, Mama," Nathan answered.

After pausing, Missy pressed forward. "Give us the news, Nathan. What happened?"

"He died three weeks ago. I helped bury him and have been trying to get back ever since. I got delayed by the weather."

Missy listened without breaking down. She had prepared herself and showed no surprise. Peter was never going to return.

"Did you mark the place?" she asked.

"Yes, Mama. They gave him a nice service, a row of soldiers with muskets pointing down. They placed him in front of the camp in a line with others. I nailed together a cross and wrote his name on it. We can replace it with a stone."

"Good," said Missy. "I want to visit. Did you bring back anything of his?"

"Just his musket and these." He took out Peter's glasses from a pocket in his blouse and handed them to Missy. "You would not have wanted his clothes. They were infected."

"Thank you, son. How bad did he suffer?"

"It was bad, Mama. I arrived just after he began the chills and vomiting. He got confused and didn't recognize me for a while. Then the pox started. They were in his mouth and then all over. He would become delirious and recover for a while. I thought he might pull through, but he went downhill. They put him in a section of tents like a leper colony, a mile from the main camp. The men there were just as bad off."

We sat for a few moments, contemplating the hopelessness of the situation. I broke the silence. "You sure you're all right, Nathan?"

"Yes, sir."

Missy wiped the moisture from her eyes and spoke firmly. "You should never have gone, leaving me here to worry for the last two and a half months."

I saw Jonathon about to speak up in defense of Nathan. I shook my head. He nodded and kept silent.

"I'm telling you, son," Missy continued, "if you know what is sacred, don't ever do something like that again." She hesitated. "Now that you're back and safe I'm sure you were a comfort to Peter and I'm glad you went."

It was Nathan who broke down not his mother. She reached out and hugged him and he buried his face in her bosom. "So am I," he said with tears rolling down his face. "No, I could never go through that again."

As we sat down to finish breakfast Annie asked, "Nathan, how did you know you would find Aunt Missy here?"

"I didn't know," said Nathan. "I went down to Chester County first. When I found no one, and the place was a mess, I figured she would probably be here."

"You walked here this morning?"

"I had no horse."

"Janie's about to have a baby," said Annie, smiling.

Nathan looked surprised and stared down at Janie's big belly.

I knew he was curious who the father was, but I left that for him to find out later. It was not a pleasant topic for me.

"Your mother is staying with us for a while," I said, "and we want you to stay here, too. Jonathon, can you clear a space for Nathan in the attic."

Jonathon looked up startled. "Papa, that's my room."

"Jonathon," I said, "That was not a question. You clear a space for your cousin in the attic. He will be staying with you until we decide otherwise."

Jonathon shot me an angry glare across the table.

"That's very nice of you," said Nathan. "I'll try not to interfere with Jonathon's things." Jonathon maintained his angry look. "How have things been going with the trading company since I left?"

"A lot has happened," I said. "Your grandfather, Uncle David and Aunt Molly all sailed for Quebec in December, and we shut down the shop. I had one good sale of flour inventory, but other than that we're pretty much out of business."

"You think you will be able to start back up again?"

The true answer, of course, was no. There were no prospects at this point. But Nathan unwittingly ventured into delicate territory. To allay any suspicion about what I was actually doing, Missy and I let it be known I was meeting daily with potential business contacts to try to resurrect sources of credit and supplies for the dry goods business.

Missy responded to Nathan. "Of course he does. He is already late for an appointment this morning, aren't you, Daniel? Why don't you go ahead, and I will have Alphonse drive Nathan over to our place to see what clothes they can salvage. Tomorrow we'll see if we can get Nathan into Jonathon's class at school."

"What is that you're carrying all your stuff in?" Jonathon asked as I got up to leave. Although upset about losing exclusive rights to the attic, his curiosity got the better of him. "It looks like a drum."

"It is a drum," Nathan said, holding it up for all to see.

"A real army drum?" asked Jonathon.

"Yes, but a drum head is missing. I thought maybe we could find some buckskin and repair it."

Jonathon looked enthralled at the prospect. He would get along just fine with Nathan.

★

I did have an appointment that morning, but my more important engagement was having after-supper drinks at the Coach and Horses Tavern in the evening. I was meeting with Lieutenant Masters, the aide to General Erskine. From the tavern we were going to a play at the Southwark Theater on South Street put on by British officers.

I met the lieutenant that evening and two colleagues with him. One was a major who served on General Erskine's staff, Major Warren. The other, to my astonishment, was Captain Cunningham, a friend of the major.

As we sat at a table, Lieutenant Masters explained we would be seeing Major Warren and Captain Cunningham in the play. "They both have lead roles. It's a play entitled *The Constant Couple.*"

I had just sipped rum from a cup. What he said did not register at first, but when it did, I choked and the rum poured out through my nose as I spat. "You mean they're actors?" I could not imagine Captain Cunningham play-acting any role, other than a cruel prison master.

Cunningham looked at me officiously. "Does my friend with a rebel sister find that surprising?"

I took my handkerchief to my face and stifled my desire to burst out laughing. With red cheeks I responded, "No, of course not. I had no idea a man of your . . . stature would find time for the arts. What's the play about?"

He gave me a frown, and I was not certain whether he was offended by my comment, but he seemed to be overcome by desire to talk about the play. "It's about four suitors who attempt to court Lady Lurewell who has to scheme to satisfy them all. It's really quite funny." He gave a little laugh.

"It sounds delightful," I said. "And what characters do you and Major Warren play?"

"I'm Lady Lurewell and he is Sir Harry, one of the suitors."

I nearly choked again, and the handkerchief came back to my face. Lieutenant Masters came to my rescue.

"Why is it, Captain, almost all of the plays have males in the roles of females?"

"There are several reasons." Cunningham looked happy to discuss. "Women can't act, is one. They have a hard enough time playing themselves, let alone someone else."

Major Warren nodded his agreement, and both giggled.

"Then again the army doesn't allow women and none of the local girls would be interested."

I had gained my composure sufficiently to ask with a straight face, "Do you enjoy playing a woman?"

"Oh, absolutely, and I am quite good at it I'm told. It's the little movements and mannerisms – sitting with your legs together and dainty steps – most men cannot master."

"I bet that's true," I said. This was killing me, but I had to think of something to say. "The plays have acquired a nice following. Which is surprising because the Continental Congress nearly banned all theatres as being scandalous and wasteful. I suspect the popularity is due to the fine acting." I threw in that last bit of flattery for Cunningham.

"That's part of it," he said with false modesty. "But it helps also that all the profits go to charities. That way the Quakers don't complain. Otherwise we would probably have to shut down. Those bastard Quakers!"

The remark gave me an opening to change the subject. "They are an odd lot, are they not? Along with a few Anglicans like my father, they dominated the Pennsylvania Assembly up until '76 and helped keep the colony from going rebel. But now that war has come and we could use them, most turn to their pacifism. They ought to fight for what they believe in."

"Some of them do," said Major Warren, "but when their church finds out about it, they get expelled."

"Have you recruited any?"

"Absolutely," said the major. "One out of every five or six recruits is or was a Quaker. In fact, we're organizing a raiding party . . . ." He paused and looked around the room. "I probably shouldn't speak of this, but we're among friends. We're getting a raiding party together in a Light Dragoon unit that is going out in a few days. They are mostly from Philadelphia and at least a quarter of them are Quaker lads."

"That's excellent, Major," I said. "Maybe they are coming to appreciate the benefits of being Royal subjects. What are you going after?"

"They'll be heading up to Middletown in Bucks County and then maybe on to Newtown. We want to show the colors and see if we can intercept some rebel supplies."

"Great idea. How many you going to send? An entire company?"

"Close, maybe fifty or sixty."

★

The play was bad. Actually, the dialogue was funny, and were it not for the poor acting, particularly of Lady Lurewell, I would have enjoyed it. But Captain Cunningham had no stage presence and I could barely understand his lines. I told him afterwards how much I enjoyed the performance.

Chapter Thirty Seven

Within a few days Janie had her baby. The birthing itself came off without a hitch. Missy took charge and ordered Jonathon and Nathan out of the house until it was over. Janie's friends from school had provided her with an ample supply of baby clothes, and we cleaned an old rocking cradle from the cellar. The baby boy would be staying with Janie in her and Annie's room for the time being. With our new arrivals of the baby and Nathan, the house started to feel crowded. At times, having so many around me felt warm and comforting, especially during the dark days of winter. At other times, I longed for solitude.

Solitude seemed especially inviting whenever I felt renewed resentment over the circumstances under which the baby boy came to us. I tried hard not to show it, but the thought kept nagging at me. My family was better than this. We deserved better for Janie than for her to get pregnant by an Indian lad we barely knew. And due to his taking advantage of my daughter, my family was now saddled with the consequences. Not to mention what our neighbors and friends must think of us. It was the kind of thing that, had it happened to anyone else, I would be thinking – with a virtuous little smile and a what-is-this-world-coming-to shake of the head – you poor bugger! Now I was the poor bugger and I could only imagine what the virtuous sons-of-bitches out there were thinking of me.

★

I arrived home late one afternoon in March of 1778 and Missy met me at the front door. She mysteriously guided me through the house, put on a cloak without saying a word and walked me out the back door to the stable, where Alphonse had Dobbin hitched to the chaise.

"What is this all about?" I asked once inside the stable.

She looked at me with alarm in her eyes. "Daniel, soldiers were here this afternoon. About a dozen of them with an officer. I think it was Cunningham, I wasn't sure. The sergeant came to the door and asked for you."

My head began to spin, trying to think what they may have wanted. "What did you tell them?"

"I told them you were not here and would not be home for a while. I think they know."

I did not have to ask what they knew. I shifted my thinking to what I might have said or done, or what hints I might inadvertently have dropped to lead them to think I was a spy. I came up blank. "What do you think I ought to do?"

"They said they would return tonight. The horse is hitched and ready to go. I put a bag of clothes and some food in the chaise. If you head out south and west you can cross at Gray's Ferry. I'll get a message to Captain Johnson to meet up with you along Darby Road."

While it was not a bad plan, I got to thinking. If the British really suspected me of spying, they would be watching. It may be they were expecting, or even hoping, I would try to escape. Finding me in a carriage with clothes and food and heading southwest would only confirm their suspicions. That alone could get me hanged. And even if I were not caught, what would become of the family of a suspected spy? Particularly Missy, whose reputation among the British was not so good?

I looked up and down the street to see if any soldiers might already be on the march. Although I saw none, I shook my head.

"Thanks, Sis, it would be too risky. If they already suspect I'm a spy, they would make sure I'd never get through. Let's take these things back inside. If they search the place, I don't want them to find clothes and food in the chaise."

She nodded reluctantly. "What do you want to do, then, when they show up here?"

"Let me think this through. If they arrest me, they'll take me to the Provost until they put me on trial."

"If you get a trial."

"True. If I get a trial. But you can't come visit me. Don't implicate yourself further. I still have about ninety pounds in silver left. Half of it is in the cellar and the other half is in the stable, buried next to Jonathon's ice pit. Use whatever you need, but don't waste it. When that's gone, we have nothing left. If you can get through to Captain Johnson, seek his advice. Apart from that?" I could not think of anything else. "We should have a nice supper. I'll say something to the kids. When the British arrive, you go upstairs and stay out of sight."

Looking at her somberly the Bible story of *The Last Supper* came to mind. I kept that thought to myself.

With Janie still upstairs with her baby, I broke the news when Annie, Jonathon and Nathan gathered in the kitchen.

"Listen carefully," I said, "because we have little time." All three looked at me curiously. Missy stood at the hearth and shook her head as I spoke. I knew she was blaming herself for my predicament. At the moment, I could do nothing to ease her guilt. "British soldiers were here this afternoon. We expect them to return tonight. They are going to arrest me for spying for the Americans."

Three pairs of eyes gawked at me.

"Papa, did you?" gasped Jonathon.

"Mama, did you know?" asked Nathan. Missy gave a non-committal look.

I had to keep them focused. "Hold on now," I said sternly, "that's not the issue before us. Once I'm in prison and you're asked questions by the British investigators, you are to tell only the truth. And the truth is, so far as you have ever known, I and my brother and father have been loyal to the British Crown. Correct? Anything untrue about that?"

"No, Papa," answered Annie.

"You will say you have never heard me criticize the British Crown. Right? As far as you know I have always opposed independence for the colonies because it would be bad for business. All right so far? I have always disagreed with your mother, Nathan, when it comes to independence for the colonies. And it would be beyond your imagination that I would ever spy on behalf of the Americans. You got it?"

All three nodded.

"Beyond your imagination." I repeated that line to make it stick.

They nodded again.

When we heard soldiers approaching, Nathan darted to the window.

"I can't tell how many," he said. "Maybe a dozen. They're carrying muskets and torches. Two officers on horseback."

Oh, my God, I thought. They came to arrest an important criminal. Their coming here was not going to be fun. I tried to act calm and grown up.

"All right, now," I said, "all of you upstairs. Don't come down until they are gone. They are going to arrest me and I will go peacefully. I don't want to give them any excuses to arrest someone else."

"But, Papa," said Jonathon, "you cannot . . . ."

"Jonathon, don't argue. Go upstairs and stay quiet."

Annie pulled him up the staircase as a thud on the front door shook the house. The soldiers meant business.

I paused, took a deep breath and shouted out, "Just a moment." I set my cup of ale down on a table and unlatched the door. I sensed the world as I knew it was about to end.

Three soldiers rushed in and secured the parlor with muskets and bayonets. Then Captain Cunningham stepped over the threshold followed by another soldier. From the torchlights I could tell other soldiers partially surrounded the house.

"So we meet again, Mr. Thompson," said the captain.

"Whatever your purpose, Captain," I said, "it need not have been preceded by armed soldiers rushing my home."

"I beg to differ, Mr. Thompson. We have come to arrest you for spying on behalf of the rebels and working against the interests of the Royal Army of His Majesty King George the Third."

"That's preposterous," I said indignantly. "How in the good Lord's name did you ever come to such charges?"

"You and that wench sister of yours."

He turned to his lead soldier and ordered, "Put the irons on him!"

Just as one of the soldiers approached me with iron cuffs, another officer entered the room from outside.

"Now just one moment, Captain." It was General Erskine's voice, speaking in a concerned and almost tired tone.

Captain Cunningham looked irritated. "General, we've discussed this. Thompson is the one."

"I know very well what we've discussed and who this is," answered the general with a glare. The captain backed off. "And I told you we were making no arrests until we had a chance to talk with the suspect."

"Yes, General."

"Go ahead and ask your questions."

Cunningham turned to me. "What have you to say for yourself?"

I stared at him blankly. "About what?"

"Captain," General Erskine broke in, "tell him why you think he's a spy and then let him respond. Come on, get on with it."

Cunningham spoke begrudgingly. "The raid by our Loyalist boys to Middletown. Major Warren told you about it the night of the play. What have you to say about it?"

"I've not heard the outcome but I trust it was successful."

"You know very well it was not," Cunningham growled. "A third of our men were killed in an ambush and half were captured. The rest barely escaped back to the City with their lives."

"I'm sorry to hear that."

"The rebels were lying in wait. They knew the exact plans of the raiding party, every step of the way."

"If you have evidence of treachery, then the perpetrator should be punished." I spoke indignantly, as a true Loyalist.

"I should say," answered Cunningham. "You are the only one outside a small group of officers and the raiding party itself who knew the plans. So how do you explain it?"

My mind swirled. Surely, I thought, they have more on me than what I just heard. Maybe they intercepted a note to Captain Johnson, or overheard me speak to someone, or captured an American officer who identified me. So far, it sounded pretty thin, and I waited for an incriminating brick to drop. But

Cunningham only stared at me, apparently expecting to hear a confession.

Eventually, I responded with genuine consternation. "I have no idea. Maybe Major Warren inadvertently spoke to someone about it."

"He did no such thing!" Cunningham looked insulted.

Accusing the major would get me nowhere. So I changed directions. "You are absolutely right, of course. What was I thinking. Might it be a member of the raiding party told a friend and that friend told someone else and the information got overheard by the wrong set of ears. The City is full of rebels. You know that. You can't always tell who they are."

"He has a point, Captain," said General Erskine. "I told you this was too far-fetched. Major Warren should never have talked about it in the first place. Even so, we have nothing on Mr. Thompson."

"He is the only source of a leak," Captain Cunningham insisted. "I know I'm right about this. Thompson heard our plans about the raid and told his sister, and she got the information to the American rebels. That's what happened, isn't it? Where's your sister?"

Erskine seemed to be on my side, and I gave him a glance. He shrugged.

"Is she here?" he asked politely. "Could we speak to her?"

"Of course," I nodded. "I will call her." I went to the staircase and shouted. "Missy, could you come down, please?"

We heard some shuffling around upstairs and a minute later Missy descended the stairs slowly. To my surprise, she carried Janie's baby. The soldiers, including Cunningham, looked on in wonder as she seated herself, baby in arms, on the parlor settee.

"She has a new baby," said General Erskine. She's not likely to have much interest in spying in that condition."

I almost corrected the misperception, but held my silence.

Cunningham looked skeptical. "You didn't act pregnant when you were a guest in the Provost," he said harshly.

"Oh really," shot back Missy, "and I suppose you know how a pregnant woman acts. Do you? Have you children?"

"I should say not," said Cunningham.

"I thought as much," Missy said with satisfaction. "I was not showing, if that's your point. My visit to your jail was three months ago. Pregnant woman don't advertise their condition to hostile strangers."

"It could have meant lenient treatment and better food," said Cunningham.

"Not likely from you, Captain." Missy's voice evidenced genuine bitterness. "Have I now satisfied your curiosity about my condition?" When no one answered, Missy took the silence as an affirmative response. "It's feeding time for the baby, and I should get back upstairs, unless you gentlemen care to watch a woman breast feed her child."

"No. of course not," General Erskine said, "you may go."

Missy was still making her way back to the top of the stairs as Captain Cunningham, staring at her back remarked, "Something is going on here. This isn't right. Do you not have a daughter?"

Before I could respond, Jonathon edged by Missy on the narrow stairway and bounded down with an excited look on his face. "Papa, is now the time? Can we find out now?"

I had no idea what he was talking about. I had instructed him to stay upstairs and be quiet. Not only was he disobeying my instruction but he acted strangely in the process.

"What?"

"You said we could ask. Nathan and me. You said we could ask, and the British officers are right here."

Nathan now emerged from the landing at the top of the stairs. "That's right, Uncle Daniel," he said. "About becoming drummer boys, with the Royal Army. You said you would be so proud if we did, to help our King and Country."

Oh, my God! I thought. What ruse were these two scamps trying to pull? I was taken completely back and had to say something.

"You boys . . ." I was about to tell them to go back upstairs, but they had taken a gamble. It was believable and I had little to lose at that point – ". . . are right. I did say I would be proud, but this is not a good time."

Both General Erskine and Captain Cunningham looked on with surprise edging to shock. Should I continue to pursue it? I would need to take it up a notch. "Unless the general would not mind my interrupting the other business we were discussing."

"Tell me what you wanted to ask, son?" General Erskine directed his question to Jonathon.

"Are you a real general?" Jonathon looked awestruck. I did not know if he was acting or not, but if he was, he was doing a great job.

The general looked pleased. "Yes. I am, my boy. My name is General Erskine, and I am happy to meet you." He gave a friendly bow.

Jonathon continued his awestruck look. "Is it all right, Papa, if I bow to the general of the whole British Army?"

"Of course, it is, son," said General Erskine. "Your papa doesn't mind. And I'm not the general of the whole army. Just a general. But an important one, I will grant you that. What is it you wanted to ask?"

"Oh, my goodness," said Jonathon, bowing to the waist. "We would like to become Royal drummer boys."

"Really," said the general, looking impressed.

"Uncle Daniel always said he wanted us to serve together," added Nathan. "We're almost the same age."

"You look like fine lads," said the general. "We might be able to arrange something."

I sensed the ruse was working a little too well. "Now, just a minute, boys," I interrupted. "I would be very proud if you served. But we should be honest with the general. What else did I tell you?" They stared at me blankly. "Come on now, what did I say?" More blank stares. "I told them I wanted them to become drummer boys, General, once they turned fifteen years old. And that will take another two years."

"Oh, that, yes," said Nathan as if remembering. He shot a quick frown at me. He already was fifteen. "But Uncle Daniel, the war will be over by then."

"I expect you're right, but the British Army will always have a place for drummers." I looked to Erskine, "Won't it, General?"

The general nodded. "Daniel is right. We don't take any boys at thirteen. But I can promise you this. If I am still stationed in the colonies two years from now, come to me. I will get you a nice assignment."

"Thank you, sir," the boys said almost simultaneously.

The general paused a moment as if deciding what to do next, and then spoke authoritatively. "Captain, we are done here. I am convinced your suspicions were ill founded."

He turned to me. "Mr. Thompson, I apologize for the intrusion. Please extend our courtesies and best wishes to your sister. We shall not be bothering you any further."

Once they left, I instructed Alphonse to make sure no one returned and called to Missy and the girls. They came down to the parlor with the two boys. I put my arms around them all, each of us laughing a little and crying a little. We all felt a tremendous release of tension.

"It was Nathan's idea," Jonathan spoke up, "us being drummer boys."

"You could not have handled it better if you had practiced for a year!" Then I asked, "Who had the idea about the baby?"

"Janie came up with it," Annie smiled.

"I really didn't want to," said Missy, "but they insisted."

"If it were not for you, all of you, I would be sitting in the Provost by now," I shook my head. "If not swinging from a rope."

"It was all my fault," said Missy. "You kids don't know this, but Daniel agreed to spy as part of the deal to get me out of prison last December."

"Is that true, Papa?" asked Jonathon.

"What Aunt Missy said is true as far as it goes," I explained. "I could have negotiated a different agreement with the Continental Army. I decided, though, the time had come for me to help out Pennsylvania in this war. Spying on the British was one way I could help."

"Papa," Janie asked, "what would we have done had you been hanged?"

I shrugged. "In many ways it was not fair to you kids for me not to tell you. But you knowing could have put you all at risk. So far as danger is concerned, though, what your Uncle Peter did took a lot more courage that I've shown up to now."

Missy shook her head and looked torn. "Danny, you are being very nice. But you don't have to say things like that. You put yourself in danger because of me. You're British at heart and always will be."

"Yes. I did it because of you. And I hope you feel guilty the rest of your life." I spoke harshly, and winked at Janie. Missy rolled her eyes. "But I also meant every word, particularly about Peter. He was a soldier to the end for what he believed in and would have been happy seeing us here today, celebrating our own little victory over the British."

"Papa," said Janie. "Oh, never mind." She looked upset.

I looked at her and asked, "What is it, honey? What's the matter?"

She sighed and started again timidly. "Papa, now don't get mad, but Lightfoot was a soldier, too. Maybe he didn't believe as much as Uncle Peter, but he was still a soldier."

Her words stunned, angered and saddened me, all at once. That wretched Indian boy! Still, she was right, of course. If now was a time for eulogizing Peter, it was also a time for eulogizing Lightfoot.

I walked over to the table where I had left my cup of ale, picked it up and raised a toast. "I could not agree with you more. So, here is to Peter and Lightfoot, two of Pennsylvania's bravest. May their memory never leave us."

Everyone raised an arm in salute and gave a cheer. "Here, here!"

Chapter Thirty Eight

Trial Proceedings

"I was wondering about that," said the Judge Advocate.

"About what?" Daniel asked, wincing.

"About what you would say about spending so much time with British officers, currying their favor. Your socializing with the enemy is well documented. You must have been aware of it?"

"Do I know people saw me spending time with British officers? I never really thought about it, but I'm not surprised. Why would they not? I made no secret of it. The only way I could acquire information was by being friends with them."

"Come now, Lieutenant, let's stop the fantasy. You were never a spy. You were a businessman. You have told us that all along. You scored a big sale with the British Army and now you were angling for more."

Daniel felt the anger building and responded with outrage. "Then why, sir, don't you ask Captain Johnson? If the theory behind this misadventure in justice is how I was betraying the American cause by trading with the enemy, then bring him here to testify. He will verify my every word. This stinking trial is a sham . . . an absolute disgrace! Have you even talked with Captain Johnson? Where is he anyway? I have repeatedly requested he be summoned."

The Judge Advocate hesitated before answering. "I thought you knew."

"Knew what?"

"He was killed in August when Camden, South Carolina fell to the British."

"You must be jesting."

"I don't jest about battlefield deaths of my fellow officers."

The news stunned Daniel. Not only had he lost a good friend, but now he realized the case against him may not be as weak as he had imagined.

"What about his commanding officer? Didn't he know the names of the spies feeding information to Captain Johnson?"

"He provided the names of spies he knew about, but yours never came up."

"I see." Daniel's heart sank.

"You have chosen your alibi well," the Judge Advocate said sarcastically.

"I never chose an alibi. Captain Johnson chose me. The spying mission was his idea, not mine. After it ended, he chose me as an officer in his company."

"Yes, we know. How did that come about?"

Chapter Thirty Nine

By early May of 1778 I had spent five weeks at Valley Forge and was on my way back for another stint. I could not believe it. Captain Johnson made it happen. After Missy wrote him about my near arrest, he promptly halted further spying activities. A few days later, I rode out to his camp.

He explained how my being suspected of spying increased the risks dramatically. While the information I provided had surpassed his expectations, he said I was free to return to civilian life.

"Still," he continued, "I would be honored if you would join my company as an officer."

I gave him a startled look.

He went on to say, "My company is one of eight that makes up the Seventh Pennsylvania Regiment. For the first couple years, every company had two lieutenants, but a lot of them are operating with just one. I'm down to none. I'm also short a fifer and ensign and my drummer is ill and may not make it. What I need most is a lieutenant. I've been waiting for the right man to come along."

"Why me?"

"Because you have proved to be reliable and resourceful. Add to that, you are educated and a gentleman."

"How do you know all that?"

"I've done some checking." He smiled.

"Those characteristics qualify me to be a lieutenant in the Continental Army?"

"Those and the fact you're a pretty good shot with a musket. I found that out, too. I need a good musket man to train my boys."

"With everything you learned, you should have become the spy."

"I'd have made a good one."

"Can't you get what you need from your other recruits?"

"I get dedication from my other recruits. They are mostly back country lads. Plus some bonded men who are stand-ins for their contract holders, a few unemployed waterfront workers, half a dozen foreign-speaking immigrants, and a couple of guys who joined up instead of going to jail. Except for the bonded men and thieves, most joined because of the enlistment bounty. That and the promise of regular meals. Which is a promise more often broken than kept."

"You make them sound like they're low life, or worse," I said.

"They are, or at least they would be if they were anyplace else. Here they are standard issue. They make up the core of the army. Who else would join at what they are paid, and defend the country under the conditions they live?"

"If that's true, I'm surprised the army has survived."

"Don't misunderstand me," he said. "Their dedication is worth a lot. And I love them all. They are my boys. Like sons, they are good fighters and they take orders well. All I'm saying is they aren't leadership material. At least not yet. I am working on some of them."

"What about Thomas Paine and his ilk and all the impassioned calls for independence that got us into this war in the first place? Where are they now?"

"A lot of them ran out of steam. That's not to say they don't still favor independence. They do. Talking and fighting, though, are two different things. If we had known in '75 the direction this war would take three years later? I'm not sure we would have chosen the same path. Yet here we are."

I sat back to think things through. "I've been a good British citizen my entire life. What makes you think I would want to join an army fighting the British?"

"To be truthful, you have not been a good British citizen your entire life. For the last few months you have been spying for the Americans."

"I did it to help my sister."

"True, you had a family motivation. I don't hold it against you. So far as being good British citizens is concerned, all of us have been, at least for most our lives. That includes General Washington. He fought alongside the British against the French back in the '50s. But for some of us sooner, some later, we came to realize we would be better off running this colony, or this group of colonies, on our own. Different people had different reasons. Family, business, political, idealism and whatever. Lots of reasons and lots of combinations of reasons. While you wanted to help your sister, my guess is that was not the only reason you agreed to spy."

I did not let on he was right. "So, you have me all figured out."

"I don't have much of anything figured out. I'm only trying to find a good lieutenant for my company."

"You have no one in the unit already who is in line to be moved up?" I asked.

"I have one sergeant and two corporals. I'm thinking about moving both corporals up to sergeant so I will have three, and promoting three privates to corporal. But they aren't officer material. I need someone who can help think strategy. And someone they will look up to."

"I've never been a soldier before."

"That's what training is for."

"Here at this camp?"

"No. We're being called back to Valley Forge. A militia unit will replace us here."

"I have my family to think about."

"What about that sister of yours you sprung from prison. She could run things for a while, and you could send her your army pay. It's not much, but it will keep the household going."

"If the pay is in Continentals, it's not going to keep the household going very long."

"You're probably right, at least while the Brits are in town. I'm hoping you still have some of the profits left from your flour sale."

"You think they are leaving the City anytime soon?"

"The most I've heard from General Washington's staff is the day is not far off, but no one knows for sure. You're aware of the treaty we've signed with France?"

"I heard something was in the works."

"It was signed in early February. It has yet to be ratified by Congress, but once it is, France and Britain are going to be in an all-out war. Then the question becomes whether the British can hold onto Philadelphia and New York and their islands in the West Indies. Our people don't think so. Something has got to give and it may be Philadelphia."

"Washington doesn't have any plans to attack Philadelphia, does he?"

"Not that I'm aware of. The Brits built some strong defenses around the City and a lot of Patriots still live there."

"How long would I have to commit for?"

"Ah, finally." The captain sighed with relief. "Now, we're getting somewhere. Down to the details. Naturally, I would like to see you stay for the duration of the war. As a practical matter, though, commissioned officers can leave pretty much any time. All they have to do is resign their commission. The longer you are in the more retirement pay you would receive, but the whole question of retirement pay is up for grabs right now. The real answer is: for as long as you can take."

I still had doubts about the prospect of joining Captain Johnson's company when I arrived home that night. I raised the subject around the supper table. To my surprise, Missy did not press me on it. She still had guilt feelings about my becoming a spy. It was actually something Jonathon said that pushed me over the edge.

"You have already chosen sides, right, Papa?"

"That's true, son."

"I don't see what's holding you back then. The trading company is not doing business now. Until the British leave, what else would you do?"

What was holding me back? I tried to put my finger on it and concluded more than anything else, I was simply reluctant to leave my family.

"I wish it was that easy, son. This is wartime. Unexpected things happen. You saw that the other night. They came to arrest me. Your Aunt Missy was arrested and held in prison. Who knows what might happen next."

"We'll be fine, Papa. Nathan and I can take care of Aunt Missy and the girls. You can concentrate on getting the war over with. We all think you made the right choice."

In the end, permission from my fourteen-year-old kid sent me off to war.

★

I furnished my own uniform. The captain said I would not need it for everyday use, since the dress code in camp was lax. But I should have one for special occasions and for when we went on the march. Waiting for it to arrive through army channels could take months. Even then, it was not likely to fit.

I talked over my plans with Elizabeth. She could hardly believe what I was about to do.

"The Continental Army? And an officer no less! Not been more than a couple of months ago you were a staunch Loyalist. What happened?"

"I don't know," I said. "Maybe, I just saw the light. Or, the darkness, I'm not sure. Don't try to talk me out of it, because you may be successful. Still, if I am going to do this, I will need a uniform. You think you can help?"

"I will make you the best darned uniform in the whole darned army."

And she did. Elizabeth acknowledged sewing uniforms for a number of local boys. Congress had chosen brown as the official army color in 1775, but by 1778 blue began to edge out brown based in part on General Washington's preference for Virginia's pre-war colors. Shipments of blue coats from France also contributed to the choice. Hence, Elizabeth maintained a supply of blue material on hand. Within a matter of hours my uniform took shape. I also bought new black boots and a dark-blue three-cornered felt hat.

The night before I left for Valley Forge I had supper with Elizabeth and her mother. After eating, we played a few hands of whist. They played with a vengeance and trounced me. When we ended the game, I enticed Elizabeth out the front door to say goodbye in private. She responded passionately when I kissed her lips, locking her arms around my neck.

"What am I going to do without you, Daniel? Seeing you is the only thing I look forward to anymore."

"Did it take my joining the army to make you think you could miss me?"

"That's how it is sometimes with me," she said. "I have to lose something before realizing how important it is to me."

"I'll be back for a few visits before we move out of camp. At least that's my plan. You'll be waiting with more warm kisses?"

"I promise. And something else, too."

"What's that?"

"We can have that discussion."

"Discussion?"

"You know, the subject you keep raising . . . our future plans."

A jolt of exhilaration shot through me. "You would talk about the future with me?"

"Yes, my love. Our future . . . together. Here, take this." She handed me the deck of cards. "You may need it to keep occupied. Think of me whenever you play. And one last thing." She spoke gravely. "Whatever you do, bring it back." I looked at her sideways, and she continued. "It's the only deck we have."

At first I thought she was serious. Then she punched me in the arm, and I could not stop laughing.

Chapter Forty

I had never before seen a large army encampment. Valley Forge in the spring of 1778 was an eye-opening experience.

A good twenty-five miles northwest of Philadelphia, the location allowed Washington to keep the British out of the interior of Pennsylvania, including the iron works at Reading. And yet, it was far enough away from Philadelphia to avoid any surprise attacks. Outposts secured every approach within two miles. Sentinels covered the outposts at a hundred yards and pickets stood ready nearer the encampment. Patrols and scouting parties moved between outposts and conducted surveillance beyond their perimeter both day and night. They all communicated with each other through ritualistic maneuvers, passwords and commands.

The Valley Creek marked the western boundary of the camp, and it flowed into the Schuylkill River that formed the northern border. These two streams of water, combined with two hills on the perimeters, curiously named Mount Misery and Mount Joy, formed easy defenses. Strategically dug trenches, stockades, long lines of double-angled pikes, and elevated redoubts provided additional security.

On the interior, the army organized itself by brigade. General Wayne's Brigade occupied an area along the southern defense line and was flanked by brigades led by General Charles Scott of Virginia and General Enoch Poor of Massachusetts. Five more brigades spread out along the south eastern line, which slanted northward toward the Schuylkill. General Knox's artillery park was located along the inner defense line to the west. In the northwest corner General Washington made his headquarters. Open space in the north central part of the camp served as the general parade and training ground. With soldiers in camp from all but two colonies, the army in residence was truly *Continental.*

The soldiers slept in six-foot square canvas tents and small log huts that could hold four or five. Parallel rows of huts and tents crammed the sunny sides of the hills inside the camp, and formed avenues.

The winter that year was not harsh, but no form of shelter afforded much protection against stiff winds, near-freezing temperatures and alternately wet and frozen ground cover. As a consequence, disease sometimes ran rampant. Yet care for the sick did not seem to be a priority, and the medical staff frequently ran short of drugs. Every brigade had its own surgeon, but he seemed to be trained mainly in not showing emotion when sawing off limbs. Not surprisingly, the fighting strength of every unit suffered due to sickness. Captain Johnson's company, for example, had forty to fifty men assigned, but those fit for duty never exceeded thirty-five until we abandoned camp in June.

The camp's population fluctuated between twelve and twenty thousand, so thousands of pounds of food rolled in by wagon daily. I did not arrive until the end of March, but I heard about the food deprivations occurring before then. The men had been served hard bread and salt pork on good days, and perhaps a few potatoes. On other days they made do with salted herrings in such a ripened condition they had to be spooned from barrels in clumps. Instead of bread, fire cake frequently sufficed, consisting of flour and water cooked on a stick. Coffee, tea and sugar never existed. If someone were lucky enough to acquire a jug of whisky, it quickly passed from mouth to mouth until empty.

Even after I arrived, though the worst of the shortages had ended, food was never plentiful. For our main meal, dinner, served at midday, we typically ate in groups of twelve. The man designated cook would be responsible for securing whatever food he could from the commissary station. Every soldier carried his own tin plate, cup and cooking utensils. If flour was available, our company could use a portable oven for baking bread, but only twice a week, for the oven served the entire regiment.

"You think you can help out?" Captain Johnson asked me after being in camp a few days.

"What do you mean?"

"Things are better than they were, but it would still be nice if we could get our hands on a few extra barrels of flour. Just for our company, I mean."

I looked at him askance. "A few extra barrels? You already got twelve out of me. Don't you think that was enough?"

"I ended up sharing some of them with other companies. They were even more desperate than we were. So we're short again."

"Is that one of the responsibilities of the lieutenant, coming up with flour for the company?"

"No, it's not. And I wouldn't blame you if you said no. I could only pay you in Continentals, and we both know what they are worth. But if your mill could donate a barrel now and then . . . hmm? Let me see. I could make a horse available to you on the weekends . . . so long as you agreed to be back in camp by Sunday night."

I had to hand it to Captain Johnson. He knew how to strike a bargain.

★

The captain initially assigned me to oversee our company's musket training. Enlisting the help of our three sergeants, I began working out some musket exercises and drills. Before actually commencing, however, he informed me of a change in plans. We were sitting inside the tent the captain used as company headquarters, sharing a boiled turnip for breakfast.

"What kind of change?" I asked.

"General Washington has put a Prussian officer in charge of training the troops. Colonel Geier tells me the guy cann't even speak English."

"I wish him good luck," I said. "It sounds like a non-starter. I say we go forward with our own company training, as planned."

"Here's the problem. The Prussian apparently came up with this idea for a model company of a hundred-twenty men. The company will serve as an adjunct to General Washington's guard for the time being. But the idea is Von Steuben – that's the Prussian – will train the model company. Then the men in the company will spread out around the camp and train everyone else."

I shrugged. "The concept sounds good. I don't understand why Washington would want a Prussian to do it. But what does that have to do with our company training?"

"Our regiment was ordered to contribute two men to the model company, and Colonel Geier wants you."

"What? I speak no German, and I don't know sign language. And besides I have my musket drills all set to go. I'm looking forward to it. Could we find someone else?"

"If it were up to me, I would," said the captain. "I just got my new lieutenant on board, and now I'm going to lose him for a few weeks. And I have no one to take charge of the musket drills."

"Could we go talk to Colonel Geier. He seems like a reasonable fellow."

"He is, but it's not that easy. He picked you because you're new to the army and won't have any bad habits. So, you can see it was not a random choice." I gave him a disappointed look. "Sorry, I can't do anything about it. If I could, I would. Now, we're left without anyone to oversee our company training. I am open for suggestions."

"Why so much training all of a sudden?" I asked in frustration. "We have a Prussian who is apparently going to, what, train the entire army? And then we have more training going on at the company level. And that's in addition to our routine regimental and brigade drills. Is it possible we're overdoing it? This war has been going on for nearly three years now. The army should have had it all figured out by now."

"You have to understand. So far, we've been surviving. That comes first. And at the moment, we have survival under control. We have a camp that's pretty well built out. The British are entrenched in Philadelphia and not going anywhere soon. And this is the first opportunity in a long time for training on a large scale. We need to make the most of it."

I sighed, trying to think of something helpful. "What you're telling me is while I'm away taking orders from a German-speaking Prussian, we need a musket man."

"Yes."

"I know a good musket man," I said absent mindedly. "Best I have ever seen. He lives not far from here."

"Can he get off four rounds per minute?"

"I have seen him do five."

"Five?" The captain looked up. "A military man?"

"Not hardly."

"He's the one we need. Can we get him?"

"I have a problem with that."

"What?"

"He's my mill manager," I said.

"So, what's the problem?"

"Who's going to run my mill if he comes here for training?"

"Come on, Daniel, you're always thinking about yourself," he said half facetiously. "Think about your captain and your company. These are your men now, not just mine. We need to put them first."

I was not about to be sucked in. "Whosever men they are, the mill needs a manager. Willie can't go anywhere without a replacement."

"It would only be for a few weeks. How about that sister of yours? She seems capable."

"'That sister of yours' you refer to knows nothing about milling. Moreover, she is strong willed. I can't predict what she would be willing to do."

"She's a Patriot, isn't she?"

"To a fault."

"Maybe, I should go meet her then."

"You have a way with strong-willed, unpredictable women?"

"I've been known to charm a few. Besides, she sounds like a manager type, and that's what you need. You can't have much going on at the mill this time of year anyway. Winter wheat won't be up for a few weeks. She just needs to keep an eye on the place for a while."

"That part is true."

"Well then, we ought to be able to work something out. I tell you what. We'll make arrangements for your sister to meet us at the mill. I can check out your mill manager and talk with your sister at the same time. And we can bring back a barrel of flour to boot. What do you say?"

"You really have it all figured out this time, don't you."

"I'm desperate, Lieutenant."

★

The captain was pushy, but in a friendly way. What made me go along with the idea more than anything, was to see what Missy would say. I knew she had no interest in the mill, especially in cold weather, but here was a captain in the Continental Army who would be making the request. I anticipated an interesting experience.

And it was. The captain sent the necessary communications and within a few days the two of us, a sergeant and three soldiers galloped our way to the mill by horseback. We towed along an extra horse for Willie to ride back, just in case our mission turned out to be successful.

We arrived near dinner time and Missy, Jonathon and Alphonse met us at the front door of the stone cottage. Once inside, Mary Jane served up big bowls of thick mutton stew. Compared with the meager faire at Valley Forge, it tasted wonderful. After eating, the sergeant and his three men fanned out on horseback to provide a lookout for British patrols.

While I had only been in camp ten days, Jonathon had a dozen questions for me. In between, I tried to get a read on mill operations from Willie. Captain Johnson kept Missy busy with inquiries about conditions in the City.

Eventually, however, we got to the purpose of our visit.

"Willie," I said, "I told Captain Johnson how well you can handle a musket. He has some questions for you."

"Yes, sir, what can I do for you?"

"How did you get so good with the musket?" asked the captain.

"Master Marvin taught me," said Willie. "Me and Mary Jane were his slaves. But they were good owners. He taught me how to shoot so I could hunt for him. He also taught me the mill business. And his missus taught Mary Jane to read and do bookwork. When he died, the missus freed us. Mr. Thompson hired us to stay on and run the mill. We're indebted for such good fortune."

"That's an amazing story," the captain said with admiration. "I would never have believed it possible."

"It's all true," I said, "and Willie and his wife have kept this place going for the last year. Despite the war. That's the amazing part."

"General Washington and the army are encamped at Valley Forge for the winter," said the captain. "You probably know that, right?"

"Everyone around here knows that." Willie nodded.

"We're looking for someone who is good with the musket to help train our men. Lieutenant Thompson here recommended you. What would you say about coming over to the Forge to teach some of those soldiers what you know?"

Willie shot a surprised look at Mary Jane. "What does Mr. Thompson say about me leaving here?"

"It's all right with Mr. Thompson if it's all right with you. It would only be for a few weeks."

"We would need to find someone to run the mill." Willie said.

"We'll work on that next," said the captain.

Willie looked again at Mary Jane. "I would be worried about my missus. Here by herself . . . being a colored lady and all."

"She won't be alone," assured the captain, turning to Missy.

She returned a suspicious look at the captain. "What do the two of you think you're up to, anyway?"

"We were wondering if maybe you . . . ." The captain paused.

"Maybe I what?" asked Missy. She was scowling.

"Daniel," said the captain, "you know the details better. Perhaps you should explain."

"Missy," I said, "we need someone to help out with the mill, while Willie is away. You are a take-charge kind of person and, like the captain said, it would only be for a few weeks."

"Is that what you told him . . . I am a take-charge person?"

"I actually told him you are strong-willed and unpredictable. But you also are a natural manager. We would not expect you to operate the mill. Maybe you could try to find a part-time operator. I know of a couple of guys over in Chester who would be great on a temporary basis, if they're available. Apart from that I would hope you could make sure someone is always here to support Mary Jane and help see that things run smoothly."

"Strong-willed and unpredictable?" Missy repeated. "That's what you think of me?"

"Now, Missy, I meant it in a positive way."

She glared at me. "You presumptuous, pig-headed little fart!"

The captain let out an audible gasp. A moment of dead silence followed.

And then . . . .

Missy gave a broad smile and said, "Of course, I'll help out at the mill. You know that, Danny. I owe you big time. And I would do anything for the Patriot cause."

Everyone sighed, sat back, and laughed. None louder than the captain.

"I bet I almost gave the captain a heart attack."

"You sure did," said the captain.

"Come here, Captain. I owe you a big hug. Take care of my little brother, will you? He is a pain in the ass most of the time, but I love him more than anything."

"I will do my level best."

We made arrangements for Missy to spend a few days a week at the mill. Alphonse would return her to the City and then back again. In the meantime she would interview for a part-time manager. Our business was resolved.

We sat back to enjoy the warmth and comfort of the stone house before making the return ride to camp.

Captain Johnson spotted Jonathon's violin in a corner and asked, "Who plays the fiddle?"

"I do, sir. Well, a little . . . I've been taking lessons."

"How about playing something for us?"

"I'm not that good. Papa says I sound like an old woman with a bad cold."

"What does he know about music? I would love to hear you. Do you know *The Blue Bell of Scotland*?"

"I know the song."

"Do you need the music?"

"Not for that simple song.

"I'm surprised at you, Captain," I said. "That's a Tory song about a young man who goes to fight for the king."

"We won't worry about the words. It's a nice old tune."

Jonathon picked up his violin and bow and began playing. He played quite well without the music, a few wrong notes, but not at all sounding like an old woman. After he played it through once, the captain asked him to play it again, hummed along, and broke into song on the last couple strains, in a gruff, raspy voice:

He's gone wi' streaming banners where noble deeds are done,

And it's oh, in my heart I wish him safe at home.

We all applauded when he finished.

"Are you Scottish?" asked Missy.

"I have a little Scottish blood," said the captain. He looked at Jonathon with renewed interest. "By the way, do you play anything else, like the fife?"

"Sure, I can play the fife. It has the same fingering as the flute."

"We could use . . . ."

"Please," I interrupted, "don't even think about it."

Jonathon caught on immediately. "Papa, I could play the fife in the army, and Nathan could play drum."

"It's out of the question." I gave the captain a sharp look.

He nodded. "The lieutenant is right. I should never have brought it up. That's a family matter and completely outside of my authority." He nonetheless looked pleased with himself, having planted a seed.

He stood up and offered thanks for the hospitality. After giving Willie time to gather up some belongings, we said our goodbyes and took off for Valley Forge, a barrel of flour strapped to one of the horses.

★

A short while into the ride, I trotted up next to the captain. "I thought you were going to ask Missy about running the mill," I said, "not me."

"You being her brother and all, I figured she would want to hear it from you."

"Great woman tamer you are." He looked at me sheepishly.

"Your sister has a nice sense of humor. She really had me going."

I nodded. "I also forgot to tell you Willie is a Negro. I hope you don't mind."

"It did take me by surprise, but it's better this way. He'll give our boys some inspiration."

Chapter Forty One

We arrived back at camp and got Willie situated into a log hut. By morning he was standing in front of our entire company beginning loading and firing drills. I had gone over with him the kind of drills I had in mind, but Willie had his own ideas. He took the loading sequence a step at a time, giving tips on the minutest of details and then combining two or three steps at a time while gradually increasing the speed. Within ten days every man had cut in half his loading time. After another week working on marksmanship and musket care, Captain Johnson asked him to start with another company in our regiment.

In the meantime, I started my own training with *the Baron*. I did not know if he was a real Baron, but the nickname we used for General Friedrich Wilhelm Ludolf Gerhard August Von Steuben, stuck.

The story I heard was he had served on the general staff in the Prussian Army, but was forced into retirement by army politics. He then offered his services to Benjamin Franklin in Paris, sailed to America with a letter of commendation, and presented himself at Valley Forge in February of 1778. His reputation with one of Europe's great armies sufficed to persuade General Washington to assign him responsibility for disciplining the sorely lacking Continental Army.

When a hundred twenty of us forming the model company showed up on the parade grounds on an early morning in late March, I was convinced the language barrier alone doomed the exercise in international army collaboration. The Baron would give orders in German to a German-speaking aide, who would translate them to a French-speaking aide, who would translate them to our company in English. The process reversed itself when a member of the company had a question or needed to tell something to the Baron. As cumbersome as it seemed at first, the communications soon progressed back and forth to what seemed an almost natural pace.

He began with a new approach to moving troops into firing lines on the battlefield. The traditional British method involved forward movement from the staging areas in single file. Von Steuben had us move forward in a column four abreast. This change allowed for more rapid deployment into firing lines and more flexibility overall. He also increased the tempo of movement, maintained by drummers, from sixty to seventy-five steps per minute, and he set double time at a hundred-twenty steps per minute. Under varying hypothetical battlefield conditions, he spent hours drilling our model company on basic column and line movements.

After a few days, I reported our progress to Captain Johnson.

"This man's perfection is amazing," I said. "One time we were marching from a column into a line, and I was supposed to turn right instead of left and messed up. He calls everyone to a halt, comes over in front of me while everyone watched. He gave me an earful in German. The German-French guy translates it to the French-English guy, and the French-English guy translates it to me."

"What did he say?" asked the captain.

"He said something like, 'You fucking son of a bitch asshole moron, don't you know your God-damn right from your God-damn left?' I have to admit, I was somewhat taken aback."

"At least the message came through clearly," said the captain laughing.

"I thought it did too, but apparently it didn't come through clear enough for the Baron. He decided it was not translated quite right. So he started over and gave me another earful. It sounded exactly the same to me. And when I hear it from the French-English guy, it comes across as 'You *mother fucking* son of a bitch asshole moron! Don't you know your *bloody* God-damn right from your *bloody* God-damn left?' This guy wanted his curses translated properly."

The captain let out a guffaw. "Good for him! You probably deserved it."

"I did, but that's beside the point. We're getting men from all over the camp coming to watch just so they can hear the Baron curse in German. They're taking lessons in cursing."

Bayonet training became another focus. Fighting with bayonets was warfare at its ugliest. The British had used it effectively for stealth assaults on a number of occasions. The Americans, on the other hand, at least up until then, relied on their ammunition for battle and used their bayonets for roasting squirrel. Von Steuben changed the army's thinking on bayonets. The barrel of a musket now became a spear and the butt became a club to be used when the enemy got close up, or when re-loading became impractical, or when silence and surprise were necessary. Within a few short days thrust, slash and butt movements of the musket became second nature to us.

Von Steuben did not limit his attention to the battlefield. He implemented basic sanitation techniques for the encampment. He issued orders forbidding soldiers from relieving themselves except in latrines, and placing latrines well away from cooking areas. He ordered the campgrounds to be kept clear of animal kill and other debris. He also insisted every soldier bathe once a week, and he saw to it that soap was distributed widely.

"I wonder if all these changes will go over that well?" Captain Johnson said after we finished our discussion of the Baron's profanity innovations. "Especially the one about only using latrines."

"What would be wrong with that one? It makes a lot of sense."

"No matter. We're not over at Aunt Suzy's fancy four-bedroom house with the big front lawn. This is an army camp. A soldier shouldn't have to walk a quarter mile to take a crap. It's one of our little luxuries of living outdoors."

"Oh, come now, Captain. It's not a quarter mile to the latrine. And it's worth it to not tread on top of some man's fresh pile of fertilizer."

"I'm telling you, it's not going to go over well with the men. Sergeant!" He summoned Sergeant Wright into the tent.

"Yes, sir," said our company's senior sergeant.

"What do you think of the new policy of having to make a trip to the latrine every time you want to take a crap or a piss?"

"May I speak freely, sir?"

"Of course, I want your honest answer."

The sergeant spoke with indignation. "I think it's full of shit, sir!"

"Sergeant," I said, "it'll keep the place a lot cleaner. Isn't that a good thing?"

"A soldier has a God-given right to take a shit wherever he damn well pleases. Sir!"

"See what I mean?" Captain Johnson smiled.

Despite Sergeant Wright's attitude, acceptance overall was forthcoming, and even I noticed an improvement in attitude and discipline. Of course, some of those improvements may have been due to the coming of spring, which can have a positive effect on anyone's outlook.

By the middle of May, the growing confidence of the army mixed with feelings of restlessness and unease. We all knew our time in camp was growing short. The captain and I looked forward to forming up and marching out to face the British. Still, we felt apprehensive about the prospects. We learned in late March General Howe had been replaced as top British commander by Sir Henry Clinton. Then in early May, Washington received news Congress had ratified two Franco-American treaties. He declared a holiday for the entire camp.

With French assistance now out in the open and more on its way, General Washington waited to see what Clinton's next move would be. Some Americans were wary of French involvement, fearing France could replace the British as colonialists in North America. The prevailing attitude at the moment, however, was the French put the Continental Army on par with the British, and maybe even gave us the opportunity to go on the offensive.

★

This turned out to be a good time for a visit home, and I got leave from Captain Johnson for use of a borrowed horse. Missy had sent me a note about a week before saying Janie was having her baby baptized at Christ Church. Missy proposed meeting me at the mill, and we would cross through the American and British lines together in the unassuming chaise.

On reaching the City, we noticed an unusual movement of carriages and people toward the waterfront. Missy explained a group of British field officers were putting on a fete in honor of the departure of General Howe at the mansion of a wealthy Quaker merchant. She had given permission to Nathan and Jonathon to help out with the preparations in a nearby walnut grove. When I questioned her about having our sons assist with a British social event, she said she was only being practical.

"All the boys in the neighborhood are helping," she said. "The British Army pays in silver. I see no harm in it."

How could I argue with that? Especially coming from a staunch Patriot.

We stopped at home for supper and then walked with the girls and baby to the church for the baptismal service. I had thought about stopping to see Elizabeth first, but decided to surprise her with a visit the following day. Trying hard not to alienate Janie, I wanted the baptism behind me. The stain on our family reputation continued to oppress me.

Janie and Annie had invited family and church friends for the service, including Margaret, to my chagrin. With four babies being baptized that evening, the Bible study room was nearly full. Reverend White officiated and went through the standard ceremonial steps. He announced the first parents' names. They stepped forward, a parent handed him the baby boy or girl, and he held the child over his head for everyone to see. The gesture gave rise to lots of "Ahs" and "Oos." On que, an altar boy brought over a bowl of water, the pastor sprinkled a little on the baby's head, and he said a prayer about how Christ Himself had once been a baby. Finally, the pastor asked for those family members and friends who would be helping to raise and guide the baby through life, to rise. A small group of audience members stood up, and he gave a further blessing before moving on to the next baby.

Janie's was the last baby to be baptized. When Reverend White called her name, she alone stepped forward with the baby.

Except for the names, the short ceremony replicated the prior three. When the pastor asked family members and friends to rise, a dozen of us stood for the final prayer.

From the back of the room, I heard shuffling and wooden chairs scrape along the floor. I turned, and to my amazement saw a group of ten or fifteen Indians also standing. They included men, women and children, all looking very much out of place. They mostly wore European-style clothes, but some had on buckskin leggings or dresses, headbands, beads around their necks, and feathers in their hair. Reverend White paused as parishioners turned to look.

I whispered to Missy, "What's with the Indians?"

"Janie invited Lightfoot's people."

I nodded, but then beheld an even greater surprise. Amongst the Indians stood Elizabeth. She looked ravishing as ever, and I could not stop staring at her. Nor could I figure out why she was here.

As soon as the service ended and as the families of the baptized babies greeted each other and offered congratulations, I went back to find out. As I approached, Elizabeth looked as surprised to see me as I was to see her.

"What are you doing here?" I asked, putting my arms around her.

"I might ask you the same thing," she said, laughing. "I thought you were off at training camp."

"I was, but I came home for my grandson's baptism. I was going to surprise you tomorrow. And you?"

She hesitated. "I received word through the tribal community a Lenape baby was being baptized. I came to show my support."

I had no choice but to tell her. "The Lenape baby . . . he's my grandson."

She pulled away from me. "Your grandson? Why didn't you tell me?"

"Because quite frankly I feel embarrassed by the whole situation." Irritation inflected my voice. "My daughter, the mother of an Indian boy." I shook my head. "Nothing much more shameful I can imagine."

Up to that point our conversation took place at the side of the room more or less in private. But now, people were turning and listening.

"So you hid it from me?" she asked.

Her tone was accusatory, and I did not like it. "I didn't hide it. I thought you would have no interest."

"Why not, it's a *part of you*." She remembered well – my own words coming back at me.

"Yes, but a part I didn't want to talk about. And why would you come here to show your support, anyway? For a Lenape boy, for goodness' sake. What interest could you possibly have?"

"I was adopted, Daniel."

"Yes, I know. Your mother told me."

"My parents were killed when I was ten-years-old."

"I'm sorry to hear that. But what does that have to do with the Lenape?"

"My parents were Lenape, Daniel. I am Lenape. I am Indian."

I stared at her, stunned. "You never . . . Why didn't . . ." I could not look at her any longer and dropped my gaze. The woman I wanted to marry. ". . . you tell me?"

"Tell you?"

I glanced up and saw mist in her eyes, turning to tears. A thought raced through my mind. The color of her face was lighter than most of the Indians in the room, but with a little sun and braided hair, she easily could pass for Indian. I was shocked, angered, embarrassed, almost to the point of paralysis. I had never noticed before.

"Tell you?" she repeated. "Why do you think, Daniel?"

I looked away again. I knew exactly why. She thought I would leave her. And I would have, too. Would I? God damn, was I that kind of person?

"After what you said about your own daughter and her son, your *shameful* grandson, you ask me why I didn't tell you?"

Yes, after what I had just said. I insulted this near-perfect woman who, until a minute ago, I worshipped. Did I still? Did her birth matter that much? I was in a daze. My confidence evaporated. My mind black. A lot of people were around us now. I could hear them talking, pointing.

"Papa," someone said. I could not think.

"Now that we are confessing all our secrets, Daniel, let me tell you another one." Elizabeth began to sob. "In front of all your friends and family so everyone knows. I do not want any more secrets."

Two Indian braves in the group came over and tried to walk her away. She resisted, holding her ground. She had something to say. Whatever it was, I knew for certain I did not want to hear it.

"Please don't. You have said enough. I'm sorry."

"No. You listen good, Daniel. The two British soldiers who murdered my parents made me watch them do it. And then they raped me, one at a time, and left me for dead. I was ten years old and they raped me." She cried uncontrollably.

"Papa." It was Jonathon.

"Elizabeth, I am . . . ." I did not know what to say. Everyone around me seemed to be moving at half speed. I could not compose myself. Too many thoughts flying through my head. Her two Indian companions were walking her away. I did not want her to leave.

"Papa," said Jonathon.

"Jonathon, I'm busy now!" I said sternly. "Elizabeth, come back."

I started toward her, but the two braves blocked my way.

"Did you really want to know . . ." she sobbed from across the room.

"Stop, Elizabeth, please."

". . . that I was a white man's whore at 10 years old?"

The words flew at me like spears across the sky, stabbing my heart.

"Papa," said Jonathon.

"For God's sake, boy, what do you want?" I was shouting.

"Uncle Daniel, it's important." Nathan stood beside Jonathon.

The group of Lenape had encircled Elizabeth and they were leaving the room. I was angry, but at the same time I sorely wanted to go after her, to talk to her, or scream at her, or hold her. I could not bear seeing her walk away.

"I'm sorry, Papa, you have to listen."

The two boys pulled me to the side, away from the crowd.

"What is it? Come on, get on with it!" My mind was elsewhere, and I kept looking her direction.

"The British are moving out a force of five-thousand men," whispered Jonathon. "They received word a brigade under General La Fayette left Valley Forge."

He had to repeat it twice before I understood. Even then I could not release my image of Elizabeth.

Struggling to clear my head I asked, "What do you know about La Fayette?"

Nothing," said Nathan. "But the British are going after him. We overheard some British officers talking about it at the party tonight for General Howe. They are dispatching five-thousand soldiers and fifteen cannon. They plan to take General La Fayette by surprise."

I had to think this through. A few days ago, Washington dispatched a brigade of two-thousand soldiers under the command of the Marquis de La Fayette to Barren Hill, about half way between Valley Forge and the City. The mission was intended to gather intelligence and reduce British foraging in the countryside. It may also have been the first step toward laying siege to the City.

If the British knew La Fayette's location and left this afternoon, they could be in a position to mount an offensive by tomorrow noon. If I could get out of the west side of the City tonight, I would have time to make it to the mill and ride the distance to La Fayette's camp in the morning light. With luck, that would be time enough to give warning about the impending attack.

I hated to leave the disaster I created. But I had no choice.

"Thank you, boys."

I went to tell Missy I was leaving immediately. She stood in a small group next to Margaret and some friends of Janie.

"What are you going to do about Elizabeth?" she asked.

I shook my head. "Wish I knew."

"You don't want to lose her. Shall I talk to her?"

I shrugged.

Margaret overheard. "You should have listened to me, Daniel," she said. "I told you she was no good for you. She's an Indian. I knew it all along."

I had had enough of this despicable woman. "Margaret," I said in a rasping voice, "let me say something I've been thinking for a long time,"

"Yes, Daniel?" she smiled expectantly.

Even now, she acted clueless. "I never want to see you again. And if you ever come close to me, I will pick you up by the back of your scruffy neck and stuff you into the deepest shit hole I can find."

I still felt sick about Elizabeth. But saying that to Margaret made me feel slightly better.

Chapter Forty Two

Trial Proceedings

"Did you talk to any British officers before you left the City?" asked the Judge Advocate.

"Of course not," Daniel replied. "Why would I do that?"

"To let them know the location of General La Fayette."

"They already knew. I can't imagine they would mobilize five-thousand soldiers without knowing where they were going."

"If they didn't know his exact location, they would need someone like you to lead them. Would they not?"

"What are you getting at?" Daniel asked in exasperation. "I didn't speak to anyone before I left the City. I certainly didn't tell anyone the way to Barren Hill."

"You're sure about that now?"

"Yes, I'm sure."

"Would it refresh your recollection if I said you were seen that night heading to Middle Ferry with someone in the chaise with you?"

"Who saw me?"

The Judge Advocate hesitated, debating as to whether he should disclose his source. "Henry Waddy, leader of the Philadelphia Sons of Liberty."

"Waddy?"

"Yes. You know him, don't you? He was there in September of '77 when your ship was burned."

"Oh, I know who he is all right. Is he the one behind all these charges of treason?"

"Lieutenant, I ask the questions, if you please. And the question is, did you have someone in the chaise with you? Yes, or no?"

"Yes, as a matter of fact, I did."

"That's interesting, Lieutenant, because just a moment ago you said you did not talk to anyone before you left the City. And now, you say you had someone in the chaise with you."

"The person I had with me was Alphonse, our bonded man."

"So you lied."

"No, sir, I did not. I didn't think you had an interest in him."

"In any event, you now admit you spoke with someone before you left the City?"

"I instructed Alphonse to come with me so he could return the chaise the next day."

"You have changed your story. Now tell us, did the person sitting in the chaise have a red coat?"

"Of course not!"

"What was the person wearing?"

"I don't know," said Daniel. "This was mid May, as I recall. Alphonse might have been wearing a cloak."

"What color was it?"'

"I would have to guess it was brown."

"You sure it was not red?"

"It could have been a rust color, but not red."

"Now you've changed your story again."

"No. My 'story' is I did not disclose General Lafayette's location to the British, if that's what you're trying to prove. And it's not a story. It's the truth. Waddy is a filthy liar."

"That's for this court to decide, Lieutenant. Now tell us, did you make it to Barren Hill?"

"The following day I did, yes."

"Did you make it in time?"

"I arrived before the British, if that's what you mean."

Chapter Forty Three

It took me longer than expected. I left the mill on horseback at dawn but stayed off main roads to avoid British troops. I eventually rode north of Barren Hill itself to Matson's Ford, where I crossed to the east side of the Schuylkill. Then, I took a little-used dirt road two miles back south. In midafternoon, I encountered a Continental Army patrol. The sergeant escorted me to a nearby outpost, where I negotiated with a captain to meet with General Lafayette.

I joined the general and his senior staff outside his headquarters tent not far from a church. From our vantage point atop the hill, I could see the Schuylkill River a quarter mile to the west with Matson's Ford upstream, and the road leading to Germantown and Philadelphia to the southeast. After a member of the general's staff quizzed me on my credentials, I informed the general five-thousand British regulars left Philadelphia the day before.

"None of our patrols reported enemy troop movements," said the general through a translator. "Why do you think they are not here by now?"

Staring at him, I had trouble believing a man so young – only in his early twenties – had the responsibility of a major general of the army. International politics, of course, was a consideration. He had come to Washington as another recommendation of Benjamin Franklin, who persistently curried French favor to secure more aid commitments. Still, I had to believe Washington would not have risked the fortunes of a large segment of his command, if he had not had complete confidence in La Fayette's abilities. He seemed amiable, but his question conveyed skepticism.

"I don't know," I answered. "My son and nephew heard they had been dispatched. They did not get a clear sense on when. Of course, the troops might not have moved out until today."

La Fayette conferred with his staff and then announced through his interpreter he would increase the number of scouting parties. Otherwise, he felt it prudent to stay their current course. After my frantic ride from the City, he disappointed me in not take more affirmative action. But I figured he knew what he was doing.

Having issued orders, the general turned to me and spoke English with a thick accent. "Thank you, Lieutenant Thompson. You have been of great service. We will provide you accommodations tonight so you can return to Valley Forge in the morning."

He gave me a little bow, which I returned. I liked him.

Another member of his staff gave orders to provision me for the evening. As I waited absent-mindedly to be shown my quarters, a well-known voice shouted at my back.

"What the hell do you think you're doing here, you Tory sympathizer?"

It was Mathew O'Leary, our shopkeeper. He immediately broke into laughter and gave me a bear hug.

"And you," I asked, "what business have you here? You decrepit old man. This army has obviously lost its standards. They let in any old body."

He laughed again. "You better watch yourself, Lieutenant, or you'll be eating warmed-over cockroach tonight."

"Why did a nice guy like you sign up for the dirty job of soldiering?"

"I was never much for the British. I guess you probably suspected it. And then, your Papa let me go, and no jobs are available in the City . . . at least while the British are there. I decided to offer my services to General Washington. To my surprise, he took me."

"Not for any fighting position, I hope."

"Why, you don't think I can handle a musket?"

"I think you could, but I know you're better suited for something else."

"You'd be right. I'm a member of the quartermaster staff. They're putting my shop-keeping skills to work. Enough of that. Come with me. You can stay in my tent tonight. We'll have a nice meal and perhaps I can roust up a bottle of rum. Then you can tell me what you're up to."

I could not have imagined a better offer.

Mathew was good to his word. After some roasted pork and boiled onions, he broke out a new bottle of rum. I knew better than to ask how he came to have it. We sat on a log outside his sleeping tent near a dozen wagons under the control of the quartermaster staff. As the sun dropped below the horizon, I felt the warmth of the rum ooze through my veins. It did not take long for him to notice I was depressed.

"So, what's weighing so heavily on your mind?"

"Believe it or not, it's a woman I've been seeing."

"Whoa, Nelly! A woman? By golly, that's exactly what you need. What could be the problem? A lover's quarrel?"

"Not really so much a quarrel. I found out something about her she didn't want me to know."

"What? She married? Another suitor?"

"No, nothing like that."

"Then I give up. What was her secret?"

"She's an Indian."

Mathew choked on his rum and began coughing loudly. "Sorry, Daniel," he eventually said. "You caught me by surprise. An Indian? What's wrong with you, boy? You couldn't tell by looking at her?"

"I'm an idiot and already know it. She's so pretty and well-spoken and lives with her adopted white mother. It never occurred to me she could be anything, but white."

"You're kind of slow when it comes to things like that." He sighed. "What do you think of Indians anyway?"

"To be honest, I never knew any until I met Elizabeth. I talked with a few but tried to avoid them because they're different and unpredictable and sometimes dangerous. Mostly, though, I thought they were inferior and not the kind of people my family had much use for."

"That's pretty much what most of us white folk think. It's rare to find someone who actually gives the Indians respect. We admire their hunting and fighting skills. Hell, La Fayette has a couple hundred Oneida in the brigade. And yet, I don't know anyone who wants one as a neighbor."

"You think that's wrong?"

"I don't know if it's wrong." Mathew shook his head. "It's just the way it is. You like some kinds of people and don't like others. I wouldn't want a Frenchman for a neighbor either."

"Why do you say that?"

"They put on too many airs with their fancy words and frilly clothes."

"They're helping us fight this war."

"Yes, but not because they like Americans. They hate the British."

I was beginning to feel the effects of the rum. "You have a point."

"I've sometimes wondered, though, if you took an Indian baby and raised it in a white family, how would it turn out? Your lady friend comes close. It makes you think. Maybe we're all the same, except for our upbringing."

"You really believe that, Mathew?"

"You're the one who never recognized a full blooded Indian. What do you think?"

I shook my head. "All I know is I can't change my mind overnight."

With that, I said goodnight. Crawling into the tent, I pressed my hand against my blouse pocket to make sure I had not lost the deck of cards.

And passed out.

★

The next thing I knew, Mathew was shaking me awake. It seemed like only an hour had passed. But through the tent flap, the sun was rising.

"Up with you, Danny, the British are attacking."

I heard musket fire and the roar of a cannon in the distance. Not being attached to any unit, I bolted out of the tent to make my way to La Fayette's headquarters for orders. The headquarters tent had already been stricken and the area was in chaos. Foot soldiers, wagons, messengers on horseback and cavalry were moving in every direction. I returned to help Mathew and the quartermaster crew, but the wagons were near loaded by the time I found him again.

"We're in a tight spot, Danny," he yelled. "The British on three sides and our backs against the river. We're in danger of losing the brigade."

He was in the process of positioning a wagon to move out as part of a wagon train once an opportunity arose. The cannon fire increased, and some of the horses began to frenzy. Our location was not in any immediate danger, but we could hear yells from retreating American militia and the beat of British drums closing in.

"Can we cross the river?" I asked.

"Matson's Ford is the only place. It's two miles up. Ridge Road and White Marsh Road are both blocked."

"A back road leads there. I rode down it yesterday."

He stopped what he was doing and looked at me. "Think you can find it?"

"For sure."

"Come with me."

Another soldier took control of the wagon as Mathew took me by the arm and we ran to find a high ranking officer.

Out of the chaos, columns of soldiers began forming into companies and regiments and positioning themselves in the staging area around the church where the headquarters tent used to be. I had never been in battle before, yet here we were about to be attacked by a much larger British force. Our guys, far from panicking, were falling into formation, readying to defend. The Baron's training methods were working.

"Are we making a stand for it?" I called to Mathew.

"Good God, I hope not. They outnumber us two to one."

We eventually found La Fayette and his general staff near a small grove of maples. Some stood examining a map spread on a small field table. Others were conferring with regimental officers, who had ridden up on horseback to receive orders.

Mathew and I were stopped numerous times as we neared the center of the gathering, but each time Mathew pushed the soldiers aside and repeated, "This man knows a secret road out of here. We must talk with the general."

I would not have given his technique much credence, but the situation seemed so desperate we got through. And when four blue-coated officers blocked our way within a few yards of the general, La Fayette himself came over to hear our news.

"Mr. Thompson," he said with his thick French accent, "you have important news for us, I trust?"

Mathew said, "He knows a secret road. It will get us across the river."

When one of the general's aides translated, the general asked, "If this is true, Mr. Thompson, it could be helpful."

"I don't know if it's secret," I said, "but it is well concealed and leads to Matson's Ford."

La Fayette listened to the translation and replied, "I want you to ride with my top aide, Colonel Lefebvre, to see if the road is clear. If it is, we will start evacuating. I will begin preparations anticipating your report to be favorable."

Someone handed me the reins to a horse and I mounted ready to ride with Colonel Lefebvre. We took off at a gallop. Trees and underbrush had overgrown onto the road, making it no wider in spots to barely allow a wagon through. We rode most of the way to Matson's Ford to assure there were no enemy obstructions. As soon as we were back within eyesight of La Fayette, Colonel Lefebvre gave a thumb up.

Columns of troops immediately began moving in the direction of the road.

While I was among those who evacuated early, I heard later how General La Fayette ordered a rear guard action to delay the British and make them believe the Americans would battle it out. The maneuver met with success, and by nightfall, the bulk of the brigade had crossed the river and returned safely to Valley Forge. The dead and wounded from the operation amounted to no more than two dozen.

The regiments at Valley Forge warmly welcomed the returning troops as brothers who had taken a close call.

Chapter Forty Four

Not until a couple of weeks later did Captain Johnson raise the subject of Barren Hill. Sitting around a cooking fire on chairs and logs near the company's headquarters tent, we were eating dinner with our sergeants and corporals. We had covered the usual topics: training, the quality of the female population in camp, and the latest palace intrigue coming out of Washington's headquarters.

The captain then said, "And rumor has it our own Lieutenant Thompson was the hero who helped to save General La Fayette's brigade from total annihilation over at Barren Hill."

The group turned my direction. "You been holding out on us, Lieutenant?" asked Sergeant Wright.

"I was over there, but didn't do anything heroic. I didn't even have a musket with me."

"You led our troops to safety, didn't you?" asked Captain Johnson.

"I found the road along the river that led to the crossing, if that's what you mean."

"It seems General La Fayette told our regimental folks you warned him about the British coming. Without you, the whole brigade might have been forced to surrender."

"General La Fayette is very generous," I said, "but he overstates my role. I will say I warned him the day before based on information I picked up when I was in the City. He listened, but didn't take me seriously."

"Holy shit, Lieutenant," said Sergeant Wright, "if someone thinks you're a hero, you ought to agree with them. I know what I would say. 'You're damned right I led those men to safety. Every last one of them. Almost got killed performing my duty.' That would get you a big fat pension when this is all over."

"I would if I could, Francis," I said, "but the closest I came to any danger was hearing the beat of the British drums."

"Speaking of drums," said Sergeant Sanders, the most junior of the three sergeants, "we were late for assembly and roll this morning. We had to rely again on other companies for drum and fife. Weren't you working on that, Captain?"

"I spoke to the drum major," said Captain Johnson, "but he doesn't have anyone to assign us. Apparently General Washington complained about fifes out of tune and drummers with no rhythm. So now, the major has to be more selective who he recruits. That doesn't mean we shouldn't try to find someone on our own. But I don't have any prospects. Do you have any ideas, Lieutenant?"

"I've not given it much thought," I said.

"You don't know anyone who might qualify?"

I paid little attention to his initial question. But his follow-up told me what he was getting at. When I did not immediately respond, Sergeant Sanders pressed me.

"You have someone we could use, Lieutenant?"

I gave the captain a look of irritation. "The captain is referring to my son and nephew. My son plays the fife. My nephew is working on drum."

"That's perfect," said Sergeant Sanders. "What are we waiting for?"

"It's not going to happen," I said. "They are fourteen and fifteen . . . too young for the likes of you guys."

"Now, Lieutenant," said Sergeant Sanders, "we have a lot of fifteen-year-old musicians here. We even have some fourteen-year-olds and younger. Your boys will be fine."

"Look, it's not happening. I'm not going to have my boys getting shot at."

"They won't get shot at," said Sergeant Wright. "The regimental drummers and fifes take us into battle, not the company's. They'll be fine. None of the younger boys have ever been hurt. They are only on duty in camp or garrison and sometimes when we're on the march. They're non-combatants. We don't shoot at the Brit boys and they don't shoot at ours."

"We have enough bad aims around," I said, "that they are never safe. But that's only part of it. You men almost starved and froze this past winter. And the camp is rampant with disease. I'm not going to do it."

"They're given favored treatment," said Corporal Hathaway. "Especially the younger ones. And they don't bunk with us soldiers. They stay with the other boys in the drum and fife corps."

All eyes looked at me expectantly. I had already said no several times, and I was not interested in arguing further. "I will think about it."

"That's fair," said Captain Johnson.

I looked at him again and wondered how long he had been planning this little ambush.

★

In early June, I visited home again. It was only my second visit since joining the army in March, and Captain Johnson again provided a horse. Elizabeth weighed heavily on my mind. In addition, I decided to at least raise with Missy the possibility of Jonathon and Nathan joining the drum and fife corps. She exercised good common sense in matters like this. I was sure she would never want Nathan anywhere near the kind of conditions that killed Peter. Once she said no, I would reject the idea for once and for all.

As we rode together in the chaise from the mill to the City, Missy surprised me by not discarding the idea out of hand. "Nathan wanted to join months ago," she said, "and I've always said absolutely not, but mainly because of Jonathon. If Nathan joins, then Jonathon will want to do the same. I know what you would say about that. I already feel bad enough about you getting me out of prison. I didn't want to put any more pressure on you."

"How can you be willing to let Nathan go like that? Look what happened to Peter."

"That's true, but the army takes good care of the younger boys. At least that's their reputation."

"Are you in cahoots with Captain Johnson?" I asked half seriously.

"No. I've not seen Captain Johnson since I met him at the mill. But here is how I look at it. This war is an historical event. Fifteen or twenty years from now, both our boys will want to look back and tell their kids how they participated. I think they should have the opportunity. And I know they would do a good job. Jonathon takes his music seriously, and Nathan already knows a few cadences."

I still had reservations but could feel the direction indicators in my head realigning. "Not more than seven months ago I was an ardent Loyalist," I said. "Now, I'm an officer in the Continental Army and am considering whether to allow our sons to join my company. Sweet Jesus."

We sat down to an early supper that evening prepared by the girls. They had taken turns cooking for the boys and

Alphonse while Missy spent time at the mill. Their preparations were tasty. Remarkably, the house was in good order, and everyone seemed to get along fine.

Midway through the meal, I took everyone but Missy by surprise. "My company commander, Captain Johnson, has been looking for a good drum and fife team. You boys have any idea where we could find one?"

Five seconds of silence followed while Jonathon and Nathan looked around the table, hardly believing their ears.

"Papa, you mean us?" asked Jonathon excitedly.

"We're going to join the army with you, Uncle Daniel?" asked Nathan.

"I can't believe it. I can't believe it!" Jonathon got up from the table and danced around. "You do mean it?" He started clapping Nathan on the back.

"Sit back down, Jonathon." I said. "We need to talk about it." The thought occurred to me that, for years, I tried to find an interest Jonathon and I could share in common. Unfortunately, this was it.

Even Nathan could not restrain himself. "We're going to play in the army?" he turned to Missy. "Mama, thank you, oh, thank you." He got up and began hugging his mother and kissing her on the cheek.

"Sit down, boys, we need to talk," I said.

"When do we leave, Papa?" said Jonathon retaking his seat. "Do we go with you tomorrow?"

"Sit down and be quiet. This is not a holiday. This war is serious business. Don't get any ideas about trying to be a hero. You two are not going to be near the fighting. You'll be ordered to the rear with the other boys your age when the bullets start flying. Do you understand?"

They both looked a little disappointed. "Yes, Uncle Daniel, that's fine."

"Jonathon?"

"Yes, Papa, we'll stay away from the fighting."

What else, now? I really had not thought this through. I realized, however, this could be my only chance to extract some iron-clad commitments before they arrived at Valley Forge.

"All right, three rules I want you to abide by, and you must promise you will. Rule number one is you stay together at all times. Most of the soldiers are pretty good guys and you will get along with them just fine. But some will try to take advantage of you. If you stay together, you're less likely to be taken advantage of by the bad apples. If I see one of you, I want to see both of you. Agreed?"

They both nodded.

"Rule number two. You're going to be in the drum and fife corps under the command of the drum major. You will be assigned to our company, but the drum major will be your commanding officer. You must always obey the major to the best of your ability. Agreed?"

No problem there.

"Rule number three. You must also obey me. No questions asked. I am responsible for you while you are in the army. If I decide you should go home, then you go home. Because you are a team, if one of you goes, then you both go. No excuses. No running away and joining another unit. No complaining. No begging. No whining. You do what I say. Understood?"

"Yes, Papa," said Jonathon.

"That goes for you, too, Nathan," said Missy.

"All right, Uncle Daniel."

"That didn't sound very convincing."

"Yes, sir!" Nathan almost saluted.

"Much better. You should go up and get ready. We'll leave by mid morning."

"Can I take my own drum?" asked Nathan.

"No," I said. "We have to get through the British lines. I would hate for them to find an army drum in the chaise if we're searched. Your major will provide what you need."

They took off like two young colts struggling for position on a race course, whooping and shouting as they stumbled up the stairs to the attic.

I looked at my twin daughters. Janie had a shawl draped over her as she nursed her baby. She had named him Scout in honor of Lightfoot's tenure with the army. Scout took after his father. He had started to crawl and actually was quite cute. His Aunt Annie doted on him and seemed content helping her sister and running the household. I knew, though, she would soon find a suitor of her own, if she had not already.

"You girls think I did the right thing?"

"I know you must have talked with Aunt Missy about this," said Annie with a mischievous look, "and if she said it was all right, I know it is."

Missy gave me a wink.

"I always knew you had confidence in me," I said. "What about you, Janie? Do you mind if Jonathon and Nathan come with me to Valley Forge?"

"That's what they want," said Janie. Her voice sounded angry, which gave me a start. I realized then she had not spoken to me since I arrived.

"What's the matter, honey?"

When she held her words, Missy spoke up. "Janie is upset over Elizabeth."

"Elizabeth?" I asked. "What do you have to be upset over?"

"The way you treated her at Scout's baptism, Papa."

"Treated her? I was not the one who kept my family a secret." The words got out before I could stop them. I knew they were not the right thing to say.

"Who are you trying to fool, Papa?" asked Janie, a whimper in her voice. "It's not her secret that caused a problem. It's the fact she's an Indian like Scout. I can't live here if you have that kind of attitude." As she spoke her voice cracked with a sob. Standing up with Scout in her arms, she abruptly left the kitchen.

Leaving me deflated.

Only Missy, Annie and I remained at the table. We sat a short while in silence, giving Janie's accusations time to incubate.

Annie said calmly, "Janie is right, Papa." She gave me a friendly grimace.

"Look," I said with deliberation, "I never wanted to have an Indian son-in-law, and I never wanted to have an Indian lady friend. Both occurred without my knowledge. If it had been in my power to stop either one, I would have done it a long time ago. You know I'm right about that. And you can't blame me for being angry with what has occurred."

"So you don't want to see Elizabeth again?" asked Missy.

"No. I don't." I said defiantly. Missy and Annie looked at me stone-faced. After a pause, I added quietly, "I don't want to see her. I want to marry her."

"You what?" they asked simultaneously.

"I can't stand being without her," I said.

They both burst out laughing, and Annie started tearing up.

"What are you crying about, you disgusting little urchin?" I asked.

"My own Papa has fallen in love again." She said it with a laugh or a cry, I could not tell which.

"What am I supposed to do? I never thought it would happen this way. Have you talked with her since I was here last?"

"Oh, my goodness," said Missy, her laughter subsiding. "I did once, but she was pretty upset. Honestly, I don't know if she will have you now."

"Believe me, I didn't want to leave her like that, but I had to go."

"I know you did, but if I were you, I would go over to her place tonight. If you want, I could come with you."

"Thanks anyway, Sis, I can handle it." I gave her a revolting look.

"Of course," she added, "you have handled it so well already." Both of them burst out laughing again. Even I cracked a smile.

I actually ran halfway to the north side of the City. I was so excited and only slowed down when I started thinking about what Missy had said, that Elizabeth might not have me back. If Missy was right, then somehow I would need to persuade Elizabeth to forgive and forget the past. I tried to think through what I would say, but before I came up with something definitive, I had arrived at her house. I would improvise.

It was then I noticed no light coming from the cottage, no smoke rising from the chimney, and the outside shutters were closed. I passed through the picket fence, banged on the door, went around to the side and banged on a window. No one was home. My hopes of seeing her that evening faded. I walked to a neighbor's cottage and asked if anyone knew where Elizabeth and her mother might be, to no avail. The most I learned was a wagon stopped by two weeks earlier. Some of the house's belongings had been loaded up and taken away, but no one seemed to know where they had gone or for how long.

I sat on the front step for a while until the sun faded and a half moon shined dim light on the City streets. In disgust, I got up and walked slowly home. Missy was still up and I reported my dismal experience to her before going up to bed. Before falling asleep, however, I wrote a short note and gave it to Missy. I asked her to place it under Elizabeth's door in case she returned.

Chapter Forty Five

The boys and I arrived at Valley Forge late the following afternoon. I got them situated with the other members of the drum and fife corps and reported to Captain Johnson.

"You have me, my flour, my mill manager and now my two boys." I let out a sigh. "Hope you're satisfied."

"It's all for a good cause," he said with a smile.

"Maybe, but you're not getting any more."

Our conversations over the next few weeks expanded from our usual topics – training, women and palace intrigue – to the question of when we would be breaking camp and moving out.

More and more we were coming to appreciate what a difference it made having the French joining up with us. The British feared the French, much more than they ever feared the Continental Army. France was one of the few world powers able to threaten an invasion of Britain itself.

A more immediate concern, however, was the threat to the British West Indies. Rumors circulated that General Clinton had been ordered to dispatch five-thousand troops to secure the British Caribbean possessions, and another three thousand to the British ports of St. Augustine and Pensacola in Florida.

The bulk of the British Army occupied Philadelphia, and most of the rest still held New York. With eight-thousand men moving south, however, it seemed increasingly likely Clinton would need to consolidate his strength in one place or the other.

"Why would they want to get up and move to New York?" asked Sergeant Sanders at one of our evening bull sessions.

Since the daytime temperatures had turned hot, our entire company spent more time outdoors in the cool evening breezes. While we took mess in groups, Captain Johnson always encouraged the company to eat in close proximity, with officers joining the rest of the men. That night's meal was no exception. Around forty of the company's active members were sitting around several cooking fires and pots of food. Willie always joined us and was treated as an honorary officer.

"What is wrong with New York?" asked Corporal Hathaway. "It has good ports and is easier to defend against the French fleet."

"But look at all the time and blood they spent taking Philadelphia," said Sergeant Sanders. "It's the capital of the colonies. It's where the Declaration of Independence was signed. And it's also the home of a lot of friendly Tories. Captain, you think General Clinton is just going to give it up?"

"Damned if I know," said Captain Johnson. "They'll be spread pretty thin if they don't do something. The only real question is whether they make the move by land or by sea. I think they would prefer sea, but I don't know if they have the ships to move all the horses and equipment."

"You think General Washington would attack Philadelphia?"

"No." The captain shook his head. "He'll never attack it. But he could lay siege to it, like Boston."

"Willie," said Sergeant Wright, changing subjects, "once we leave camp, what are you going to do? You've done training for what now, four, five companies?"

"Five," said Willie.

"You going to go back and run the lieutenant's mill again?"

"I expect I will at some point," Willie nodded. "I might just stay on with you fellas for a time, though. I have a lot invested in your shooting. I'd like to see how it all turns out. If the captain lets me."

"Let you? We'd be honored!" said Captain Johnson. "You're the best musket man in camp."

We heard a drum roll. Though it was not the time of day for drum signals, we all looked over to where Jonathon and Nathan stood in their musician uniforms with peacock feathers in their hats. They had been playing Reveille, Assembly, Troop, Retreat along with other calls and signals for our company for the last several days now.

Once the drum roll stopped, Jonathon gave us a lively rendition of *Billy Boy* on the fife, accompanied by Nathan on the drum. They played it through once, paused, and Jonathon shouted out, "Sing along!"

To my surprise, everyone did. They sang loudly and out of tune. And at the end of two verses, the entire company let out a huge roar of approval and called out requests. Jonathon held up his hand defensively.

"We can only take one at a time."

Someone yelled for *Old Dan Tucker*, and since he yelled louder than the others, Jonathon looked at Nathan, and they began playing the tune, accompanied once again by about twenty to thirty sour voices from the company. When that concluded, cheers erupted again, along with more requests. I had the impression this could have gone on all night.

After another song or two, however, Jonathon wisely held up his hand and said, "We can only do one more. Nathan and I have to get up early for Reveille." Someone shouted out *Girl*

I Left Behind Me, and Jonathon responded, "I'll need the fiddle for that one."

He picked up the fiddle, gave a short introduction, and nodded for the singing to begin.

The whole concert lasted only twenty minutes. When it finished the boys marched off to the beat of Nathan's drum, along with shouts and whistles from the entire company. It was one of the first times I recalled being genuinely proud of Jonathon. The failed horse race, the disaster of a bear hunt, the bullies he ran from at school, and a flood of other disappointments all made little difference to me now. My son stood up fearlessly and entertained the troops in Captain Johnson's company with his fife and fiddle. It may not have been a big deal, but I would never forget it. And if he decided he wanted to be a musician rather than a musketeer, it was time I encouraged him.

★

A few days later we were on the march. It was the day after we received word the British were evacuating Philadelphia by land, moving across the Delaware and into New Jersey toward New York. Washington planned to give chase.

In early morning, Captain Johnson formed up his company and made his inspection. He then marched it into the regimental parade for inspection by the regimental field officers. After that, we joined other regiments and marched out of camp by brigade. The main army was preceded by a detachment of advance guards, and followed by a rear guard with flanking platoons on the sides a hundred yards out. Other than high ranking officers and cavalry, few soldiers rode horses. We stretched out in a column four to six men wide. With the wagon train at the end, the artillery park at center, and cavalry and dragoon units interspersed throughout, the column measured a good five miles long.

We moved quickly due east through farmland and forest as fast as the artillery could roll. We had about two days' distance to close up between us and the British. As night approached, scouts would select a camp site, the lead brigade would form a color line, each unit pitched its tents along the color line, and outposts would form and sentries post. Those not assigned to guard duty would eat supper and get a few hours' sleep. Then off again at daybreak.

On the third day out we crossed the Delaware River at Coryell's Ferry. Once in New Jersey we left our tents and heavy baggage behind so we could step up the pace. On the fourth day, during a morning break, Captain Johnson returned from a briefing to give our company an update and new orders. We clumped together under what little shade we could find in the sweltering late-June sun.

"Here's the deal," said the captain. "The Brits are moving slower than expected. In four days they have only covered twenty miles." A little cheer rose up. Everyone seemed eager to fight. "Part of the reason is the heat. Part of it is the sandy roads. Part of it is the fact that they have a wagon train a good ten miles long."

"What do they have in all those wagons?" someone yelled out.

"Best our guys can tell," said the captain, "they have blacksmith shops and boats and bakeries along with all sorts of stuff they looted from Philadelphia. Plus, they have a couple thousand Tories with them who decided the City may not be so hospitable after the redcoats left."

"Any word on what shape they left Philadelphia in?" I asked.

"It's intact and not much worse for the wear, except for a few damaged houses and what the Brits took with them. A lot of shopkeepers are pretty sore because not all their accounts got paid. Washington sent in a regiment under General Benedict Arnold. He'll keep things safe until we get back.

"When do we meet up with the Tory Army?" someone asked.

"I'm getting to that," said the captain. "We're close. They have been heading north and east. But General Washington is convinced they are going to turn due east any day now and head toward Sandy Hook off the Jersey shore. We expect they'll board ships and sail the rest of the way to New York. From where we are now they are only thirty miles away, and we're on course to intersect them in a few days, even after they turn east."

"So why don't we just turn south now and end it all here?"

"Let me put it this way. The Brits are running from us. They may think they are marching north to reinforce New York, but in Washington's view, they are on the run, and it's the first time that has happened in this war. So let them run a while longer. It's good for public morale. It also gives us an opportunity to harass them and wear them down.

"And that's where our company comes in. We're going to be a part of a detachment of three or four thousand troops to move south as an advance force. We're leaving the 7th Regiment and joining up with the Pennsylvania 9th temporarily in a brigade forming under General Scott. After that, we'll rendezvous with the rest of the army if we have a general engagement."

"What do you mean if?" asked Sergeant Wright. Of all the men in the company, he seemed the most anxious for a fight. "If we don't take them now while they're on the run, we're a bunch of friggin' cowards."

"No one here is a coward, Sergeant," replied Captain Johnson, "so get that out of your head. There is, though, a disagreement at the top over strategy. Washington, La Fayette and Greene all want a general engagement. General Lee wants to hold off until the French arrive. But that's none of your concern for the time being. We'll be heading south to take some shots at the British column. Pack your haversacks with two days' provisions. Keep it light because we'll be moving at double time until we see the redcoats."

Sergeant Wright looked triumphant. "Finally!" He threw a fist in the air.

That morning, a dozen or more regiments fell out of the main column, formed up into new brigades to the right and began moving south.

Captain Johnson's promise of double time proved accurate. We covered a good twenty miles that day over rolling hills, stopping only occasionally to let our few artillery pieces catch up. We stayed together as a small army for the first day. But early the next our scouts reported the British column not more than a few miles away. At that point two brigades disbursed along a several-mile stretch, while others prepared to attack the rear guard of the baggage train.

★

I got my first glimpse of the British Army on the march as Captain Johnson and I crept up to the the peak of a ridge where we peered down at the long British column a quarter mile away. Pulling out his spyglass, he gave me a look. The thousands of stoic-looking soldiers wearing heavy red coats, cumbersome leather belts, long leggings and hats with cockades – were a sight to behold. They carried firelocks and haversacks while maintaining neat-looking formations in near-ninety degree temperatures. In the Continental Army, those of us with uniforms had shed them days ago. What we lacked in official appearance we made up for in personal comfort.

"We're on our own," Captain Johnson said as he and I sized up the British line. "We'd best split up the company. I'll take half the men and move upstream to the left. You stay here with the other half and see what you can do. We'll meet along this ridge by late afternoon. You think you can handle that?"

"I expect so." This was my first actual combat command. I knew he was testing me, but was grateful the test came here, far removed from the chaos of a general engagement. We would shoot, run and hide . . . then shoot, run and hide again. We would expose ourselves to danger, but it was a manageable danger, and small-scale tactics would play a big role.

"I'm going to give you Sergeant Wright and his men, along with Sergeant Sanders and half of his men," said the captain. "Wright is your most experienced man. Make good use of him. You also get Willie, our best shot."

We slid down the ridge away from the British Army and stood up. "We'll do our best." I was nervous but tried not to show it as I barked out orders to the sergeants to split up the company.

"Good hunting, Daniel," said the captain.

"Thank you, sir," I responded as I took off my hat and gave him a formal salute. "Same to you."

Chapter Forty Six

Once the captain left with his men, I stood there thinking: Holy fucking shit! What do I do now? There I was with 23 soldiers, and not more than a quarter mile away marched the whole God-damned British Army. All the training at Valley Forge had not given me a clue about how I was supposed to mount an attack.

Trying not to exhibit utter incompetence, I asked my sergeants to join me up on the ridge, and turned to my most experienced man.

"What do you think, Francis?" I asked Sergeant Wright. That was the best I could do to get the ball rolling.

"The problem is the flankers. You can see them, there, a hundred-twenty yards out from the column, moving slowly along. Ten or twelve men. Once they get wind of any suspicious activity they'll discharge their muskets and a regimental commander will send out reinforcements. If it looks serious, the situation can escalate."

"I take it they're supposed to prevent harassment details like us from getting too close."

"Exactly."

Well, then, we could rule out my best idea, which was just waltzing up close and taking a few shots. So, where do we go now? I tried to think of something intelligent to say, and at least appear like I may have a plan. "What do you think the interval is between them and the next group of flankers?"

"Half mile maybe."

Not a bad question, or answer, I thought to myself. At least it gave me something to work with.

"So, if we want to get in close enough to fire on the column, we'll have to take out one set of flankers, move in, make our strike, and get back out, all within twenty to thirty minutes at the rate they are moving."

"Or, we could just take out the flankers and retreat," offered Sergeant Wright. "Be a lot easier."

"Yes, but that won't do much good. We want to take a few shots at the main body, don't we?" In all honesty, I was not sure myself, although I assumed that was our goal.

"How do you plan to do that, Lieutenant?" Sergeant Sanders asked.

The honest response was: Beats the hell out of me!

But saying that would get us nowhere, and also reveal how clueless I really was. So I surveyed the area between us and the flankers, and between the flankers and the column. A couple hundred yards in front of the flankers as they moved east I noticed a barn, more or less in their path. It looked to be about midway between us and the marching column.

"How about this for starters," I said, hoping for input from the sergeants. "We make our way to that barn. All twenty-four of us. By the time we get there, the flankers will be almost upon us. We'll try to take them quietly. If we end up getting into a fire fight along the way, we back off."

"Even if we get close to the column," asked Sergeant Sanders, "what is to stop them from dispatching a regiment or two to chase us down?"

Beats the hell out of me!

But, once again, I restrained myself from saying what I was actually thinking and offered, "Nothing, but I don't think they will." Of course, I had no idea, but continued, "They might send out a few men, but their interest is keeping the column together and moving east, not chasing after every diversion." At least that sounded logical. "What do you think, Francis?"

"You're probably right about that," agreed Sergeant Wright. "But I'm still thinking about the flankers. Once we get to the barn, what do you have in mind?"

In truth? Not a God-damned thing. Nothing! But I managed, "We'll see what happens." I just hoped all military planning was not this haphazard.

With hills and trees populating the landscape, running undetected to the barn proved easy enough. The barn itself brought us to within a hundred yards or so of the slowly moving British column. To fire effectively on them we needed to move to within fifty yards. But first things first. I had been trying to think how to disable the flankers. An idea began to form and I gathered everyone into the barn.

"Here is what we'll do. One of us will go find the flankers, tell them a bunch of rebels are over here in the barn and lead them over. Once they arrive, we will surround them, hopefully without firing."

"Just like that?" asked Sergeant Wright. "You think those British boys are going to follow someone over here and walk right into a trap?"

Dammit, Sergeant, I thought, you put it like that, you make me sound like an idiot. Well, it was the best I could do. "You have a better idea?"

"No."

Ah, I thought, he's almost as dumb as me.

He continued, "But whoever is going to lure them over here will have to be a pretty good talker. Who is that going to be?"

I looked around, praying someone would speak up. But no one did, and I did not have time to cajole anyone into the task.

"That's my role, Sergeant," I said with as much bravado as I could muster. "And here is what you do. Assign four of your men to stay inside the barn." I pointed to the area inside the open double doors on the north side of the barn. "They will be our decoys. They should talk loud like rebels getting ready to make a strike. I want to hear them as I'm bringing the British platoon close. You got that? They also should look busy, like they are cleaning their muskets."

"And then what?"

"The Brits and I will sneak up on them from the sides. That's why I want our four guys inside. It will look and sound real."

"The rest of us?"

"You and the rest of the men surround the barn keeping most here in front. They have to stay hidden. If they see you, it's all over. So stay hidden until I give the signal. The signal will be . . . 'Drop your weapons and disarm.' At that point you show your muskets, but don't fire unless you have to. Questions?"

Silence. Either they thought the plan flawless, or they had not been listening at all. I was not sure which.

"Willie, I want you to follow me as backup. Stay out of sight, but stay on my tail going out and again when we come back in. Make sure all the British lads are with us. I don't want a straggler to foul us up."

Willie was the one man I could trust for such a job. He could track bears, deer, my daughter, and almost anything else. I did not have to worry about him blowing the whole operation.

"Yes, sir. I got you covered."

"Sergeant Wright, you're in charge of making sure this works. Just stay back out of the way until the whole British platoon is in front of the barn."

I took off in search of the flanking patrol, wondering vaguely what I had gotten myself into.

While the British Army column occupied the relatively flat and passable main road, the flankers had no road to follow and had to make their own pathway through, over, and around all kinds of terrain, from tall grasses to thick groves of trees, stone fences, creek beds, and craggy hills. I soon spotted their lead men ascending a shallow ravine.

Approaching them from an angle, I held up my hands to show I was unarmed. "Hey you, soldiers," I said in what I thought sounded like a friendly voice, "can you come with me? Some rebels are holed up in a barn over there."

I was immediately surrounded by a half dozen redcoats carrying muskets, their bayonets now pointed at me. All were sweating profusely and looked none too happy to be diverted from their main task of keeping pace with the column. My heart was pounding.

"What you say, Mate?" asked one of them. "Rebels in the area?"

"Yes, sir," I said. "You the man in charge?"

"I'm in charge of this platoon here, yes," said the redcoat. "I'm Corporal Maxwell. How do we know you're not the rebel?" He pressed his bayonet against my chest.

"If I were a rebel, I don't think I'd come here looking for you, would I? I'd shoot you instead." That seemed to satisfy him. Maybe the British rank and file were not as smart as they looked.

"What about the others you were talking about? What makes you think they're rebels?"

"I saw them sneak into my barn. With our British Army so close, it seemed odd they were sneaking around. That make any sense? I would have gone over to the main army column but I saw you boys first. I think they are up to no good."

"How many?"

"I don't know, Corporal, a bunch. How many you got in your platoon?"

"Twelve."

"You can take them by surprise. I will help."

One of the other redcoats said, "Be careful, Corporal, it could be a trap,"

"Look," I said, "I came over here out of duty. They aren't going to hurt me. I'm a civilian. If you want to let them go, fine with me." I started to walk away.

"Hey, you, what did you say your name was?" asked Corporal Maxwell.

"Daniel."

"Take us to them, Daniel."

"All right," I said reluctantly, "you see the barn? It has a double door on the north side, and that's where they are gathered. I will lead the way. When we get to the barn, we'll surround it."

The Corporal looked at me, still not sure what to think, but he nodded. "Lead the way. You men in the back, tighten it up and stay together."

As we neared the small clearing around the barn, I stepped back to whisper to the corporal, "If you send half the men around to the other side, we can take them from both angles."

The corporal seemed to like the plan, whispered something to one of his men and five or six split off and began circling the south side of the barn. We moved up the sides of the barn, slowly turned the corner around to the north face, waived to the men approaching us from the east, and stealthily closed in on the doorway. Voices coming from inside the barn door gave assurance the rebels were actually there. Once we reached the door, I stepped out in front of the doorway and said in a firm voice, "Drop your weapons and disarm!"

Several redcoats pushed in beside me with muskets pointed while more clustered behind them. The men in the barn seemed genuinely surprised and raised their arms in surrender. I looked behind me and saw a dozen muskets pointed toward the redcoats from behind trees, rocks and shrubbery.

I turned to Corporal Maxwell standing with musket at the ready. To his surprise, I gently lowered the barrel of his musket, put my arm around him and spoke softly in his ear. "Corporal, I am going to have to ask you to order your men to place their muskets on the ground and raise their hands above their heads. You do the same."

He gave me a confused, dismayed look and jerked his flintlock to break my grip. "You are quite out of your mind."

I held onto the barrel and motioned with my head toward the row of muskets pointing from behind. "Corporal, let's not have any bloodshed here."

He looked behind him and then at me with a hateful expression. "You bloody son of a bitch."

"Give the order now," I said. "Some of my boys are trigger happy."

"Lay down your weapons, men," he said, "and raise your arms. That's an order."

His men acted confused but looking behind them, they did as ordered.

"Sergeant Wright," I called out, "have your men check the back of the barn."

"Already done, sir," said the sergeant. "We picked up two more."

I turned to our guys inside the barn. "Take their muskets, cartridge pouches and haversacks. Distribute them to whoever needs them, and everything else pile inside the barn. Sergeant Wright, make a count of our guests. We should have twelve."

"Lieutenant, I count eleven."

I looked at Corporal Maxwell. "Where's your last man?"

"How the fuck should I know?"

"Oh, here we go, Lieutenant." Sergeant Wright smiled. "Willie is bringing him in now."

"This one almost got away," Willie said matter-of-factly as he prodded the captive with his bayonet,

I marveled at what I saw. "Willie, you're worth your weight in gold. Take his belongings and put them with the others.

I turned to Sergeant Sanders, "Assign four of your men to guard the prisoners until we return."

"Yes, sir."

"Corporal Maxwell, you and your men are to stand at attention in a single row on the outside of the barn until we return. I'm giving orders to shoot anyone who falls out of attention. Is that clear?"

The corporal scowled at me.

"After shooting the soldier falling out of attention, you will be shot next for allowing it to happen. Understand? So, line up now."

I then turned to the rest of our company. "We now will get down to the real business at hand."

★

"Got to hand it to you, Lieutenant, I never thought you'd pull it off," said Sergeant Wright as we gathered on the side of the barn.

Disarming the flanking patrol did not make me any smarter, but it did raise my confidence a notch or two.

"We've been fortunate so far," I said. "Now, what next?" I paused to think. If our goal was to take some shots at the marching column, that did not seem too complicated. "I say we move toward the column in groups."

"Without the four on guard duty, we have twenty men. How about four squads, five men each. You will lead one squad, I will take another, Sanders the third and Corporal Hathaway the fourth."

At least the sergeant was not second guessing me this time. That was refreshing.

I turned to the group. "You heard the sergeant. Four squads. My squad and Sergeant Wright's will move out together. Sergeant Sanders, your squad will follow me. Corporal Hathaway, yours will follow Sergeant Wright. We'll work our way to within forty to fifty yards of the column. When we're set, we'll fire by squad. We'll keep it up until they start chasing us or we're backed out of range. Got it?"

We split up and started forward. At first, we moved quickly, but the last stretch got tricky. Since the sight barriers between us and the column did not allow for rapid movement, we ended up having to crawl through open areas and dash one-at-a-time between trees to avoid being spotted. Fortunately, the redcoats in the column seemed less concerned about an attack than being trampled by comrades from the rear. Even the officers on horseback did not maintain a vigilant watch on the flanks. They were more concerned with keeping everyone moving.

Once our two lead squads reached to within fifty yards, I was tempted to go further. But Sergeant Sanders' earlier question lingered in the back of my mind: What was to prevent the British from sending a substantial force to chase us down? Chase-and-shoot tactics were out of character for the British. They preferred firing in formation on an open battlefield. Still, I had no guarantee they would not have a change of heart on this day.

We positioned ourselves with two squads in a line up front and the other two behind, all facing the British column.

I glanced over at Sergeant Wright, nodded, and the front two squads stood up and fired in unison. Through the black powder smoke, I saw a few redcoats fall, an officer's horse rear up, and soldiers scatter off the road. Others turned in confusion and tried to pinpoint where the shots came from.

Before the British organized to return fire, our second two squads stood and fired. Those shots sent the British into further disarray. I watched for any sign of movement of forces toward us, but saw none. Within half a minute the first two squads had reloaded and we stood to fire again. The two squads in the rear got off another round, by which time the segment of the British column under attack had come to a complete stop. Everything behind them halted. Officers on horseback rode forward to consult with those on the scene. Within minutes, a unit began to form to come after us.

We kept up our assault for two or three more volleys. But once the unit detached, we began our withdrawal. It was not the regiment-sized force predicted by Sergeant Sanders, but even at what looked liked forty soldiers, it was more than we could handle.

High-tailing it to our rear a hundred-fifty yards or so, I saw a place where we could make a stand. It was a dry creek bed with sufficient width and depth we could again form two firing lines. We concealed ourselves until the British detachment approached.

The redcoats came at us from an angle, either unaware we were in the creek bed or unwilling to break from their disciplined march.

Whichever the case, our two squads let loose once they came within range, followed by our second two a few seconds later. By the time the first line reloaded, the detachment scattered into an unorganized retreat.

We took a few more pot shots, but it was time for us to withdraw to the barn. From there we moved with our prisoners out of the vicinity entirely, lest we find ourselves having to deal with the next flanking patrol arriving from the west.

Good Lord Almighty, was I glad that was over!

Chapter Forty Seven

Trial Proceedings

Given the lateness of the hour, the court adjourned for the day without further questions. The court's president warned Daniel not to talk to anyone about his testimony until reconvening the following day.

On returning to his cell, Daniel realized his testimony would soon come to an end. The members of the court would then deliberate and announce their decision. More than anything, he wanted for this trial to be over.

Having testified all day, he felt tired but not hungry, and ate little. Sleep eluded him for most of the night as his mind re-played segments of the day's testimony. He kept thinking of things he should have said, and many he should not have. Eventually, he realized he would have little opportunity to rectify his mistakes, and decided to stop keeping track. He then relaxed and his mind shut down for a few hours' sleep.

On arriving back in the Hall the next morning, Daniel spoke before being asked a question.

"Sergeant Wright can verify our assault on the British column."

"I imagine he can," said the Judge Advocate.

Daniel frowned, not sure whether the Judge Advocate understood the significance. "Traitors to the American cause don't lead assaults on enemy forces."

"Oh, I'm not so sure. General Benedict Arnold led many attacks on the British. And yet, he is going to be hanged if we can get our hands on him."

The Judge Advocate had a point. General Arnold had been an American hero at Saratoga and he had been one of Washington's ablest generals. The reports of his defection to the British had become public just within the last two months, and they shocked everyone.

"True," Daniel said, "But so far as I'm aware, he didn't lead any attacks after he turned traitor. Under your theory, my allegiance has always been with the British. Yet not only did I lead a harassment patrol but I fought ably against the British at Monmouth a few days later."

"Come, now, Lieutenant, maybe you had second thoughts, or you were keeping up appearances. The fact you engaged in some conduct to the benefit of the colonies doesn't mean you should not be punished for your acts of disloyalty."

"I've made many mistakes, but none have evidenced disloyalty to the cause for independence. Since committing, moreover, I never wavered. There is no 'maybe' about it."

"We'll let the court decide, Lieutenant. Did you meet back up with the other half of your company after the raid?"

"Yes. We did."

"You have mentioned Monmouth. When did you rejoin General Scott's brigade?"

"Late afternoon on the same day. After we reconnected with Captain Johnson, we spotted a convoy of soldiers and wagons heading east. A rider then dispatched from the convoy headed in our direction."

"What did the rider report?"

"He asked if we were part of General Scott's detachment. When we assured him we were, he told us to join the convoy because General Scott had new orders to move immediately to Englishtown. There we would merge with the advance force under General Lee."

Chapter Forty Eight

"General Lee?" Captain Johnson asked the rider. "I thought he wanted to delay until the French arrived, so La Fayette took command of the advance force."

"That was yesterday," answered the rider. "When General Washington increased the size of the advance force to five-thousand men, General Lee could not resist."

The captain nodded. "All right, we've put in a full day and have prisoners. I hope you're not going much longer tonight."

"Maybe another hour."

We double-timed it to the rear of the convoy before slowing down to a moderate walk. It gave me a chance to bring the captain up to date on our activities, and he relayed his to me.

"We were not as successful as you," he said. "We went forward a couple of miles and saw a gap in their column coming onto a wooden bridge. We tried to slip in and destroy the bridge before the lead units arrived. We got behind the gap and disabled it all right. But as we were leaving the site, a company of dragoons on horseback gave chase. While a couple of our guys got hit by musket fire, we came out in decent shape."

"Sorry to hear about the injuries."

"They will be fine. But I'm really proud of you, Daniel. You created a major disruption in the column and came away with a dozen prisoners to boot."

"Beginner's luck," I said. "What do you make of General Washington increasing the size of the advance force?"

"I'm not sure. That's almost half our entire army. Sounds like we're in for a battle."

"And replacing La Fayette with Lee?"

"Makes no sense. He is Washington's senior general, and that's the only reason Washington let him replace La Fayette. Unfortunately, Lee is in it for the glory of leading an army. Let's hope it doesn't turn out a disaster."

As we walked, I began to feel the wear and tear from the day's events. Looking around, I could see our entire company struggling to keep up. The time was near six in the afternoon, and yet the sun gave no sign of weakening. I sensed some urgency to make it to Englishtown by early tomorrow. Nonetheless I was hungry and thirsty and my eyes kept closing.

I began to think about our raid on the British column. It went well, and Captain Johnson was pleased. Even Sergeant Wright seemed impressed. Still, something bothered me about it. All the killing we had done that afternoon. They were good British boys some not much older than my own son. Some could even have been my relatives from England. I was not against killing things in general. People killed animals all the time, for food. Animals killed animals. It was the way of things. But I had never shot at a human being before, and found it repulsive. This was war, true enough, and I was a soldier. So, what did I expect? I volunteered for it. But soldiering was a disgusting occupation. I was glad I did not have to kill up close that day. Could I have, if needed? I did not know and hoped I would not be put to the test. The Quakers had the right idea. No killing people. I admired that.

★

We reached Englishtown the following day, picking up a number of units along the way. By the time we arrived, we were close to the full fourteen-hundred men assigned to General Scott's detachment.

Englishtown itself was not much of a town. It had a couple of taverns, two or three commercial shops and perhaps four hundred citizens in scattered residences with large gardens and backyard pens for chickens and pigs. The locals were friendly enough and everyone seemed supportive of the independence cause. Of course, how could they not be with five-thousand Continental soldiers descending upon their town? They nevertheless went out of their way to make us feel welcome, opening up two churches and a school house for temporary quarters, and sharing their stores of food.

That night, companies and regiments clustered together in their own marked-off boundaries while various units practiced marching drills, their sergeants barking orders while wagons moved supplies from one location to another. Since we lacked the fortifications and redoubts at Valley Forge, security was tight with lots of outposts and checkpoints. After all, we were only five miles from the British Army in Monmouth. Our stay in Englishtown would be short. Quarters were tight with no open spaces. Even the artillery park was compacted with only fifteen heavy guns. The rest remained with the main army contingent a few miles to the west.

Our orders were to be in formation and ready to move out by 4:00 a.m., and a lot of anticipation permeated the air. But for what? No one seemed to know. Were we getting ready to stand our ground and defend if attacked? Were we in for more harassment duty on the British column? Were we actually going to engage the British in an open-field battle?

Our company was assigned to outpost duty until 9:00 o'clock that evening. When we returned to our assigned camping area for supper, Captain Johnson was not in a good mood.

"Nobody knows nothin' about nothin'," he said with frustration. "We have no reconnaissance on the ground conditions between here and Monmouth. We have no battle plan for tomorrow morning. No one knows the order of march once we break camp. The only orders coming out of Lee's headquarters are that the generals not dispute rank. What kind of a plan is that? No one disputes rank. Then what do we do? This is the most half-assed operation I have ever seen."

"Why is Lee concerned about rank all of a sudden?" I wondered aloud.

"I don't think he has ever worked with these generals before. He was a prisoner of war for almost a year until he was freed in March. Prisoner exchange. That's all the more reason he ought not to be leading this operation."

"What does our regimental commander say?"

"Colonel Butler? He's just as befuddled as everyone else. He's not even sure what units he is going to have in his regiment."

I did not know if this was just a display of the captain's night-before jitters, or if he really had a legitimate concern about the lack of planning.

"Sounds as if there is nothing else we can do at this point," I said. "Why don't you just relax a bit and we'll deal with it in the morning."

He gave me a wry look. "That's a rather fatalistic approach, the night before a looming disaster. I think we should stay up all night and worry about it."

I was not sure if he was serious or not. "We could, if that would make you feel better."

"No. It would make me feel worse. How do you propose relaxing?"

I thought a moment. "Women and rum would be my first two choices, but I've not seen either one lately. As an alternative . . . how about a game of whist? I have a deck of cards."

He looked at me incredulously. "You have a card deck. I cannot fucking believe it. We're going into battle tomorrow and my lieutenant wants to play cards. A game of whist, no less."

I gave a little shrug.

He took a deep breath, and I almost thought he was going to throw me out of the company.

Instead, he said, "I have the shits. Give me five minutes. In the meantime you find a few other players. And then, I will whip your ass. But we're not playing whist. That's a game for old spinsters. We'll play brag."

Brag was a betting game. Each player received three cards, and the betting would begin with everyone either putting money into the pot the same amount as the previous player, increasing the bet to a higher amount, or folding. The betting continued until all but two players folded. Then, the player with the highest hand would take the pot. Since the pots could get huge quickly, the captain dictated starting bets of a penny with maximum bets of five.

Finding players was not a problem. We ended up with ten. Even playing with pennies, some of the pots grew to a pound or more, which for some was a tidy sum. For those with the drive to make a little money, the incentive to stay in was strong.

I did not worry about winning. For me, the game was a way to socialize and take my mind off other things. I looked around at the men sitting in our company. There was the captain, of course, the authoritative father-figure, who usually had a clear head and plan of action. He rarely became flustered over anything. Tonight was an exception.

We had a dozen men in the company who were seasoned battle veterans, and several now were focusing on their next bet in our circle of card players. I could not tell the veteran players from the others by looking at them. But they seemed to have a certain confidence and distance about them absent from others. They also seemed to swear a lot more and complain a lot less. They included Sergeant Wright and Corporal Hathaway.

A few of our "back country lads," as the captain liked to call them, were boys from rural farm areas and now playing in the circle. Two of them were the Warner brothers, John and Jerry . . . one barely twenty and the other a year or two older. They came from Bucks County and told about their family farm. They planted forty acres in grain, and before the war they tended a small herd of dairy cattle and a dozen hogs. Having six siblings, the two brothers worried about how to divide up the farm when their parents left.

The half-dozen immigrants in the company were from almost as many countries. They all spoke with noticeable accents. One catching my eye playing cards was Erick Strauss, a Mennonite from Prussia. Before the war, he worked as a tanner in Philadelphia. I once asked him what he thought about fighting against his Hessian brethren from the old country.

He responded, "What do you think about fighting all those redcoats from England?" I told him the truth. I did not feel good about it, and he said he did not feel good about the Hessians either.

One of our bonded men, Kinder Peterson, turned out the biggest winner of the night. He had not even known how to play brag, but being unfamiliar with the rules, he hardly ever folded and had a string of good luck with the cards. His winning pleased me. Of those in the company, he was the neediest. He had been promised his freedom by his contract holder from New Castle if he fought out the war. He was on his own with no family.

The captain had been right in describing those in the company as good lads. They were. And in just a few months I had come to have respect and affection for each one. I could talk with any of them as if I had known him for years. I found even the waterfront workers and former thieves were not much different from anyone else. Each had joined the army for good reasons, although not necessarily because of independence.

★

The game finally ended, and we managed a few hours of sleep, but 3:00 o'clock came awfully early. We rose quickly to the drum beat of Reveille, ate a light breakfast, and were summoned into formation by the Assembly beat. Our company found its place in Colonel Butler's regiment. His regiment became first in a column of four regiments and a small artillery company all led by General Scott.

That was the easy part. Finding out where General Scott's detachment would fit in with the other detachments and brigades was a lot more challenging. The generals and colonels had to negotiate their place in line.

Once in formation we moved forward, stopped, fell out of formation, fell back in, started forward, only to stop again, and repeat. Multiple times. Of course, we never received an explanation for the delays.

"Here's what I think it is," said Captain Johnson. "That asshole Lee is just now wising up to the need for some reconnaissance of the ground ahead."

I shook my head. "We could have gotten another two hours of sleep."

"We're going to need it by day's end."

Finally, about 7:00 a.m. we actually began traversing the five miles southeast toward Monmouth. Without a drumbeat, we marched mostly through forested areas, which helped to conceal our position from any watching British scouts. Word filtered back that part of the British column had begun moving east out of Monmouth toward Middleton. Troops under the command of General Cornwallis were still in Monmouth near a courthouse. Cornwallis was known to lead some of the most elite troops in the British Army.

For two hours, we marched mostly south before turning east along a road crossing a deep ravine by way of a causeway leading to Monmouth Road. It ran north and south. On reaching it our scouts reported Cornwallis and most of his division had vacated the village to the northeast. He left only a rear guard of close to thirteen-hundred men under the personal command of General Henry Clinton, the commander-in-chief of the British Army.

General Lee immediately deployed our units to the left and right, north and south along Monmouth Road. General Wayne's unit took up a position to the right near the courthouse on an open plain across which, at about a hundred-fifty yards, stood the British rear guard. My detachment under General Scott was posted to the left and furthest north along the road, to cut off a British retreat. General Lee's remaining troops occupied the center area between Generals Scott and Wayne. Our position on the north gave us an opportunity to view what was happening along the road and near the courthouse.

I could not follow exactly whose units were which, but I did know General Wayne's troops began advancing and other Continental units moved around to the south of General Wayne to try and outflank the rear guard under Clinton. Then the British opened up with cannon fire.

Simultaneously, Captain Johnson shouted, "Alert to the northeast! British division on its way."

It was a huge British division doing double time to Monmouth on Middleton Road. They were moving in our direction although a few units were angling south to assist Clinton.

"Cornwallis?" I asked.

"That would be my bet," said the captain, "to help out the rear guard."

The cannon fire to the south continued and some of the American units began taking cover as a few began to retreat. The retreating soldiers were mainly from General Lee's force at center even though not under attack.

General Scott's detachment to the left continued to stand its ground, waiting for orders or for Cornwallis's men to come within range, whichever came first. General Scott consulted with Captain Johnson and some other company and regimental officers.

Captain Johnson reported a few minutes later. "General Scott has no orders to advance," he said. "He sent a messenger to get some direction from General Lee."

"So we stand our ground?" I asked.

"Until we hear different."

Cornwallis's division stopped before coming within range.

"Must be a thousand of them," I said. "You recognize their unit?"

"The Royal Foot Guard Brigade," said the captain. "They are reforming for battle. Get ready."

In the meantime, the British rear guard under Clinton began pushing toward General Wayne's detachment near the courthouse. I glanced back at General Scott, who again was conferring with officers.

If there was a time to advance on Cornwallis's troops, now was it, before they were fully organized. With no orders to advance, however, General Lee was gesturing with wild, frustrated movements. The center line units to our right were not just retreating, they were collapsing altogether.

"Look at this," said Captain Johnson. "The Foot Guards are formed up. They are about to attack. We've lost the opportunity."

"What do we do, Captain?" I asked. "Attack? Stand our ground? Retreat?" I began to panic.

The captain ran back to the rear to find Colonel Butler. When he returned a few moments later he said, "The colonel ordered retreat."

I shouted out the order and heard it repeated almost simultaneously by other lieutenants and sergeants in nearby units. We retreated in an orderly fashion with deliberation at first and moved back a few yards. When the Foot Guards moved toward us, we took a few rounds of shots at them and they at us, the two sides being mostly out of range. We then moved back a few more yards.

"This is crazy," said Captain Johnson. "We outnumber them and can outflank them. We should be attacking."

"Our whole line is retreating," I told him. "Lee must have ordered it."

"Yes. But why? Most of the line is not under pressure. We're retreating for no good reason." Turning, Captain Johnson spotted Colonel Butler, our regimental commander, now trotting in our direction.

Captain Johnson asked, "Colonel, what's going on? Why are we retreating?"

"We're retreating because we have no orders to attack and no backup units, and the line to our right is crumbling," answered the colonel.

"What happened to our backup?"

"General Lee never ordered them."

"Can you order an attack?"

The colonel gave him a friendly but disgusted look. "Not without orders from General Scott, who needs orders from General Lee." Butler trotted off.

I approached the captain. "You want me to order the company forward?"

One company out of the whole regiment, against a brigade of British Foot Guards? It was a bad idea. Not to mention doing so would have been against orders and I would risk court martial. I must have been thinking if we started forward, others would follow. As bad as it was, Captain Johnson gave it serious consideration.

He eventually threw his hands up and said in frustration, "No, everyone is retreating. We need to go."

By that time, our entire detachment was no longer backstepping and firing in formation. Rather, we had turned our backs on the enemy, walking fast and running in disarray to the south and west, where we met up with other fleeing units.

"Lieutenant," said the captain, "do what you can to keep the company together. With any luck, someone has sent for Washington. The day is young, and we may still have a fight of it."

I shouted to the sergeants at the top of my lungs, "Form up the company!"

Having backed off Monmouth road, we formed into a disorganized column with other advance force regiments now turning quickly onto the road leading back west. We slowed almost to a walk as the column narrowed to re-cross the causeway over the ravine. It was then I spotted General Washington on a white stallion forty or fifty yards away on our side of the ravine we had yet to cross.

"Look!" I pointed and called out to Captain Johnson. "Washington is here."

Washington's presence meant the remainder of the army was not far away and the day had not been wasted. Generals and aides, including Lee, all on horseback, stood in a cluster. Although we were too far to hear what was being said, their animated motions displayed frustration and anger.

When the cluster broke up, Washington and a few of his aides rode toward the approaching British. A few minutes later, he returned and began ordering troops into blocking positions to allow our retreating column to stream back across the ravine. To my surprise, troops broke out of the chaos, shuffled into marching units, and moved into position with precision. It was a beautiful sight to behold. Once again, those hours of training under Baron Von Steuben were paying off.

Chapter Forty Nine

Once across the ravine, Washington integrated many of Lee's units into the main regiments still a half mile further to the west and began moving artillery into place. By that time, Lee himself was nowhere to be seen.

Our positions organized along a hedgerow that served as a fence in peacetime. The hedgerow itself ran from north to south a hundred yards or so from the foot of a hill that sloped up about forty feet. I learned later it was known as Perrine's Ridge. Four or five of our regiments and two heavy guns formed up on the west side of the hedgerow with backs toward the ridge, facing the British arriving from the east. Captain Johnson's company, however, reorganized as part of two other detachments General Wayne commanded at the edge of a woods on the north end of the hedgerow, facing south.

No sooner were we in place when Captain Johnson gave the order, "Prepare for battle and fire at will!" We were being attacked by the same brigade of Royal Foot Guards who forced our retreat an hour earlier.

This time, however, we stayed to fight. At first, we exchanged volleys of musket fire at close range. Being near the woods, our guys were able to use trees for partial protection when reloading, while the Guards, poor bastards, were out in the open and had only their bodies to absorb our musket balls. That did not stop them and within a few minutes they came at us with bayonets. Our line was still well formed at three men deep, but no one could reload fast enough to ward off the redcoats. We resorted to our own bayonets for defense. Even Willie, our fastest and most accurate shot, became overwhelmed and I saw him fall.

But I had no time to check on him. Redcoats were everywhere. Having climbed over the bodies of their fallen comrades, the British line reached us in tight formation. After their initial onslaught, the fighting disintegrated into a chaotic melee. This was not the time to start ordering troops around to strategize for position. Indeed, there was no strategy. The most I could do was focus on the enemy soldier most threatening to me at any given moment. If no one threatened to me, I assisted the closest man in my company who was under attack. Nothing else mattered.

Fighting at close quarters was both easier and more difficult than I had imagined. I found it easier because I felt none of the moral trepidations that concerned me earlier. The rule was simple: kill or be killed. It was harder because my throat was burning with thirst, sweat soaked my clothes, and a sickening panic drove me to move with speed and force I never thought possible. If I lost my concentration, I would be cut down like many around me.

I can still recall the first man I killed that day. He was a British officer coming at me with a saber. I assumed the attack position Von Steuben taught us in bayonet training with my musket out front at a slight angle, hands a foot apart on the barrel and stock, feet at shoulder distance, knees flexed. It was the best position not only to strike at an enemy soldier but also for parrying a sword or bayonet attack. The officer signaled his intentions a little too clearly, and I caught his sword with the wood of my musket stock. Stepping forward, I smashed the butt of my musket into his head. That set him back a step, allowing me to straighten out the musket and thrust forward with my bayonet. He crumpled to the ground.

I had time to reload and get one shot off, but then another Redcoat rushed me with his bayonet. I again took my attack stance as he raised his musket to his shoulder as if to shoot me at close range. I figured he was bluffing. If his piece was actually loaded, he would have discharged it at me well before then. I took the opportunity to jab at his musket with the butt of mine but was not successful in dislodging it. Seeing we were at something of a standoff, we ended up pushing and hitting at each other with our musket stocks, trying to angle for an opportunity to thrust or slash with the bayonet. The tussling came to an end only when I was able to trip him backwards over the body of a dead Continental soldier and inflict a fatal stab.

The worst of the melee lasted only twenty or thirty minutes, but they were the longest minutes of my life. At that point, we received orders from officers behind us, "Retreat toward the hedgerow!" And that's what we did, joining the units south of us along the hedgerow.

The upclose fighting continued sporadically, but then we heard the roar of artillery open up on top of Perrine's Ridge. It was firing over our heads and reaching the British positions beyond.

"That's a pretty sound," I heard the captain say. The firing cannons meant the main army atop the ridge had finally organized and our advance units below could join them. All of us along the hedgerow made a disciplined retreat in short order across a bridge over a brook and shallow marshes, until we climbed to the safety of the ridge top. As we moved up the hill, I saw Willie in front of me and clapped him on the back.

"Holy shit!" I said. "Can't tell you how glad I am to see your gorgeous face. I saw you go down over by the woods."

"Just got the wind knocked out of me." Willie smiled. "The fellow who did it got a musket ball in his chest. We held them. How'd you come out?"

"Thirstier than hell. Come on, let's get to the top."

"You think I'm gorgeous?" he asked half smiling.

"No. You're ugly, but I'm happy you're alive anyway."

We lumbered in behind the front line units at the top of the hill and found mess wagons set up in a clearing. My first wish was for water and the second for a shady place to drink it. Fortunately, we found both. Accompanying the army atop the ridge were a half dozen women who had been hauling water to the mess wagons from a nearby spring. I got my hands on a bucket half full and gulped down two canteens full before slowing down.

I then grabbed a couple of apples from the mess wagon and found Captain Johnson and Sergeant Wright sitting next to a tall growth of bushes near the mess area. It was the first I had sat since morning. Others in the company were scattered nearby.

The sergeant wore a blood-soaked bandage around his arm. I turned to him first. "Bayonet?"

"No. Musket ball. I think it's out. I should be fine. You?"

"Somehow I escaped with no more than a few scrapes, but plenty tired," I said. "I saw Sergeant Sanders take a bayonet in the ribs. I'm sure he never made it. Do we have a read on other casualties?"

Captain Johnson spoke up. "We're missing eight or nine. I didn't know about Sanders. That makes ten. Of those, we now have five confirmed dead. I'm hopeful the rest will still show up.

"Who's dead?" I had to find out.

"Other than Sanders, we lost one of the Warner brothers, also Strauss and Higgins. Who else, Sergeant?"

"Hathaway."

I was surprised. "Corporal Hathaway? He was a good man."

"They are all good men," said the captain. "We have another half dozen wounded including the sergeant here. Most are mobile, but they will be out a few weeks. A couple more collapsed from the heat."

"That heat is really something," I said. "I don't know how those British boys stand it in those wool uniforms."

"They've lost more to heat than us," said Sergeant Wright. "And they must be a lot more tired. Some marched half way to Middleton before ending up here."

"What happened to General Lee?" I asked.

"Washington ordered him to the rear," said the captain. "He has led his last army."

★

The captain received orders to join back up with our old 7th Pennsylvania Regiment. It had become part of one of the brigades assigned to Major General Stirling, sometimes referred to as Lord Stirling based on a Scottish title he inherited. Lord Stirling's brigades, along with an artillery company of eight cannons, formed the left, or north wing of the American forces atop Perrine's Ridge. General Wayne took over command of the center units, which consisted of General Lee's former troops. General Nathaniel Greene took charge of the right wing.

In the short while we rested, a fierce artillery battle had gotten under way. The British rolled up ten big guns shooting six and twelve pound cannonballs from three or four-hundred yards out from the base of our hill. They tried to use the artillery as cover for troops charging up the hill toward Lord Stirling's left wing position. The Continental guns were only capable of shooting four and six pound balls. From the top of the hill, though, they proved an effective counter to the British fire power.

Near the Continental cannons, Captain Johnson's company helped fill a gap in the front line of musket men who scattered behind trees, rocks and trenches for cover from incoming cannonballs. We were close enough, however, to prevent any massing of British soldiers at the foot of the hill. None of the redcoats ever made it very far up.

The artillery battle raged on for a good hour until Lord Stirling decided it was time to try an offensive maneuver. He selected three regiments to move through the woods to our left and north and try to infiltrate the flank of the attacking British units. While the 7th Pennsylvanian stayed on the ridge, due to the departure of the regiments assigned to the flanking exercise, we adjusted our location. The forty men in Captain Johnson's company still able to fight moved closer up to the edge of the ridge. Lying prone on the grass a short distance to the right of our artillery.

From that vantage point, we had a good view of the action. To our far right, we saw General Greene's men move artillery pieces to a hill on the south side of the battlefield facing north. The maneuver added a new angle to the Continental bombardment. Repeatedly Cornwallis' troops tried to take down the artillery, but to no avail. To our immediate right, waves of British troops tried to overwhelm General Wayne's troops in the center. Each time, Wayne waited until the British came breathtakingly close and then let loose with multiple rounds of musket balls.

On the left where we were, the artillery battle continued while we awaited the outcome of the flanking attempt. In the meantime, we dodged incoming cannonballs and kept watch on the regiments of redcoats who had mostly pulled back from the base of the hill and now clustered near their artillery. We also took potshots at British patrols navigating within range as they tried to assess our strength and the prospects of rushing our position.

"Who do you think owns this land anyway?" I asked Captain Johnson as we kept an close eye on the landscape below.

"I heard it's owned by different farm families. The Perrines, the Cobbs, the Sutfins. I don't know who else."

"I hope today was not planting day."

"They have their crops in by now. Being trampled by horses and cannons, though, will not do much good."

"A lot of debris will be left behind for anyone interested in a good souvenir."

"It will tangle up plows and ruin horses' hooves for years to come." He held up his hand. "Watch it now! This one is coming our way. Heads down!"

Within seconds a twelve-pound cannon ball landed in the grass to our rear and rolled forty yards before disappearing into the under bush.

"That will make a nice souvenir, when someone stumbles across it ten years from now," he said matter of factly.

"You never told me about yourself, Captain. You a farmer by trade?"

"I've done a little farming. I had forty acres in Delaware, New Castle County. It was actually not far from the Brandywine. When we marched down there last summer, I hoped to get a look at it, but never had time."

"Who runs it now?"

"I have a sharecropper. My wife left me a few years ago because I spent too much time in the militia. Which meant she ended up having to do all the farm work. Can't say I blame her. She took my daughter with her. So rather than trying to run the place myself, I rented it out."

"How long were you in the militia?"

"On and off for sixteen years. I always liked it. I acquired some military skills, but I was not full time. I became a captain and knew Franklin. After the war started in '75, he asked me if I would like to have a Continental commission." He held up his hand again and called out. "Willie!"

"Yes sir, Captain," Willie answered from a short distance.

"Come over here. I have a job for you."

I saw Willie slide back off the ridge. Staying in a crouched position he trotted over to where we were and slid up on his stomach to the other side of Captain Johnson.

"You see those guys?" The captain pointed to five redcoats huddled together down the ridge near a tree. They were pointing in our direction.

"Yes, sir, I see them."

"How far away do you think they might be?"

Willie looked around for a marker to judge their distance. "Hard to say. Hundred-ten, maybe a hundred-twenty yards."

"I don't know what they are up to but it's not anything good. You think you could reach them with that flintlock of yours?"

"I could come close."

"Give it a try."

Willie backed off the edge to re-load his musket, adding extra powder and adjusting the wadding. He slid back up next to the captain.

"You're not overloaded, are you?" The captain looked worried.

"No, Captain, I know what this baby can hold."

"Fire when ready."

Willie took a minute to take careful aim. He fired and an instant later one of the redcoats fell to the ground. Being helped up by a comrade, the injured man and other four quickly fell back off their position.

"Great shot!" The captain looked at Willie with admiration. "All right, back to your post." After Willie left, the captain said to me, "That was amazing. I thought he might come close, but not actually hit anyone."

"He has talent and a good eye."

"You think he'd be interested in moving up to sergeant?"

"Technically, he's not even a soldier. He is a contractor of training services. Remember?"

"I'll change that with a little paperwork. He'll set a good example."

We watched the British a while longer before I asked, "You think you'll go back to New Castle County when this is over?"

"No," he said, "I'm going to sell the place. I bought a hundred acres out west, near Pittsburgh. So cheap I couldn't say no. What about you? Going back into the merchant business in Philadelphia?"

"I suppose, but I don't know if I can get back into dry goods business. Our London supplier might be a little testy, me becoming a rebel and all."

"Let him smell an opportunity to make money, he'll be your friend."

"You're probably right," I said. "What I would like to do, though, is get married."

"You got a prospect in mind?"

"Yes. If I can find her. And if she'll have me."

He looked at me skeptically. "Sounds a little half baked."

"It's a long story."

★

We heard a barrage of musket fire forward to our left. The British regiments resting in the afternoon heat near their artillery began forming up and moving back. Lord Stirling's flanking maneuver was having an effect. The British cannons stopped firing and joined the withdrawal while other British units to our right began to pull back.

Retreat! The British were actually backing away from the Americans. Then we saw troops under General Wayne to our right begin to form up into a column. We heard shouting from officers behind us.

"Form up! Form up! We're going after them!"

Our artillery continued the barrage as the regiment formed and started down the ridge. By the time we reached the lower ground, nearly half a mile separated us from the British. The redcoats now appeared to be in full retreat. Our big guns on top of the ridge had gone silent. We were approaching the British in a half dozen different columns from different angles over varied terrain. Passing through a patch of marshland, our column slowed down and Willie came up beside me.

"You think they're running from us, Mr. Thompson? Or, maybe they decided to get on with their business of going to New York."

"I was wondering the same, Willie. My guess would be they're not running but decided they can't outflank us, and are just giving it up for now. Washington is pretty good, though, making the redcoats look like they're on the run."

By now the British had moved to the other side of the same ravine we had crossed and re-crossed that morning. As our columns reached the ravine, we spread out along it just out of range of British musket fire. If we were going to make a battle of it now, we would have to descend the ravine and charge up the other side. Could that be what our commanders had in mind?

I hoped not. I was tired. I had been up since 3:00 in the morning and did a lot of marching and fighting. Charging up the ravine, of course, was not the only way to get to the British. We could march some regiments around it and attack the flanks, and I was sure Washington's strategists were mapping out such a plan. But dusk was beginning to fall. By the time we got into a position for any sort of fighting, we would be doing it in the dark.

So, for the moment, the two sides were at a standoff, sizing up the other across a ravine a hundred-fifty yards apart. As darkness filled the air, supply wagons with food and water moved up from the rear. Washington ordered units not involved in guard duty to sleep on the battlefield, the battle to resume in the morning.

★

I've had many a sleepless night thinking about the close calls, gory sights and many deaths I experienced that day. Still, for three or four hours that night I slept well, out of sheer exhaustion. Then, upon waking, I began thinking about the precariousness of our current position. Whatever had happened the previous day, would all be repeated today. While I continued to lay there, tired as I was, I could sleep no more.

The stars faded with the faint glow of early morning sun rising behind the eastern hills. But even before the moon disappeared and the refreshing early morning mist melted away, the entire Continental Army looked across the ravine in utter amazement.

The British Army had evacuated.

General Washington had assigned a Connecticut regiment to maintain watch, but somehow the British left under their very noses. To me this was welcome news. A few senior officers grumbled about not having another crack at the redcoats. But I also heard many expressions of relief at not having to charge up the ravine. My sentiments were in the latter camp.

Captain Johnson officially brought us the word.

"The new moon last night didn't help," he said. "The Connecticut boys were probably more concerned about a sneak attack than the British getting up and leaving. In any event, they're gone."

"We going after them?" asked Woods, our sole remaining able-bodied sergeant.

"Probably not," said the captain. "They'll be in Middletown soon and well dug in. Also they'll have protection from Admiral Howe's fleet just offshore. So, the consensus at this point is to let them go for now."

"What does General Lee say?" someone asked, giving rise to snickers and jeers.

"General Lee never got a vote on this one," responded the captain.

"So what are we in for today?" I asked.

"Rest and recuperation. We have cleanup to do and need to re-supply. Also we need to organize a burial detail. The general orders so far are to go slow and take it easy. We'll probably start for White Plains tomorrow."

"How ironic," I said.

"Why so, Lieutenant?"

"Here we are in the summer of '78. And we're going to end up in White Plains with the British in New York. The same place the army was, and the same place the British were, at the end of '76."

"Good thinking."

"So has all of our training and fighting really made any difference?"

"Yes," answered the captain.

"How's that?"

"Back then, we were in a position of weakness. Now, we're in a position of strength."

Chapter Fifty

"Papa!"

I looked up and saw Jonathon and Nathan waiving, trying to work their way my direction. Stepping over equipment, dodging soldiers, avoiding horses, and running around stacks of supplies and wagons along the way, they both attacked me with big hugs.

"Are we glad to see you!" Nathan said, releasing his grip. Jonathon held on a little longer. Tears rolled down his cheeks, and he wiped them away a couple times before he let me look at him.

I was privileged to have a family reunion on the battlefield. A few others reached out to touch a brother or a son, or maybe even a wife assigned to the women's support unit. But not many.

"Where have you boys been? I lost track of you days ago."

"They kept us clear to the rear, Papa, back with the commissary wagons. We could not even get close enough to see what was happening. We heard the cannons and musket fire, but that was all."

"We thought it was all over in the morning, when Lee retreated," said Nathan. "Then the fighting kept going on, and we didn't know who won or lost until this morning."

"What did they tell you," I asked, "did we win or lose?"

"We won!" They both exclaimed simultaneously.

"What was it?" I turned to Captain Johnson. "A victory or defeat?"

"We controlled the battlefield in the end." He looked pleased. "It was a victory. No question about it. You boys can sit here with us. We'll celebrate by rustling up some vittles and extra tea. Your father deserves it. All the men in the company deserve it. Corporal!"

Corporal Richards, one of our two remaining corporals, took charge of tracking down breakfast. Soon our entire company feasted on muffins, eggs and tea, along with our fifer and drummer.

"Tell us about the battle," Jonathon asked once the eating was underway.

I gave him the short version. "After the retreat in the morning, we organized over yonder by the hedgerow and woods. That was the tough part of the day. Those Foot Guards came at us with bayonets. We had a lot of casualties and lost one of our sergeants."

"Not just a sergeant, but four other men as well." said Sergeant Woods."

"Willie fell to the ground," I said, "and I thought he was a goner. But he got back up and we were able to move to the top of that ridge. After that it was mostly artillery for a couple of hours, at least in our sector."

"Captain, you have any information on overall casualties?" asked Corporal Richards.

"Nothing definite. Early estimates are eighty or ninety dead on our side, somewhat more for the British. Two to three-hundred wounded on each side. A lot still missing and suffering with heat-related injuries."

After breakfast the first order of business was locating the dead from our company for burial. General Washington designated an area close to the forest beneath Perrine's Ridge for a cemetery near where many of them were killed. The medical corps gathered the bodies and wrapped them in blankets, but members of every company had the grisly task of identifying them.

The boys played their instruments during the burial ceremony. As they played, each body was carried past our company's line of soldiers standing at attention with musket muzzle on the left foot, left hand on the stock, and right hand atop the butt. An officer from Washington's staff sat on horseback with saber drawn pointed down. Each body was placed in a grave facing the direction of the British attack. After Captain Johnson said a few words, the officer on horseback gave an order and three musket volleys fired. We then moved to the next grave.

★

That afternoon the captain asked me to take charge of a convoy of eight horse-drawn carts the quartermaster's unit was sending down to a docking facility on the Shark River.

"It's only four or five miles south of here," he said. "We're trying to lay in more supplies for the march north. The quartermaster was able to have them shipped in by barge. We received word this morning they are ready for pickup. All the wagons are tied up, but carts and horses are available. I agreed to supply the manpower." Captain Johnson smiled. "It was either that or help bury the British dead. I figured you would prefer to make the river trip."

"What happened to the rest and recuperation?"

"As soon as you get back. I guarantee it."

I had to admit the supply mission was better than digging more graves. "What are we picking up?"

"Mostly food. A few dozen cured hams, some livestock, and I don't know what else. You can take your boys with you if you want."

"Thanks, they would probably like to go."

"Assign one or two men per cart. The boys can take one of them. Take along a corporal and someone on horseback for security."

Within the hour we were rolling. I led the way on horseback, with Corporal Richards riding up and down the column to keep everything in line, and Willie bringing up the rear. A pair of draught horses pulled each two-wheeled cart, some up to eight feet long. Having wheels in the middle, they were easily maneuverable, unlike a Conestoga. Some of the carts had boards on which to sit. Jonathon and Nathan rode on one of those. Drivers for other carts had to walk along side or hop onto one of the horses.

The road to the river consisted of a rough track of sand and dirt, pocked with big stones that had worked their way to the surface over the years. We passed a roadside tavern at a crossroads and a couple farm houses, but saw little else apart from the peaceful New Jersey countryside. It was refreshing to get away from the stench of burnt powder and decaying bodies.

The dockmaster had the supplies waiting in a ramshackle warehouse next to the dock. They included not only the hams wrapped in burlap bags, but also barrels of salt fish and pork, hundred-pound bags of dried beans and rice, bushels of green apples, barrels of flour, big wheels of cheese, a few crates of rum and six head of cattle.

As we pulled the first cart into the warehouse area, the dockmaster asked, "You run into those fellows who just left here before you arrived?"

"No," I said, "we didn't see anyone. Why do you ask?"

"They were acting a might odd is all."

"How so?"

"Two came in on horseback and another two on a wagon with a bad wheel they tried to fix. When I asked where they were headed, they were real unfriendly about it."

"What kind of a wagon was it?"

"Kind of like a Conestoga with a curved wagon bed and the ends arched up, but a lot smaller. No bigger than one of your carts."

"A farm wagon?"

"No. It would not be much use on a farm. Too small. I don't know what the British use them for, but I've seen them before."

The description piqued my curiosity. "I will keep an eye out for it."

★

After loading up and starting back, the cart on which Jonathon and Nathan were riding hit a stone damaging a wheel. Repairing it would not be difficult, but we lacked the tools. Looking around for a nearby farmhouse, I saw the tavern we passed on the way out.

"Corporal, here is what we'll do," I said. "I'll take the boys and cart over to the road house. They ought to have some tools, and it should not take us long to fix it. You take everyone else and livestock back to Monmouth and try to get some of that rest the captain keeps talking about. We'll meet you in an hour or so. Willie will stay to help us out."

After Willie temporarily repaired the wheel, the four of us slowly made our way down the lane to the tavern. It was a large, pleasant-looking log structure with a water trough out front and a frame barn to the side. There were two horses tied to hitching posts, and near the barn stood an unusual-looking wagon fitting the description given by the dockmaster. Along with missing a wheel, its bare axle rested on a wooden sawhorse. Crouching nearby, a frustrated looking man worked to fashion a part for the wheel assembly while a second man watched from behind.

We pulled our cart next to the wagon and I gave them both a friendly nod. "Seems we got the same problem. It's these roads. You mind if we share some of your tools?"

The man crouching on the ground stared up at me, shifted his glance to our cart convoy on the main road heading north, and looked back at me. "Whatever you can find," he said. The other man said nothing.

The dockmaster was right. They were unfriendly. Their wagon, however, drew my greater interest. It was shaped almost like a boat but with a squared off bow and stern. The wagon bed itself was only a foot and a half in height and had a five-foot wide wooden cover over the entire top. The cover had hinges near the front end to allow it to be lifted. It was secured at the back by a padlock. From the stability of the wagon bed on the sawhorse, I had the impression a heavy load occupied the interior. The padlock suggested something valuable. I wanted to find out what.

"You boys stay here with Willie and try to get that wheel fixed." I started for the door. "I'll go see who we're dealing with."

Walking through the tavern door, I entered the great room. Through the dim light, I saw a dozen thick, rough-finished tables surrounded by heavy chairs and benches. A stone fireplace took up the far end of the room, and a wooden bar stood along another wall with stools along the front. Behind the bar stood a large man, presumably the proprietor. The kitchen area looked dark and vacant. We had arrived between meals.

Two patrons sat at a small square table on the far side of the room drinking ale. They got up when I entered. One grabbed for his musket while the other picked up a flintlock pistol off the table. It was the size of a horse pistol, the kind military officers carried in their saddles.

Both wore civilian clothes, but their boots were military issue. I sensed from their stature they were officers. I carried my own musket and when I saw them point their weapons at me, I held up my hands to show I meant no harm. To my amazement, I recognized the two.

"Major Warren and Lieutenant Masters," I said. The major was on General Erskine's staff in Philadelphia and the lieutenant had served as the general's aide.

"Who are you?" The major squinted. "Thompson? Daniel Thompson?" I stood my musket near the bar, and they lowered their weapons.

"What a surprise," I said, and it really was. What were these two British officers doing here? Out of uniform? And how was I to act? On whose side did they think I was?

I gave a formal bow and they returned it, laying down their weapons.

"What in bloody hell are you doing here?" The major forced a laugh.

I needed time to think of something to say. "I was about to ask you the same thing," I said disarmingly. "You haven't played a suitor to Captain Cunningham in any plays lately, have you?"

The major shifted his eyes to the lieutenant and back at me. "Not hardly. We got separated from the main column and then our wagon broke down. As soon as we get it fixed, we'll be re-joining the army. And you?"

I restrained my curiosity from asking what they were doing several miles south of Monmouth when the entire British Army was northeast of here. And why out of uniform with that little odd-shaped wagon? His story raised more questions than it answered. Still, it was a good enough story for me to use.

"I know what you mean. The same thing happened to me."

"Really?" He did not look impressed. "You were traveling in the British column?"

I had to think if that was where I wanted to place myself. "Of course," I said, "along with friends from Philadelphia. I would not stay in that bloody City after the army pulled out."

"You have a wagon outside?"

"It's only a cart, but a wheel came off, just like yours. We're trying to get it fixed."

"Why are you down in this area?"

"We had gone down to the river to pick up some supplies before the battle yesterday."

"You mind if we take a look at your cart? Maybe we can help you out."

From the tone of his voice, he was not offering help. He wanted to check out who I was traveling with and what we were carrying.

"That would be mighty nice of you. We pulled it up right next to yours."

The three of us stepped outside and walked over to the two vehicles. Willie was down on his knees working on the broken wheel and the two boys stood nearby stabilizing the cart. One of the men working on the British wagon was hammering away. The other continued to look on.

I spoke as we approached, to give the boys and Willie some warning. "Boys, look who I ran into inside. This is Major Warren and Lieutenant Masters, two of my friends from Philadelphia. Both worked closely with General Erskine. You remember? He came to our house last March with Captain Cunningham."

The two boys looked at me with alarm not knowing exactly how to react. Nathan recovered first. "Of course," he said affably. "How are you, sirs? General Erskine, he was so friendly. I trust he came through that awful battle yesterday."

The lieutenant nodded. "I'm sure he did. He told me about you two. You still want to become drummer boys?"

"It's our fondest dream," Nathan answered. "We have just another year to go and we'll be old enough."

The major glanced in the cart. "Bags of grain?"

"We have a lot of mouths to feed," I answered. "No telling how long it will have to last."

"And who is this?" asked Major Warren pointing at Willie. "Your property?"

I had to think quickly. Should Willie be slave or free? "Yes, he is," I said, "and a lazy piece of property at that. Come on, boy, get a move on. Once you're finished with this cart, you are to help on that wagon. You understand?"

Willie took it in stride without flinching. "Yes, master."

I shook my head and clucked my tongue. "Good help is hard to get in wartime."

"What is he doing with a musket?" asked Lieutenant Masters, nodding at Willie's musket leaning against the cart a few feet away.

Jonathon piped up. "That's not his. It's mine." He immediately grabbed it.

"I told you never to stand it so close to Willie," I said. "You just never know what he might try." I gave Willie another frown and clucked a little more.

"Yes, Papa."

"The major and his men got separated from the British column and had a wheel problem, just like us." I let the boys in on my little lie. "Once they have it fixed, they will join back up with the army. I'm thinking maybe we can all ride to Middletown together."

"It will be nice to have the company." Nathan smiled.

Major Warren did not respond. He only turned to the man hammering on the wagon. "How much longer, Jake?"

"I gotta rebuild part of the assembly." He was now sitting on the ground next to the wheel axle. "At least an hour."

"Make it sooner if you can," the major said in disgust.

"Your cargo must be heavy," I said, trying to get an idea of what his wagon was carrying.

"What if it is?"

I shrugged. "Hard on the axle. Well, we might as well go back inside, if it's going to be a while."

Chapter Fifty One

Before leaving the wagons, I bent down near Willie as if to examine his progress, and whispered, "Keep an eye on us." He nodded.

"Let me buy you a pint," said Major Warren as we moved inside toward their table. He brought three large mugs of ale to the table and made a toast. "To the better times in Philadelphia."

"To the better times indeed." I raised a mug and took a swallow. "How would you gents like to play some cards?" I pulled out my deck. "Just to pass the time. Maybe a friendly game of brag?"

"How about whist?" asked Lieutenant Masters.

"That's a game for old spin- . . ." I caught myself, ". . . for old soldiers. Sounds good to me. We can play with three-person rules."

I looked at Major Warren for his approval. "Deal them up!"

Lieutenant Masters won the first round, which we played without conversation. He began dealing the second round when Major Warren asked in a conversational tone, "You know what I think?"

"No. what?"

"I don't think you got separated from the British column at all."

I tried not to look surprised and began sorting my hand. "Come now, Major, my story was no less believable than yours."

"Maybe, but you were never with the British column."

"It's your play, Lieutenant," I said, and he laid down a card.

"Were you?" The major persisted.

"What difference does it make?"

The major played a card. "It would mean you lied to us about why you are here. If you were under my command I would see you got ninety lashes with a cat-o-nine tails."

"I am fortunate then not to be under your command."

"Are you going to tell us the truth, now?"

"You don't know I lied."

"Oh, but I do. We tried to locate you a few days before we left Philadelphia to see if you had more flour available. You were nowhere to be found. And your sister – your rebel sister – was making no preparations to leave."

"Of course not, she's a rebel. She would never leave the City. And I could have joined the column after you left."

"True. But you didn't."

I tried to shift the focus. "You know what I think, Major?"

"What is that?"

"You have no intention of rejoining the British Army at Middletown."

"Your play. Even if that were true, what business would it be of yours?"

I played a card, picked up the trick, and laid down another card. "It would mean you lied to me."

"Touché then. Now, that you've had the satisfaction of accusing me of lying, I trust it was for a good cause."

"It just raises the question of what are you doing here. Are you defecting to the Continental Army?"

Both officers burst out laughing.

"No. Mr. Thompson," said the major, "I can assure you we have no interest in that second rate, ragtag Yankee Army."

"That second rate, ragtag army held its own against the best that the British Army had to offer yesterday." While it was not the wisest thing to say, I could not help myself.

"So, you were there." Major Warren nodded. "Did you have a westerly view or an easterly view?"

"I didn't say I was there. News travels fast. It's your play, Lieutenant."

The lieutenant played a card and said, "It pains me to say this, Major, but I think Captain Cunningham was right. I think Mr. Thompson was spying for the Americans last March. He lied to Captain Cunningham and General Erskine back then and lying to us now."

The major nodded. "You are now accused of being a double liar, Mr. Thompson. What do you say to that?" He laid down a card.

We were getting into dangerous territory, with two of them to one of me. I would try again to shift attention. "Here is what I say. If you're not going to Middletown, and if you're not defecting to the Continental Army, then you're on a frolic of your own. The two of you plus your comrades in the yard."

"That's an interesting observation," Major Warren smiled. "What do you regard as the nature of the frolic?"

"It looks as if you are stealing whatever is in that wagon you have padlocked."

"Oh, so we're being accused of stealing." The major glanced over at the lieutenant. "First lying, then stealing. That's not very friendly."

"Well then, I take it all back. We want to keep this on a friendly level."

We each played our turn in silence before the major asked. "What do you think is in that wagon?"

"Something important," I answered. "But instead of me guessing, why don't you just tell me, since we're among friends."

Major Warren sighed, placed all his cards on the table and reached down to pick up his horse pistol from the empty chair beside him. "I'm afraid we cannot do that, Mr. Thompson, because we're not friends." He now aimed the pistol across the table at my heart.

Oh, shit! I had engaged in a full day of combat yesterday and escaped too many close calls to count. Just as I began to think destiny was shining on me, now I hung on the cusp of death once again. Destiny be damned. I tried not to betray my emotion and looked down at my cards.

"Why are you pointing that pistol at me, Major? You think I've been cheating?"

"I am pointing the pistol at you because your curiosity has gone too far. As soon as our wagon is ready, we'll be leaving here. I want to assure we will have no trouble from you."

"What makes you think I would give you trouble?"

"Because you are a rebel. And whatever we may be up to, we cannot take any chances with you."

I heard a movement at the front door and a voice said, "Put it down now, or you're a dead man."

It was Willie, his musket aimed at Major Warren. The major froze and I barely breathed. Surprised, Lieutenant Masters jerked back in his chair.

I was not sure if he was going for a weapon, but Willie stepped forward and had both of them covered.

"Whichever one of you two makes a move is going to get it the head," he said. "Makes no difference to me which one. Now put the pistol down, or it's going to be you, Major."

The major lowered the pistol to the table and raised his hands. "It looks like your property knows how to handle a musket."

"Looks like it." I stood up slowly and moved around the table to retrieve his weapon.

Before I got close, we heard a scuffling at the door. The two wagon tenders, one brandishing a musket and the other a saber, burst into the room. Willie swiveled and fired at the man with the musket. As he fell, the other man, Jake, grabbed the musket and moved in my direction.

I picked up a chair and hurled it in Major Warren's direction, hoping to knock the pistol to the floor and give me some running room. I grabbed another chair and swung it at Jake now coming toward me with a musket and saber. The chair temporarily knocked him off balance.

"Let's go!" I shouted to Willie, pointing toward the tavern door. We both made a dash, but as I stooped to snatch up my musket, I heard a bang and felt an excruciating pain. A lead ball from Major Warren's pistol hit me on the inside of my leg above my left knee. I dropped like a rock behind a table and chairs, unable to budge.

Willie picked up my musket and up-ended the table to give us cover.

No sooner had he done so than in charged Jonathon and Nathan each carrying a pistol, apparently retrieved from the horses in the yard.

"Down, boys, down!" yelled Willie.

They hit the floor and scrambled over to join us behind our table-and-chairs barrier. In the next second a musket fired from the other side of the room. Its lethal charge harmlessly whizzed overhead.

The situation momentarily stabilized, with the two boys, Willie and me behind our hastily created fort, and the two British officers and Jake behind a similar structure not more than fifteen yards away. Agonizing pain burned in my leg as I tried to maintain a presence of mind. Another shot fired from across the room landed a lead ball with a thud into the table.

Nathan fired back blindly.

"Let Willie do the shooting, boys," I whispered, "at least until you have a clear shot. Do we have any extra cartridges?"

"Yes, sir," said Nathan, holding up a cartridge box.

I looked inside the box and saw only musket cartridges. "We have to make do for the pistols. Give me yours, Nathan. I will see if I can make it work." I struggled to a half sitting position.

"Papa, you all right?" asked Jonathon, panting from nervousness.

"Barely," I whispered. "Stay calm and you'll be fine. Willie, can you get off a shot?" We had two muskets and two pistols with no more than a dozen cartridges.

"Can't tell what's happening." Willie peered around the over-turned table to look at the shadowy far side of the room. "Got a pile of chairs stacked up."

"Fire into the cracks just so they don't get any ideas about rushing us."

Willie fired, quickly reloaded and let loose again. The British returned like fire. After a pause, we heard a voice from across the room.

"Thompson." Major Warren called out my name.

"What is it?" I tried not to reveal my pain.

"It doesn't have to be like this."

I looked at Willie and the boys, shook my head and whispered, "Keep a close watch," pointing in the direction of the Brits. I hollered back, "You drew the first weapon."

"I did," said Major Warren. "And then you killed one of my guys."

"It was shoot or be shot at."

"I'm not saying I blame your man. I am just saying maybe we've gone far enough. All we want to do is leave here in peace. Just give me your word you won't shoot, and we'll be gone."

"I cannot do that," I said."

"Why not?"

"You are British soldiers in territory controlled by the Continental Army. You are now our prisoners."

"We're not your prisoners until we've surrendered our arms. And that's not going to happen."

"Well then, we'll have to fight it out."

"Your boys are with you," the major reminded. "Do you want them hurt?"

I looked at Jonathon and Nathan. Warren was right, but I could not stop now. "We're well armed. The boys will be fine."

"Have it your way."

With that, three shots fired at close intervals. Two came from muskets and one from a pistol. I suspected that was all the fire power they had without reloading. It would have been a good time to rush them. But I could not lead the charge, and I had no intention of sending Willie by himself or either of the boys. I motioned instead for Willie to return fire.

A few more shots were exchanged, after which I could hear heated discussion from the other side of the room. Warren spoke again.

"Thompson."

"What is it?"

"I propose a momentary truce."

"What for?"

"To see if we can work this out. The small table in the middle of the room. We can meet there. You and I will sit. The others can stand behind."

"You make the first move." I did not trust him.

We waited until Warren, waiving a white handkerchief, moved to the middle table and took a chair. I whispered, "You boys walk beside me, and Willie, prop me up from the back. I can barely walk."

The four of us moved awkwardly to the middle table. If Warren noticed anything wrong, he did not let on.

Lieutenant Masters and Jake emerged from their fortress to stand behind Warren.

"Nice to see you again." Warren looked at Jake. "Retrieve our steins from yonder table. I could use a refreshment."

My leg felt on fire. I did not know how long I could sit. "What do you have in mind?"

The major waited upon Jake's return. After he took a swallow, he said, "I want to make a deal."

I sipped my ale. It tasted so good I took another. "The only deal I can make is for you to surrender your arms. In return, we will treat you to all the courtesies due an officer of the British Army."

His tired eyes looked at me. "No. That's not going to happen. I and my men are not surrendering anything. There is plenty for us to share. And then part company."

I did not have to ask what he proposed to share. My suspicions were confirmed. They were on a frolic and making off with something valuable. I asked, "How much?"

Warren hesitated. "Sixty-thousand pounds."

Holy Christ in Heaven! I realized these fellows were thinking big. It had to be an army payroll. Willie, the two boys and I were the only ones standing in their way. "Treasury agents following you?"

"I don't know. Maybe."

"Coin or bills?"

"Silver and gold coin."

"What's your proposal then?"

"It's packed in four strong boxes inside the wagon. We'll take three, you get one."

I sensed they were desperate to get moving. Negotiating surrender would be futile. On the other hand, I thought we could do better than one strong box. "We split it fifty-fifty."

"You're too greedy, Thompson. It's three for us, one for you."

"No deal. Half and half and you can take our two horses. You will have four. You can pack one with coin and distribute the excess on the other three. We'll take the wagon and draught horses. You'll move a lot faster."

He looked at the men behind him. Each nodded.

"All right then," Warren nodded. "We'll go out and retrieve two boxes."

"No," I said, "everyone stays here."

"You will have to trust me."

"That will not work."

"So what are you saying? The deal is off?"

We had to come up with a way to retrieve our portion of the payroll without sacrificing our security.

"Where is the proprietor?" asked Jonathon. "Maybe he can help."

"Mr. Proprietor," I shouted, "are you still with us?"

"What do you want?" He had been waiting out the shooting from behind the bar.

"We need your help."

"Doing what?"

"There's a wagon out in the yard. It has a padlock on it. Major Warren has the key. Take his key and open up the back of the wagon. It contains four heavy boxes. Bring two to me. They will be heavy. You'll have to bring one in at a time. Leave two boxes there and the wagon unlocked. Then return the key to me. Will you do that for us?"

"All right."

As we waited for the proprietor to return, I could feel myself fading. My pants leg was soaked with blood and it continued to flow. I needed to tie off the wound. I could not retain consciousness much longer. Without giving away the seriousness of my injury, I had to get the British quickly on their way.

"I know I winged you, Thompson," Warren said as we waited. "Are you badly hurt?"

"Barely nicked," I said. "How about you fellows? Our musket fire get through the cracks?"

"No. We're all fine."

"How much time you need to pack up?"

"Not more than ten minutes."

"How were you able to take it?" I asked.

"During the battle yesterday. The paymaster left it unguarded, just long enough. Now, let me ask you a question. You sold all that flour to the army last January. Why did you end up going to work for the Americans?"

"Well, you know, business is business."

It seemed like an eternity, but the proprietor finally returned with the second strong box.

"We have our boxes, Major," I said. "If you leave without any sudden moves, you will be safe for the next ten minutes to pack up and head out."

Warren stood up and the three soldiers cautiously made their way across the room. Lieutenant Masters walked behind the other two when I noticed something. His left arm hung limp. One of Willie's musket balls found its mark.

They reached the front door without a word. Warren then turned, nodded back to us and said. "To better times."

I told the two boys to watch them carefully until they rode off. At that point, I could stand the pain no longer and collapsed from the chair onto the floor.

"Willie," I said, "get me some rum and help me tie off my leg."

He retrieved a bottle from behind the bar and helped me take a swig. He found a blanket, tore it in strips, and cut off my left pant leg above the wound.

"How does it look?"

"Nasty," said Willie. "Is the lead ball still in?"

"I can't tell. Just tie it off."

"We gotta pour a little of that rum on it," said Willie. "It will kill the infection."

I handed him the bottle. As he poured an agonizing pain shot through my entire body.

"Son of a bitch . . . Stop! No more. Holy bloody shit. Just give me the bottle. What do you think you're doing?"

"That will get you back to camp," said Willie.

The pain and loss of blood were taking their toll. I took another swig. "You guys are going to have to carry me out to the cart. Is it fixed?"

"It will get us to Monmouth. What do you want to do with the wagon?"

I was beginning to fade again. "What wagon?"

"You know, the Brit wagon out by the barn."

I nodded. "Is the wheel on?"

"I think so."

"Reload the strong boxes. You drive it."

Willie left and the two boys came over to help.

I felt groggy. "Is Warren gone?"

"Yes, Papa," answered Jonathon.

"I'm going to pass out."

The next thing I remember they were placing me in the back of the cart on top of a bag of beans. The pain briefly revived me. I motioned Jonathon to come close so I could speak into his ear.

"Don't let them take off my leg."

"Don't worry, Papa."

Just before we pulled out, Willie leaned over the cart and said, "Lieutenant, the boys are going to take you on ahead. I have another strong box to load. What do I do with the payroll when I get it back to camp?"

"Take good care of it," I said, or something like that. I cannot be sure.

Chapter Fifty Two

Trial Proceedings

"It's your testimony this encounter with Major Warren and Lieutenant Masters was unexpected and a coincidence?" asked the Judge Advocate.

"Yes," said Daniel. "I had never been more surprised."

"Your version of the incident differs from what Lieutenant Masters said happened." He looked back through his notes of earlier testimony.

"Lieutenant Masters didn't testify in this trial," said Daniel.

"True. He was captured five months ago during the battle for Charleston. And the soldier who captured him testified. He told us what Lieutenant Masters revealed before dying from a bayonet wound."

"I heard what was said. Lieutenant Masters admitted he lost his arm as a result of the shootout in the roadhouse."

"Yes, but that was not all. Masters re-joined the British Army after a falling out with Major Warren. More importantly, though, he confessed to conspiring with you in stealing the payroll, and said you agreed to arrange a passage west for him and Major Warren. *His statements led to your arrest.*"

"None of what Lieutenant Masters supposedly said is true.

"Why would he lie?"

"How do I know? Maybe out of vindictiveness because he lost his arm. Maybe to protect Major Warren. Or maybe he was having delusions. You said he died a few days after being captured. I don't know why he lied. I do know this: Masters and Warren were crooks. So the real question is why would you believe him in the first place?"

The judge advocate brushed aside the question. "In any event, you admit making another deal with the enemy?"

"Another deal, what do you mean?"

"You earlier negotiated for the sale of flour. Then you bargained for the British payroll."

Daniel shook his head. "We've been through this. Yes, I made a deal with rogue officers of the British Army for the payroll. They were not really the enemy, though."

"You were fighting against them, were you not? Does that not make them the enemy?"

"They were deserters and not the enemy of the Continental Army."

"You had four men. The Brits had three. And instead of overpowering them, you made the decision to negotiate. Is that not true?"

"No. I was wounded with two fifteen-year-old boys, who had no combat training. While Willie was very capable, he was in no position to rush three combat ready soldiers on his own."

"You have told us you put your share of the British payroll in Willie's charge and ordered him to take good care of it. In effect, you were ordering him to hide it. Were you not?

"Not in the least," said Daniel. "We were in possession of a fortune in silver. I assumed he would return to Monmouth. And I was just telling him to take precautions along the way."

"The silver you recovered was not yours to keep. It was not like a prize at sea. It was property recovered from an enemy state at war, and belonged to the United States. You understand that, did you not?"

"I understand it was not mine, yes."

"But you didn't order Willie to return to Monmouth."

"I don't remember exactly what I said. I was half-drunk with rum, trying to kill the pain in my leg."

"Do you know where he went?"

"No."

"Did he ever return to the mill?"

"Not that I'm aware of."

"Did he contact his wife?"

"I don't believe so. I've asked her, and she denied hearing from him."

"By the way, Willie's wife? What's her name, Mary Jane? Where is she?"

"She stayed at the mill for a while. After Willie didn't return, she moved to the City."

"And you hold to your statement that since June 29, 1778, for over two years, you have not seen nor heard from Willie Howell?"

"That's correct. I have not."

"You expect me to believe you have had no contact with this man who has possession of over thirty-thousand pounds in British sterling."

Daniel paused. "Mr. Judge Advocate, I don't expect you would believe in Jesus Christ himself if he were standing here."

A commotion erupted in the Hall causing the president of the court to bang his gavel. "Lieutenant, you must refrain from disdainful comments or I will sentence you to twenty lashes. Is that understood?"

"Yes, sir."

The Judge Advocate appeared irritated but continued. "Even though you cannot remember whether you told Willie to return to Monmouth, you state he never did come back, correct?"

"I never saw him and assume he did not."

"Therefore, he disobeyed your order? At the very least, he acted contrary to the expected conduct of a soldier acting under your command, correct?"

"That's a difficult question. As you know, Willie never enlisted. While he took orders from me and other officers, I couldn't say whether he was obligated to obey me."

"Are you trying to tell this tribunal that if we tracked the man down and brought him to justice for absconding with thirty-thousand pounds, we could not prosecute?"

"I don't know. I'm not a lawyer. I would guess if he never joined the army, you would have a problem with jurisdiction. You're the lawyer, not me."

"You have no idea what happened to Lieutenant' Master's share of the payroll?"

"If it was not with him when he was captured, then no."

"Or, Major Warren's share?"

"No."

"You have no idea where Major Warren is?"

"I've not seen nor heard from him since the day after the battle."

The Judge Advocate frowned and looked over at the president, who shrugged. Pressing forward he asked, "How long were you in Monmouth?"

"I was there nearly two weeks in the field hospital. I lost a lot more blood when they removed the musket ball. My son and nephew stayed with me. Once I was well enough to travel, we returned to Philadelphia."

"Did you resign your commission?"

"Not then."

"Why not?"

"An officer at the hospital told me to hold off resigning. It would improve my chances for a pension."

"A pension? You're not serious, Lieutenant. You don't honestly expect to receive a pension, do you?"

"I was wounded in the service of my country. Why would I not?"

"You were wounded while in the process of stealing the Brit payroll."

"I did no such thing. I was wounded by a British officer the day after the biggest battle of the war. He was stealing the British payroll. All I did was try to recover a portion for the benefit of the Continental Army."

"The portion you say you tried to recover is missing, is it not?"

"Yes. It's missing, but I didn't steal it. And nothing Willie did constituted stealing. He assisted in removing a portion of the payroll from British custody during wartime. He performed a great service to our country, even if it didn't end up in the coffers of the Continental Congress."

The Judge Advocate scowled. "By the way, is it possible any of the payroll ended up with the Oneidas who are supporting the British?"

"Most of the Oneida Tribe took the American side, I believe. I don't know what you're asking."

"You know what I'm asking," said the Judge Advocate. "That squaw you have been seeing? She is Oneida, is she not?"

Daniel stared at the Judge Advocate. "That squaw I've been seeing is more American than you are. *Sir.*" He said "sir" with emphasis.

The Judge Advocate flinched but did not pause. "I don't think you answered my question, Lieutenant. She's Oneida, is she not?"

"No, she is not Oneida. She is Lenape, as I said earlier. You haven't been listening." Daniel looked to the president of the court and added, "Who is on trial here, me or my wife?"

The president looked surprised and asked, "Did you marry the woman?"

"I did, your honor."

"Did she have Loyalist leanings?" asked the president. "I think that's what the Judge Advocate is getting at."

"Absolutely not. I already made that clear. She hates the British."

"What about her people?"

"Her people? Her adopted mother and brother feel the same. Her Indian friends, I don't know for sure. They came to our wedding. As to whether they are Loyalist? I don't know, but I will ask her."

"What do you mean?" asked the president.

"That's her sitting in front." Daniel pointed to Elizabeth.

"I thought she was your sister."

"Elizabeth is sitting to the right of my sister." Daniel looked over at her and smiled. She smiled back. "Are your Indian friends Loyalists?"

"Not that I am aware of," answered Elizabeth.

Silence followed. The Judge Advocate stared at Elizabeth as if spellbound by her presence. The pause lasted awkwardly long.

"Sir, have you further questions, or, are we finished?" asked Daniel.

The Judge Advocate came out of his trance. "Tell us what happened after you returned to Philadelphia."

"A lot happened. What do you want to know?"

"Start with how you tracked down your Indian wife?"

"My *Indian* wife? She's my only wife. As a simple courtesy, please refer to her as Mrs. Thompson."

"Let's not quibble."

Chapter Fifty Three

It was pushing mid-July and the doctors were debating whether the infection in my leg required amputation. I insisted not, but they never gave my opinion much weight. When the swelling began to diminish after a few days, the doctors noticed an improvement. Breathing a sigh of relief, I pleaded for permission to continue my recovery back in Philadelphia. I still could not walk, but we learned of a Conestoga train heading to the City. The owner was willing to let wounded soldiers ride in open cargo space. Aboard that wagon, I felt every rock in the road along the way, and three days later in early August, we crossed the Delaware and pulled into Philadelphia.

Many changes had taken place since early June. Redcoats no longer patrolled the waterfront. Blue-coated Continental soldiers took their place. While the City as a whole welcomed the Continental soldiers, the civility between Patriots and Loyalists existing before the British arrived had evaporated. Many Patriots who suffered deprivations during the British occupation realized the tables had turned. They now sought vengeance from those who still might have pro-British leanings.

The most ardent Loyalists, expecting the worst, had left the city with the British Army. The main targets of vengeance now were those less vocal in their support of the British crown, who lacked political connections to protect themselves from thugs bent on doing harm. Hardly a day went by without a suspected Loyalist house being torched, or their property confiscated.

Business in the City had ground to a near standstill. The shops able to remain open during the occupation were accustomed to being paid in sterling, which most Philadelphians lacked. What business occurred in Continental or Pennsylvania paper currency took place at prices that were all-time highs and nearly double from before the occupation.

Many shops folded under the weight of unpaid receivables. The British Army was not shy about buying goods on credit. Much of the debt it ran up stayed in the City when the army left. Also leaving with the army were the foreign traders attracted to the City by the British. Some Patriot merchants were beginning to return, but their foreign suppliers had cut off their inventory shipments. It would take months to re-establish connections. Vacant houses dotted the streets and added to the depressed economy.

For me, the first couple of weeks back home nearly spelled the end. Two full days of jostling in the back of a wagon aggravated my wound to such an extent I began questioning my resolve not to have the leg amputated. I could not escape the pain to fall asleep unless I was in a drunken stupor. As often as not I had nightmares about the bayonet attack at the edge of the hedgerow. Waking up terrorized and hung over, I usually vomited whatever nourishment I took in a few hours before.

Whether sitting or lying down, I constantly shifted positions in my relentless pursuit of that particular body angle to ease my pain. I needed assistance to rise, sit, dress, relieve myself and bathe, and I sorely tried the patience of my family members.

Getting up in the morning, I puttered around the kitchen while complaining and fidgeting. Soon, those nearby looked as aggravated as I felt. Then I would pick up my crutches and awkwardly work my way to the back yard or garden. There, I tried to sit for a while on a cushioned chair in the shade. After a while I would give up and amble back into the house to become a menace once again to anyone coming too close. I did not feel like reading, nor going anywhere, nor seeing friends, nor doing much anything other than complaining about my miserable condition.

One day late in August, I sat in the back yard watching Alphonse tend the garden. Vegetables were ripening, and he gathered them up while pulling weeds at the same time. Gardening was an activity that never appealed to me. I thought a moment wondering why not. The answer came quickly: Papa never cared for gardening, so neither did I. It occurred to me how much I had become like my father, and the dislike of gardening was only a small aspect of it.

He enjoyed hunting and so did I. He chose to be an Anglican and so did I. He became a merchant, lived in the City and had four children. I was the same in all respects except my fourth child died at birth. Try as I might to please the man, he always expected too much and never expressed his appreciation, save for that one occasion before he left for Quebec. Even then, he coupled his praise with an expression of disappointment. I had the same expectations for my son and rarely conveyed my appreciation. Papa acted terrible when he was ill and showed no tolerance for those around him. I emulated Papa a hundred times over with my wounded leg.

I also found myself close to Papa in yet another way. My mother died in child birth when Papa was close to the age I was when Sarah died. He never remarried. Instead, he took up with Mrs. Pickering . . . neither one willing to make the marriage commitment. I, too, felt a need for female companionship. Yet my prospects for doing anything differently from Papa looked bleak. I began thinking about Margaret. I did not like her much, but I could tolerate her part of the time. She would come back at the drop of pin.

In the midst of my pathetic ruminations, I heard a voice. "Hey, soldier!"

It was obviously my imagination. But then I heard it again.

"Hey, soldier."

Louder this time, I recognized it and turned. There stood Elizabeth not ten yards away. I could not take my eyes off her afraid she would disappear. She was wearing her ruffled white blouse and gray skirt, the same she had on a year ago when I walked her home from the Continental Army Parade. I continued to stare, partly in awe, partly because I did not want to wake up and find she was just a dream.

"Did you hear me, Lieutenant?"

I nodded. "Where do you think you have been?"

"I have been around."

This was Elizabeth all right. Stubbornly evasive when she wanted to be. Just like me. "What are you doing here?"

"A birdie told me you had something to say to me."

"Really. Did the birdie have a name?"

"Her name is Annie."

"I never could trust that little scamp."

"She takes after her father."

"We both know he can't be trusted."

"Well, what is it then?"

"You have to come closer," I said.

"I have already come across town. You come over here."

Knowing I had a bad leg, she challenged me. I hated her for it, yet loved her all the more. Glancing down at my crutches, I almost bent down to pick them up. Something told me I should try it on my own. Placing my hand on the back of the chair, I slowly got us with most of my weight on my good leg. My wound hurt like the devil, but I was standing. I let go of the chair and took a step with my good leg. It was not more than a shuffle and I pulled up my bad leg up even. Shuffling forward three or four more steps, I realized it was all I could take for the day. Without warning, my wounded leg collapsed under me, I fell forward, and Elizabeth caught me in her arms.

We both were startled and my instincts told me to straighten up and get back to looking respectable. But she felt so good holding me like that. Christ! I did not want to move. The nagging ache in my wounded leg temporarily halted, and I wondered if all it needed was to be moved around more to increase the blood flow. With my cheek against her shoulder and her arms clasped around my waist, I turned my head up, brushed my cheek against hers, and stared hard into her eyes.

"Don't ever leave me like that again," I said.

"Is that what you wanted to tell me?"

"No, but it's a start." I put my head back against her shoulder.

"No need to worry, soldier, I'm not going anywhere . . . without you."

★

We were married a month later, the wedding held in our back yard. It was not an elaborate affair, but comfortable. Reverend White officiated. He now headed Christ Church as his predecessor, Reverend Duche, had fled to England.

Apart from family, we invited forty guests from around the City, including a half dozen of Elizabeth's Indian friends. The twins, with Alphonse's help, built a six-foot trellis and covered it with leaves and vines. It served as backdrop for the ceremony where Elizabeth, in a blue dress, and I in a waist coat, stood to read our vows. Before the ceremony, Jonathon and Nathan played fife and drum, and Jonathon switched to violin for the reception. Missy, Elizabeth and Elizabeth's mother prepared all the food. We had beef pie, venison and pork, along with tea, ale and rum. Missy baked a cake with a piece of nutmeg planted inside. She gave the nutmeg slice to Annie, a sure sign Annie would be next to marry.

I was still limping at the reception, but the gathering gave me an opportunity to catch up with old acquaintances. Although I had been a prominent fixture in the City during my months of spying, I then just disappeared as far as our friends and neighbors were concerned. Missy told some of her Patriot confidants how I had received a commission in the Continental Army, but many of our wedding guests had no idea I joined either army. If they had to guess which side, they would have made me a redcoat.

John Lawrence, a good friend from church, was one. He put his arm around me and said, "Daniel, can I talk to you a moment?"

"Sure, John." He ushered me away from the guests. I had a premonition about what was coming.

"First," he said, "I know this is your wedding day and I don't want to do anything to ruin it. I wish you the best. You have a beautiful bride. I know she's an Indian, which I suspect might create some issues down the road. If anyone can handle it, you can. So, congratulations."

"Thank you, John." He clasped my arm.

"I came here today for a second reason. I was going to make you an offer, now I'm not so sure."

"What did you have in mind?"

"Before I get to that, let me just ask about some nasty rumors."

I looked him in the eye. "They are probably true, John."

"About your fighting in the battle over at Monmouth?"

"Yes. I was in the battle."

"Fighting on the rebel side?"

I nodded.

He shook his head. "Well, I will be a bloody son of a bitch. And all that running around entertaining British officers early in the year? What was all that about?"

"You don't want to know."

"I suspect I don't." He shook his head again. "After all these years, Daniel. What would your father say if he knew about this?"

"He would be interested to know whether I fought well, and if I had good reasons for joining the rebels. He would also be upset."

"Doesn't it mean anything to you? That you are disappointing your father?"

"Yes, it does."

"What happened that caused you to cross over? The Thompson and Lawrence families have known each other for decades. We thought alike on most everything."

"John, it was a long process and I got there gradually. That might not sound convincing, but it's the truth."

He sighed. "There goes my offer then. Good luck." He turned to go.

I felt like shit, this old friend of the family walking away. "John, tell me what you had mind. Perhaps, I can help in some way."

"No. That's all right."

"This war has been hard on everyone. No reason exists why we can't still be friends when it's over."

"I'm not so sure." He turned away.

"Try me."

He turned back to look at me. "We're leaving. My wife and I and our two kids and their families along with a half dozen other families. We're packing up and moving out. We can't stay here. It's too dangerous for Loyalists. We're no longer welcome. Threats of being tar and feathered, house burnings and other humiliating bullshit. I never thought I would see this day. I was going to invite you to come with us. There's safety in numbers. But now, you have no reason to leave."

"Where are you going?"

"We have our sights set on Fort Niagara. I have relatives in that area. We'll see how far we get."

"A lot of rebels between here and there."

"I know, but what can we do? We'll try to avoid as many as we can."

"Maybe Elizabeth can help."

"What do you mean?"

"You'll be traveling through Iroquois territory. A lot of Mohawks, Oneida, Seneca and they're all part of the Iroquois nation. She has connections with all those tribes. She might be able to arrange an escort, or at least some guides to help you avoid the worst dangers. When are you leaving?"

He brightened. "A few days. We could delay it, if that would help."

"Let me talk to her."

A look of concern came over him. "Daniel, we can't pay much. I don't want you to be obliged because of us."

"Come up with a few gifts for the guides along the way. Elizabeth will have some suggestions. You'll be fine."

He put his hand on my shoulder. "You anger me, Daniel. Still, if we have to have rebels in this world, I wish there'd be more like you."

That night I made love to my new wife. I decided my family needed enlarging, and I intended to get the job done in one night. Elizabeth was agreeable.

Chapter Fifty Four

Trial Proceedings

"Again, you admit aiding the enemy?" asked the Judge Advocate.

"No." Daniel answered. "I lent a hand to an old friend."

"He was a Loyalist."

"He was not my enemy. He was looking for safe passage to Niagara."

"Friends of our enemies are our enemies," said the Judge Advocate. "And you, sir, were an officer in the Continental Army. You should know that."

Daniel thought about how best to respond. "I facilitated the departure of forty Loyalists from the City of Philadelphia. Had I not offered assistance, they might have changed their minds. Now, we can rest easy with forty fewer traitors to the American cause."

"You don't believe that," said the Judge Advocate with a dismissive look.

"I admit to feeling conflicted," said Daniel. "Still, what I did was not contrary to the interests of Pennsylvania or the Continental Army."

The Judge Advocate continued. "Let me see if we can wrap this up. Did you go back to active service?"

"Yes. I went back on active duty in November of 1778, almost two years ago. Since my days of marching twenty-five miles a day were over, I requested garrison duty in Philadelphia. General Arnold's staff accommodated me. That was before he turned traitor. They assigned me to the prison where I am now, and what was formerly the British Provost. I was second in command."

"How many prisoners being held there?"

"When I resigned my commission a year later, we had 125 British and another hundred or so Hessian."

"The same prison where your sister was held, right?"

"It was."

"Did you take a pound of flesh on her behalf?"

"What do you mean?"

"She witnessed the mistreatment of many Americans. Did you make sure those Americans were avenged?"

"Not in the least."

"And why not?" The Judge Advocate expressed genuine surprise.

"Because of my sister. She wanted the prisoners treated humanely. In fact, she organized women in the community to make quilts and to bring over extra food for the prisoners at Easter and Christmas."

"You allowed that to happen?"

"Of course I did. These were rank and file British soldiers. Whatever they did, they did at the direction of their superiors. I had no reason to make their lives miserable."

"You don't consider providing treats on holidays as giving aid and assistance to the enemy?"

"I didn't then nor do I now. I regarded them as future Americans. If we treated them with respect, they might stay when the war ends."

The Judge Advocate chose that as the point on which to conclude. "I'm finished with this witness, Mr. President."

★

A few more witnesses testified before the trial came to an end. They included Missy, who corroborated Daniel's testimony about her spy reports to Captain Johnson. Sergeant Wright appeared as a witness and told about Daniel's leadership under Captain Johnson. Jonathon and Nathan provided support for the events concerning the British payroll.

In his closing argument, the Judge Advocate minimized the importance of all these witnesses. He argued they were biased and lacked knowledge of Daniel's true motives.

"It is undisputed, your Honors," he stated in summation, "the accused made many public pro-British statements. It is undisputed he resisted the necessary destruction of his family's ship to keep it from the British. It is undisputed he repeatedly sold flour to the British Army. He cavorted openly with British officers during the occupation, and now claims he was on a spying mission. A spying mission for which he produced no proof.

"He led the British to Barren Hill. He denies it, of course, but he was seen leaving the City with a redcoat. What other purpose could he have had? He claims to have heroically saved the day by finding an escape route for General La Fayette. The story lacks credibility, but this much I can tell you for sure: by the time he found the escape route, the whole Barren Hill mission had already failed because of the lieutenant's actions.

"I do not dispute the man fought at Monmouth. But that only demonstrates, at most, that he was not truly committed to either side. No, he was in this war for himself. I suggest, moreover, his true colors are shown by what occurred thereafter. He conspired with friends who were officers in the royal army, to reach a deal to facilitate the theft of the British payroll for their own private gain. Unfortunately for Lieutenant Thompson, he learned the hard way that no honor exists among thieves. Whatever the cause of the dispute between him and his fellow brigands, the capture of this huge wartime prize of sixty-thousand pounds in silver and gold, which even now would be of enormous benefit to the Continental Army, has been lost.

"Lieutenant Thompson engaged in a continuing effort to sabotage the efforts of the Continental Congress and Army in their quest for independence, and to assist the British to the extent of providing holiday treats to British prisoners of war. What further proof is necessary?

"I ask that you find him guilty of treason, violation of our spoils-of-war laws, fraternizing with the enemy, and other high crimes and misdemeanors."

The Judge Advocate spoke for forty minutes. Daniel prepared to speak for a similar duration. At the last minute, however, he decided the most persuasive argument for his innocence was the testimony he had already given.

Rising to speak, Daniel looked up at the judges and simply stated, "I am a loyal citizen of Pennsylvania and America. It is true I was not among the first of those answering the call for help in this war. But I answered nonetheless, and once I made the commitment, I served with unwavering dedication. Thank you."

With that the president announced the case would be taken under advisement, and the trial came to an end. The verdict would be rendered the following day. The prisoner remained under arrest.

★

When Daniel arrived at Carpenter's Hall the following afternoon, he found his entire family sitting in the first row behind his table. Taking a seat, he turned around to face them while awaiting the judges' arrival. He had done nothing wrong, or so he felt, yet he knew some of his actions could be misconstrued. If worse came to worse, this would be one of the last times he would see his family. He would hang in a dishonorable death.

He prayed that would not happen as he looked at each one individually and smiled. Janie was at the end of the row with Scout on her lap, squirming as usual. She gave the boy a toy horse to keep him occupied. Annie sat next to her. She had a suitor, who sat to her side. He was a nice young man and son of a mid-level merchant in the City. They would be married in a few months. Daniel thought it a good match, and he prayed he would stand up at her wedding. Seated next were the drummer and fifer. October weather had turned cold, and they sat with cloaks draped across their laps, whispering and fidgeting sporadically. Daniel's sister came next, a mixture of determination and anger showing on her face. Beside her sat his precious Elizabeth, closest to him and almost within reach. She gave him a confident smile and nod. Each knew the gravity of the situation, but no one betrayed anxiety. For that he was grateful.

The thirteen members of the court filed into a packed Hall. Militia and Patriot groups had spread the word that the verdict was forthcoming. Predicting a guilty verdict, some of their members intended to use the outcome to provoke charges against others they regarded as insufficiently pro-American. Waddy himself, surrounded by a dozen supporters, sat behind the Judge Advocate's table and talked loudly about the convincing nature of the evidence. A few onlookers came as friends of the Thompson family to show their belief in his innocence. Not many, though, because no one wanted to be seen as supporting someone disloyal to the American cause. Curiosity seekers showed up in abundance hoping to witness a spectacle.

The president of the court wrapped his gavel and the room quieted. He shuffled some papers, finding what he was looking for. Then he spoke.

"Would the accused please stand." The president looked at Daniel gravely. "Mr. Thompson, this court has reached a verdict. But before I announce it, let me ask one more time about the British payroll. You have testified that sixty thousand pounds in gold and silver were split between you and the two British officers, is that correct?

"Yes, sir," said Daniel.

"I cannot expect you to know what happened to the portion taken by Major Warren and his colleagues. Yet do you have any idea about the portion you entrusted to Willie Howell?"

"I do not, sir. And let me just add, if I knew the whereabouts of 30,000 British pounds, and had access to it, my family and I would never have suffered the kind of lifestyle we have these last two years, when we, like many others in the City, experienced financial challenges on a daily basis."

"I am sure you are right. But let me ask you to speculate. What is your best guess about what Willie Howell might have done with the treasure?"

Daniel paused before speaking. "With him being a lone colored man driving a wagon on a country road, I can only believe he met with foul play. I surmise no other possibility."

"And if he were to show up at your doorstep today with the treasure in hand, what would you do?"

Daniel wrinkled his brow, trying to make sure he understood the question. "Willie has not shown up at my door, and I have no reason to believe he would at this point."

"Humor me again, Lieutenant. If he did show up with the treasure, what would you do?"

"My intention at the time was to turn the silver over to the Continental Army. Nothing has caused me to change my mind."

"Thank you," said the president. He looked around to the members of the court. "Does that change anyone's mind? I guess not. So let me announce the verdict. It was not unanimous. But each judge considered the evidence carefully, I can assure you. A majority of the judges found the evidence presented . . . was insufficient to prove wrongdoing." He paused and stared at Daniel. "You are found *not guilty* and you are *free* to go. I wish you the best, Lieutenant."

Over. Just like that.

★

Expressions of surprise mixed with disappointment and delight erupted from all corners of the Hall. The ordeal had finally ended. Daniel breathed a huge sigh of relief and felt a profound sense of exhaustion . . . and anger. He had spent several months in unnecessary confinement and a pointless state of tension. It was time he could have spent with his family and getting re-established in business. As his loved ones rushed to him with hugs and congratulations, he glanced over at Waddy. For once, that short, stocky ogre of a man had stopped talking. He looked shocked.

The Hall cleared except for a couple of sergeants at arms. Daniel and his family prepared to leave when the president of the court, now re-arranging a pile of papers on his table, glanced up and caught Daniel's eye.

"Lieutenant," he called out, "have you a moment?"

Daniel decided it would do no good to offend this prominent figure. "Yes, sir." He stepped toward the seated officer.

"This was a capital case, and required nine to convict," said the president. "Only three voted against you. Don't ask who they were. I'm not allowed to say. But you handled yourself well and came through strong. I've seen verdicts go the other way with less evidence."

"Thank you, sir. Naturally I am pleased to have been acquitted. I cannot help but think I should never have been charged in the first place. I did nothing wrong and served the American cause honorably."

"You did. And for that you have my thanks and the thanks of General Washington. I intend to make a full report. As for being wrongfully charged, it was a sign of the times. The war has engendered a lot of bitterness, and some of those who acquire positions of influence do not use good judgment. Take Mr. Waddy, for example, whose heart is in the right place, but his head is up his ass, if the ladies will pardon my expression."

Daniel shook his head. "No sir, his heart is up there too."

"Maybe, but if I could offer you one small piece of advice, it would be this: Rise above it. Once this war is over, these united colonies have a lot of promise. Difficulties lie ahead, but overall the future is bright. So don't let yourself become blinded by bitterness from your trial."

Probably good advice, thought Daniel, but not something he would need anytime soon.

On leaving the Hall, Daniel noticed something bulky filling the inside pockets of the cloaks the two boys were wearing. He turned to Jonathon and asked out of curiosity, "What's that you're carrying?"

"It's nothing, Papa. Just . . . extra wraps if the weather turns bitter."

Chapter Fifty Five

As much as Daniel wanted to believe his acquittal vindicated his reputation, he knew the verdict would have no impact on that segment of the population who viewed everyone with suspicion except for the most ardent of Patriots.

Times remained tough, with prices in Continentals now fifteen times higher than before the occupation. Unable to re-open the retail shop, his family was surviving on the flour trade alone, and even that was becoming more challenging. Parts for mill repairs were increasingly difficult to come by. Farmers were demanding higher prices for their wheat. And with the British in full control of sea lanes, the market for the sale of flour had drastically shrunk. In the City, discontent ran rampant and someone had to be blamed. Roving bands of troublemakers no longer patrolled the streets as they did a year ago. But self-appointed militia groups still formed to make arrests and dish out local justice to those they deemed insufficiently patriotic.

To add insult to injury, Alphonse's indenture had expired months earlier, and Daniel lacked the funds to continue his services or hire other domestic help. The days of what seemed like luxurious living were gone.

Thinking about these and other problems, Daniel was chopping wood alone back of the stable one afternoon shortly after the trial, when someone shouted from a distance, "There he is!"

He looked up and saw to his surprise an angry troop of militia men. Fueled by strong ale and rum, they were marching up Walnut Street from the waterfront carrying torches, clubs, and sabers.

Seconds later a half dozen men rushed the yard encircling Daniel, led by Henry Waddy.

"Are you responsible for this intrusion, Waddy?" Daniel demanded.

"Oh, indeed I am. I and these other fine Patriot lads."

"You and your lads are trespassing. I ask that you leave."

Waddy smiled back. "We intend to. And we're taking you with us."

Daniel looked at him askance. "Where would you be taking me?"

"We're taking you to the State House Commons where we'll put you on trial for treason. If we find you guilty, you'll be punished accordingly."

"I've been tried by a military tribunal and found innocent. You know that. You were there."

"Yes. You were tried by the military, but not by the people of Philadelphia. We intend to put you on trial for crimes against the City."

"Does Joe Reed know about this?"

"Ah, our esteemed Executive Council President. We'll tell him in due time. When it's all over."

"No, you'll tell him now. If Joe Reed orders it, I'll do as you ask. Not otherwise."

A well-known radical, Joseph Reed was every bit as strident in his views on independence as Waddy himself. As president of the Pennsylvania Supreme Executive Council, however, he had taken on a heightened sense of responsibility to restore order to the City. Daniel found him fair in his dealings with both Tories and Patriots.

"Maybe you didn't hear me, asshole. I said we'll tell Joe later. Now, are you coming with us quietly or do we have to use persuasive measures?"

"I'm not going anywhere, asshole. I told you to get off my property. Now leave." Daniel took a threatening stride toward Waddy.

Stepping back, Waddy shouted out, "Tie his hands, boys."

With rope in hand someone approached from the front as two others grabbed his arms. Daniel broke free twice and got in a couple of good hits before a fourth man put his arm around his head and neck, forcing him into a headlock until his hands were tied.

Daniel straightened up, breathing hard. "Come on, Waddy, let's settle this right now. Just the two of us. Fists, pistols, whatever you choose."

"Don't be naive, Thompson. This isn't between you and me. This is between you and the people of Philadelphia. The people will have their say."

"You mean you and the drunken hoodlums you brought with you?"

"Hoodlums? I should say not. We are the sons of the revolution, the loyal supporters of the Declaration of Independence."

"Yes, and where were you and the loyal supporters during the British occupation? How many British soldiers did you take down? How many days did you spend on the march going after the British Army?"

"My job," said Waddy, "was to nurture the flame of independence and keep it alive here in the City."

"The flame didn't need your nurturing. You stayed back with the women and children and let someone else do the fighting. You're nothing but a God-damn coward."

"Coward? Why you son of a bitch! At least I didn't sell contraband goods to the enemy. And after we put you on trial, we'll see just how brave you are when standing with a rope around your neck."

"Without proof of guilt?"

"Come now, Thompson, it's just a matter of taking a vote and carrying out the sentence." Waddy gave a hearty laugh. "We already heard the evidence, haven't we, boys?"

A cheer went up as several men pushed and punched Daniel while someone else kicked him on his bad leg causing him to fall. When he tried to get up, a free-for-all of punching and kicking broke out, leaving him back on the ground, hands tied, scrambling to avoid more blows.

The struggle stopped when a voice rang out, "Stop there!"

Daniel looked up and could hardly believe his eyes.

His father stepped out from the front of the stable. Steven, his father!

His hair a shade grayer, a few extra wrinkles to his cheeks, but his eyes as sharp as steel. What in God's name was he doing here?

He stood with musket pointed at Waddy. Behind him, Elizabeth held a second musket ready to pass to his father once he fired the one he held.

"That's my son you have tied up," said Steven. "Untie him now and clear off this property."

"Back from Quebec, eh, Steven," Waddy said in a mocking tone, "where you fled with your Tory friends. Maybe you've forgotten. Philadelphia is no longer under the protection of King George."

"King George or no King George, you'll be the first to go, Waddy. Clear out or take your chances."

Waddy froze for a moment, and then began in an affected conciliatory voice, "Steven, my friend. You must know if you pull that trigger, you're a dead man. Not only are you a Tory, but you are an armed Tory, and you are threatening me." As he spoke he turned his back to Steven and made eye contact with his compatriots. "My guess, though, is that, without the boys in red at your back, you're no more going to shoot anyone than . . . ." As Waddy turned further, Daniel saw him draw a pistol from his belt and pull back the hammer.

"Watch it, Papa!" shouted Daniel. "He has a . . . ."

Waddy spun and fired, hitting Steven in the chest. He sank to his hands and knees, shook his head anger, and collapsed to the ground onto his back.

Almost instantly, a second blast filled the air, "Bam!," louder than the first.

"Where did that come from?" yelled Daniel, struggling to his feet. Elizabeth stepped to his side, handed him the second musket, and pointed in the direction of Waddy. He staggered with blood rushing from a neck artery and fell face down, his flintlock still in hand.

Daniel glanced about and saw the shooter in a cloud of black-powder smoke, musket still in one hand, brandishing a pistol in the other.

"I have one shot left," yelled David menacingly, approaching from the street. "Who wants it? Come on, fuckers, who wants to see me shoot again?"

Daniel had never seen his brother so angry.

Carefully, David surveyed Waddy's militia men. With Waddy himself down and the pistol threatening, they looked bewildered.

“Go check on Papa,” David told Daniel without lowering his pistol.

Daniel handed David the loaded musket and rushed to his father’s side. Although he was breathing heavily, dark red blood oozed from his chest.

“Papa, why’d you do it?” Daniel implored, his voice barely audible.

Steven looked up, and in a gravelly voice said, “God damned Yankees.” He then grimaced, winked at Daniel, and became still.

From Walnut Street three men on horses galloped toward them, the middle man waving a saber and shouting,” What goes on there?” On seeing Daniel and David, Joseph Reed dismounted and asked, “How did this happen?”

Without taking his eyes off his father, Daniel replied, “Hi, Joe. Waddy and his crew came to arrest me. When Papa tried to stop him, he shot Papa. David tried to stop him by shooting Waddy, but it was too late. Waddy is down over yonder.”

Reed shook his head in disgust. “I guess it was bound to happen. Henry always pushed things to the edge. Why were they trying to arrest you, anyway?”

“They claimed I was a traitor.”

“But you were already tried and found innocent.”

“He knew that, but it made no difference. What brings you here?”

“I try to keep an eye on Waddy and his gang. They attack anyone who looks at them cross-eyed. Unfortunately, I lost track of them today.” Reed paused, thinking what to do next, and continued. “Even though I disagreed with your father on everything, he was an honorable man. I am sorry for your loss. If you wish to press charges against the other militia men, I will have them arrested.” He paused and then added, “Maybe you want to take a moment to gather yourselves.”

Daniel turned toward David.

"Papa?" asked David.

Daniel shook his head, distraught. Looking at his brother, he then asked quietly, "What are you doing here?"

"Papa heard you were on trial, and wanted to do what he could to help. So, when he found out he knew a couple of the officers on the court, he decided to try to come here and say a few words at the trial on your behalf. But our ship got delayed, and we just arrived this morning. Fortunately, you didn't need him, and got acquitted anyway."

"And he dragged you along with him?"

"He didn't drag me, Danny. I wanted to come. We're family."

Daniel put his arm around his brother. "Well, you're wrong about one thing. I did need him. And you. You saved me from a lynching. You couldn't have arrived at a better time. I know you were very close with him."

Daniel looked up at Reed. "Joe, I'm not sure we gain anything by having the militia boys arrested. Things might go better if we show a little reason. Just make sure they don't bother us again."

David nodded.

Reed looked at him approvingly. "I applaud your decision." He began to mount up, hesitated, and turned back to Daniel. "I will issue a burial detail in the morning and assist with arrangements."

Chapter Fifty Six

Over the next few days, Daniel, David and Missy buried their father. For once in his life, Daniel actually found David's presence comforting. David took charge of the funeral preparations and contacted the few close family friends still left in the City who had known Steven well. Realizing his presence as a Tory could spark further incidents, he moved about the City discretely.

David also brought them up to date on the business in Quebec. The city had an influx of refugees from the lower colonies and Logan had come through with shipments from London. The dry goods business was thriving. Their sales were not what they had been in Philadelphia, but David, Molly and their father had decided to make Quebec their permanent home. David asked Daniel to consider joining him and Molly, but Daniel declined.

"I have the mill," he told David, "and my family is entrenched here. I promise we'll come for a visit once it's safe."

Following David's departure, Daniel became severely depressed. His father's death, the military trial, the desertion of many close friends, his business anxieties, and the whole incident with Waddy, caused Daniel to shrink into a near state of paralysis at times. Over the last three years he had never second guessed his decision to support the independence movement. Of course, he realized, good men and women stood on both sides of the divide. But he had confidence in his ability to think things through, and was convinced he had made the right choice for himself and his family.

Now, however, he was not so sure. Having put himself in physical danger for the benefit of his country countless times, he had expected to live in the City where he grew up with respect and security. Yet since resigning his commission from the army, one obstacle after another thrust itself before him. And, while Waddy no longer threated, others like him still did. Daniel could not walk a block from home without looking over his shoulder to see if some self-righteous "Patriot" might be watching for an opportunity to show how suspected Loyalist sympathizers should be treated.

★

Before October's end, an unexpected visitor banged on the front door of the house as Daniel, Elizabeth and Jonathon were eating supper. A wide-brimmed straw hat covered the visitor's head and a raggedy cloak concealed most of his face.

"Mr. Daniel."

Daniel could not believe his eyes. "Willie Howell?"

"Yes, sir."

Daniel had so many questions he did not know where to begin. He said the first thing that came to mind. "I told you never to call me 'Mr. Daniel.'"

"Sorry, Lieutenant."

"I'm no longer a lieutenant either. Where in God's name have you been for the last two years?"

"It's cold out here, sir. Could I come in? It's a long story. By the way, do you know where my Mary Jane is?"

Sitting at the kitchen table, and eating his first square meal in weeks, Willie told his story. After he left the tavern near Monmouth, the wagon he was driving continued to have problems with its wheels. Given its precious cargo, he pulled the wagon into a wooded area, unhitched the horses, and covered the wagon with brush. He then began riding one of the horses bareback toward the Monmouth. Almost immediately he encountered a half dozen Continental soldiers on leave from the army heading south to Virginia. Seeing a Negro riding solo on a horse without any provisions, they took him for a runaway slave, confiscated his horse, and forced him to join the group.

"I cannot tell you," said Willie, "how many times I gave them your name and Captain Johnson's name and begged them to check out our regiment. I told them about the battle at Monmouth and gave them details. They knew I was telling the truth because they were there. But they paid no attention and took me to Richmond with my hands tied behind my back the whole way."

Upon arrival, one of the men forced Willie to work in the tobacco fields. He looked for opportunities to escape, but between being locked up at night and closely watched during the day, he had no chance.

Willie continued to work in the fields for the next two years. After a few months most of the fighting in the war began shifting from the mid-Atlantic colonies to the south. At that point, Willie's assumed owner joined a Virginia militia unit as an officer. Having come home on leave in August of 1780, he returned to duty and took Willie with him. The militia unit was assigned to a force of some four thousand men under General Gates to re-take Camden, South Carolina, from the British.

"We were about a day's march from town," said Willie, "and who do you suppose I run into?"

"Captain Johnson," said Daniel.

"Yes!" said Willie. "How did you know?"

"I didn't, but that's where he got killed."

"Yes, a day later. But before that he set me free and gave me papers to prove it. I thought it was a miracle. He had been assigned temporarily to a Delaware regiment for the fight in Camden. So it was a pure accident he saw me."

"How did the battle go?"

"A disaster. General Gates screwed up. Half our men got killed. I stayed on for a while with what remained, and left six weeks ago to make my way home. I walked the whole way."

"I am sorry you had to go through all that," Daniel said. "Many things have gone wrong in this war, and what you went through is one of them. I'm beginning to have second thoughts about a lot of things."

Elizabeth exchanged glances with Jonathon, and they both looked at Willie, who wrinkled his brow in surprise.

"What you mean second thoughts?" asked Willie.

Elizabeth answered, "Daniel has been through a lot lately, too. His father was recently killed by a Patriot militia gang, and before that he stood trial for treason. He was acquitted, but it caused a lot of stress."

"Treason? What did they accuse you of?"

"A lot of things," said Daniel, shaking his head. "But a main one is they thought I collaborated with those British officers in Monmouth to steal the British payroll."

"That's just crazy."

"It was crazy," said Elizabeth. "And with everything else going on, Daniel feels as dispirited now as he did when he came back with a wounded leg."

"Some good things have happened, too," said Jonathon, trying to cheer up his father. "I mean you got married to Elizabeth. That was pretty nice. And your leg has mostly healed. So things aren't all that bad, are they, Papa?"

Daniel ignored the question and looked at Willie. "Your wife lives about half a mile from here. I will walk you there. Tomorrow we'll ride out to the mill in the chaise."

★

Late the next morning, Willie appeared in front of Mary Jane's cottage, shaved, cleaned up, and in a fresh set of clothes. The day was sunny and warm for late October, and he smiled broadly when Daniel pulled up in the chaise.

"She has a nice little place here," he said, climbing in next to Daniel. "My, oh my, she is one fine woman and has not changed a bit. It was like I never left. She sat me down and made me eat a second supper before we turned in, and then fed me a big breakfast this morning. I've never eaten better in my life. And after I told her what happened, she made me promise...."

"Willie, stop," said Daniel. The chaise was nearing the edge of the City on a road to Middle Ferry.

"What, Lieutenant?"

"I'm happy for you. I am. But I want to talk some business with you."

"Sure, Lieutenant, I didn't ask her about moving back to the mill, but I know that would not be . . . ."

"Just stop, Willie. Please. The mill is not running because we need new parts. But that's secondary at the moment."

Daniel paused to gather his thoughts, and continued. "I don't minimize the problems you have had for the last two years. By comparison, my problems may seem small. But hear me out.

"Like Elizabeth said, I've been very down lately. The City has changed. The people in it, the mood, the government, business, the rules, everything has changed. It used to be fun to live here. You could say whatever you wanted and disagree with people. No one cared. Life went on, traffic in the streets, people happy, they celebrated everything, color everywhere. But not any more. The streets are dead most of the time. Everyone is under suspicion for something. No one has enough of anything. I can barely make ends meet, even when the mill is up and running. Waddy was about to hang me, and might have, if my father had not intervened. And then he shot my father."

"I'm sorry to hear that."

"Two weeks ago my brother asked me if I and my family wanted to move to Quebec, and I told him no. And I still don't want to move to Quebec. But I am not sure we can live here any more."

"What are you going to do, Lieutenant?"

"Let me ask you this, Willie. You said last night on your way back to Monmouth with the British payroll, you hid the wagon in the trees under some brush. Is that right?"

"Yes, so it would be safe when we returned."

"How well did you hide it?"

"You would have to be looking to find it."

"You think it's still there?" asked Daniel.

"I've not thought about it. I reckon so."

"You remember where?"

"Probably."

Willie looked closely at Daniel and did not have to be told what Daniel was thinking.

"You looking to split it up?" asked Willie.

"Fifty-fifty."

Willie nodded.

"If you make your presence known in the City, though, it can never happen. People will start asking questions. The army will be all over you."

Willie nodded again. "I guess we both will have to leave. I mean, not just you and your family, but me and Mary Jane too."

"A rich black man in Philadelphia? Some day, hopefully, but not now. Yes, you would have to leave, too."

"With all that silver, you think we would be in danger?"

"There are risks, yes. Especially if the American Army were to find us out. We would probably be arrested. Loyalist territory might be safest."

"Is that what you want, Lieutenant, to turn Loyalist?"

"I don't know, Willie." Daniel sighed. "A few weeks ago I would have thought all this nonsense. Now I don't know. The way I see it, the Patriot cause has turned against me, not the other way around."

"It's what we fought for."

"It is, I know." Daniel paused, looking off into the distance. "Let's think about it for a while. In the meantime, you should stay low and out of sight."

"Yes, sir."

★

Over the next few days Daniel raised the subject with Elizabeth. He continued to feel depressed, but did his best to sound upbeat.

"Of course," he said, "we would bring your mother with us. I hope my kids would come as well, but I can't force them. They're old enough to make their own decisions."

Daniel's state of mind caused Elizabeth genuine concern, and she placed her hand on his. "Daniel, I cannot blame you.

Things are bad. Your father's murder horrible. Have you talked with Missy about any of this?"

Daniel looked at her skeptically. "You and I need to decide what's best for us. She doesn't get a vote. We'll tell her, and she and Nathan might decide to come with us, but that's unlikely."

"Yes, I agree. Still I would like to get her insight on what is happening. She has been close to some of the pro-independence people who are causing the problem."

"If you think that would be helpful," said Daniel, trying not to sound dismissive, "then go ahead and call on her."

"What prospects do you think we have once we leave? Wherever we go we'll be refugees starting anew."

"We'll have the British silver to get us started. It doesn't matter where."

With the trial having focused on the missing silver, that aspect of the plan worried Elizabeth most. For the moment, though, she simply asked, "Has Willie actually found the payroll wagon?"

"No, he hasn't been back to look."

Two days later Elizabeth visited Missy at the print shop and invited her and Nathan over for supper. Apart from Steven's funeral, they had not gotten together since the trial. Jonathon, Janie and Scout joined the group around the kitchen table while Missy brought them up to date on the printing business. Daniel remained quiet and sullen until Missy turned to him.

"Well, brother, I understand you're thinking about abandoning this great City of ours."

"It was a great City," said Daniel without looking up.

"It still is, Danny. You can't expect everything to return to normal right away. First one side gets driven out, and then those people return and drive out the other side. People on both sides getting killed and wounded. Waste and corruption all over. Leaders turning out to be less than competent. The money system getting messed up, so now no one knows what anything is worth, and we're all paying too much, and getting paid too little. I've not lived through many wars, but I imagine this is all pretty typical. You have to give it time."

"Missy," said Daniel in a low angry voice, "I'm quite familiar with the whims of wars. But our father was killed by the very people I was fighting for. I was arrested, prosecuted, and almost hanged by the very people I was fighting for. I continue to be held in contempt and under suspicion by the very people I risked my life for. Under those circumstances, my family remaining here is an act of utter insanity."

"It is not!" shouted Missy. "Those things happened. But the cause you fought for was the right one. And what's important is not that many people around this City don't know their asses from holes in the ground." Janie flinched and placed her hands over Scout's ears. "What is important . . . is that the people who know you best *still believe in you*."

"And we believe in you, Uncle Daniel," said Nathan without pause.

Daniel gave an exasperated look and shook his head. "It's not that simple."

"Jonathon, do you still have them?" asked Nathan.

"Upstairs in the attic," said Jonathon. "I'll get them."

"What are you boys talking about?" asked Missy.

"Just hold on," said Jonathon. A few minutes later he returned and placed two horse pistols in the center of the kitchen table. "So there."

"What's this all about?" asked Daniel, gesturing skeptically at the firearms.

"Papa," said Jonathon, "you remember on the day of the verdict, as we were walking out of the Hall, you asked me what I was carrying in my cloak? And I said something like, nothing important, it was just a cold day."

"Get to the point, Jonathon."

Nathan spoke up. "Jonathon had these two pistols stuffed in pockets inside his cloak. I had three more in mine."

"Why were you carrying pistols into the Hall?"

No one answered, until Janie broke the silence.

"I know why. In case the verdict came back guilty."

The gathering hushed, as her words sunk in.

Daniel frowned, and began in an exasperated voice, "You mean you planned to . . . ." The gravity of what the boys had in mind overcame him. "You planned to . . . . How in God's name would you have gotten me out?"

Missy looked as surprised as Daniel. "They must have had a plan, did you, boys?"

"A plan?" said Daniel. "Any plan would have been suicidal."

"Then they would have died trying," said Janie, astonishing herself as much as anyone else.

"It was foolhardy," said Daniel with anger.

"Papa," said Jonathon in a weak voice, his face flushing, "we had a horse waiting." With tears flowing down his cheeks, he added, "Like Aunt Missy and Nathan said, we believed in you. No way we would let them hang you."

"Believed in . . . . The guards had muskets!" exclaimed Daniel, now shouting. "There were fifty people in the room. It was God-damned foolhardy!"

Nathan faced him with a hard, determined look. "You were worth the risk, Uncle Daniel."

Daniel rose, shaking visibly. "God damn it, you boys. You have no fucking sense! No god-damned fucking sense!" He left the room wiping his eyes.

Chapter Fifty Seven

Ever since his father and two siblings left for Quebec, Daniel had used his own parlor as his counting house to store books and records and conduct whatever business he could. It was there he found Mathew O'Leary sitting patiently the next morning after Daniel arrived late from oversleeping. He could barely get to sleep, reluctantly yielding to a profound sense of gratitude for the boys' shaky escape plan, and at the same time feeling mortified about everything that could have gone wrong had they tried to implement it.

But once he drifted off, he slept unusually well. He woke with the intent to further his plans for leaving the City, albeit with waning passion. He concluded that Missy was right . . . once again. What mattered most was not what those who barely knew him thought. What mattered most was whether those closest to him believed in him and the righteousness of his actions.

In that frame of mind he welcomed his family's long-time shop keeper.

"The last time I saw you," said Daniel, "you were driving a team of horses down Barren Hill like a wildfire in hell, and half the British Army on your tail."

"Maybe so, but you were a mile ahead of me and going twice as fast."

Daniel burst out laughing, the first time in weeks. "It's good to see you anyway, you old horse trader." Daniel gave him a hug. "You still working for the army?"

"Hell no. I gave that up a few months ago. They said I was getting too old, and anyway I had enough time in for a small pension."

"So you living back here in the City?"

"No, just here on a visit. I've been staying at my daughter's place in Boston. But I ran into Logan the other day and thought I better give you warning."

"Logan, what's he doing?"

"What do you think he is doing – he's peddling the same shit from London he has always peddled."

"Not in the lower colonies?"

"Anywhere he can find a buyer."

"How does he get the stuff here?"

"You know Logan. Where there's money to be made, he finds a way. In any event I told him to look you up when he gets to Philadelphia, so you should expect a visit anytime soon now."

"Thanks, Mathew, you are always welcome here."

"Well, when you get the dry goods shop back up to speed, just give me a holler, and I'll come running."

★

Seeing Mathew, even but for a few minutes, caused Daniel to reflect further on whether leaving was the right thing to do. His doubts increased after a meeting later that day with the Quaker haberdasher, the same judging official that called the shooting match back in April of 1775. Daniel had seen him around the City from time to time and nodded cordially. But they exchanged few words and never did business together. He thus found it odd the man showed up in the counting house requesting to talk with Daniel confidentially.

"But first let me ask you," said the Quaker, "can you still get off four musket rounds in a minute?"

Daniel had to smile. "Way out of practice. I'd be lucky to do two."

"Too bad," said the Quaker, smiling and thinking back. "What an amazing day that was. That black fellow. He sure could shoot."

Daniel nodded.

"Oh, well. Back to reality. I am here on a mission for the Quaker community, or what's left of it. We're looking for a candidate we can support for the Pennsylvania General Assembly. We Quakers, as you know, have not done much to earn the trust and respect of those in the independence movement, even those of us who favor separation." He gave a near-genuine look of contrition, and continued. "So we do not think now is the time to try to elect one of us and are looking for someone to work with us. You have a good business background, you served in the army, and with your father having been in the Assembly for years, you have good name recognition. And, by the way, I am sorry to hear about your father."

"Thank you," said Daniel. "But you're aware he was killed by one of the local Patriot leaders, who himself was then shot by my own brother. Surely that cuts against my qualifications."

"We are aware, and do not think so. We believe there are enough rational, moderate Patriots in the City, like yourself, who would welcome a candidate with your background. At least we ask you to consider running, and if you do, you'll have our support."

"I am honored by your confidence. Let me think it over."

So, thought Daniel after the haberdasher left, a few rational people still live here.

★

The final blow to his departure planning came as Daniel shared an early morning breakfast with Elizabeth before church on Sunday. The conversation started with his telling her about returning from an errand to the local wheelwright the previous afternoon and being approached by an agent from Willing & Morris, the City's largest trading firm.

"He told me Mr. Morris was out of town but would be back next week and wanted to set up a time to meet with me. So I asked what it was all about, and he said Morris has an offshore market for the sale flour and wants to talk about a business proposition."

"That sounds wonderful, Danny."

"I was surprised as hell. The flour market has been god awful, so I was not sure he was serious. The only thing I could think to say was that I would never accept payment in Continentals. Morris himself offered me that advice a couple years ago. So, the guy gives me kind of a wry smile and said, 'Mr. Morris will remember that,' and we set up an appointment."

Elizabeth nodded, but she was not smiling, and her face showed pain.

"What's the matter? You don't like my little story?"

"No, I like it . . . it is just that I have woken up with an upset stomach the last few mornings."

"Have you been to see Dr. Wagner?"

Elizabeth sighed, shut her eyes, and placed her hands over her face. "I am sorry." Daniel could hear sobbing in her voice and became instantly alarmed.

"Tell me, have you seen the doctor?

"Yes, Danny," she said between sobs. "He was not sure either and wanted me to hold off telling you anything."

"Telling me anything? Tell me something, please. What does he think it is?"

Elizabeth uttered some words between the sobs, but with her head in her hands he did not understand.

"He said what?"

Finally she got it out. "He thinks I might be pregnant."

Daniel stood straight up, knocking over his chair in the process. "He thinks you might . . . ." He was not sure he heard right. "You said pregnant, right?" She nodded, forcing a smile.

Daniel fancied himself a stoic person with emotions always in check. But the thought of a new baby struck at his heart-strings. At least for the moment, it pushed aside his resentment of Patriot zealots like Waddy and the underbrush of anger and grief he'd been carrying for weeks. Suddenly he felt a release of tension, and his voice turned almost hysterical with sobs and laughter.

"I can hardly believe it!... After all we've been through, and all that's gone so God-damned wrong, finally, something turned out ... God-damned right!" He knelt down beside her, sobbing for real and bumping his head against her shoulder.

She put her arm around him. "Oh, Danny, I am glad you are happy. But I cannot leave the City in this condition. I am sorry."

"Sorry? Don't be. We'll stay and do whatever we have to do to make things work."

★

That afternoon Daniel went to see Willie. Having proposed the plan to leave the City in the first place, he felt uncomfortable telling Willie about his change of heart. He took a deep breath and explained simply that, after some soul searching, he had decided to stay.

"But that doesn't mean you have to," he quickly added. "A wagon load of silver may still lie hidden not more than two days' ride from here. So far as I know, you and I, and our families, are the only ones who know. If you want it, it's yours. Your secret will be safe."

Willie looked at him in awe, unprepared for what he heard. "You staying?"

Daniel nodded.

"Well, then, Lieutenant, you will not . . . ."

"Please, Willie, call me Daniel, all right?"

"Yes, sir, Daniel, then you won't mind my telling you. I'm not leaving either."

Daniel looked at him doubtfully. "Why not, Willie? I would do what I can to help."

"No need for that. Mary Jane talked me out of it. And she didn't have to do much talking. I've been through a lot lately – forced to work on a tobacco farm, as a free man no less, for nearly two years, just because I'm a black man. I told her the risks involved with the Brit silver, and she tells me that something is sure to go wrong. And if I don't end up back on a tobacco farm, I'll spend the rest of my life in jail. And jail for a Negro is no place to be.

"She's right about that."

"I know she's right. She's educated, that Mary Jane. She read me that Declaration of Independence. And the part that stuck in my mind is where it says, 'all men are created equal.' Well, I'm a man, but I'm not treated equal to you white folk. So I don't know what those fellows who wrote it were thinking."

Daniel pondered a moment and responded. "Maybe they thought writing it down would help make it come true some day."

"Maybe. I guess saying it in that Declaration is better than not saying it. And if that's what we fought for, we fought on the right side. But saying it, alone, doesn't make it true. And it's not true for black folks most anywhere, including right here in Philadelphia." Willie paused, then added softly, "I will say, though, Mary Jane and I would rather take our chances here than in a lot of places. So, we plan to stay."

"I'm glad to hear it." Daniel placed his hands on Willie's shoulders and looked at him squarely. "And as long as you are here, I promise you this. I will treat you both well, and as equally and fairly as I treat anyone else. That won't change the world much, but it's the best I can do."

"It won't change the world. Still, it means a lot to us."

Daniel released his hold and sighed. "I have a mill that needs a manager. The job is yours if you wish it."

"Starting when?"

"As soon as you and Mary Jane are ready."

★

"Rise above it," the president of the court martial had said. If that were only possible, thought Daniel, as he walked with Elizabeth along the waterfront. They took Scout along, each holding one of his pudgy hands and swinging him along over unfriendly terrain. Commercial activity along the wharves had not reached its pre-war levels, and would not until the war ended, but at least it had improved somewhat. Scout seemed captivated by the last of the tall ships arriving before the harsh winter weather set in.

Daniel did not believe so much he was rising above anything, as just doing his best to live through the current round of life's difficulties. At least for the moment he felt contented, more so than he had in a long time. It reminded him of similar feelings he experienced at the Quaker picnic more than five years ago. "Now to His temple draw near." He still could sing it, word for word. Much had happened since then, and more changes were to come. He did not relish more disruptions. But the thought he would live out his days with his family in the City of his birth gave him satisfaction.

★

The last major battle of the war took place at Yorktown, Virginia in October of 1781.

The war officially ended with the signing of the Treaty of Paris in September of 1783.

Benjamin Franklin returned to Philadelphia from Paris in 1785. He died at age 84 in 1790.

George Washington became the first president of the new nation in 1789 and served until 1797. He died in 1799.

About the Author

Don Sampen is an appellate attorney in Chicago who writes for a living. He has written many articles, book chapters, and briefs in court on non-fiction topics. The WHIMS OF WAR is his debut novel of American historical fiction. Two considerations inspired Don to write the novel. One was an interest he developed to write the kind of historical novel he would want to read. The writing turned out to be a labor of love. He is convinced, moreover, that others will enjoy the final product as well. As a second reason, Don wanted to present a not-so-simple picture of the American Revolution, an event of huge historical significance that many people take for granted. He tells the story from the perspective of a business and family man, in a city, Philadelphia, whose citizens were conflicted over the prospect of independence.